# Prophecies

an FFSG novel

Bill Dughaille

# Contents

# Prologue

## September: The first wedding

The wedding was almost perfect. All the women cried. All the men were merry, from tipsy to totalled. If anyone had noticed that the bride was two months pregnant no-one had mentioned it. Despite a raging hangover and not having slept at all the previous night the best man had delivered his almost perfect speech like a trouper, and now lay comfortably asleep under a side table, along with one of the bridesmaids who was chatting happily, if incoherently, to his comatose body.

There had only been one fracas and that had finished almost before it started: shortly after the service had concluded and the guests and happy couple had moved on to the celebrations, the father of the bride had taken offence at a remark the father of the bridegroom had made about the ample girth of the bride's mother. It was an understandable misunderstanding, the two hardly knowing each other. The father of the bride had offered to thump the father of the bridegroom. The mother of the bride had sarcastically suggested he use his four-iron on the father of the bridegroom, a reference to his complaint that the wedding had interfered with his golfing schedule. The father of the bridegroom had replied that he would meet any such action with a nine-iron. Having established that they both played the game the two men had gone off to swap stories from the fairway, leaving their wives in a very unfair way.

The post-nuptial celebration was almost perfect. After the bride and groom had led the first dance – an almost perfectly executed waltz – the others had taken to the dance floor which was now packed with what could be described as gyrating bodies, though several wobbled enthusiastically rather than gyrated. Desk Sergeant Eric Johns, wearing a suit which had last seen the light of day several years and quite a few pounds before, had been dragged out to dance by Constable Sam Nightingale to the blaring out of Abba's "Mamma Mia". It was a sight to make sober minds wonder, had there been any present. She was probably an inch taller than him in her bare feet. Wearing four-inch high heels only increased the disparity and incongruity. To add to this her girlfriend sat watching without the slightest hint of jealousy in her laughing eyes. While the word "gay" could have described all present, it had more than one meaning for Sam Nightingale and her official partner.

Possibly the happiest person there sat looking after the administration of the refreshments. Agnetha of the police canteen, frustrated many years before in her own family life by the death of her fiancé before their wedding, was never happier than when one of her boys or girls got married, and here two of them had, to each other. Only someone who knew her well, however, would recognise the dour look on her face as a kind of spiritual or emotional ecstasy.

'Cheer up, Agnetha,' Phil Walthers told her as he came to the heavily laden table in search of a sausage roll. 'It's a wedding, everyone has a duty to be cheerful.'

'I am cheerful,' Agnetha replied, taking a sip of sherry. 'Don't know why everybody keeps telling me to cheer up.' She gave him a keen look. 'And when will you be tying the knot?'

Phil Walthers choked on his sausage roll, which was a pity, because it was a very tasty sausage roll.

'I think I'm a little old for that sort of thing, Agnetha. I'm a confirmed bachelor.'

'Excuses. Men are never too old.'

'Tell you what, Agnetha, I'll get hitched when you do. How's that for a promise?'

Only the gaiety of the festival air and his lack of knowledge of her history made it an acceptable challenge. He smiled and left to continue his unofficial duties as photographer, not noticing a small pork pie which flew past his head, coming from the rough direction of Agnetha's left hand.

There was an official photographer, but Phil Walthers found that carrying a large camera helped him avoid landing in the sort of situation that Eric Johns was now in. You obviously could not, if you were involved in the serious business of recording such a happy event for posterity, waste time with frivolous pursuits such as jumping around a dance floor. That was understood by almost everyone.

'A marvellous occasion,' Detective Chief Inspector Hunter was saying to Detective Inspector Percy Hanson and Detective Sergeant Pete Phillips as Phil Walthers came up beside them, finding them loitering at the back with the intent of not going anywhere near the dance floor.

'Great bash,' agreed Percy. 'Even though young Harry looked petrified to begin with.'

'Nothing a couple of stiff whiskies can't cure.'

'Or three or four, come to that,' noted Pete Phillips. 'That's what I needed to calm myself down when I got married.'

'And what might you two gentlemen be doing lurking here?' asked Phil Walthers in a good-humoured manner.

'The same as you're doing carrying that camera, Mr Walthers,' replied the Chief Inspector in similar vein. 'Avoiding being corralled into making a fool of ourselves on the dance floor.'

'I heard Mrs Blower was looking for you for that precise reason,' Percy Hanson said. 'To dance, that is, not to make a fool of yourself.'

'Now that,' noted the Chief Inspector, 'would be an interesting experience. I have always admired Mrs Blower's enthusiasm, though preferably from a distance. If her dancing is in any way similar to her conversation I fear her partner might well sustain multiple injuries.'

'A fine woman, sir,' said Phil Walthers. 'A lady with a heart of gold, if you'll excuse the cliché.'

'Oh, I fully agree,' replied the Chief Inspector. 'A heart of gold. She just has a certain eccentricity in her speech, and her attention span has been known to occasionally be of short duration.'

Phil Walthers nodded.

'That, I am afraid, nobody can deny. I will rely on her attention span to forget that she wanted to dance before she manages to find me.' He looked around. 'Wonderful things, weddings. The one time you can really celebrate and let yourself go with friends and family. There isn't the same pressure as, for example, Christmas.'

'Unless you're single,' joked Pete Phillips. 'I remember when I was single everybody kept asking when I was going to get married. The worst were family weddings. All those aunts and great-aunts and grandparents demanding to know when I was going to pop the question and who to.'

'And when your daughter's grown up they'll be asking you when she's getting married,' Percy Hanson said. 'You can't escape it.'

'Aye, fortunately it's a long time till that happens. I must say, Mr Walthers, that was very kind of you to set up that kiddies' playground outside the Blue Bliss.'

The Blue Bliss had originally been a night club on the outskirts of Wellbury, most famous for its strippers. Mrs Blower and Phil Walthers having taken it over, it was no longer clear what it was, apart from being popular.

'Every pub should have a family area,' Phil Walters said. 'We've decided to make it permanent. Make it more of a family business.'

'Keeping the strippers going?'

'Yes. No reason why stripping can't be acceptable. More erotica than erotic, if you see what I mean. Keeping the children away, naturally.'

'The council will be demanding that you apply for a licence for change of business use,' laughed Percy Hanson.

'They wouldn't dare. Firstly they know that I know a lot more about them than I've printed. Secondly I'll let Mrs Blower deal with them.'

Along with running the Blue Bliss Phil Walthers constituted the entire staff of the Wellbury Herald. Although "running" was perhaps not the best description of his duties at the Blue Bliss. "Keeping Mrs Blower from getting carried away with unique and impossible schemes for new ventures" would be more accurate.

'There you are!' cried a voice from behind them, the very same Mrs Blower. 'Come, Mr Walthers, give your camera to the Inspector, we are going to dance. At least one dance, I haven't danced for ages. Isn't this wonderful?'

Reluctantly, but recognising defeat before it came, Phil handed his camera to Percy and allowed himself to be led away.

'Strange how a wedding can concentrate a woman's mind,' noted the Chief Inspector. 'She did not deviate for a second. Unusual, that.'

'And Mr Walther's reluctance did not appear totally genuine,' agreed Percy Hanson. 'I think he has a soft spot for her.'

They stood in silence for a few seconds at the enormity of this idea.

'To the happy couple,' proposed Pete Phillips finally. 'The other happy couple, that is, the wedding couple.'

'The happy couple,' agreed Percy.

'Allison and Harry,' said the Chief Inspector.

'And we'll be having another soon,' said Percy. 'Where is young Frank and his betrothed?'

'Betrothed. Nice old-fashioned word, that.'

'I thought I saw him in the crush on the dance floor.'

Frank Summers was indeed on the dance floor, next to the happy couple, Allison and Harry (now both Wheatley). The music had moved to a slow ballad, and Allison had rested her head on Harry's shoulder. They were tired, both from emotional and physical stresses of the day and the long lead up to the wedding. For months Harry had been afraid that Allison would suddenly change her mind, especially lately, two weeks ago, after he had been arrested for being drunk and naked in public in the streets of Dublin where Pete Phillips and a group of them had gone for his stag night.

The Gardai, he had discovered – a little too late, since it was the morning after, when he woke up to find that he had a splitting headache, was wearing only a blanket, and was lying in something that looked and smelled, only too familiarly, like a police cell, though he was normally on the outside looking in rather than how he found himself that morning – no longer took an easy-going approach to planeloads of young men intent on drunken debauchery to celebrate their last days of bachelor freedom. Dublin's tourist authorities were aiming at a more genteel and upmarket approach, and anyone who thought that staggering through the city's fair streets naked and blind-drunk while singing Molly Maguire at the top of their voices was an acceptable pastime was in for a rude shock.

What saved him from a court appearance was the fact that he was a police officer, just like the Gardai. This was a double-edged advantage though, because, in order to confirm that he was who he said he was they had faxed his photograph to Wellbury police station.

Sitting in his cell, wearing only a blanket, face deathly pale, his eyes bloodshot.

All he could be grateful for was that it was in black and white, and he looked more like a tramp than his own self did when in uniform. As it was he returned to find that Eric Johns had pinned the fax on the announcement board in reception where all and sundry could see it, with the caption "Do you know this man?", to which someone had added "Do you really want to know this man?".

The only person who did not find this hilarious was Allison, especially when someone suggested that the blanket did not entirely hide his modesty, followed by comments not of a maidenly nature. The night he and Pete Phillips had flown back (twenty-four hours later than planned) they had been treated to a couple of pints of Guinness at the airport by two members of the Gardai (who drank Beamish), and he had left in a mood of euphoria that his recent problems were behind him, only to discover that they had been faxed ahead.

To describe Allison as "not happy" would not be an understatement, it would be an economy of the truth beyond parsimony. "Furious" would be an understatement. If Harry were to be in the doghouse it would seem luxury compared to the abuse she hurled at him. She told him she wasn't speaking to him, which was technically accurate since it turned out that she was speaking at him, and he had no right of reply.

She told him that she didn't know why she had agreed to marry such a worthless specimen. She asked someone not there (God, possibly, the devil perhaps) what she had done to deserve this wretched creature. He was the recipient of the silent and the non-silent treatment, both excruciatingly loud, for an entire week, until he was close to deciding that it would be better to call the whole thing off, join a monastery, throw himself into the deep dark waters of the river Wellbury, join the Foreign Legion – anything to escape.

As a police officer Harry should have been expected to notice little details. Such as the fact that she had not thrown her engagement ring at him and told him in which part of his anatomy to position it, including a reference to the shining sun, something one might expect had Allison truly meant what she shouted at him.

Such as the fact that, after a week of purgatory (hell, actually) he appeared to be forgiven and suddenly granted a pardon for his offences.

What he did not realise, just as Allison had not realised was the case with him, was that Allison had for months been afraid that Harry would decide against wedlock and that ominous phrase "we can still be friends" used. Even more so when she discovered that she was pregnant. She had spent almost every minute of every hour of every day since then agonising over whether or not to tell him. She owed it to him as the father.

But what if he decided it was a ploy to entrap him, to ensure that he could not wriggle out of his promise? She would rather he married her willingly than as a sense of duty. Being a single mother was not that great a problem these days (she thought), and she loved him too much to put him to trial. "If you love something let it free, if it returns to you it is yours, if not it never was" was her earnest belief.

Though not one she employed as a police officer. In her professional incarnation "Nail the bastard" was more likely to be employed.

There was also the question of her hen night. There had been another party celebrating their hen night nearby at the time, and their behaviour, especially when the male stripper turned up – oiled six-pack glistening when he removed his shirt – was quite shameful. Disgusting. Quite unacceptable. Chavs. Tarts. Sluts. That business with the whipped cream …

'Let's face it,' said her chief bridesmaid alongside, 'we'd be doing the same if it wasn't for you-know-what.'

This was accompanied by the pointing of a thumb towards Allison's stomach. Concerned about the child she was now carrying, she had limited herself to two glasses of wine, and even then she remained unsure. They had chosen a pub with a no-smoking area, and her doctor had assured her that there was little danger in the occasional glass of wine, but she had read recently so many articles on the meat and drink a mother-to-be should be allowing herself to consume in order to ensure a happy, healthy baby – apparently the slightest drift towards too many tomatoes or too few tangerines could result in the production of a circus freak – that she no longer knew what to think.

And she knew her chief bridesmaid was right. She would also be three sheets to the wind and licking that whipped double-cream from those pecs had she not suddenly acquired the haloed and hallowed status of mother-to-be.

Come to think of it, she rather fancied some double whipped cream right at that moment.

She bought six tubs on the way back home and devoured every single one. She felt sick the next morning, but then she felt sick most mornings.

That day was the day she forgave Harry Wheatley.

And tomorrow she would reveal her secret to him, now that they were officially man and wife.

It would be a shock to both of them. He didn't know, and she, despite his protestations that he loved children, did not realise how exuberantly he would react to the idea of becoming a father. His love would turn into adoration. She wouldn't be able to make a cup of tea without Harry jumping up to make it for her, and protesting that she should take things easy "in her condition".

All in all he was going to be a right pain in the neck about it.

'How do you feel about becoming a granddad?' her mother asked her father as they sat watching the happy couple, his father having been dragged away from his enjoyable golf discussions under the argument that he was ruining the wedding, and could only make it a success by sitting next to her and being bored to death.

'Oh, no need for them to hurry. They're still young, plenty of time to be thinking about having children.'

The mother of the bride and the mother of the bridegroom looked at each other, shook their heads in unison and raised their eyes upwards as if to say "Men!". Their partners looked at each other and just shrugged.

'I still say that Gary Player was the best golfer of all time,' the father of the bride said, apparently continuing a dispute that had not been satisfactorily resolved.

'Not a patch on Jack Niclaus. Now there was a – '

'That's enough!' cried the mother of the bride. 'Stop talking golf and start enjoying yourselves, this is their day.'

The confused fathers rolled their eyes and reluctantly turned their attention to those on the dance floor.

'Happy, Harry?' Frank Summers asked the groom next to him as they held their respective partners on the floor.

'Never happier, sir,' a tired but beaming Harry replied. Allison opened her eyes to smile at her husband as the song ended.

'I could do with a sit down and a cup of tea, darling,' she said. Both couples began to move back to their respective tables.

'And I could do with a good whisky,' Frank commented to his partner.

'Who was that man you were talking to? The one with the white quiff of hair?' the mother of the groom asked as the new husband and wife took their seats.

'That's Mr Summers,' Harry replied, taking a deep draught from his beer.

'Oh, so that's Mr Summers,' said his mother, as if expecting something more impressive. 'He doesn't look like what I thought he would look like.'

Harry looked at his bride and winked. She smiled back. They were both used to bickering parents, to mothers who were perpetually prepared to be disappointed in the reality of something someone else had praised. It was the kind of attitude bred in some born into less-wealthy families who scorn what they cannot afford, and gradually come to scorn most things no matter how much their own situation might improve. Harry and Allison had already agreed that their marriage was going to be different. There would be no bickering, just eternal love and light. They would have been astonished to discover that their own parents had made exactly the same promise many years before.

Cupid has a lot to answer for.

The wedding reception had in fact been a grand ceremony, one that neither had expected they would be able to afford. Originally the aim had been to get married in a register office and move on to a pub for the post-nuptial celebration, pretty much as their own parents had done all those years ago. Then Mrs Blower and Phil Walthers had stepped in with the offer of the free use of the private members' bar at the Blue Bliss. Agnetha had volunteered the station canteen staff to look after the refreshments, and, judging by the spread, had probably quietly volunteered quite a bit of the canteen's stock. The usual raiding party had been sent across the Channel to ensure that no-one's throat should turn dry. By and by and bit by bit, as requirements were established, it turned out that someone knew someone or was related to someone who could provide the requirement at a generous discount. The legal provenance of some of the satisfied requirements was not questioned. Wellbury's police officers knew when to turn a blind eye.

Almost all staff from the police station were there, with only a skeleton force left on duty, and those would turn up when their shifts ended. Whether or not their replacements were in a suitable state to take over was a moot point, though the word had been spread amongst the criminal fraternity that it would be a bad idea to take advantage of the situation, as any such abuse would be repaid with interest at a later date. So far things had indeed been quiet.

'No calls, so far, touch wood,' Pete Phillips said. 'Or, nothing major, anyway.'

'Aye, it's quiet out there,' the Chief Inspector said. 'Two slight accidents and one break-in at an empty house. Nothing serious.'

The other two men showed no surprise that he should be so well informed, despite not having visibly received news of the state of the nation, or having been seen near the station for quite a long time, officially being on leave, fishing.

'Speaking of such things, it's the first wedding I've been to where the vicar's had a black eye,' said Percy.

'Yes, you have to hope it isn't a portent of some kind,' suggested Pete Phillips.

'Apparently he's gone to visit the sick tonight. Not sure whether having a vicar with a black eye turning up at my bedside would be a comfort.'

'Sam's got hold of Frank now,' chuckled the Chief Inspector. 'That woman certainly knows how to – what's the word – boogy?'

'Something like that,' replied Percy. 'Last time I was on a dance floor it was called disco.'

'Another good thing about weddings,' noted Pete Phillips, 'is you can enjoy Abba without being embarrassed about it. Any other time anyone under thirty would be afraid of losing their street cred.'

'It's a good band,' the Chief Inspector put in. 'They seem to be able to mix the slow and fast pieces. Unusual, that. Most weddings I've been to the slow stuff is the signal to wind things down.

'About time for me to do exactly that,' commented Percy, looking at his watch. 'If I'm going to be in any reasonable state for early shift tomorrow.'

'Hello, I think they're about to be off.'

The band had finished and a bleary-eyed best man was tapping a glass for everyone's attention. He had been resuscitated with a glass of cold water applied externally and a strong brandy applied internally.

'Hello! Silence, please, folks. I would like to announce that the hippy couple, er, the happy couple that should be, our own Allison and Harry, are about to leave on their honeymoon. Let's all give them a good send-off.'

There were enthusiastic cheers as those present followed the couple out to the front where their chauffeured car awaited. There were even more cheers as the bride threw her bouquet over her shoulder. Wolf whistles greeted the sight of her right leg as Harry removed her garter and threw it over his shoulder.

'Think they planned that?' asked Percy Hanson as Harry held the car door while Allison slipped inside, denying an indignant chauffeur the pleasure.

'If they didn't, they should have.'

'Frank doesn't seem to know what to do. That's a first.'

A bemused Frank was holding the garter, looking at his fiancée who was holding the bouquet, blushing.

'Well, if he wasn't already engaged he would be soon. No getting out of it now. That's fate, that is.'

The crowd waved as the car drove off, trailing a selection of old boots and tin cans.

'Where's his kitten? Little Squishy?' asked Percy as they moved back indoors.

'Not so little any more. It's growing fast. He left it with Aggie.'

'Ah, I wondered why he popped in to the cemetery before the service. I thought he might be going to ... Well, typical Frank. Only man I know who could come up with a kitten-sitter like that.'

'It'll be October soon,' noted the Chief Inspector thoughtfully.

The other two nodded.

'Still, it's September now. A gorgeous evening, summer at its best. Carpe diem, I say.'

Pete Phillips presumed he was talking about fishing.

'To the next happy couple,' he said before the other two could get carried away with their angling conversations. 'To Frank and his betrothed.'

'Frank and his betrothed,' they echoed and drank.

'Who would ever have thought of it, Frank getting engaged.'

'The next miracle will be him getting married.'

This brought a sudden quiet. There were several concerns on that score. A prophecy had been made that Frank would never reach the altar. Mentioning the fact was not appreciated by some standing there.

'Eric's face was a picture when he heard,' Percy Hanson said to break the silence. 'What is it, almost three months ago? Seems like only yesterday.'

'You're right, it does feel like only yesterday. When that toddler went missing.'

But it had indeed been three months ago. Back in June.

# Chapter One – Seven Days

## Monday Evening: A missing toddler

Detective Sergeant Frank Summers switched off his computer in preparation for going home. He had spent the day on odd jobs, waiting for a call to report to Inspector Frieda Garold's eyrie for the worst bollocking of his life. The previous day, at Sunday lunchtime, he had revealed to a group of assembled officers in the private members' bar of the Blue Bliss, amongst other things, the identities of those who had been behind a practical joke played on him.

The miscreants in question had been his boss, the afore-mentioned Detective Inspector Frieda Garold, Detective Constable Gertie Gregson, who reported to him, and pathologist Doctor Susan Pleadle, all three of who were striving for a romantic interest in him, and who had indeed demanded that he should choose one of them, to let the others put the past behind them and get on with their lives.

As repayment for the practical joke, and a form of *encourager les autres*, he had sabotaged their handbags; Gertie discovered what appeared to be a dead mouse in hers; Susan found herself showered with pieces of paper; Frieda received the worst treatment – he hadn't sabotaged hers. Despite knowing logically that there had been no time for Frank to have done anything to it at the time, it had taken her half an hour to pluck up the courage to prove this, and finding nothing, she spent the following hours in nervous anticipation of discovering what he had planned for her.

He had committed an even more heinous crime. Each had taken his invitation for drinks that Sunday as a personal invitation, only to discover that half the station were there, and they all knew that each of the three believed they were there for a romantic tête-à-tête with Frank. Thus were the three publicly humiliated, with the added indignity of their discovery of his handiwork in their handbags carried out in front of their colleagues.

By the Monday morning Gertie had forgiven him. She even managed to see the funny side of it for a few hours. Susan had also telephoned to make sure that he understood that she bore no grudge. Only Frieda had remained ominously silent.

Gertie's mood lasted until lunchtime, after which she appeared struck with a strange lethargy, almost apathy. By the end of the day, when Frank switched off his computer, she would have made Ophelia appear a bubbling extrovert.

'Fancy a drink, Gerts?' Frank asked as she put on her jacket.

'If I must, I must,' she replied in the manner of a condemned man being invited, since he wasn't doing anything else at that precise time, to pop down to the chamber where a short rope and a long drop awaited him.

With impeccably bad timing Susan appeared in the doorway.

'Hello, Frank. I was just passing and thought I'd pop in to see if you fancied a drink when you've finished for the day.'

He looked from Susan to Gertie, and then back to Susan. Susan looked at Gertie. Gertie looked at Susan.

'Hello, Susan,' said Frieda, walking in on this looking game, dressed as if she was about to leave the office, unusually wearing shoes with flat heels, and what could only be described as an even more unusual air about her, similar to Gertie's depressed mien. 'Frank, Gertie, a toddler's gone missing on the river bank. We need everyone we can get to help search.'

'A toddler?'

'One Johnny Whittle, just over two years old. His parents went for a walk after the husband had finished work, with Johnny in his pram. At some stage they stopped and discovered that he was missing. He must have climbed out while they weren't looking. We got their call about five minutes ago. They're rather frantic.'

'I'm not surprised. We'd better get there straight away. Come on, Squish, lazybones, we need to get going.'

This last was addressed to a little kitten curled up sleeping in his in-tray on a scrap of towel. He had originally discovered the kitten left outside the door to his flat, and believed that he was just looking after it until its rightful owner turned up to reclaim it. Until then he had punched small holes in the large pocket of an old leather jacket, and transported Squishy in the pocket, carrying the jacket, in the warm weather, over his shoulder. In the beginning the scrap of towel had been the kitten's security blanket; it had now added Frank and his jacket in a similar role.

Frank Summers was a walking example of the law of unintended consequences. He had little thought of the effect a man turning up at the police station with a little kitten in his pocket might have on his colleagues. He found his office suddenly very popular with the female officers, and quite a few of the men turned out to be "just passing" when they popped in for a word, and just by coincidence noticed the kitten. Hard-boiled old hands, cynical to a point, could be found tickling her under the chin and asking whether she wasn't the cutest little kitten ever. Part of the car park, a covered section, had been cordoned off with cardboard as a feline "Ladies' room", with special litter tray. Squishy had developed a special miaow indicating that she needed to go.

Needless to say it was rarely Frank who carried her out.

Even Eric Johns approved of Squishy, though for different reasons.

'In the old days every police station would have its own cat, to keep the mice down. I reckon this one will turn into a pretty good mouser if we train her properly.'

'Squishy will not become a mouser,' Gertie had retorted. 'Squishy is a well brought up, decent little kitten, aren't you, Squishy? You wouldn't go chasing nasty little mice, would you? No, you're going to grow up like a little princess, aren't you my lovely, wubbly, liddle puddy cat?'

Eric Johns had wisely recognised a good moment to change the topic.

'Hey, have you heard the latest excuse for speeding?' he had asked Frank. 'A bloke last Saturday – well, almost early Sunday morning, anyway – one of the patrol cars stops him, and he claims he's over the speed limit because he's trying to escape a ghost.'

'An interesting concept,' Frank replied. 'Apart from proving it, there is the rather interesting question of whether you can escape a ghost by accelerating. The physical versus the spiritual, as it were.'

The question caused Eric Johns to blink his eyes and pause for a second, before dismissing it. Eric Johns was very good at interpreting reality in his own way.

'Anyway, he claimed he'd been on his way home from the pub, needed to go all of a sudden, had popped into the cemetery and was relieving himself when he felt this sudden blast of cold air, and a ghost shot out from behind a gravestone and attacked him. He legged it, but the ghost chased him right out of the cemetery.'

'I don't blame the ghost. Using a cemetery as a public convenience? The phrase "taking the piss" comes to mind. If I'd caught him at it he'd think twice before doing it again.'

Everyone knew that there was a certain grave at the cemetery which was the cause of Frank's reaction.

'Still, when they breathalysed him he was well over the limit, so I don't think his story of a ghost will help much,' Eric Johns concluded.

'I think I may know who the ghost is,' Frank said. 'But I don't think she would have attacked him. Probably just surprised him and scared the daylights out of him. Or nightlights, in this case.'

'Who?'

'Someone called Aggie. She looks after graves there. I'll tell you about her sometime. Squishy knows her, don't you Squish? You like Aggie, don't you Squish?'

Squishy looked at him, head cocked to one side, as if wondering why Frank was talking like a toddler.

Nor had Frank considered how he was going to look after the kitten during the day while he worked, but that too proved to be of little consequence. Squishy loved playing what Frank called "football"; chasing and batting a table-tennis ball around the room. There was no lack of volunteers to join Squishy's squad. Even Detective Inspector Percy Hanson could be found at one time on his hands and knees encouraging the kitten. And, should Frank need to go out and need to leave the kitten behind, Tricia Leigh, Frieda's secretary, had begged the privilege of looking after Squishy before anyone else might get the idea.

She could not at the time, unfortunately, inform Frank of Frieda's mood or planned retribution, and seemed, with her concentration on the kitten, not to much care. In a way it was a bit of a blow to Frank's self-esteem. He was used to being the centre of attention, no matter how little he realised that this was actually the case. Now he had been supplanted by a kitten.

The biggest effect Squishy had was on Agnetha in the canteen. She had long been a fan of Frank's, and the kitten had merely raised him in her eyes. She did not normally venture out of her own domain and empire, to whit the kitchen and canteen, but in this case she made an exception, coming several times during the day with tasty morsels for Squishy.

Having said that his position had been supplanted by a kitten, there was more to it than that. As the day grew on it seemed that the various visitors were looking at him in an almost accusative way, as if he had done something they disapproved of. Frank, in his own inimitable way, totally missed the looks, just as he invariably missed people's opinions and feelings towards him.

And now Squishy was working her magic on Susan and Frieda, who crowded around Frank as the kitten yawned and stretched in his hands. Gertie would have been there as well, but she had all day in the office she shared with Frank to cuddle and stroke the kitten, and now it was their turn.

'Ooh, hello little Squishy, who's a cute little kitten,' cooed the usually impeccably professional Frieda, as if Squishy had come there expressly to make her miserable day more cheerful.

'You are the most adorable little thing, aren't you?' Susan chimed in competition.

Squishy suffered the tickling and stroking of outrageous fortune while looking pleadingly at Frank. The kitten, whose past was unknown but presumed to be not of the best, was as yet unused to humans being pleasant. Football was fun, they could forget the fawning.

'Better get used to it, Squish,' Frank said, slipping first part of her little towel and then the kitten into his pocket in a practised manner. Squishy sat happily looking out, a paw hooked on top of the pocket, looking rather like a queen regally surveying her queendom from her carriage.

'What more do we know about this kid?' Frank asked as he, Gertie and Frieda walked to her Range Rover, Susan having promised to follow them in her MG.

'No more than I've told you,' Frieda said as she switched the ignition on and drove out of the parking lot at the back of the station. 'Two patrol cars are on their way, and I've asked Tricia to round up whoever she can find, on duty or off duty. We could probably leave it to uniform, but I think it's best to get as many people there searching as soon as possible. I don't like the sound of a toddler that age being lost close to the river.'

'I agree. Have the river wardens been alerted?'

Wellbury was too small to afford a dedicated river police unit. Initially someone had come up with the idea of training certain officers to be able to handle a boat should the need arise. All that had resulted in was four soaked, unamused and disgruntled police officers, and an appreciative crowd on the riverbank shouting advice, amongst other things, on how to right their capsized boat. After that a volunteer, civilian, group of river wardens had been formed to provide assistance should it be required.

'They should be there now. I'm hoping we'll get there to find little Johnny safe and sound, but if he hasn't been found I'm afraid they're going to have to start dragging the river.'

Frank looked at his watch.

'About three hours of light left, maybe four,' he mused.

'There'll be a near-full moon tonight,' Gertie offered.

'Yes,' noted Frank, 'but if we don't find the kid in three hours I wouldn't put too much money on his chances.'

The thought remained unspoken that, if the parents and the officers in the patrol cars hadn't found Johnny by the time they arrived, his chances were not good even then. A two year-old could hardly wander far. If the child wasn't found soon the likelihood would be either that he had fallen into the river and been swept away, or, a possibility they did not want to mention too soon, had been abducted.

They found the two unoccupied patrol cars down a gravel road, parked on the grass verge near a large clump of trees and bushes, vegetation that extended for about fifty yards, forming a dense little wood, hiding the river from their sight.

'The ground's a bit soft,' Frank noted as Frieda pulled up behind the patrol cars.

Soft was a slight understatement. Recent rain had left the land that sloped down to the river soaking wet. To step off the compacted path that led around the wood was to risk stepping into mud disguised by a topping of bright green grass.

'They probably couldn't have chosen a worse spot,' noted Susan as she joined them. 'This area was left to grow wild, you could easily get lost in that wood.'

There was a little-known history behind the area. The council had agreed that it should be left to its own devices as an experiment, somewhere for naturalists (the original recommendation had mentioned "naturists", which had led to some confusion and a number of embarrassed encounters), environmental students and school pupils to study. Unfortunately the committee given the job to implement the recommendation – and why create a committee to oversee a job of doing nothing? – had brought in a landscape designer who had decided that the land should be redeveloped as it would have been in the Mesozoic era, though why the landscaper thought this, or that most of the area would have been below the river level during that period, was anyone's guess. Perhaps because the Jurassic period fell within the era, and the area had the resemblance of a park, a connection had been made in his mind. Suffice to say that it was left in a condition that anyone who took a few moments to think about it would realise that, come the first rain, it was going to turn into a bog, or worse.

The builder contracted to create the network of paths had originally intended to run things according to his usual business approach – minimal outlay which would later require maximum maintenance, for which he would, of course, be given the contract. On immediately realising what the landscaper had done, rather than gleefully accepting that that it had made his own aim far easier, he indignantly reversed his usual policy at the insult of the simplicity, and determined on constructing paths which would survive a biblical flood. In this he had been extremely successful. So long as people kept to the paths their feet would remain dry, no matter how much of a quagmire the rest of the area became.

'Sounds like someone's in there,' Frank said as the sound of calls came to them.

They walked around the edge of the wood, listening to cries of "Johnny!". Once around the edge they could see the river. Between the wood and the river lay the river path, then some twenty yards of clear grass, with the occasional willow tree leaning into the water. Two boats, each containing two men, were tied up to one of the willow trees.

There was a noise in the undergrowth and a uniformed constable stumbled out of the undergrowth and came to a stop in front of them.

'No luck, Bobby?' Frieda asked.

'No, ma'am. You could hide an elephant in there and no-one would spot it,' Constable Bobby Stang replied, taking his peaked cap off and wiping his brow. 'We're trying to do a line search, but the undergrowth is so thick it's impossible to keep a line going. You think you're going straight and then find you've wandered out, just like I did now.'

'Are you sure this is where little Johnny is?'

Bobby shrugged.

'It seems the most likely place, most of the rest is pretty open. But the parents aren't sure when Bobby was last in his buggy. They've walked about two miles up to here, from the car park. They were just beyond the wood and about to turn back when they discovered he was missing.'

'Two miles? How can you walk two miles with a baby and not realise he was missing?'

Bobby gave another shrug.

'When they last saw him he was asleep. He was wearing a hat with a bobble on the end of it. They could see the bobble – the hat had become snagged to the buggy canopy. They didn't think that the boy might not be wearing it anymore. Added to that – well, apparently it was one of these low-slung buggies with a hood, and the mother had bags of baby stuff slung on either side, so I suppose that made up the weight. Guess the bags would have obscured their vision, too.'

'Reinforcements arriving,' noted Frank at the sight of a mixture of uniformed and plain-clothes officers coming towards them. 'I don't think it's going to be enough to search two miles, though. You'd need a small army just for this wood alone.'

Another uniformed constable came crashing out of the wood, blinking as if surprised to find himself out in the open.

'Blimey,' he informed Bobby Stang, 'that's a ruddy jungle in there.' He turned to find Frieda looking at him, an inspector whose intense dislike of even the mildest form of swearing was well known. 'Oh, evening, ma'am, didn't see you there.'

It was Harry Wheatley. He had a reputation for saying the wrong thing at the wrong time. Allison Hardbury had belted him with her handbag on a number of occasions purely for that reason.

'Are those the parents?' Frieda asked, referring to the continued calls coming from within the wood.

'Yes, ma'am.'

'I think it's time we interviewed them properly. Harry, you get back in there and bring them out. Bobby, those are the river wardens under that willow, I take it.'

'Yes, ma'am. They're waiting for orders.'

'Okay, tell them to start searching, inlets, that sort of thing, they should know where. Tell them to drag wherever a body is likely to turn up.'

The two constables hurried off on their tasks. Frieda turned as the others came up. Detective Inspector Percy Hanson led the group. He was wearing a loud Hawaiian shirt, khaki shorts, knobbly knees, socks and sandals, an ensemble some might have felt that he should have been arrested for, the charge being disturbing the peace on a quiet summer's evening.

'I was just about to relax in the garden with a beer,' he said in explanation. 'What's the situation? I hear we've got a missing child.'

'Johnny Whittle, aged about three. Disappeared somewhere between here and two miles back.'

Percy whistled softly.

'That's bad,' he said, squinting as if he were an experienced tracker as he looked down the path. 'Probably the worst stretch of the river for it to happen. Isn't it, Frank?'

Frank nodded. There were three of them who knew the river well, from their almost daily fishing expeditions. Two – Frank and the Chief Inspector – fished without bait or hook and lived in fear of catching anything. The third – Percy Hanson – used both hook and bait and never managed to catch anything. If it were an afternoon he would often visit the fishmonger's on his way home, not to pretend that he had caught his purchase, but rather to point out that that was what it would look like when he finally achieved his aim. And he would, one day. After all, everyone knew the river was teeming with fish of the best specimens, and other anglers were often going home with prize catches, so why shouldn't he? Eventually.

'We're going to have to split into two teams,' Frank said. 'One to search the open land, another to do the wood here.'

'I'm on your team,' Tricia Leigh said, putting an arm around him and peering into his pocket. 'Hello, Squish, it's your Auntie Trish here.'

Frank had an unsettling feeling that he could have led into battle an army of Roman legionnaires against hordes of Hannibal's elephants, so long as they could peer into his pocket for Squishy's approval before going off to battle.

'Right,' said Frieda, giving Frank a look which clearly showed what she thought of his trying to organise things instead of leaving it up to her, and that he had better behave himself, 'Inspector Hanson and I will take charge of each of the two teams. Choose which team you want to be in and we'll get started.'

It wasn't Frieda's way to be democratic but she seemed strangely out of sorts. Unfortunately almost everyone joined her team. Or, knowing that Frank would be in her team, they joined Frank's team. Or perhaps, given that most of them were giving him disapproving looks, they joined Squishy's team. The only person left with Percy was his loyal Detective Sergeant Pete Phillips, and even he looked as if he might desert given a quarter of the chance.

'No! You can't do that! Stop them! They can't do that!' screamed a voice close by.

It was Mrs Whittle, pointing at a boat in which two men were ploughing the water with poles and hooks close to the opposite bank, looking for a terrible harvest.

'Allison, take care of Mr and Mrs Whittle,' Frieda ordered, her jaw set. 'Take them out of sight, back to where the patrol cars are, I'll join you there in a second.' She turned to Tricia and handed her her car keys. 'Bring my Range Rover down here, we'll use that as a control centre for the moment. And organise a mobile canteen. Tea, at least. And start arranging for night equipment, arc lights, torches and the rest, just in case it comes to that. Harry, you give Allison a hand.'

The three named moved unwillingly to their tasks. Tricia Leigh would have preferred to have been part of the search party, especially with Frank – or perhaps Squishy – but she was a civilian, she knew she had good organisational skills, and that, if the search were to continue into the night there were many things to think of.

Allison and Harry, for their part, would rather not have been chosen to look after a hysterical woman whose child had gone missing. They had only decided on a wedding date recently, and such circumstances were a reminder that married life carried potential pitfalls not included in their rose-tinted view of the future.

'I'll be back in a few seconds,' Frank said.

'And just where do you think you're going, Frank?'

'Squishy needs to go.'

'Squishy needs to go?'

'She's shy. She doesn't like going when people are looking at her. I'll just take her behind that bush over there. Won't be long.'

Frieda shook her head in disbelief.

'Whatever you do don't let her wander off. We've come to find a child, not lose Squishy.'

'I'll get Trish to look after her once she's finished,' Frank promised.

'Right, all of those from Steve's right hand on, join Sergeant Phillips. Percy, I think it would be best if your team started at the last known point where Johnny was in his buggy, the car park, and work towards us. We'll handle the wood. If we don't find anything here we'll start working towards you.'

Percy nodded.

'If it's two miles we'd better get moving. It might not take long to walk it, but a proper search will take hours. Okay, Sergeant, back to the cars. We'll drive to the car park and start working back towards here.'

As Percy led his team back to where their cars were parked Tricia drove up in Frieda's Range Rover.

'It's just been on the radio,' she told Frieda as she got out. 'Zack the Prat was calling for volunteers to help the search.'

'Oh, dear heavens no,' muttered Frieda.

Zack was a local radio presenter known to himself as Zack the Man, and to the rest of society as Zack the Prat. He knew all the evils of the world, and their solutions, amongst which were bringing back hanging and flogging, and making firearms available to respected members of society such as himself.

'I thought he presented the early morning show,' Frank noted, returning after Squishy had completed her toilet.

'He does a morning and an evening show these days,' Tricia replied, 'so he can wind people up going to work and going home.'

'That means we're going to have to keep a couple of people back to handle tourists,' noted Frieda. 'Did the Prat have anything else to say to make our lives more difficult?'

'He said that we should publish details of all paedophiles in Wellbury. That he knows of at least a dozen, but can't give their names or addresses for legal reasons.'

'Well,' said Frank, 'in that case we'll have to pay him a visit. If he has information relating to a crime it's his duty to inform us. A couple of hours down the station should do, perhaps three or four.'

'I shall look forward to that,' Frieda said. 'For the moment let's get this search going. Fall in line, everyone. Frank, you get things moving.'

'Here you go Trish,' Frank said, handing her his jacket, 'look after Squish for me.'

'Ooh, yes please!' she exclaimed, taking his jacket as if it were delicate china. 'Auntie Trish is going to look after you, little Squishy.'

'Do you think that's wise?' Frank asked Frieda. 'Bringing your Range Rover down here? It's likely to sink in, the earth is pretty soggy.'

'I think I know what I'm doing, Sergeant Summers,' Frieda snapped. 'Gertie, you come with me. Susan, you'd also better come along. I want a word with the parents, and from the reaction of the mother I think a doctor might be needed.'

Frank's eyebrows rose as the three walked away. Gertie reported to him. It was the first time Frieda had separated them while working. He shrugged and turned back to the matter in hand. Frieda was in a bad mood for some reason.

Wondering why was a waste of time. Asking why would be a waste of a life – his.

'Just so long as you don't mention that I'm a pathologist,' Susan said as they walked.

'That would be somewhat of a faux pas,' Frieda acknowledged. 'I'll only mention that you're a doctor if that woman becomes hysterical again.'

'You sound a bit down in the dumps,' Susan noted. She turned to Gertie. 'And you look like your pet goldfish just drowned. What's up?'

'You haven't heard the news?'

'What news?'

'Frank's getting married.'

There was a pause.

'What?'

'And not to one of us.'

'What?'

'He asked me out for a drink this evening,' Gertie said. 'I bet he was planning that well known "we can still be friends" routine. No doubt you'll get your invitation soon.' She sighed. 'I thought the day would never end. Him going around cheerful as ever, me feeling like the end of the world has come.'

'What?'

There was no reply that could be made to a third "What?", so neither of the other two made it, trudging forward, leaden footed.

'What? Who – who is he going to get married to?' Susan finally asked when the shock wore off.

'We don't know,' Frieda replied. 'We just know that he's proposed to someone.' She sighed, deeply. 'And it's all my fault. We pushed him too hard. He hadn't recovered from his accident, not fully. And then we demanded he should choose between us, and now he's gone for someone else, probably the first option he could find. He probably thinks that getting married will solve all his problems. A version of falling for someone on the rebound.'

'How did you find out?'

'Keeping a secret at the station is impossible. I think the only person who doesn't realise that everyone knows is Frank himself.'

They walked on in silence for a few yards.

'Rubbermats!' Frieda uttered under her breath.

'Rubbermats?' asked Susan.

'You know I don't swear. But sometimes you just feel that you have to say something – something, I don't know, something.'

Susan nodded.

'Yes,' she said. 'Rubbermats.'

'Yes,' agreed Gertie, 'rucking rubbermats.'


'Right,' said Frank, rubbing his jaw while looking at the dense wood in front of them. 'You all know the drill. Keep a straight line, stay close to the people either side, make sure you don't miss an inch.'

Eric Johns looked sceptically at the thick undergrowth.

'Keep a straight line, Frank? Bloody impossible, if you ask me.'

'We are Wellbury's finest, Eric. We can do what no mere mortals can.'

'You haven't been drinking, have you?'


'What's this I hear about Frank getting married?' Percy Hanson asked Pete Phillips as their search line straggled slowly forward.

'It's true, everybody on the station knows by now. He's got engaged to someone. We don't know who to, we just know it isn't who we thought it might be.'

'What, someone from outside the station?'

'Could be. Probably is, I reckon. Everybody reckons he shouldn't have done it, he should have chosen between the Inspector, the Doctor and Gertie, but you can understand he might jump for someone else just to get rid of the pressure.'

'Be interesting to find out who it is,' Percy murmured.

'Why don't you just ask him, sir?'

'Ah, well that's just it. As a senior officer it might appear that I was interfering in his private life. Impolite, to say the least. Why don't you ask him, you're the same rank, and his mate.'

'Ah, well that's just it. A mate shouldn't ask a mate a question like that because it's the sort of thing a mate would tell a mate without being asked, so if a mate needs asking then the mate shouldn't ask because the mate will tell his mate when he's ready to tell his mate.'

And, Pete Phillips did not add, he would probably have his head bitten off if he tried.


'I think I know who it is,' Gertie said angrily. 'The little tart he left Squishy with. '

'Tricia Leigh?' exclaimed Frieda. 'Surely not!'

'He left Squishy with her,' Gertie repeated. 'He would only leave Squishy with someone who was special to him. And she's being going around like the cat who got the cream. And she's been down to our office five times today.'

They continued walking in silence as they considered this damning evidence. Frieda hadn't noticed any difference in her secretary, Tricia had been just as cheerful as she always was.

Then again it had been through Tricia that she had learnt the news, happening to overhear Tricia on the phone to someone. And Tricia hadn't actually told her. And there had been a certain light in her eyes for most of the day ...

And what was it she'd overhead Tricia saying? "Frank ... yes, engaged ... I'm so happy!"

And Tricia had certainly been absent from her desk quite a few times that day.

But, no, it couldn't be Tricia.

Could it?

She had originally taken Tricia on as her secretary on Frank's suggestion. Five minutes after the interview in which she had offered Tricia the job she had found Frank in his office with Tricia's lipstick smeared all over his cheek.

And a few days later he and Tricia had gone out for drinks. Nothing further had happened on that front after she had made clear her disapproval.

But had nothing happened?

Back at the Range Rover Tricia noticed Squishy struggling to get out of the jacket pocket.

'You want to stretch your legs, little Squish, my sweet?' asked Tricia. 'Come, let me help you.'

She eased the kitten out and put her on the grass, laying Frank's jacket next to the front wheel of the Range Rover. She turned around at the noise of someone bursting out of the wood.

'Flaming Nora!' exclaimed the man. 'You don't know where you're going in there.'

Squishy shook a paw at the damp grass. Then she found a comfortable place to sit, underneath the Range Rover. Tricia failed to notice that the wheels of the car had already begun to sink into the soggy earth.

'I wouldn't have minded it so much if it had been one of you two,' Gertie said. 'It just seems totally unfair to lose him to some floozy who just happened to pass by and took his fancy.'

'Whoever it is, I think we owe it to Frank to persuade him against rushing into marrying someone unsuitable just because he wants to escape his problems,' Frieda said, still undecided as to whether Tricia – her loyal secretary – could be the culprit, and consequently unsure whether or not to reprove Gertie for suggesting that Tricia was a "passing floozy".

'You mean sabotage her?' asked Susan.

'No, not that. Of course not, no. It's just – well, I feel a bit responsible. And we all know the saying, marry in haste and repent at leisure. I just wish there was a way to – well, warn him, I suppose.'

'Maybe there's something about her background we could find out,' suggested Gertie.

'Gertie! No! Frank may well be in love with her – whoever she is, and I'm not convinced it's Tricia. If he is, then, well, it would be wrong to interfere.'

'But if he isn't then it would be right?' suggested Susan.

'Well, yes, you could put it that way. Anyway, enough of that later. We've got a job to do here.'

They had come in earshot of Allison and Harry attending to the parents of the missing toddler. The man was standing with arms folded and legs spread apart, glowering at the ground while Harry asked him a question, notebook in hand. The woman was sitting bent on the rear seat of a patrol car facing out, her feet on the grass, blankly looking nowhere, her hands tearing at the sleeves of her blouse, Allison crouched next to her. Seeing them coming towards them Harry and Allison came to meet them.

'Right, what's the story?' asked Frieda.

'This is Mr and Mrs Whittle,' Harry said, speaking softly. 'They came down to the river for a walk, parked their car at the car park a couple of miles away, and started walking, with the child, Johnny, in the buggy. Along with them were Mrs Whittle's mother and their daughter, Gina, aged six. Apparently Gina can be a bit of a handful, and Mrs Whittle's mother an interfering old buzzard – I quote Mr Whittle there. They haven't quite said so, but my guess is that they were arguing the whole way. This pair have been having a go at each other every opportunity they can.'

'Which partly explains how they managed to miss the fact that they had lost their child,' Frieda noted. 'Where are Gina and the mother-in-law now?'

'The mother-in-law took Gina home when they realised that Johnny had gone missing.'

'Gina hates her brother,' said Allison. 'Her mother told me that Gina felt that she had been pushed aside for Johnny even before he was born. She's always finding ways of putting him in danger.'

'And Johnny's an adventurous lad,' contributed Harry. 'His father claims that he was always off to investigate, ever since he could crawl.'

'If his parents are arguing all the time I'm not surprised,' noted Frieda. 'He's probably been trying to crawl away from them ever since he was born.'

'It's families like the Whittles that put me off the idea of marriage,' Susan said. 'Might as well stay single.'

'You know,' Frieda replied, 'you've just given me an idea.'


Squishy sensed danger. Something was crowding in on her. She mewled faintly and instinctively sought deeper cover underneath the car.

Another officer wandered out of the wood, looking surprised to be there, shoes muddy and uniform covered with leaves and moss. Reluctantly he turned around and pushed his way back in.

Tricia looked up, shook her head in bemusement, and continued her conversation on her mobile phone. Organising a mobile canteen to deliver tea and coffee had been easy. The other equipment was proving more elusive.

'Know what I reckon?' said Pete Phillips.

'I have this feeling you're going to tell me,' Percy Hanson replied morosely.

'I reckon it's that new WPC – Sam Nightingale.'

'Don't be daft. She's gay.'

'Ah, that's what she says, doesn't necessarily mean it's true. Maybe she's a closet straight?'

'Sergeant,' sighed Percy, 'why don't we just concentrate on the job in hand?'

'Yes, sir.'

They walked in silence for a few yards, heads down.

'Anyway, I think it's that student he met, the twin,' Percy said. 'The one he got to clean his flat.'

Along with exposing the coven's – a nickname given to Frieda, Gertie and Susan by some officers, but only in private and very quietly – practical joke, Frank had caught twins, a girl and a boy, students at the university, playing their own practical tricks against him. As punishment he had made them clean his flat from top to bottom.

'Symbolic, that is, a woman cleaning your flat,' Percy noted. 'Very symbolic. Strikes to the very core. Maybe not consciously, but very attractive to the subconscious, the primordial part.'

Pete Phillips did not reply. To his mind there had to be something very wrong with a man who found a woman cleaning his flat an erotic or romantic stimulant.

He had known Inspector Hanson for some years. It just went to show how little you really knew your fellow man.

He wondered if Inspector Percy Hanson didn't have a secret

stash of magazines and photographs hidden in his garden shed.

Cleaning Women's Weeklies. With suggestively placed aprons.


'So, we have a number of possibilities,' Frieda noted. 'They stop somewhere to enjoy an argument, Johnny crawls out of the buggy somehow unnoticed, wanders off behind a nearby bush somewhere and they carry on.'

'Unless he fell into the river,' Gertie suggested. 'He might have cried out, but they could have been arguing too loudly to notice.'

'If Johnny is adventurous,' added Susan, 'he might not have realised that he was in trouble until it was too late to cry out. He could have gone under, tried to scream, and taken a lungful of water instead.'

'True,' noted Frieda. 'Second possibility. Gina takes the opportunity while her parents are arguing to take little Johnny from his buggy and hide him somewhere, thinking perhaps that some other family will find him and adopt him.'

The others nodded at this idea of an innocent six-year-old living out an illusion. They preferred that to the possibility that Gina had hidden Johnny and just didn't give a damn.

'And then, of course, our nightmare scenario,' Frieda said. 'Someone abducted Johnny, either from his buggy, or after he had wandered away from it, or after Gina had hidden him. Did the parents see anyone else about?'

'There was a couple close to the car park, sitting on a bench,' Allison replied. 'They also had a buggy with a baby in it. They stopped to chat with them. Apparently they had a very pleasant chat about babies before moving on. They would have stayed longer, but Gina had leaned out over the river, holding on to the branch of a tree, to get sight of a kingfisher, and almost fell in. All of them rushed to catch her before she did, though Mrs Whittle thinks it was just attention seeking, so she decided they should walk on, out of hearing distance, so that she could give Gina a talking to. When they were a little distance away the other couple began to have an argument. From the sounds of it the two groups interrupted their own quarrels to be polite to each other, and then carried on.'

'Nice to know that politeness still exists,' Frieda commented. 'Anyone else?'

'An old man with a walking stick,' Harry said, consulting his notebook. 'Mr Whittle thought he looked a bit strange – shifty-eyed. He thought he looked at Johnny in his buggy in a funny way.'

'Oh, great, our good-old, old, shifty-eyed old man. Call him a pervert and slap the cuffs on him. Story over.'

'You know, he might well looked at the buggy in a funny way if it was empty,' Gertie said. 'Three adults, a child of six and an empty buggy. Why push an empty buggy along the river path?'

'Excellent point, Gertie,' said Frieda. 'Any other strange passers-by, Harry?'

'Two joggers, male and female, aged about eighteen or nineteen. One single female jogger of about sixty. One single female walking her dog, aged approximately fifty – the woman, that is. Two men fishing, about a hundred yards apart – they were still there when we arrived. That's it.'

'Have you interviewed them? The two men fishing.'

'We spoke to them when we first got here. They hadn't noticed anything. They were either lost in thought or engrossed in their fishing. They didn't even notice us until we stood right next to them.'


Frank burst out of the wood, Eric Johns following shortly.

'See, I told you we could keep together,' said Frank. 'Although I grant you we're supposed to be in rather than out.'

'This is bloody daft,' panted Eric Johns. 'If the kid was in that wood it would be screaming its head off by now.'

'I know. But we have to keep at it.' He paused and held up a hand. 'I thought I heard something.'

'I can hear something. The sound of a bunch of heavy plods crashing around a wood. Playing blind man's buff.'

'No, it sounded like Squish. Tricia's probably playing with her. Still, once more unto the breach.'


'Are you just going to stand there doing nothing having a chat?' demanded Mrs Whittle, standing up, her patience exhausted.

'Yeah, what you doing gassing there?' added Mr Whittle. 'Our Johnny's gone missing and you're just gassing like a bunch of old women.'

'Mrs Whittle,' Frieda replied in a frigid tone, 'I am Detective Inspector Garold. I believe I am good at my job. Perhaps if you had been better at your job as a mother we would not need to be here now. And as for you, Mr Whittle, I suggest you might need to examine your own parenting skills as a father. However, as we are here now I intend to ensure that nothing gets in the way of our work, and that includes interference from the two of you. Do you understand?'

If they did understand they did not say so. Both their mouths were open, too stunned by the attack to reply.

'Right,' Frieda said, speaking to the group next to her, 'much as I dislike it, we're going to have to get Zack the Prat to request anyone who was along the river path earlier to contact us. How much good it will do I don't know, since he's already invited any vigilantes out there to do whatever they feel like doing. And he's told his listeners, who I hope don't number more than two, to join the search party. So you'll have to stay here, I'm afraid, Harry, Allison. If anyone turns up to offer help, thank them politely and tell them to wait here until further notice.'

'We could do with some more people,' Susan pointed out.

'Yes,' agreed Frieda, 'of the right sort. Unfortunately quite often they turn out to be the type who know what to do, only it's not what should be done, but they do it anyway. Especially when it's the sort of person who listens to Zack the Prat.'

The looks in Gertie's and Susan's faces showed clearly that they were wondering why Frieda's radio in her Range Rover had been tuned to the local station on which she could listen to Zack the Prat.

'Hello, looks like our first visitor,' said Allison as a car pulled up behind the patrol cars. An elderly man with a walking stick got out.

'We must be desperate if the geriatric squad are coming to help us,' noted Harry.

'It's im!' shouted Mr Whittle. 'It's that bloody old pervert!'

44

He ran towards the old man.

'I'll bloody teach you! Tell us where you've taken him, you bastard!'

Harry and Allison did not need to be told. They immediately ran after him.


'Squishy?' asked Tricia, hearing the kitten mewl. 'Where are you? Squish?'

She noticed the Range Rover's wheels now sunk deeply into the mud-like grass. The calls were coming from underneath it.

'Oh, my God! Squishy, come out. Squishy!' Her first thought was to drive the car away. But there was no guarantee it would get out of the mud. And she didn't know where Squishy was. Moving the Range Rover could kill the kitten.

She flung herself at the car, trying to pull it up. 'Help! Help! Somebody help me, please!'


Eric Johns, having lost Frank somewhere or other, stumbled into a small clearing to find himself facing Constable Sidney Feeler.

'Ere, lad, you're going the wrong way,' he informed the constable.

'Er, Sarge, are you sure it isn't you going the wrong way?'

'No, lad, because I'm a sergeant and you're a constable. Stands to reason, doesn't it?'

Faced with this logic all Sid Feeler could do was turn around and begin forcing his way back where he had come from, clearing the brambles for Eric Johns.

'Here, Sarge, this business with Sergeant Summers'

engagement. Not right, is it?'

'Not up to us to jump to conclusions when we aren't in the full knowledge of all facts, lad,' replied Eric Johns, a man who did not jump to conclusions, he tele-transported himself to them at a speed faster than the speed of speed.

'I suppose you're right, Sarge. Not much we can say before we know who he's got hisself engaged to.'

'Exactly, my son. Why don't you ask him when you get a chance?'

'You're joking, incha, Sarge?' asked Sid Feeler, a constable so in awe of Sergeant Summers he wouldn't dare ask him the time of day, let alone such a delicate question. 'Why don't you ask him, Sarge, you know him quite well.'

'Ah, my son, the fact that you should even suggest that shows why I am a sergeant and you are a mere constable.'

'How d'you mean, Sarge?'

'I mean, lad, I would never be that daft. There are far more pleasant ways to commit suicide.'


Allison and Harry managed to restrain Whittle, but not before he had swung a punch which felled the old man.

'Are you okay, sir?' asked Gertie, kneeling down beside him.

'Okay? Let me get up,' the old man gasped. 'I'm going to thump that ignorant young thug.'

'Calm down, sir,' Frieda told him. 'I'm Detective Inspector Garold. We'll sort out this little difficulty later. At the moment we need to concentrate on finding a lost child.'

'That's why I'm here,' the man said, standing up slowly with the support of Gertie and the boot of a patrol car. 'I passed them – those two, with another woman and a young girl – on the river path. Their pram – buggy, pushchair, or whatever they call the things these days – was empty when I passed them. I thought you might want to know.'

'He's lying!' shouted Whittle, for no apparent reason.

'Where was this?' asked Frieda. 'Where did you pass them? Next to the wood?'

'Oh, no, long before that. About a mile from the parking area.'

'Right,' said Frieda, turning to the others. 'We can pull everyone out of the wood and move down to meet Percy's lot. Now we've got a chance of finding the child. Harry, Allison, you stay here. Oh, and arrest Mr Whittle for assault. Cuff him and put him in one of the patrol cars. Come on. Sir, we'll need you to show us the spot.'

She led Susan and Gertie quickly back past the side of the wood, the old man hobbling after them as fast as he could, supported by Mrs Whittle. A reluctant Mr Whittle was forcibly assisted into the back of a patrol car. The leading women came around the front of the wood to find a strange sight. Tricia, Frank and Eric Johns were straining at the side of her Range Rover, apparently trying to turn it over.

'What on earth are you doing?'

'Squishy's trapped underneath,' gasped Frank. 'It's sunk in the mud. She's stopped calling. I just hope she's okay. Come on, on the count of three, heave!'

Gertie and Susan didn't hesitate. They immediately lent their efforts to the task, but the muddy ground gave no purchase, and their feet slipped from underneath them as they pushed.

Frieda did hesitate. There was a child missing, and they now had a much better idea of where that child might be. The child had been on its own for over an hour, possibly two. There was no time to waste.

Such as rescuing a kitten stuck underneath her Range Rover.

As a professional police officer she often had to take difficult decisions. And she would be crucified in the press if it became known that she had allowed her officers to rescue an animal while a child's life was at stake should that child come to harm while they were busy.

To aid her thought processes Mrs Whittle, coming around the edge of the wood with the old man, some thirty yards away, saw them struggling with the Range Rover, let go of the man and ran up to them. The old man, surprised by his sudden lack of support, fell over.

'What are you doing? Why aren't you looking for my baby?' she cried.

'There's a kitten trapped underneath,' Frank grunted.

'My baby is missing and you're trying to rescue a kitten?' she screamed, becoming hysterical again. 'What about my baby? What about my baby?'

Frieda tapped Gertie on her shoulder.

'Gertie, get everyone out of the wood, immediately.'

She turned to Mrs Whittle.

'We can't do anything until that man who saw the buggy empty gets here. I suggest you go back and help him. And if you start screaming once more I will personally smack you. Now go.'

Then she put her own back in, struggling with the others to prevent the heavy vehicle sinking further.

As the others left the wood and were alerted to the situation they ran to the car. Within minutes there was a group of hefty police officers desperately struggling in the mud. They managed to lift the car a few inches, sufficient for Frieda to lie on the ground, put an arm in and pull out a wet, muddy and trembling lump of fur.

Squishy's wide eyes looked up at her as she cradled the kitten. The kitten miaowed at her as if to ask what had taken her so long. The others crowded around to assure themselves that the Squishy was unhurt.

'Okay, okay, that's enough,' Frieda said. 'This man here – I'm sorry, sir, what did you say your name was?'

'I didn't. Jenson, Arnold Jenson.'

He looked at them. They were all muddy to a certain degree. The front of Frieda's blouse and skirt were ruined. All of them had streaks of mud across their faces, not to mention their clothes which were stained green and brown in places from their sorties into the wood.

'I must say, I'm most impressed,' Arnold Jenson said. 'The way you all piled in to rescue the little kitten like that. Not a moment's hesitation. It does you credit, it really does.'

Mrs Whittle looked at Frieda and kept her mouth shut.

'Yes, well there are more important things to think of right now,' Frieda said. 'Frank, Mr Jenson here passed the Whittles and noticed that their buggy was empty. We'll have to presume that that means the child had already gone missing, and isn't in the wood. You take the others and follow him. When you get to the spot spread out and start working towards Percy's group.'

'Right,' Frank said, giving Squishy a tickle, 'you'd better stay out of trouble for the rest of the evening, Squish, or you'll be confined to quarters for a week. Come on, let's get moving.'

'Squish?' asked Arnold Jenson as they moved off, Mrs Whittle trailing miserably behind.

'Short for Squishy,' Frank replied. 'She was left outside my flat all on her own. She was such a small, frightened bundle I decided to call her Squishy.'

'Admirable,' said Arnold Jenson. 'Absolutely admirable. I shall write to the press to commend you.'

'Please don't,' Frank requested with some feeling. 'I always end up in trouble when that happens.'

Four women watched them move off, each in various moods of dismay.

'Oh, yes, bloody admirable,' said Gertie.

'He is admirable,' said Tricia Leigh. 'I just hope he forgives me for letting Squishy get into trouble like that. Can I have her back please?'

'Well, there is that,' said Gertie more happily as Frieda frowned at an imploring Tricia Leigh. 'I don't think he's going to forgive you lightly for that. Squishy means more than the world to him. He'd put Squishy before anyone else.'

Tricia's face fell at the suggestion.

'Here you go, Tricia,' Frieda said, handing Squishy to her. 'Put Squishy in my car. And see if you can get the car out of the mud. If you can't, get a truck out here to pull it out. But before you do that, get on to someone at the local radio. Tell them we need to speak to anyone who was out here this afternoon, anyone who might have seen the child. Tell them it's urgent.'

Tricia began to do as she was told while the other three followed the first group.

'This is turning out to be a farce,' Frieda noted as they walked. 'We were supposed to be a professional police force responding immediately to a problem which would be solved within minutes of our arrival. Now we look like a bunch of kids after a mud fight, and all we've managed to do is rescue a kitten which wouldn't have needed rescuing if we hadn't brought it here in the first place. If it wasn't so serious it would be hilarious. I would say things couldn't get worse, but they always do when you say that sort of thing.'

'Just as well you didn't then,' Susan said. 'I spy with my little eye something beginning with "P". Or "E", if you want. Namely Phil Walthers, editor of the Wellbury Herald.'

Phil Walthers, editor, only journalist, photographer and effectively the Wellbury Herald was indeed coming down the river path. He had already joined Frank and was talking to him.

'Oh, rubbermats,' said Frieda. 'Come on, let's catch them up.'

'No comment, I'm afraid, Mr Walthers,' Frank was saying to the other man. 'You'll have to speak to Inspector Garold. She's in charge here.'

As he said this he turned and smiled at Frieda. She glared back at him. Typical of the man. Tries to take over when he wants, dumps everything in her lap when he doesn't.

'Inspector Garold,' Phil Walthers said, 'any official comment? Or unofficial, if you like.'

Frieda explained the situation briefly. Unlike Zack the Prat Phil Walthers was a friend of theirs, almost part of the force sometimes. Partly this was because of shared interests and experiences, partly because of gratefulness that he had not held it against them that Pete Phillips had once emptied the magazine of a rifle at him, only just managing not to kill him. It hadn't really been Pete Phillips' fault. He hadn't known that it had been Phil Walthers he was firing at.

'What do you think the child's chances are?' Phil Walthers asked.

Frieda checked her watch.

'Not good,' she said grimly. Phil Walthers nodded unhappy agreement.

'Right here,' called Arnold Jenson. 'This is where I passed them.'

'Right, spread out,' called Frank. 'Let's get moving, there's only an hour and a half or so of light left.'

They spread out quickly and began moving forward. The line was held up every few minutes as someone discovered something, but invariably it proved to be a false alarm. Sweet wrappers, old scraps of clothing, a discarded shoe hidden underneath a bush, anything but the sign that a small child had recently been there. An hour passed before they met up with Percy Hanson's group coming towards them.

'No luck?' he asked Frank, his eyebrows raised at the condition of Frank and the others.

'Not a sausage.'

'Nothing on your side either, I take it?' asked Frieda. Percy's eyebrows almost disappeared into his hair at the sight of her clothes.

'Not a nibble. I'm pretty sure the child isn't here.'

'Which means someone's taken him. Or he fell into the river

and was swept away.'

'Not swept away. Carried away, perhaps. The river doesn't flow fast enough to get swept away.'

'Stop being pedantic, Percy, you know what I mean.'

They stood in silence for a few moments, each of them hoping someone else would come up with an idea of what to do next. Anything that did not hold the thought that the child might have been abducted.

'Nothing in the wood, then?' Percy asked.

'Mr Jenson over there saw the buggy empty before the Whittles got to the wood. The child must have gone missing some time before that.'

Just then Frieda's radio beeped. She took it out and answered.

'Inspector Garold, over.'

A pause.

'What? Repeat that, Control.'

'He did what?'

'Are you sure?'

'When?'

'He is?'

'Yes, we'll bring the parents back to identify him. We'll be back shortly. Out.'

She switched the radio off, looked at it in growing fury, and shoved it back into her pocket.

'You are not going to believe this. There was a couple with a young child in a buggy, close to the car park, sitting on a bench. The Whittles stopped to chat with them. After they had left the couple started arguing – or perhaps continued an argument the Whittles had interrupted. The woman left, taking the buggy. The man stayed there. He spotted a toddler next to the bench and presumed it was their own child which had crawled out of the buggy. He decided to slip away and take it home – they're estranged, apparently, and he hardly ever sees his daughter – and not tell his wife as a form of revenge, let her have hysterics when she got to her car and realised the child was missing. It was only when he got around to changing the child's nappy later that he discovered that their baby daughter had suddenly become a he. A he! What sort of man can't recognise his own child, never mind the difference between a baby boy and a baby girl?'

Vaguely Frieda knew that she had not been entirely fair, but she allowed her fury to continue.

'The man is down at the station now, with the child. Apparently he's terribly sorry for the mix up. Which is nothing compared to how he'll feel when I've finished with him.'

There was a silent pause. Then Bobby Stang muffled a chuckle. Frieda glared at him. A repressed laugh burst from Percy Hanson.

'I'm glad you find it amusing, Percy.'

'Look on the bright side, Frieda,' he said. 'Phil Walthers is over there taking photographs of our noble expedition. I'm wearing this horrendous shirt an aunt gave me last Christmas. You're covered in mud, your lot look like they've been pulled through bushes backwards – after a tour of duty in the trenches – and all for nothing.'

'We should have a group photograph taken,' Frank said. 'Have it framed and put it up in reception.'

'Excellent suggestion, Frank,' agreed Percy. 'And after that I am going home to my garden and my beer.'

'Yes, I must get back to Tricia and Squishy. She'll be wondering where I am.'

There were three women there who had no wish to appear in such a photograph. Frank's last words had removed whatever little urge they might have had for saying "Cheese".

Frieda was tempted to say something of the form of "We must do something about it" to Gertie and Susan. But that was precisely what she had originally said that had got them into this mess. She wasn't going to make the same mistake again.

'We must do something about it,' whispered Susan. 'For Frank's sake, of course.'

'Of course,' agreed the other two.

## Tuesday Morning: Domestic 1

Frank drove towards work humming happily. In the foot well of the passenger seat Squishy was patting her table tennis ball around. The sound of Ravel's Bolero was gradually gaining momentum, and Frank tapped the steering wheel to its accompaniment.

'Da-da-da-daa-dum!' he broke out. Squishy interrupted her playing to give him a look of concern, as if the kitten thought he might be in pain.

'Cheer up, little Squish,' he said. 'It's a bright June morning, the sun is in the heavens, and it feels good to be alive. What adventures do you think we'll have today, eh?'

His radio squawked at him.

'Control to Sergeant Summers, come in Sergeant, over.'

'Well, well, so early. We'll soon find out. Summers here, over.'

'Could you attend a domestic for us, Sarge? Everyone else is busy at the moment, and it's on your way in, over.'

'A domestic? That's uniform's job. If I tried that they'd go on strike. They'd be marching down the High Street with banners saying "No domestics for Frank Summers". I can hear them now, "Death to Summers! Domestics are for uniforms only".'

'I know, Sarge, but we're really short-handed at the moment, over.'

'Okay, give me the address.'

Frank did a U-turn and drove to the given address, noticing a patrol car parked outside of a transport caff, and wondered what crime could have taken place. Probably some idiot had tried to rob it, he decided, someone not being intelligent enough to realise that the till would be almost empty at that time of day.


'All domestics?' asked Bobby Stang, on radio duty and known for the period as Control.

'All domestics,' Frieda replied. 'Frank is up for promotion. The board want to know that he can handle difficult situations.'

'Poor sod,' said Bobby. 'Promotion isn't worth it.'

'The responsibility of rank, I'm afraid.'

'Tell you what, though, Inspector, by the time he's through wall to wall domestics he's not going to be so enthusiastic about getting married.'

'You know, that thought hadn't occurred to me.'

Bobby Stang checked his watch. In an hour he would be off duty and Sid Feeler would take over. He hoped the hour would pass quickly. He had a nasty feeling that he was about to be caught up in something that would not be very pleasant.

And he had jumped at the chance of being Control. Such a cushy, safe job, including hearing all the latest gossip first.

Now he was not so sure.

'It isn't right,' Pete Phillips said to Eric Johns in the canteen. 'Frank should have chosen between Fabulous, Gertie and the Doctor.'

'How do you think I feel? I nearly lost money on it.'

When the news that the three women had demanded that Frank should make a decision had reached the ranks, Eric Johns had opened a book on the likely result. Betting had been brisk. Fortunately for Eric Johns, as the odds on that particular possibility had been quite high, few had bet on the chances of Frank's escaping all their clutches.

'I'm serious,' said Pete Phillips. 'He's a mate, and when a mate does something wrong it's up to the other mate to see he doesn't go through with it. He's done me a good turn a number of times. I owe him more than one.'

Eric Johns had been serious about his close call with a financial disaster, but he also agreed with Pete Phillips.

'Not much we can do about it,' he noted sadly, 'apart from giving him the advice of older, more experienced men.'

'There may be something. You've heard who he's got engaged to?'

'No. Who?'

'Tricia Leigh, Fabulous's secretary.'

'You're joking!'

'Straight up.'

'Well, I never. Tricia Leigh.'

Eric Johns pondered this unexpected news.

'Not surprising, really, when you think about it,' he said. 'She's good looking, a lovely lass, always cheerful. I suppose you just tend to think of her as being so young, you know, more like a girl than a woman.' He smiled. 'Still, that will put the pigeon among the cats.'

'You mean the cat among the pigeons.'

'I know what I mean.'


Frank parked his car outside the address he had been given. Unlike most of Wellbury this was a dingy terraced house, the front garden overgrown and neglected, strewn with remnants of bicycles, rusty pieces of iron and an old, stinking mattress. The pebble-dashed walls were drab browny-grey, the paint on the front door had started peeling so long ago there was little left to peel. Loud voices were coming through the open front window, the curtains of which were probably best not washed, as the dirt was all that was holding them together. Guessing that the door-bell would not work he hammered on the door itself.

A voice inside invited him to "Eff off". He hammered again. Eventually it was opened by a bleary-eyed, pot-bellied man wearing only a pair of shorts and several amateur tattoos.

'Yeah? Wotcha want? If you're from the Social you can get

lost. If you're Jehovah's witnesses you better get lost before I shove your bloody bibles somewhere the sun don't shine.'

Frank showed the man his warrant card.

'Detective Sergeant Summers. We've had a report of a domestic argument disturbing the peace.'

''Ere, where's your uniform?' the other man asked, puzzled. 'You lot always wear uniforms.'

''Oo is it?' asked a voice from inside.

'It's the coppers, only this one ain't wearing a uniform,' the man said without turning his head, fascinated by this visit from a non-uniform-wearing police officer.

A head poked itself underneath his arm to confirm this sight, a thin, grey-haired woman who was at least a week late for a bath or shower.

'Bleeding 'ell,' it said, 'and he's on his own.' She looked at him. 'The others always come in pairs. Why you on your own?'

'I'm not on my own,' Frank replied. 'I've brought my kitten.'

Squishy's head popped out of his jacket pocket, awake and curious.

'Well blow me down,' whispered the man. 'See that, he's got a kitten.'

''Oo, it's lovely. I want a kitten like that.'

'Well you can't 'ave one, kittens need looking after.' He looked at Frank. 'She's a bit simple, you see. Doesn't realise how much work pets are.'

It was fortunate, Frank decided, that the man at least seemed to understand that fact, otherwise some poor animal might end up as neglected as the front garden.

'So,' he said, 'what's going on? We've had a complaint about noise.'

'Oh, we've just had our morning row,' the man said. 'She's bloody useless until I shout at her. Tires me out, it does, tires me out for the rest of the day.'

'You argue every morning?'

'Every single morning,' the man said proudly. 'Except bank holidays and Christmas, of course. Every man needs a rest now and then.'

Frank considered this. He wasn't surprised that the neighbours had called the police. He was just surprised they hadn't moved out. Probably because they couldn't find anyone foolish enough to buy a house close to this couple.

'You know there's a law against making a loud noise before eight in the morning?' he asked, at a loss for anything else to say.

'Yeah, well, sorry about that, mate, she was a little worse than normal this morning. Don't worry, we'll keep it down from now on.'

Frank guessed that that was what the man said whenever the police were called, and that would be on a regular basis. He also guessed that there was nothing else he could do here.

'Right, well, I'll be off then. Oh, by the way, you know that two gold doubloons were lost somewhere around this area? There's quite a reward for anyone finding them.'

'Gold dublunes? What's them when they're at home, mate?'

'Gold coins from the Spanish Armada, quite small coins, but very valuable. Collectors' items. The old man who owns them lost his way and was walking around here when he lost the coins too. They must have dropped out of pocket and rolled into someone's garden. Anyway, must be off.'

'A copper with a kitten,' said the woman in wonder as he walked back to his car. 'Don't see many of 'em these days.'

'You haven't seen one of 'em before, you daft cow,' the man replied. 'Now stop talking daft and get the shovel.'

Frank grinned to himself as he drove away. At the same time he wondered what the use of getting married was if you ended up like those two.

Still, they were undoubtedly an exception.


'You're looking cheerful this morning,' Frieda said as Tricia Leigh brought her her eleven o'clock cup of tea.

'I'm always cheerful,' Tricia responded – cheerfully.

'More so than normal, I would say.'

Whether this was true was debatable. Some unbiased observer might have suggested that it was Frieda who was less cheerful than Tricia. Though a wise observer would not have said so aloud.

Tricia pondered the question for a few seconds, smiling.

'Maybe I'm in love without realising it,' she said. 'They say that can happen. You meet someone, at first it doesn't seem special, then something happens and suddenly everything changes. I think that's what's happened.'

'Well kindly take your cheerfulness somewhere else,' Frieda snapped, slamming down a file in front of her. 'I have work to do.'

Tricia's face registered a sudden hurt. She closed the door and sat down behind her desk, miserably wondering why Frieda was being so sharp with her. She had never done that before.

She was allowed to be happy, wasn't she? She had experienced happiness so little in her life, why couldn't she have just one chance? And yet the whole station were treating her as if she were a pariah, from the moment she had turned up for work that day. No-one seemed to want to speak to her.

She decided to skip lunch that day. She couldn't face a canteen full of people deliberately trying to avoid her.

'At least I've got you,' she said to the many fluffy toys crowding her desk. 'At least you don't let me down.'

She picked up a bright pink rabbit and nuzzled it.

'You still love me, don't you, Pinky?'

Inside her office Frieda stood up and went to look out of the window. She shouldn't have been so short with young Tricia Leigh. It wasn't the girl's fault.

She sighed. It had all gone wrong, everything. Three years – was it three years? – ago when she had been posted to Wellbury she had been an ambitious, professional police officer, burying her ex-marriage to a fellow police officer and wife-beater in her work. Frank had arrived in Wellbury around the same time, and she had known from the start that he would be trouble.

She had not realised just how much and what sort of trouble.

Gertie had been right the previous evening. Had Frank chosen Gertie or Susan she, Frieda, could have lived with it.

If only just.

Instead his attention had lighted on Tricia Leigh. Everyone in the station knew, and everyone in the station disapproved.

Well, almost everyone. Apparently Sam Nightingale and Pete

Phillips had already had a slanging match. Sam had told him to keep his nose out of other people's business, that Frank had the right to make his own choice without his colleagues interfering, and that there was nothing wrong in Frank's choosing Tricia Leigh, after all, it was his choice. It was the longest sentence Sam had made since arriving at Wellbury, which showed how annoyed she was. She was, after all, a uniform constable and Pete Phillips a detective sergeant. Normally she would have avoided all contact with him.

Where previously there had been a camaraderie now there was dissension. And she, as an Inspector, would have to do something about it. Though she could hardly be described as an unbiased spectator.

It was all Frank's fault.

But was it really Frank's fault? Tricia was a bubbly young thing, loyal, happy, outgoing, the sort of woman that would suit Frank down to the ground. They would almost undoubtedly have a very happy marriage, three bubbly little children, get into debt, get out of it, laughing their way through their troubles and woes.

No, it wasn't Frank's fault, nor was it anyone else's. It was just life. And now it was time to get on with her own life. For three years she had forgotten about her ambition, her drive towards promotion. It was time to get back on track. Much as she loved Wellbury, it was time to move on. There would be no promotion here. There would certainly no longer be any enjoyment here.

She would ask for a transfer. Reason? She wanted to get ahead in her career. They would understand that. A transfer to somewhere larger would not take too long to organise. A couple of months at most and she could be gone, taking only memories of a better time.

Eric Johns was fond of pointing out that most people transferred to Wellbury initially hated the idea of being sent to such a small force, but they soon changed their minds, and no-one ever left until they retired. Well, now there would be one.

There was a knock at her door. Tricia must be away from her desk. She invited the knocker to enter. Gertie came in and closed the door.

'Could I have a word?' she asked.

'Go ahead, Gertie,' Frieda said without turning around from the window.

'It's just that – well, I don't know how to put this, it's not that I'm unhappy here, not with the job, that is, but ... I'd like to ask for a transfer.'

Frieda smiled thinly, turned around, went to her desk and sat down.

'Funny, that, I was just thinking of how Eric Johns always claims that people never want a transfer out of Wellbury. And now, suddenly, there's two doing just that.'

'Two? You mean ...?'

'Yes, I do mean. I'm going to request a transfer myself.' She sighed and put her chin in her hand. 'I've been arguing that Wellbury needs a larger force, another Inspector at least, with due sergeant and constables reporting to him – or her. Now I'm going to have to say, yes, we still need the extra resources, but can I leave, please?'

'It's better, this way,' Gertie said after a pause. 'I've been studying for the sergeant's exams, but I haven't really been paying much attention to it, or to my law studies. This way we can get on with our lives.'

'My feelings exactly.'

'I feel a little sorry for Susan. She can hardly request a transfer anywhere.'

'No, I suppose not. And even when Frank leaves, which I presume he will do, sooner or later, she'll be reminded of him wherever she goes.'

'I don't think he'll ever leave.'

Frieda nodded.

'No, I suppose he probably won't. He and Wellbury fit each other too well.'

'How long do you think it will take? A transfer, I mean.'

'Oh, not too long. A month, maybe two, if I can push things through fast enough. I could probably get it done within a week if we had a better reason, harassment or something like that. Unfortunately we'd only be laughed at if I gave the real reason. Anyway, you don't want anything on your file which might do your career any harm.'

'I bought two tickets for the fancy dress ball in September from Eric Johns,' Gertie said mournfully. 'It sounded like a great idea. Now I just want to be away before it comes around.'

'I suppose I'll have to buy a couple of tickets, to set an example, if nothing else. Just thinking about it makes me feel depressed.'

Gertie twisted her fingers as if there was something else she wanted to say.

'I don't suppose I could be transferred back to uniform until my posting comes through?' she asked finally.

'Not a good idea, Gertie, not if you want to get ahead. You've always wanted to be a detective, don't throw it away now. Just keep your head down, lose yourself in work, plod on until the posting comes through. I'll do my best to make sure you don't have to spend too much time with Frank.'

Gertie nodded miserably and left. She walked past Tricia Leigh without a word, just as she had when she had come through to Frieda's office.

Tricia squared her jaw and tried not to let the tears show. She could handle some of the others being nasty, she'd had that sort of thing before in her previous job, but she liked the Inspector and Gertie, she'd always thought of them as friends.


'Here, Eric,' Frank said in the canteen, 'I understand that you're organising the Policeman's Ball in September.'

'It's officially the Police Ball, not the Policeman's Ball, Frank. And, no, I'm not organising it, I'm not that stupid. I'm just selling tickets.'

'It's a fancy-dress ball, isn't it?'

'Got it in one, Frank. Can't say I'm looking forward to it, but the missus is. And the profits go to the police widows' and orphans' fund, so it's a good cause.'

'Didn't they change that to the police widows', widowers' and orphans' fund? Anyhow, no matter. I'll take two tickets. For the first time in my life I am planning for the future. I intend to bring a very special someone.'

Eric Johns looked at him mournfully.

'I thought you might say something like that,' he said. He put his teacup down solemnly. 'Frank,' he continued, 'now I don't want to come across like a father figure, but I really think I ought to give you some words of advice from someone who is older than you, someone who has seen a lot more of life.'

Frank's tea paused on its way to his mouth. It seemed as taken aback as he was. While Eric Johns was well known for being happy to dispense dubious advice to naive constables, he hadn't made that mistake with Frank before.

'No, don't interrupt, Frank,' Eric Johns said to a man who was obviously too surprised to interrupt. 'Only, you know the saying, marry in haste and repent at leisure. Now I've been happily married for almost thirty years, and you know why? Because the missus and I knew each other for many years before we tied the knot. We were childhood sweethearts. We knew each other better than anyone else. No, now, let me finish. I've seen a lot of failures in my time, and it's always been a case of people jumping into things without thinking, without taking time. '

Frank put his cup of tea down.

'Eric,' he said slowly, 'what are you blathering on about?'

Eric Johns raised a hand.

'The old sayings still hold true, Frank. Look before you leap.'

'What about "he who hesitates is lost"?'

'A fool rushes in where angels dare to tread, remember that, Frank.'

Eric Johns finished his tea, stood up, patted Frank on his shoulder and said:

'Remember, trust the advice of your friends, Frank. They only want what is best for you.'

'And don't forget the well-known aphorism of the great Roman Cicero,' Frank said. 'Dino, dinat, donner.'

'Precisely,' said Eric Johns.

Frank's radio beeped as he watched him go.

'Summers,' he answered.

'Control here, Sarge. Could you attend another domestic for us? Over.'

Frank looked around the canteen. He could count five uniformed officers having a tea break.

'Sid, I can see five uniforms sitting doing nothing.'

'Er, sorry, Sarge, they're all assigned to other things. Over.'

'Okay, Sid,' Frank sighed. 'Just this once more.'


Frank parked his car outside the house where the supposed domestic was taking place. He got out with his jacket, Squishy happily in the pocket, peering out at the world. As he locked the car a solidly-made ashtray came flying through the left side of the front window, scattering cigarette butts and ash. The window, being closed at the time, burst into smithereens. The ashtray just missed Frank, leaving a dent in the side of his car. Squishy immediately hid in his jacket pocket. She didn't approve of smoking.

'You bloody idiot, you almost killed me with that thing,' shouted a male voice from within the house.

'That's what I was trying to do, you bastard,' screamed a female voice. 'And if you don't leave I will kill you.'

Frank bent down and picked up the ashtray.

'Leave? This is my bloody house. You can leave. Go on, get out.'

'Don't you dare touch me.'

Frank weighed the ashtray in his hand. He nodded thoughtfully.

Then he flipped it back through the window, taking some more fragments with it.

He strolled up to the front door as two incredulous voices asked, in various flavours, what precisely was going on. He rang the bell. He noticed a young girl of about six crouched next to a bush, hiding out of sight of the doorway, holding a baby of about two years old. He winked at them.

An angry man wrenched the front door open.

'Ah, Mr Whittle, maybe you remember me, Sergeant Summers.'

'What the hell do you want? Piss off, I'm busy.' He was about to shut the door when something struck him. 'Hey, it was you what threw that ashtray through our window, wasn't it? I'm going to have you for that, I am.'

'Ashtray?' asked Frank innocently. 'What ashtray was that? I noticed that your front window was broken. You didn't throw an ashtray through it, did you? You could get arrested for that sort of thing. Especially as it hit my car – a police car. I wondered what that was – it bounced straight back through your window.'

'I didn't throw it, the missus did.'

'No I didn't,' came Mrs Whittle's voice. 'It was him. Go on, arrest him. He's been beating me up, he has.'

'Beating her up? I should be so lucky. She's been trying to kill me, the bitch.'

'Okay, that's enough,' Frank said. 'I hope that, while you two are acting like a pair of two year-olds your own two year-old is safe.'

'Oh my god, Johnny,' cried the woman, running back into the house.

'Stupid bloody woman,' Mr Whittle muttered, rushing after her.

Frank smiled and strolled over to where the six year-old sat.

'You must be Gina,' he said, squatting down next to her. 'I'm Frank Summers.'

The girl merely looked at him, a hint of mistrust and fear in her eyes.

'Someone told me you don't like your little brother,' Frank suggested.

'That's not true! I love little Johnny. But he wanders all over the place and gets into trouble, and I get blamed. I can't keep my eyes on him all the time, I have things I want to do as well.'

'What about your Nan?'

'She lives on the other side of town. Anyway, she's too old. She's over fifty.'

'Do your mummy and daddy argue a lot?'

'They never used to. But then daddy lost his job. He got a new one, but he always seems to be angry. They're always fighting these days. I look after Johnny when they do that, he doesn't like it, he runs away.'

'Johnny!' cried Mrs Whittle at the front door.

'Thank god for that,' muttered Mr Whittle. Frank stood up as Mrs Whittle ran to her child, barring her way.

'Not just yet, Mrs Whittle,' he said.

'That's my baby! Get out of my way!'

'I told you, not just yet. Now stop your nonsense or you'll be spending the rest of the day in a police cell. And that goes for you too, Mr Whittle. The Social will have to look after your children.'

'You won't send them to jail, will you?' pleaded Gina. Frank turned and winked at her.

'They've been very naughty,' he said. 'Now I want you to take little Johnny inside and look after him while I have a word with your mummy and daddy. Will you do that for me?'

'Oh, yes, of course!' she cried, her face grinning at the secret wink. She hurried indoors with Johnny while Frank held Mrs Whittle by the arm.

'Now listen the pair of you,' he said softly. 'I'm not a social worker, I'm a copper. But I don't like seeing two kids scared because a pair of muffins like you two like having a go at each other. So if you insist on disturbing the peace I will take you down the police station and lock you up. Trust me. I'll make sure that, whenever anyone from the station has to come here to sort you out, both of you will end up in the cells. I wouldn't like anyone to accuse me of favouritism. And believe me, it will happen. I'm a sergeant. If I tell any constables to nick you whenever they get the chance, they will do it. Apart from that they all know that I'm a really nasty sod when crossed, so they wouldn't even think of not doing it. Understand?'

The two looked down at the ground, each with their hands crossed in front of them, as if they were two unruly school children being chastised by the headmaster. Each muttered something. Squishy, deciding that the danger had passed –

that there were no longer any smokers in the vicinity with dangerous flying ashtrays – popped her head out to enjoy the spectacle.

'Sorry, didn't quite catch that.'

'I said I was sorry,' said Mr Whittle.

'I said we was sorry,' said Mrs Whittle.

'Yeah, that's what I meant,' corrected Mr Whittle. 'I meant we was sorry.'

'And there's the little matter of a large dent in my car.'

'I'll pay for that,' Mr Whittle said to the ground.

'Don't be a bloody idiot,' Mrs Whittle said, also to the ground, 'we can't afford that. What are you going to do, spend the money we don't have on a copper's car and let Johnny and Gina starve?'

'Okay, we'll forget the car,' Frank decided.

'No,' Mr Whittle said, looking up at him, in his eyes. 'We dented your car, it's only right we should pay for it. We might be poor, but fair's fair. I might not be able to pay for it right now, but I'll get the money sooner or later. There,' he continued, turning to his wife, 'I've said it. We're poor. You can throw that in my face whenever you want. I admit it, we're poor. And it's my fault. Happy now?'

'Oh, Johnny,' she cried, looking up at him, tears in her eyes, 'it's not your fault, it isn't your fault. I just wish you wouldn't get so angry about it all the time.'

Frank rolled his eyes.

'Right, just so long as we understand each other,' he said, rather uselessly, as they were no longer listening. He returned to his car, placed the jacket with Squishy on the passenger seat and drove off.

'He had a kitten in his jacket,' said Mrs Whittle, still looking anxiously into her husband's face.

'Don't be daft,' said Mr Whittle. 'You're a right little muffin, you are.'

'So are you. We're both just two little muffins.'

It was as well for Frank that he did not hear that conversation. Having to handle domestic arguments was bad enough. The idea of going directly from a perfectly good argument to sweet mutterings in sixty seconds flat would not have sat happily with him.

'You know, Squish,' he said, 'I am really beginning to wonder about this marriage lark. Somehow I wonder if men weren't designed to stay single all their lives. Or maybe it's just me. Maybe I'm destined to be a bachelor.'

He paused.

'That's not a very rational thing to say, is it, Squish? Destiny, fate, karma. Load of bollocks, isn't it, Squish?'

Squishy miaowed at him. She didn't know what karma was, but if it was edible she was prepared to try it. It was waaay past lunch time.


## Tuesday Afternoon: Domestic 2

'Control to Sergeant Summers.'

'Go on, Sid, tell me you've got something interesting for me.'

'Sorry, Sarge, another domestic, I'm afraid. But you'll like this one, Sarge. The vicar's cleaning lady is having a go at him.'

'The whosits is doing whatsits to whomits?'

'You know St Mary's church, Sarge? The one next to the cemetery?'

'Know it? Intimately, Sid, intimately.'

That was perhaps not strictly true, but he had occasion to visit the church previously, when it turned out that the incumbent at the time had in fact been a psychopathic killer living under the guise of a vicar. And the cemetery was where Jean Candour was buried.

'Could you attend, Sarge? Vicar's name is Cringely.'

'Certainly, Sid, it will be a pleasure. After all, a vicar named Cringely, who could refuse?'

And it would give him a chance to make sure Aggie was okay.

Aggie was what the Social Services termed "a problem case". No-one knew anything about her past. She had apparently been a bag lady of sorts when she was discovered in a woman's garden shed just before the previous Christmas. The woman had given her a meal and a hot bath, in return for which Aggie had demanded that she be given something to do in repayment. The woman had, eventually, agreed that Aggie should help her tidy her husband's grave. After the festive season was over the woman discovered that Aggie had taken up residence in the cemetery, dedicating her time to looking after any untended grave, especially those of children.

The reason the Social Services found Aggie a problem was that, though she was obviously old, with a hideous scar disfiguring her face, she believed herself to be twelve, and that when she turned twelve and a half in October, would be joining her brothers and sisters, those buried in the cemetery, in the peace and light of the Lord. A further problem was that she was quite self-sufficient, using the facilities of the church to keep herself clean, with twice-weekly hot baths at the house of the woman who had originally discovered her, as a treat. Visitors to the cemetery, mainly the elderly, gave her what money they could afford as payment for keeping the graves in a tidy condition.

The ultimate problem for the Social Services was that Aggie appeared, if you ignored the facts, to be a happy, if reserved and shy, twelve year-old.

Frieda and Frank had each originally encountered her, on separate occasions, as she was placing wild flowers on a grave. They had each jumped to the conclusion that she was stealing them, and waded into the attack, thoroughly terrifying the poor woman. When the facts were explained to them they had been so shocked that they had each decided to atone by looking after her as best they could.

Such as on this occasion. Frank intended to settle the question of the vicar's problems with his cleaning lady, and then pop in to the cemetery to check on Aggie.

He found the vicar in the vestry, sitting on a chair while a tight-lipped woman of about forty wearing black bandaged his head.

'Detective Sergeant Summers,' he introduced himself. 'I hear there's been a bit of bother.'

'Oh, dear,' said the vicar, 'it wasn't Mrs Haggerty who called you, was it?'

'Mrs Haggerty?'

'My cleaning lady. She might have misinterpreted the situation.'

'And what situation is that?'

Vicar Cringely paused before replying.

'Mrs Barton here takes care of a number of what I term as the secular requirements – looking after the flowers, making sure the vestments are in order, that sort of thing. This morning she brought cleaning materials in to shine up the thurible – we only use it on rare occasions.' He motioned towards a half-shined thurible lying on the floor. 'She was cleaning it when it slipped out of her hands and hit me on the head. I'm afraid that Mrs Haggerty might have jumped to the conclusion that we were having an argument.'

'She was cleaning it when it went off?' suggested Frank, not believing a word the vicar had said.

'Sorry?'

'Never mind. So long as it was just an accident there's no need for me to stick around. Look after yourself, vicar, Mrs Barton.'

He nodded and left. There was no way that thurible had accidentally slipped out of Mrs Barton's hands and clocked the vicar on the head. The man would have to have been lying on the floor for that to happen.

Unless he had been lying on the floor. Perhaps that was the latest position to pray in.

But how, then, had Mrs Haggerty mistaken it for an argument?

Unless Mrs Barton had flung it.

He gave a mental shrug and headed towards the cemetery entrance. To his surprise Frieda was just coming out.

'Hi there,' he said.

'Ah, Frank,' she replied, just as surprised to see him, and not, apparently, pleasantly surprised, more nervous. 'What are you doing here?'

'Someone reported a domestic at the church. I thought I'd use the opportunity to pop in and see that Aggie was okay.'

'A domestic at the church?'

'A divine domestic, presumably. Anyway, the vicar claims that it was all a misunderstanding, he just had an accident with a levitating thurible.'

'Right. Good. Well, so long as it's all under control. I'd better get back to the station.'

'What were you here for? Anything interesting?'

'I was just checking up on this ghost business. I must rush, I'm late for a meeting. I'll see you later.'

Frank watched her go, a surprised frown on his face. She was obviously avoiding him, or at least avoiding being alone with him.

He shrugged and walked into the cemetery. People were behaving rather strangely, but, to his mind, people always behaved strangely. Which made it perfectly normal.

The idea that his own behaviour might ever be deemed to be strange never crossed his mind. After all, if other peoples' strange behaviour was normal, then so must be his. There was probably a Latin tag for that sort of thing.

He found Aggie hard at work on a grave towards the back of the cemetery. Aggie was perhaps some peoples' idea of the ideal worker, with no thoughts on her mind other than what she was concentrating on, no idea of holidays, with perhaps just the tiny flaw of thinking of roaming the neighbourhood after dark hoping to hear some music.

'Hello, Aggie, how are things?' Frank asked.

'Hello,' she said neutrally, much like a girl of twelve might speak to an adult male she was not entirely sure of. 'Have you brought Squishy?'

'Of course,' replied Frank, lying his jacket on the ground to let Squishy out.

'I'll get her some water,' Aggie said, jumping to her feet and running off to the stand-pipe.

Frank perched himself on the raised side of a grave and watched as Aggie stroked a Squishy gratefully lapping at the cup of water.

'So, everything okay, Aggie?'

'Yes. Squishy is getting fat.'

'Not troubled by ghosts, then.'

'There are no such things as ghosts, only spirits. Spirits can't harm you, only ghosts can.'

Frank wondered whether, should he spend the time thinking about it, whether that statement would ever end up making any sense.

'When is the lady in white leaving?' Aggie asked suddenly, her concentration on Squishy. The "Lady in White" was Aggie's name for Frieda. Frieda always visited her after Sunday tennis, wearing her white tennis clothes.

'Frieda? Frieda's not leaving,' Frank replied, surprised. 'What gave you that idea?'

'She said she might be leaving. When people want to be polite they say "might", but it means they're going do to what they say.'

'I'm sure Frieda isn't going to leave Wellbury.'

Aggie ignored his sureness.

'Do you think she'll leave before October?' she asked.

Being sure that Frieda wasn't about to leave Wellbury at all allowed him to be confident of his answer.

'I'm sure she won't leave before October, Aggie.'

'Are you going to leave?'

'Of course not, Aggie. I like it too much. I intend to settle down and become an old man here. I shall grow old disgracefully, as they say.'

'I'm sure you won't, you're just teasing me.' She tickled Squishy. 'Will you come and see me before October?'

'I'll be here at least once a week,' Frank promised.

Aggie stood up reluctantly.

'I must be going.'

She gave him a brief look.

'He was wearing black, and flying,' she said. 'The ghost they're talking about. Bye-bye, Squishy, come again soon.'

Before Frank could say anything she was moving quickly away, seeming to disappear amongst the tombstones, even though they weren't tall enough to hide her.

### Tuesday Evening: Still Friends

Gertie did not seriously pray for another missing toddler to delay the "quick drink" she knew would be Frank's invitation that evening, but she wouldn't have minded something less serious. As it was she was out of luck, and reluctantly followed Frank to the Hangman's pub near Heading Square, a name she felt more than appropriate under the circumstances.

'I know what you're going to say,' she said, playing with Squishy as Frank brought their drinks and sat down next to her. 'We can still be friends, but that's it.'

'Well, more than friends, Gertie. You know I've always thought of you as a younger sister. I am very fond of you. You know that, don't you?'

'I suppose so,' Gertie sighed.

The barmaid behind the counter was new. She had noticed them come in. Such a nice, attractive couple. The barmaid was a dreamy sort. At that moment she imagined that the young man with the quiff of white hair was telling his girlfriend how much he had looked forward to meeting her tonight.

And that cute little kitten that had popped out of his pocket. She wasn't sure if it should be allowed in, but it was so cute she had decided to pretend not to have noticed it.

'You really need to get out more, Gerts. Meet people, that sort of thing. People who aren't police officers. What about your studies, Aikido classes, that sort of thing? You haven't been going to Aikido much lately, have you?'

'Not really. Anyway, the people there are either happily married or gung-ho eighteen-year-olds.'

'What about the Open University? Surely you must meet loads of people on your course?'

'It's distance learning. You never get to meet anyone.'

Frank could recognise an uphill struggle when saw one. Normally he would have abandoned it as a waste of time. But he had been truthful when he had said he was fond of Gertie.

'They must have social events, Gerts,' he said. 'Get togethers, that sort of thing. What about these famous summer schools I've heard of? Dens of iniquity, so I'm told. Drinking till the early hours and then orgies before breakfast.'

'None of my courses have had a summer school,' Gertie replied in a sad voice which suggested she wouldn't have minded the odd orgy before breakfast, if only for the social side.

'Well, can't you take one with a summer school then?'

'I suppose so.'

Frank was close to sighing, not a practice he normally indulged in.

'Come on, Gerts, buck up. Life's not that bad. You're young, very attractive – and usually full of the joys of spring.'

'It's just that – well, I wish it had been someone else.'

'How do you mean, "someone else"?'

'You know what I mean.'

'No, Gerts, haven't a clue. Enlighten me.'

'You know what I mean,' Gertie repeated.

Frank gave it up as a bad job. When a woman says "you know what I mean" and refuses to expand on that statement a wise man leaves well enough alone.

There, thought the barmaid, a little tiff. A little lovers' tiff. All lovers had them.

'Harry and Allison are getting married in September,' the wise man said, promptly putting his foot in it. 'Eric's organising a collection. I've always wondered what you buy a couple for their wedding these days, normally they've already got crockery and cutlery and all the rest.'

Gertie burst into tears.

'Oh, come on, Gerts, come on, please don't cry,' he said, putting an arm around her.

'You are a total bastard, you are,' she said through her tears. 'I hate you, I really hate you.'

Well, that went well, he thought.

See, thought the barmaid, they've already got over it, she's in his arms and crying happily.

## Wednesday Morning: Domestic 4

'And may you stay forever young,' Frank sang to himself as he drove to work. Squishy, fortunately, was too young to have heard Bob Dylan sing the same words, and point out that Frank's attempt at imitation was so far off the mark it had entered another, non-musical, universe.

'Control to Sergeant Summers, Control to Sergeant Summers, over,' warbled his radio.

'Flippin' Ada,' he muttered. 'Second day in a row. Summers here, over.'

'Could you attend a call for us, Sarge? It's another domestic.'

'What, another one? What's wrong with these people? First thing in the morning and they're already having it out. What do they do for the rest of the day? And where are the uniforms? Has there been a mass breakout of crime, or have they all called in sick?'

'Sorry, Sarge, just the way things go, sometimes.'

'Oh very well. Give me the address.'


In the radio room Bobby Stang stretched his neck to relieve his muscles.

'I do not like this,' he said to Sid Feeler, who had just arrived.

'Has to be done,' Sid replied. 'Can't let the poor bloke make a mistake like he's trying to make.'

'You don't think anything we do will make a difference to Sergeant Summers, do you?'

'Bobby, with Wellbury's finest on his case, he hasn't got a ghost's chance.'


At least this time, thought Frank, the address was in Lords Acres, a wealthier part of town. Though how, with large gardens and the houses far apart, a domestic could disturb the tranquil peace it was difficult to guess.

He drove up a long drive, parked in front of the house, picked up his jacket, slipped Squishy in the pocket and got out.

'Come on, Squish, let's see how the other half live and fight.'

As he closed the door to his car the reason for the complaints became obvious. There was the sound of twin blasts of a shotgun going off at the back of the house.

'Oh, no, Squish, that doesn't sound good. I do not like guns. Nothing personal, just that someone tried to kill me with one, once, before you came along. Which is why I have this white quiff of hair you like playing with when you get the chance.'

He hesitated for a moment, pondering on whether to call for backup or not, as he knew he should do.

'Let's just have a quick gander, Squish. If it looks dodgy we'll get out sharpish.'


In the station reception Eric Johns sat on a stool behind the counter with a book of quotations in his hands.

'Sissero, Sissero,' he muttered to himself.

'What's up, Sergeant?' Sam Nightingale asked as she entered in her pre-shift uniform of motorbike leathers and crash helmet.

'I'm looking for a quotation by that Roman bloke, Sissero.'

Sam looked at the book.

'I think you'll find Cicero begins with a "C", not an "S",' she suggested. 'C-i-c-e-r-o.'

'Course, I know that. I was just distracted for a moment.' He rubbed the side of his temple with a finger. 'You know that well known quotation of his, dino, deenat, donner? I was just making sure I had the spelling right.'

'Well known? I've never heard of it. It doesn't even sound like Latin. Or "donner" doesn't, anyway. That sounds German.'

She leaned down towards him.

'You don't suppose someone's been taking the Mickey out of you, do you Sergeant?' she asked in a low voice, her eyes twinkling, her lips curved.

Eric Johns gave her a sour look.

'Bloody Frank!' He slammed the book closed. 'You think a bloke's a mate, and then what does he do? Gets engaged to someone he shouldn't, and then acts as if he's so high and mighty and superior.'

'If he chooses to get engaged to someone it's his own choice. Nothing to do with any of us. We should all be happy for him.'

'Love, you might say so, but you're the only one who does. You're new to Wellbury. We've been his mates for a long time. We only want what's best for him. We want to protect him.'

Frank walked warily around the side of the house. At the back there was a large, normally neatly-kept lawn now littered with dining-room chairs, most in tatters, the others awaiting their end. A man stood reloading a shotgun, his back to Frank. As Frank watched the man lifted the shotgun to his shoulder and blasted two more chairs, one and two. Frank put his jacket and Squishy down to one side and moved forward as soon as the shotgun was broken open for the next round.

'Police,' he called out, warrant card in hand. 'Put the shotgun down and keep your hands where I can see them.'

The man whipped around.

'I told you, put the gun down, now.'

'Who the hell are you?' asked the man. 'And what the hell do you think you're doing on my property.'

'I'm a police officer, and you have three seconds to put that gun down.'

'Oh, really? What if I don't?'

'I'll break your jaw for you, how's that?'

The fierce look in Frank's eyes and his bunched fist convinced the man that laying down the shotgun was a good idea. He did so with a bad grace.

'How dare you speak to me like that?' he demanded. 'I shall complain to the Chief Constable.'

'You'll be able to do that from a prison cell if you don't have a very good reason for using a firearm in a built-up area.'

'Oh, thank heavens you've come,' said a refined woman's

voice from the steps at the back of the house. Frank turned to find a well-dressed woman of about forty emerging from the rear French windows. 'He's gone quite mad.'

'You get back inside!' shouted the man.

'Okay, okay, enough of that,' Frank interrupted, deeply relieved that the gun was out of action, surprised to find that he was short of breath and his hearting was pumping wildly. 'Care to tell me why you're shooting these chairs? It isn't the season for it, as far as I know. Chair shooting season starts in October, everybody knows that.'

'Very funny, Constable.'

'Sergeant, actually. Detective Sergeant Frank Summers.'

'Sergeant, then. If you must know, they were a present from my mother-in-law on our wedding day.'

Frank considered this. It hardly seemed a good reason for shooting them, and the couple did not look recently married, so if there had been a reason surely it would have been done long before?

'Well, that isn't the chairs' fault, now is it? Not really.'

'My mother was planning on staying with us for a couple of weeks,' the woman explained. 'Charles absolutely refused to let her into the house. When I insisted that I have the right to have my mother here he just went totally berserk and began shooting the chairs.'

'If she does have the temerity to turn up she won't have anywhere to sit down to eat,' the man said with a good deal of satisfaction. 'And her meals will consist of sawdust from those horrible chairs.'

'She was right about you. She told me I should never have

married you. She told me I would regret it and how right she was.'

'She's a whingeing old harpy who should be burnt at the stake along with the rest of the witches in your family, and you've turned out to be just as a much a witch as the rest of them. My mother warned me about you. I just wish I'd listened to her.'

'Your mother is an interfering old harridan.'

'Your mother is a leathery old bat.'

They paused, having run out of insults. The man turned to Frank.

'Well, there you have it, Sergeant. Since the chairs are my own property I have committed no crime. I apologise for using the shotgun, I should have thought of the neighbours. I'll use an axe instead.'

'I'm sorry, sir, I can't allow you to do that,' Frank replied.

'Why ever not? They are my property. If I want to smash them up you can't stop me.'

'The trouble is that they are also your wife's property. If you both agreed to destroy them, yes, that would be quite acceptable. I'd even offer a hand, if I had the time. Breaking things can be very therapeutic. As it is, I doubt if your wife would agree, so, it's a no-go, I'm afraid.'

'Ridiculous!' said the man in a tone that showed he had realised that the argument was irrefutable.

Frank shrugged his shoulders.

'Sorry, but that's the way it is.'

'Aren't you going to arrest him for the damage he's already done?' asked the woman.

'I'd rather not. It would mean having to take both of you down to the station, spend a lot of time and effort on paperwork, and all it would result in is a caution.'

'I will most certainly not be taken down to the station, as you put it,' declared the woman.

'So there you have it,' Frank said, retrieving Squishy and his jacket. 'I'll leave you two lovebirds to sort yourselves out.'

'That's it? You're leaving?'

'Absolutely. You've already interrupted my morning, and my kitten is dying for a saucer of milk. Come on, Squish.'

'You're bloody useless as a wife,' Frank heard the man say as he walked around the side of the house, back to his car. 'You could at least have offered the officer's kitten a saucer of milk.'

The reply to this was the crash of the French windows slamming closed.

'See, Squish, they've got loads of money, a lovely house, no doubt good jobs, security, all the rest, and even they can't get along. What hope for the rest of mankind, eh?'

Squishy had become quite the philosopher under Frank's tutelage. She considered this for all of half a second before miaowing to point out that she was hungry.

'Exactly, Squish, you have it in one. Carpe Diem. Let us live as Epicurus did.'

Squishy frowned. She wondered if this Epicurus was a new dish, and whether or not she would like it.

### Wednesday Lunchtime: Say That Again Sam

Frank sat in the canteen enjoying a cheese omelette, Squishy sitting on his jacket next to the table leg, waiting for the next passer-by to offer her a titbit or a pat on the head or tickle under the chin. Squishy, Frank noticed, was getting all the petting and plaudits, while he was getting almost none.

Not that he actually wanted to be petted, of course.

And, anyway, he thought, interrupting someone absorbed in one of Agnetha's creations was tantamount to interrupting a person at prayer. Agnetha had a way with herbs and spices that transformed a simple cheese omelette into heaven, plus she had included little pieces of roast potato in a way he had only heard the Germans do, yet German cuisine could never have hoped to attain the sublime heights Agnetha did. Agnetha even made porridge for breakfast sound appealing.

Not appealing enough to try it, though. Not even Agnetha could break through memories of boarding school porridge.

'Mind if I join you, sir?' asked a voice next to him.

'Not at all, Sam,' he replied as Sam Nightingale slid into the chair opposite. He sighed with the air of a man replete as he pushed his empty plate away, and in the manner of a man who wishes his stomach were larger. 'Tell me something, Sam, I'm not wearing the wrong kind of deodorant or aftershave, am I?'

'How do you mean, sir?'

'Well, I just have this strange feeling that people are avoiding me. Or am I imagining things?'

'You know why that is, sir.'

'No, I don't. Go on, Sam, give us a hint.'

She looked at him dispassionately and began tucking into her lunch.

'You know why, sir. And I do not get caught up in other peoples' personal problems or interfere in their decisions.'

Frank sighed. If Sam was going to do the equivalent of "You know what I mean" it was time to give up.

'Squishy!' she exclaimed, looking down at the kitten miaowing at her and tugging on her leg. 'You want to sit on my lap, do you? Come on then.'

She picked Squishy up and put her on her lap, where the kitten sat purring and watching the world go by from underneath the table, accepting the occasional morsel from Sam.

'I've never thought of you as an animal person, Sam.'

'I'm not. But Squish is a friend now. She's coming on quite nicely isn't she?'

Squish was, indeed, "coming on nicely". Within the space of a week she had turned from a terrified scrap of a kitten into a plump little thing no longer entirely afraid of the world – as long as Frank was around, and even that was changing – and no longer in fear of food deprivation but quite possibly the opposite.

'She's going to have to go on a diet soon, if she's not careful,' Frank noted. 'Everybody insists on giving her something to eat, just a titbit, but it all adds up.'

'She'll be fine if she gets enough exercise, she's still young,' Sam replied, concentrating on her own scrambled eggs on toast. It was a point they shared in common: fear that Agnetha's delights might turn them into mirror images of Eric Johns. Strangely enough, Agnetha, whose only wish, apart from keeping her boys' and girls' stomachs happy, was that they should all marry, settle down and have happy families, had quite taken – if you knew how to interpret Agnetha's dour lack of emotion – to the new, gay, Constable Sam Nightingale.

So had Frank, after the initial power struggle. That had ended in what might be described on paper as a score-draw, but despite her distance and her insistence on calling him "sir", Sam had come to like this eternal boy.

So much so that her new girlfriend was becoming jealous of him.

Silly woman.

'I think an afternoon siesta for her,' Frank said, 'followed by a strenuous game of football.'

'1986, but with Maradona out with an injury?' suggested Sam.

'Hamstring, I think,' replied Frank. 'He always was such a ham actor.'

'We could have won that year,' Sam said, finishing off her scrambled eggs and pulling her sticky-toffee dessert towards her.

'Maybe next time,' Frank replied wistfully.

'Mind if I join you?' asked Pete Phillips, tray in hand, ending the domestic harmony.

'The more the merrier,' said Frank. 'Pull up a pew, Pete.'

'Ah, that's better,' Pete said, sighing as he sat down. Sam sucked on her dessert spoon and watched him with the look of a subordinate who doesn't think much of her superior officer, but is far too polite and intelligent to say so.

'You look a bit knackered, Pete,' Frank said sympathetically. 'Not been overdoing the overtime again, have you?'

'It's this bloody ghost,' Pete replied, taking a bite of one of

Agnetha's original hamburgers with cheese (to call it a cheeseburger would be an insult).

'What, not the graveyard ghost again? What's it done this time, attacked another passer-by?'

'You heard about that?' Pete asked, surprised.

'You know me, Pete, I'm psychic. So, tell me all about it.'

'Phil Walthers of the Herald heard a call come in last night. So he gives Percy a bell to find out what the story is – he's planning a front page story about it. So Percy calls me and asks me to have a look. Well, I haven't much choice, have I, not if I want to be an inspector some day. So I toddle off and spend most of the night sitting in the car outside the cemetery. It was both bloody boring and bloody tiring, I can tell you.'

Now that, thought Frank, explained quite a few things. Such as why Frieda had been at the cemetery the previous day. Both Frieda and Percy were hungry for their own promotion. It had taken Percy a while to catch on to Frieda's approach: while he knew that getting his name into the newspapers was a good thing, he had presumed the best way of doing that was to handle the normal run of break-ins and burglaries. Frieda had always known that it was the more unusual stories that made the front page, and remained in people's memories long after. Nicking a ghost would be ten times as valuable as nicking a tealeaf.

'I warned you about that lust for promotion, Pete,' he said. 'It won't do you any good.'

'It's okay for you,' moaned Pete. 'You don't want promotion. You're quite happy as you are.'

'Oh, it's not that I don't want it, just that I'm not willing to pay the price of doing silly things like sitting outside a cemetery all night to get it.' He closed his eyes and pressed his fingers to his forehead as if in sudden concentration. 'I'm getting a psychic thought coming through here – yes, yes, it's becoming clearer, yes, I see a woman, a married woman, very unhappy with her husband because of his dedication to ambition.' He looked up at Pete. 'Am I right?'

'Very funny, Frank. In fact, there's something I wanted to say to you about that. Now I've been happily married for quite a few years – okay, maybe not always that happily, there have been one or two rough spots, but the reason we've got through them is that we know each other well. We knew each other for years before we took the plunge. If you ever look at the reasons for couples splitting up, ninety-nine percent of them rushed into it without thinking.'

'It's a good day for my voices, you know, Pete. They're telling me that you're about to say "look before you leap".'

'Well, strange you should mention that, Frank, actually – '

'No, wait, the next is "fools rush in where angels dare to tread".'

'Well, I was going to say – '

'"Marry in haste, repent at leisure"?'

'That's exactly – '

Frank stood up and patted his shoulder.

'See, Pete, I can read your mind. Don't worry, I won't tell your missus what you were thinking when you were interviewing that blonde the other day.'

Pete Phillips watched Frank as he collected his jacket and Squishy and walked away.

'Bloody hell,' he said softly. 'I knew Frank was good, I didn't know he was a mind reader.'

'So what were you thinking when you interviewed the blonde the other day?' Sam Nightingale asked with a sweet smile.

Pete Phillips frowned at her and busied himself with his hamburger with cheese. The blonde had been a right looker. Such a pity it had turned out that she was carrying the proceeds of a lucrative shoplifting expedition when he had released her without a caution, and without a search. It was Sam who had discovered the proceeds when she had arrested the woman less than an hour later in a different shop.

It was not the sort of thing that led to promotion.

There was something wrong with this Sam Nightingale, he decided. She seemed to see things other people didn't.

'Don't worry, Sergeant,' she said, standing up, 'we all make mistakes.'

I'll bet you don't, thought Pete Phillips as she walked away. Not ever.

He decided that he would have to keep an eye on Sam Nightingale. She had an aura of someone who knew something, something more than any normal person. At least more than a certain ambitious detective sergeant. And it was only logical that an ambitious detective sergeant would want to make sure that he found out what she knew and he didn't.

## Wednesday Evening: Still Friends (2)

It was Susan's turn at the Hangman's. She had been tempted to decline or defer Frank's invitation, but had decided in the end that it was best to get it over and done with. She had come to accept that it was their fault that things had come to this point, the three of them had pushed Frank too far and she was not the type to attempt to avoid her own responsibility.

'I know what you're going to say,' she said, playing with Squishy as Frank brought their drinks to their table. 'We can still be friends, but no more.'

The new barmaid was puzzled. She recognised the man – even with a bad memory for faces, you couldn't mistake that quiff of white hair, it gave him the look of someone older and wiser in experience than his face otherwise suggested. Trustworthy. The type of man a woman could only dream of meeting. Yet here he was with a different woman.

A work colleague, no doubt.

'Let's face it, Sue,' he said, sitting down next to her, 'whenever we get together we end up arguing. I've seen quite a few domestics over the past few days, and believe me, we don't want to end up like that. At least as friends we can argue without hurting each other.'

'That's true enough,' Susan said ruefully, thinking that Frieda's strategy had at least one unexpected side-effect. 'I just wish you had chosen someone else.'

'How do you mean?'

'You know what I mean, Frank.'

There was that phrase again. This time the wise man decided to steer well clear of any mention of marriages.

'There you go, we haven't been together five minutes and you're mad at me,' he said instead.

Susan gave another rueful grin.

'Yes, you're right. But I do love you, you know that, don't

you.'

'And I love you, Sue,' he said, putting an arm around her and kissing her on her cheek. 'We just aren't compatible as partners. But I meant what I said about staying friends. I hope that, when we're old and grey, I'll still be doing things that irritate you, and you can tell me off for being a naughty little boy.'

Now that wasn't the kiss of a work colleague, the barmaid decided. She hoped it wasn't some woman he had picked up off the street. She didn't look like that sort of woman, but then she had heard that high class hookers always appeared outwardly respectable.

If it was going to turn into that sort of pub she was handing in her notice.

Susan smiled weakly.

'You'll be staying in Wellbury then?'

'I certainly hope so. I mean to have a lot of fun, create havoc, grow old disgracefully, and end up haunting the corridors of the police station telling the youngsters how much better it was in the old days.'

'I suppose I'll end up being a dry old spinster, snapping at young staff for not doing their job properly.'

'I bet you won't. Some bloke will come along and sweep you off your feet. You'll be married within a year, just watch.'

'Don't be silly, Frank.'

'Ten quid says you are.'

'Done,' she said. 'I shall claim my ten pounds a year to this day. I shall have it framed and point it out to everyone to show what a useless detective you are.'

'Let me try my psychic powers: I see you at the policemen's ball dressed as Marie Antoinette, dancing in the arms of a handsome man dressed as the Lone Ranger – or Zorro, perhaps.'

'I don't think I'll be going to the ball. Not really my cup of tea.'

He smiled and took a sip of his pint.

'Since we're going to be friends, how about a weekly game of badminton?' Susan asked. 'There's no-one at the club now to have a really good game with. They try, they're great company, but none of them are really fit enough or good enough. It's fun, but you don't get the exercise.'

'An excellent idea. I've been meaning to get fit again for ages. I haven't done any sport since I got out of hospital. I've even thought of joining a tennis club.'

'Not entirely compatible sports, tennis and badminton,' she replied, looking at the white quiff of hair above his forehead. 'But I suppose you'll manage. How's the head, by the way?' she asked, stroking the quiff gently.

Ah, thought the barmaid, his sister, no doubt. She was obviously in love with him one way or another.

'Never felt better,' Frank replied.

That was what had caused the problem, Susan thought. You couldn't blame Frank. He had taken a bullet in the head, it had put him out of his character totally for almost a year, and now he wanted to return to his old ways, without a reminder of that bad time. That was why he had jumped at the choice of someone who wouldn't daily remind him of then. After all, who would want to wake up next to someone to see a face that instantly brought back the time that he had almost died and Jean Candour had been killed next to him?

'I do just want you to be happy, Frank,' she said.

'I fully intend to be happy, very happy. I promise, you can count on me.'

She smiled wistfully. She knew he was making a mistake. Everybody knew. But there was no stopping him. All she could do was to be around to help him pick up the pieces afterwards.

A thought which left her in a certain quandary. On the one hand she rather wished that he would not be making a mistake, that he might marry and live happily ever after. On the other, if it was a disaster, and she was there to help him pick up the pieces afterwards, maybe ...

No, it was better that it was over. It was time to put the past behind and look towards the future.

And, who knows, maybe she would meet someone to sweep her off her feet. It would be worth ten pounds to be proved wrong.

But in her heart she knew it would never happen.

Agnetha of the police station canteen had lost her fiancé, an Australian killed in Vietnam, an experience that she had turned into dedication to what she thought of her boys and girls, the police officers, accepting that she could never love another as she had loved the first.

Some years before she met Frank, Susan remembered painfully, her then boyfriend had died the day she believed that he was going to propose to her. Killed in a senseless motorcycle accident.

She would do as Agnetha had done. Give up on love and

dedicate herself to the happiness of others. It would make life so much easier.

She could understand why so many women became nuns and shunned the illusions of the modern world.

## Thursday Morning: And Another Domestic

'You see, Squish,' Frank told the kitten as he drove them into work to the accompaniment of Chubby Checker urging them to twist again, 'it's something to do with the music. Yesterday was Bob Dylan, the day before was classical, and we ended up spending the day sorting out domestic difficulties. So today we'll start off with good old Chubby, and we'll twist and dance our way away from domestics.'

'Control to Sergeant Summers, come in Sarge, over.'

'Noooo,' moaned Frank. He picked up his radio. 'Ja, Hauptman von FlinkelPinkelHofffenToffen hier.'

There was silence for at least three seconds.

'Er, is that you, Sarge?'

'Nein, I am telling you das ist Hauptman von FlinkelPinkelHofffenToffen. Off ze Bundesmundes polizei. Iben Munchen.'

'Er ...'

'Vy are you calling me on my polizei radio, liddle Englishman? Hier in Chermany das ist illegal to use das polizei radio frequenzees. You wants to go to chail, hein? You noddy, noddy little Englishman.'

'Er, sorry, sir, strangely enough I'm actually a police officer in England, I think somehow our signals have got crossed.'

'Ach, so! Das ist der atmospherics for you, nicht warr? Gross grot glebe, have a happy day, ja? Break an harm und ze leg.'

Frank tossed the radio onto the passenger seat.

'See, Squish, told you Chubby would swing it for us.'

Chubby Checker assured them that there would be a time and place for them.

'Control to Sergeant Summers, come in Sarge, over.'

'Don't give up easy, do you? Oh, well, no matter.'

He picked up the radio once more.

'Zis is Hauptman von FlinkelPinkelHofffenToffen hier. Is tot tot little Englishman vunce again?'

'That is you, isn't it, Sarge?'

'Nein, I am telling you this is Hauptman von FlinkelPinkelHofffenToffen of ze Berlin polizei. At zis very moment I am driving past ze Brandenburg Gate. Look, you zee, I am even now waving at it. It is ein very nise liddle gate.'

'You were in Munching a few seconds ago, Sarge.'

'Ah, zat is because my Mercedes has four sprung duck technology. Ein minute ago I was motoring in Munching und now I am bombing along in Berlin. Desen ducken ist sehr gut idea, ja? Zo long as you getten your ducken in a row, as you English zay, nicht whar?'

'That's vorsprung durch technik, Sarge, and it isn't Mercedes it's Audi.'

Frank gave a deep laugh which could have come from a castle in Thuringia or a coffin in Transylvania.

'Ah, you English like your liddle choke, nein?'

'Aw, come on, Sarge, stop mucking about. It's an interesting one this time. Some woman's got a bloke up a tree, and she's standing underneath it holding a meat cleaver.'

Frank gave up on Hauptman von FlinkelPinkelHofffenToffen. You just couldn't get the right Chermans these days.

'Bobby, you want me to investigate a woman holding a meat cleaver on my own? With no body armour? I wouldn't want anyone to think I was a coward, but there's a difference between being a coward and being downright stupid.'

'She's probably only dangerous to the bloke up the tree. And you can call for backup if you need it.'

'That will be backup from the people we don't have at the moment, will it?'

Bobby Stang had a high regard for logic. He just didn't like it when it was used against him.

'Er, they'll just have to drop whatever they're doing, Sarge.'

Frank sighed again and requested the address. He made a U-turn and drove to the house, noticing a patrol car parked outside of the same transport caff as the day before, wondering how strange it was that the same place had called the police in two days in a row. No doubt another hold-up. There were some criminals who would just never, he decided, be able to use the brains they were born with.


Bobby Stang sighed with relief as the door to the radio room opened and Sid Feeler walked in to start his shift.

'Boy, am I glad to see you. I've just sent Sergeant Summers off to another domestic. Sooner or later he's going to cotton on, and then there's going to be trouble.'

'We're going to be in it big time,' agreed Sid, taking the seat

Bobby had just vacated. Bobby paused on his way out.

'Hey, you heard the one about Tonto and the Lone Ranger? They're in this gully, Red Indians all around, war paint on, looking down on them, about to start with their bows and arrows, and the Lone Ranger says, "Looks like we're in trouble this time, Tonto". Know what Tonto replies?'

'No, what does Tonto reply?'

'What's this "we" business, paleface?'


Frank pulled into the pavement outside the address he had been given, a neat, would-be middle-class terraced house, struggling to be upper while only just managing lower, with an almost-well-kept garden in front, much of which was taken up by a straggling tree. Standing beneath the tree was an extremely large woman, well-built rather than fat, wearing a dressing gown, and holding, not a meat cleaver, but a butcher's knife. In the tree there was a small man with a neat, clipped moustache, wearing what probably would have been a smart suit had it not had the slept-in, rumpled look – unless, as was entirely possible, that was the latest fashion.

'You'd better stay here, Squish,' Frank told the kitten. 'That woman doesn't look like an animal lover to me.'

He lowered the window just sufficiently to let air in, opened the door, got out and closed it. Immediately Squishy climbed up onto the passenger seat, ran across to the window and protested at being left alone.

'Stay, Squish,' he said. 'I won't go out of sight, I promise. You're going to have to get used to being left alone for a few minutes, you know.'

He turned to the woman standing a few yards away. Normally

Squishy's pathetic appeals would have softened his heart, but the sight of the knife in the woman's hand held his attention. And made him far more nervous than he would have preferred.

'Detective Sergeant Summers, Wellbury police force,' he introduced himself. 'Would you like to explain why you're standing there with that knife? And why that man is up the tree?'

'This is my garden,' said the woman in a voice that spoke of tweed, horses, hunting dogs and being in control. 'I can stand here holding a knife if I want to.'

'Not if you're intending to use it to inflict harm. Which, from my reading, is exactly what you intend. So, what, precisely, is going on?'

She turned and glared at him, the first time she had bothered to look at him.

'Precisely? That thing cowering in the tree like the real coward he is, is my husband. He didn't come at all last night. This morning I found him sleeping on the front step, with lipstick all over his face and shirt. He's having an affair with some little tart at his office. I've suspected it for some time now.'

'Please, my darling, you don't understand, I haven't done anything wrong,' the man pleaded.

Frank leant against the front wall and folded his arms as if calmly evaluating the truth of the woman's claim.

'I hate to point this out,' he said, 'but if he's having an affair he's not a very good philanderer, is he? Coming home with lipstick all over him?'

'It's all a misunderstanding, my dear,' the man up the tree called. 'I just had a drink or two too many.'

'Kindly go away, it's none of your business,' the woman told Frank. 'Henry, you'd better bloody well come down right now, and get what's coming to you,' she shouted at the man. 'Or you'll really be in trouble. You're embarrassing me in front of all the neighbours.'

'Would you mind telling me your name, madam?' Frank asked.

'My name? I wasn't aware that we were living in a police state. This is private property. I asked you to leave. If you don't understand allow me to put it in language you might understand: get lost. Henry, are you coming down or do I have to come up and get you?'

The tree seemed to shudder at the thought.

'Madam,' Frank said, 'allow me to explain something to you. If you do not put that knife down and go indoors I am going to arrest you for threatening behaviour.'

'Threatening behaviour? I'm not threatening anything, I'm promising it.'

'Look,' Frank said, 'the first thing I do on getting to work is have a cup of tea. Because of you I haven't even had that pleasure yet. You have one final chance. Put the knife down and go indoors. Otherwise I am going to arrest you.'

'Arrest me? You wouldn't dare.'

'Please don't arrest her, officer,' the man pleaded. 'It'll only make things worse. She doesn't mean it, she's just a little over-excited.'

'I warn you, I shall defend myself to the death,' the stout woman said, waving the knife vaguely at Frank.

'Right, that's it. You are under arrest for threatening a police officer. You do not have to say anything but anything you do later rely on in court may, or may not, be used against you.'

He had never quite got the warning right. He would have far preferred to be able to declare, "You're nicked!" It seemed to say it all in so many fewer words. Fortunately he had managed to get away with it. So far anyone in the dock, on being asked if he had had his rights read to him, had always replied "Yes", with a confused look in their eyes.

'Go ahead then, make my day,' the woman said.

Frank took out his radio.

'Summers to Control, over.'

'Control here, Sarge, over.'

'Sid, I need a couple of uniforms in a van. Make sure they're wearing body armour. We've got a dangerous woman wielding a butcher's knife, and she's refusing to put it down. She's even threatened me with it.'

'Blimey, sorry about that, Sarge. I'll get them over to you right away.'

'I thought it was you who were going to arrest me?' asked the woman, both scornfully and pompously. 'Afraid to do it on your own? Typical man, cowards to the last one.'

Frank smiled easily and kept quiet. And his distance. The woman sniffed at him and turned her attention back to her cowering husband.

'Henry, I demand that you come down right now. Otherwise it will be the worse for you.'

'I'll come down if you put the knife away, my dear.'

'Put the knife away? I'm going to cut it off, you horrible little man.'

The patrol car that Frank had last seen at the fast food restaurant pulled up as this threat was offered.

'Blimey, Sarge, what's she doing with that knife?' Harry Wheatley asked as he got out of the car, Allison shortly behind.

'She wants to give the bloke up the tree a circumcision, only a little closer to the bone than normal.'

'Ouch. Big lass, isn't she?'

'Lend me your baton, Harry.'

'You aren't going to take her on, are you Sarge?' Harry asked, handing Frank his extendible baton. 'Not without body armour? Hey, we could use the Taser. I'll get it out, shall I?'

'Watch and learn Harry,' Frank replied, pulling the baton out to its full length. 'Madame, en garde.'

The woman turned in disbelief as Frank opened the gate and approached her.

'Keep away or you'll regret it,' she warned, holding the knife in front of her.

There was a flash of light as Frank whipped the metal tube like a rapier. In a second the woman was holding her wrist and looking down at the knife lying on the grass as if wondering what had happened.

'Okay, you two, cuff her and take her down the station,' Frank ordered.

'You should have got her on the elbow,' Harry said critically as he and Allison took the stunned woman each by one of her arms, handcuffed her wrists and pushed her towards the patrol car.

'We'll have a contest sometime,' Frank suggested. 'You try

your way, I'll try mine.'

'Er, no thanks, Sarge.'

'Just one thing, Harry.'

'What's that, Sarge?'

'There's something going on at the station, something I don't understand. For some reason I suddenly get called out to every domestic going. But I'll tell you something. I might not understand it at the moment, but when I do, whoever's behind it is going to wish they weren't born. Got it?'

'Er, yes Sarge. We're just obeying orders, Sarge, honest.'

'Orders, eh? Well you can tell Eric Johns that, if he's behind it, he'll choke on every cup of tea he drinks between now and Doomsday.'

'I'll pass that message on, Sarge,' Harry said, grateful that he was able to escape with the madwoman in the back of the car. A choice between a cuffed madwoman and an angry Sergeant Summers was no choice at all.

'You can come down now,' Frank told the man in the tree as the patrol car left, at greater speed than necessary.

The man descended reluctantly.

'She will blame this on me too, you know,' he said sadly.

'Care to tell me what this is all about? Your name might be a good place to start.'

'Henry Smith,' he sighed. 'My wife's name is Hilda. It's a long story. Well, perhaps not a long story. She comes from an old established family, you see. Unfortunately they'd lost all the money they ever had – her father was going to be tried for fraud before he disappeared. Anyway, Hilda agreed to marry me, and she's blamed everything on me ever since the day of the wedding.'

'What happened this morning?'

'I went out for a few celebratory drinks with colleagues from work last night. The business has been going through a bad patch recently, and they couldn't afford a normal raise, so they gave me a promotion instead. Secondary chief assistant to the chief account's clerk's assistant,' he said proudly. Then his face fell again. 'I asked Hilda to come along, but she thinks my colleagues are beneath her. And then I think I got carried away. I don't even remember getting back here.'

'Why don't you just divorce her? Your wife?'

'Oh I couldn't do that. I love her, you see.' He sighed again. 'Love is a tyranny, Sergeant, in many ways. And I'm sure she's fond of me, in her own way. She wouldn't get upset with me if she wasn't, would she?'

'I can think of better ways of doing it,' Frank commented.

'It isn't her fault, it's the way she was brought up.' The man gave another deep sigh. 'What will happen now?'

'She'll be taken down to the station and booked. If she behaves herself she'll be given a caution and sent home.'

'Oh dear. She's never behaved herself. She's eccentric, you see.'

'Threatening people with a butcher's knife is not eccentricity, Mr Smith. Doing cartwheels down the street blind naked while throwing away twenty-pound notes is eccentricity. Waving knives around is just stupidity.'

'She wouldn't have used it, you know.'

'You've heard of the fifth horseman of the Apocalypse, Mr Smith? The first four are Death, Famine, War and Pestilence.

The fifth is called Whoops. I've seen too many situations where people say "Whoops, I never meant that". And I don't intend the last thing I hear on earth to be Whoops. Now, if you'll excuse me, I can hear my kitten calling.'

He paused as he opened the car door and allowed a distraught Squishy to scramble up his arm.

'It's not my place to give advice on domestic arrangements, Mr Smith, but I'd advise you to keep your wife under stricter control.'

He chuckled as he drove away.

'That was naughty of me, wasn't it, Squish? Still, at least we know he'd never try it.'

### Thursday Lunch: Introducing The Ghosts

'"Speedster Flees Spectre"' quoted Pete Phillips, sitting in the canteen reading the front page of the Wellbury Herald. 'Not bad, that. Old Phil Walthers' headlines are improving.'

'And what does he say about Percy?' asked Frank.

'"Detective Inspector Percy Hanson of the Wellbury Police Force admitted that they have as yet no clues as to the identity of the ghost, but assured us that he would have some of his finest officers put onto the case, and that Wellburians could sleep sound at night",' Pete Phillips read. Frank chuckled.

'He does give hostages to fortune, old Percy.'

'How do you mean?'

'Well, put it this way, why do you suppose it was Percy who got interviewed? Rather than Frieda?'

'He just got one step ahead of Fabulous this time, I suppose.'

'Okay, let's say that Frieda had been interviewed. What do

you think she would have said?'

Pete Phillips considered this. He thought he was beginning to see where Frank was coming from. Percy had effectively said "sorry, we haven't a clue" and then followed that up by promising some activity – activity which would need to be reported on later. Frieda would probably have just given a "no comment", or made some remark about ghosts not falling within the remit of official police work. Later, if it did transpire that there was anything to the case she could, while announcing a conclusion to the affair, point out that she never commented on cases while they were ongoing.

'What you're saying is that Phil Walthers will be back to hear what Percy's finest officers – for that, read me – have been doing? Whether we've achieved any results?' Pete Phillips asked, a sour look on his face.

'Not just Phil Walthers,' Frank replied, smiling. 'Locally we have Zack the Prat with his phone-in show, and I hear it's been reported in a couple of the national newspapers too. There's even been some discussion as to whether or not seeing a ghost – or believing you've seen a ghost – qualifies as extenuating circumstances. That's the quality argument. The tabloids, I hear, are debating whether it might not have been an attack by aliens.'

'Great,' said Pete bitterly. 'So most likely I'll end up having to answer silly questions from reporters looking for a story.'

'Do what I do, Pete.'

'And what's that?'

'Raise your eyebrows, look puzzled, and refer them to someone senior.'

Pete Phillips nodded. He knew it was the right thing to do, he didn't need Frank to tell him that. The problem was remembering to keep his mouth shut. He was too inclined to be blunt and tell any reporter who turned up to stop asking stupid questions, which would then be made to appear as if he was in disagreement with Percy, something he really could do without. Frank, on the other hand, was a past master at the looking puzzled and dropping issues into senior officers' laps.

'You know something, Frank?' he asked. 'I've never understood how you do so well as a copper, but manage to balls up your private life so well.'

It was Frank's turn to look puzzled.

'How do you mean, Pete?'

'You know what I mean, Frank.'

So now Pete Phillips was at it as well. Time to give up.

'Don't worry, Pete,' he said, winking. 'I've managed to scrape through so far. I dare say I'll manage again this time.'

'Not this time, Frank. This time you've really blown it.'

'Trust me, Pete, there's a secret to my success.'

'And what's that, oh great one?'

'It's a combination of a number of things. Rationality. Logic. Clear thinking. But the most important is: don't worry, be lucky.'

'Easy for you to say, Frank,' Pete Phillips replied morosely.

Frank smiled and winked. He knew the importance of appearing confident, despite all the odds. However much, or perhaps especially when, inside his mind his personal doubt demon was doing overtime.

**Thursday Afternoon: Now The Vicar Has One**

'Control to Sergeant Summers, come in Sarge, over.'

'I'm not here,' answered Frank, driving back from the Blue Bliss. 'I'm out of the country on an undercover case, incommunicado.'

'In where, Sarge?'

'Incommunicado, Sid, it means I can't be contacted. Ask Squishy, she's right next to me, she'll tell you.'

'But I've just contacted you, Sarge,' Sidney Feeler pointed out perfectly reasonably.

'No, you haven't.'

Sid was silent as he tried to work this one out. In the end he gave up and tried the direct option.

'It's the vicar again,' he said.

'What's the vicar again, Sid, a submarine?'

'Eh? What you on about, Sarge?'

'Not enough, Sid, I should be earning a lot more.'

'You ain't been taking any funny pills, have you Sarge?'

'Loads of them, Sid, green and pink and blue and purple and – hey, an orange alligator is flying next to me. You ever seen an orange alligator, Sid?'

'Come on, Sarge. This should be the last one before knocking off time.'

'I know something I'd like to knock off,' Frank muttered. 'Okay, Sid, I'm on my way. At this rate I might even join the church, I seem to be spending so much time there.'


He walked into the church and initially presumed it to be empty. It was only when his eyes became accustomed to the semi-darkness that he saw a black-clad Mrs Barton standing watching the vestry door, a pile of missals held in her left arm, one in her right hand. There were two missals lying untidily in front of the door.

'Afternoon, Mrs Barton, me again, I'm afraid,' he said in the soft voice people who rarely attend church tend to use when in one. 'We've had a report of a disturbance. I don't suppose you might know what it could be about?'

'Everything is quite in order, Sergeant,' she said, not taking her eyes off the vestry door.

'Right, then, I'll just nip along,' he said, rapidly taking the opportunity to turn to leave. 'Sorry to have bothered you.'

Just then there was a creak and the door opened slightly. Mrs Barton's hand came up immediately and the missal she was holding in her right hand flew straight at the door, bounced off, and joined its companions on the floor.

'Please, Mrs Barton,' came the vicar's pleading voice from behind the door. 'I do think you're overreacting just a little bit.'

'What, exactly, is going on?' asked Frank, reluctantly turning back.

'The vicar and I are having a disagreement about clerical policy,' she replied, the next missal ready. 'No need for you to get involved, Sergeant. Theological questions do not, I believe, fall within the purview of the police.'

'Attacking someone with a guided missal could be construed as assault, Mrs Barton. I would say that that falls within the police force's secular role.'

She gave him a look which told him exactly her opinion of him.

'That, Sergeant, is what I presume is supposed to be a joke? Guided missal?'

'Not a good one, admittedly, Mrs Barton, but I'm afraid an accurate one. Why don't you put those missals down and tell what this is all about?'

He received a repeat of the look, but she put the missals down on a pew, reluctantly recognising that his response, should she continue, was unlikely to be as mild as the vicar's.

'I will be back later, vicar,' she promised, still looking at Frank. Then she walked out of the church giving no appearance of someone leaving the battlefield, defeated.

The vestry door creaked open again, wide enough to allow the vicar to peek out.

'Has she gone?' he asked.

'She's gone,' replied Frank. 'Care to tell me what this is all about?'

The vicar sighed and sidled out of the vestry.

'It's a little embarrassing,' he said.

'Not as embarrassing as having uniformed police officers coming around to pay a visit. You're lucky they asked me to pop around. Next time it's likely to be a couple of uniforms in a car with "police" written all over it. The neighbours are likely to talk. I can't see that being very good for the reputation of the church.'

'That's true, I suppose,' he agreed sadly.

'So why was Mrs Barton attacking you with the good word?'

The vicar sighed and sat down on the pew. Frank sat down on the next pew.

'The thing is, you see,' he said, 'I'm a bachelor.'

Frank pondered this statement for a few moments. If Mrs Barton had some inexplicable grudge against bachelors there were quite a few men in the town who should be going in fear of their lives. Including, for the moment, himself.

'She was attacking you for being a bachelor?' he asked finally.

'No, of course not. The thing is, you see, I'm thinking of getting married.'

'And she thinks you should stay single?'

'No, not at all, she believes that a man of the cloth should marry and settle down, otherwise he receives too much attention from the spinsters of the parish. No, the thing is, she doesn't like the woman I'm seeing. She's divorced, you know.'

'Mrs Barton is divorced?'

'No, no, the woman I'm seeing is divorced.'

'Ah,' said Frank, 'I see. She has something against divorced people. Mrs Barton, that is.'

The idea seemed to surprise the vicar.

'You know, you could be right, I believe her husband ran off with a divorcee. She claims that he died, but I'm told that that isn't the case, it's just a pretence she likes to keep up. But that's by the by. The thing is that Mrs Barton is terribly conservative in Church matters. For example, she considers the idea of women priests heresy of the first order. I think she leans more to Rome than to Canterbury. And she is totally against someone in my position marrying a divorcee. Whenever I go to see her – the divorcee – well, you've seen Mrs Barton's reaction.'

He sighed again.

'And to make it worse she's American.'

'Mrs Barton – '

'No, no, the divorcee. Mrs Lucy Galapogos.'

'Well, that isn't her fault, is it? After all, she was just born there.'

'Eh? Oh, yes, I see what you mean.'

'Your first name isn't Edward, by any chance?'

'Well, it is as it happens. Why do you ask?'

'Oh, no real reason. I seem to recall the same thing happened to someone called Simpson or something like that. But you know that you could take out a restraining order, bar her from entering the church?'

'Mrs Galapogos?'

'No, Mrs Barton.'

'Ah, of course. Yes, I know, I know, but it feels a bit like surrendering, somehow. Ideally I'd like to present her with a fait accompli. Once I was married there would be nothing she could do.'

Apart from taking a thurible to both you and your new wife, thought Frank. It would give a whole new meaning to the word "incensed".

'That's a bit drastic, isn't it?' he asked. 'After all, are you sure you really want to marry this divorcee?'

The vicar nodded agreement.

'That's another problem. Normally I would like to get to know her better before taking the plunge. I only get a chance to see her once a week normally, after I've done the hospital round. Mrs Barton follows me like a shadow, but never to the hospital. I think she believes that illness is a sign of God's disfavour. Saturday is my usual night for that, but I told her I'd decided to switch to Wednesday this week. Unfortunately her suspicions must have been roused.' He sighed. 'But can you really get to know a person properly, enough to know you want to get married, when you only ever see them once a week?'

'Well, you know what they say. Look before you leap.'

'Ah, but he who hesitates is lost.'

'Marry in haste, repent at leisure.'

'Faint heart never won fair lady.'

'Fools rush in where angels fear to tread.'

'He who hesitates is lost.'

'I think we've already had that one.'

The vicar sighed.

'Have we? Oh, you're right, I think. Ah, well, I shall have to admit defeat on that one. What to do, that's the question.'

'Perhaps you could remind her that Jesus forgave Mary Magdalene, and she was a fallen woman, worse than a divorcee, if I remember my Sunday School classes correctly.'

'Oh, no, I've tried that. Unfortunately Mrs Barton is not overly impressed by the bible. Given half a chance she would probably rewrite most of the New Testament. To be honest I rather think she'd prefer to keep religion entirely out of the church.'

'Well, whatever you decide to do, I'd advise you to get Mrs Barton sorted out soon. Otherwise my lot will be around again, and both you and she could end up in court. We do have better things to do than get involved in theological domestic disputes.'

Frank left the vicar considering his options, himself wondering why he had the feeling that, for a moment, he had suddenly changed sides.

And was it just for the moment?

## Thursday Evening: Tricia's Troubles

'Hello, Tricia my love,' Frank said, walking into the outer office of Frieda's eyrie. 'Fabulous in?'

'She's gone for the day,' Tricia said, her face a sign of misery.

'What's up, Trish, you don't seem very happy?'

'I'm not. I'm totally miserable. I hate this job. Everyone's treating me like a total leper. I'm going to take tomorrow off sick and find another job.'

'Ah, don't be down, Trish. Come let me give you a hug. Everything will turn out for the best in the end.'

Tricia stood up, came around her desk and put her arms around him.

'At least you're not angry with me.'

'Don't be silly, how could I ever be angry with you? Come on, I'll buy you a drink.'

'Will you?' Her eyes brightened. 'Can I play with Squish while we're having a drink?'

'Of course you can.'

The barmaid at the Hangman pub was by now thoroughly confused. The young man had brought a totally new girl this time, quite a young one. He sat back with his arms along the back of the bench he was sitting on, the girl playing with that adorable kitten he always brought along.

She couldn't make it out. You might have thought that he was the girl's uncle, but he wasn't old enough for that. But it wasn't unusual for uncles and aunts to be much younger than you might expect. Or was that nieces and nephews being older?

He was her brother, that's what it was. That's why he had that protective look in his eyes.

'I'm still taking tomorrow off sick,' Tricia said, trailing a piece of string for Squishy to attack. 'I don't care what you say. Tomorrow I start looking for a new job. Somewhere I can find some friends. Real friends.'

'You do that, Trish, my sweet,' Frank said, squeezing her shoulder. 'But I think you'll find that you have some good and true friends at the station. Once I've sorted them out, that is.'

'I don't want you to sort them out for me. I can stand on my own two feet.'

'I know you can. But I'm going to do it anyway. I'm going to sort this mess out. Wait and watch.'

Tricia believed he meant it. She just did not believe he could do it.

She had seen the forms Frieda had tried to keep secret from her, forms requesting the posting of both Inspector Garold and Constable Gregson to pastures new. Frank didn't know about that. And even if he had, there was nothing he could do about it.

Wellbury was about to enter a new phase, and she didn't want to be part of it.

**Friday Morning: Strange Sounds Of Silence**

The CD player in Frank's car was playing Onward Christian Soldiers.

'See what we've come to, Squish, religion. Resorting to superstition to ward off calls about domestics. Oh, how low we've sunk. Still,' he continued, tapping out the tune on the steering wheel as he pulled up at a red traffic light, 'it sounds good. Let's just hope it works.'

'Control to Sergeant Summers, over.'

'Now that's what gives religion a bad name. Promising miracles and not delivering. Well, Squish, let us adopt the approach of the Enlightenment, let us rely upon rationality – and the gullibility of the average copper.'

He picked up the radio.

'Hellaw, Superintendent Jones here,' he said in the broadest Welsh accent he could come up with.

'Aw, come on, Sarge, stop mucking about.'

'This is Superintendent Taffy Jones of the Cardiff CID. Who the hell is that?'

'Er, ah, sorry, sir, I think we have a crossed signal.'

The radio went dead. But not for very long.

'Control to Sergeant Summers, over.'

'Chief Superintendent MacMaginty here.'

'Stop mucking us about, Sarge, please?'

'This is Chief Superintendent Hamish MacMaginty of the Aberdeen Fraud Squad. Who the divil is that?'

'That is you, isn't it, Sarge? Aberdeen don't have a fraud squad.'

'Aye we do, the noo,' replied Frank, guessing that Bobby

Stang was guessing about Aberdeen having a fraud squad.

'Come on, Sarge, be reasonable. It isn't my fault.'

'I tell you, this is Chief Superintendent Hamish MacMaginty here. We MacMagintys are known for taking our revenge on constables who disturb us. Ye'll have me caber about yer ears afore long if yer not carrrefull.'

'Please, Sarge, this is my last early shift. I go on evenings tonight. One last time, Sarge, please? It really isn't my fault.'

Frank sighed. He felt that he was getting good at sighing first thing in the morning.

'Okay, Bobby, give me the address.'

When Bobby gave him the address he felt like cursing. It was the address of the Whittles.

He parked outside the Whittles' house and sat listening for a while. There were no sounds to suggest that anyone might be having a strenuous disagreement, just the peace and quiet of a summer's morning interrupted by the trilling of an enthusiastic bird somewhere nearby.

He picked up his radio.

'Summers to Control, over.'

'Control here, Sarge, over.'

'Bobby, who made the complaint? This place is quiet as the grave.'

'One of their neighbours, Sarge. A woman at number fifty-two.'

'Thanks, Bobby, out.'

He got out of his car, the window slightly open, leaving

Squishy sleeping happily on the passenger seat, closing the door quietly. He knocked at the door to number fifty-two. An old woman answered, peeking out with the chain still on.

'Detective Sergeant Summers,' he introduced himself, showing his warrant card. 'I understand that you made a complaint about a problem next door?'

'Yes,' the woman answered eagerly. 'He's gone and murdered her. Or she's gone and murdered him.'

'How do you know that?''

'It's too quiet. They're always having rows first thing in the morning, and at night too. But not this morning, not a sound.'

Frank considered this concept. It had a certain logic to it, but it was the first time he'd ever been called somewhere because it was "too quiet".

'I'll have a look,' he told the old woman. 'I'm sure everything is okay, but I'll have a look just to make sure.'

'Here, that girl of theirs is trying to break into your car.'

Frank turned. Young Gina was trying the handles on his car.

'You stay safe indoors,' he told the woman. 'I'll handle this.'

'No fear,' she replied, shutting her door. 'I'm still in me dressing gown. I'm not taking the chance of being found murdered in public in me dressing gown.'

Frank could understand her feelings. He wouldn't want to be found murdered in public in her dressing gown either.

'And what do you think you're doing?' he asked Gina as he approached his car.

'Your kitten wants to get out,' Gina explained honestly. Squishy miaowed at him. It wasn't a "why did you leave me alone" miaow, more a "I want to go for a walk" miaow.

122

'Good girl, Squish,' he said, opening the car to let the kitten out, 'you're getting used to having me away for a short time, aren't you?'

Squishy stood on the edge of the car seat, looked down, pawed the seat once or twice, and then looked up at him and miaowed, as if to say, "Yes, I know I'm a good girl, but I am still only a little kitten, after all, and it's a long way down to that pavement, so, if you wouldn't mind?"

'Okay, Squish, hop aboard,' Frank said, holding his hand out for Squishy to climb onto. She tested his palm with her paw, and then swiftly stepped onto his hand. He lowered her down to the pavement and she stepped off her personal elevator, regally sniffing the air and looking around at this part of her queendom.

'She's lovely,' said Gina. 'I wanted a puppy, but my Daddy said they needed a lot of care and attention, and I've got to wait until I'm ten before I can have one.'

'Pets are a lot of hard work,' agreed Frank, blithely ignoring the fact that he invariably arranged for others to do most of the "hard work" as far as Squishy was concerned.

'It just seems like forever until I'll be ten.'

'Oh, I wouldn't worry, that'll come soon enough. Are your mummy and daddy in?'

'Yes, they're having breakfast. I must go now, I've got to get to school. Goodbye, Squishy.'

Frank watched her skip towards the house, wondering whether he should follow to make sure that everything was as quiet and peaceful as it appeared.

'No, leave well enough alone, Squish,' he said. 'Come on, let's get back to the nick for a cuppa and a nice saucer of fish.'

Squishy might have wanted to explore for a little longer, but a saucer of fish was a saucer of fish.

## Friday Afternoon: You're Going To Regret That

Frieda walked into Frank's office to find it empty. She had some good news to pass on, and wanted to get it over with, finish for the day and get away for the weekend. She also wanted Frank to get his "we can still be friends" spiel over and done with, without the charade of going for a friendly drink. She had deliberately ducked out of that the previous evening, knowing what was coming, but now she intended to force the issue.

But Frank was not there to force the issue with.

She decided that she would leave a note asking him to come to her office immediately he returned from wherever it was he had got to. She opened his desk drawer in search of a piece of paper. She immediately noticed something she might have expected.

A small jewellery box.

She opened it. A gold ring with a small diamond twinkled back at her. It was gorgeous, large enough to show off, not large enough to get in the way of daily tasks.

Now why was it in his desk? Why not on Tricia's finger?

Of course. Tricia had taken it to the jeweller's to have it altered to fit properly. She was off ill today, so Frank had collected it instead.

Frieda did not feel good about that. She had a good suspicion that Tricia Leigh's supposed illness was a fear of coming to work to face the hatred of her colleagues. A fear that she, Frieda, had helped enforce.

What is happening to me? Frieda asked herself. When my marriage broke up under the blows of a wife-beating – rubbermats – I vowed that I would become a professional police officer, looking after all in my charge, caring for them as if they were my children.

But Tricia Leigh was not a police officer. She was a civilian.

A rather nasty thought appeared in her brain. What if the ring was not in its box when he took it around to Tricia's flat later that evening? What if he took the box back home and opened it to find the ring missing?

Oh, Mephistocles!

There would be panic. Rushing around. Where could it have gone? Had it been stolen? What bad luck! It had to mean something. The engagement was doomed!

It was not a nice thing to contemplate doing.

In fact it was an extremely evil thing to do. Especially for a woman. Hiding, even for a moment, another woman's engagement ring.

But.

It would achieve what she had been aiming for. Frank would be forced to think of what he was rushing into.

Sell your soul to the devil. And the devil you are selling your soul to is yourself.

Yes, she would sell her soul to the devil. She might be damned, but Frank would be saved. It was a price she was prepared to pay.

Yes, she would see him in her office later, get this "we can still be friends" nonsense out of the way, deliver her good news, wait until he had gone home, and put the ring back into his desk drawer in such a way that it would look as if it had fallen out of the box at some stage. It would be found after the weekend, or even if he rushed back to search for it later, after opening the box and finding it missing, but then it would be time for pointing out what bad luck it was for the engagement ring to go missing for even the shortest time. However he might scoff at the idea, even Frank in his blind folly would be forced to ask himself if he was doing the right thing. Especially if everyone he spoke to pointed out what bad luck it was, and she had no doubt they would.

She would make sure they did. Often.

She walked back to her office, feeling extremely guilty, but also convinced she was doing the right thing.

The right thing. A last, hopeless gesture. Still, that was what lovers did, wasn't it? One last hopeless, pointless gesture.

She could never take Ophelia's route. Drowning herself in despair.

But, was not leaving Wellbury to drown herself in her ambition a modern form of Ophelia's desperation?

Stop being silly. Frieda Garold was an extremely rational, logical person.

She entered her office and sat down at her desk.

Now, the question was, did she lock it in her desk drawer, just in case its disappearance came to light, and she could claim to have found it lying around somewhere and had put it away for safe-keeping, or did she keep it in her pocket?

She opened her desk drawer.


In his office Percy Hanson checked his watch. It was not

quite knocking off time – it was well short of knocking off time, although at least on the right side of lunchtime – but it had been a long week, and he needed a drink.

'Fancy a quick pint, Pete?' he asked.

'Sounds good to me, sir,' Pete Phillips said.

'This business with Frank,' Percy said, putting on his jacket. 'I've been wondering if there wasn't something more we could do.'

'I reckon there must be. Why don't we have a get-together with the others? Throw a few ideas around?'

'Good thinking, Pete. Spread the word. Drinks at the Blue Bliss in half an hour.'

'Not too many, though, sir, my missus is expecting me home before seven. And we're on duty over the weekend.'

'Plenty of time before seven, Pete. I just hope it's enough time to come up with a plan to prevent Frank making the worst mistake of his life. Whatever happens, we have to stop him.'

'I agree, sir. We have to stop him.'

'And, if we put our heads together, nothing can stop us stopping him.'


## Friday Evening: A Proposal

Frieda sat behind her desk as if it were a fortress protecting her. It felt a very weak fortress. She would have preferred something three times the size for the meeting that was to come.

There was a knock at the door.

'Come in,' she said to the enemy.

Frank came in.

'Shut the door, Frank, and take a seat. I have some news for you.'

Frank shut the door and took a seat, a half-smile hovering around his mouth.

God, but she hated that smirk of his.

She really did.

Really.

'I don't know how to put this, and I see you've probably heard the news already, so I'll be brief. Your promotion's come through. You are now Inspector Summers.'

Frank's eyebrows shot up.

'Inspector? Blimey, that's a surprise. I'd given up on that. I took the exams yonks ago.'

'You didn't know? The grapevine hasn't been working?'

'No, not a clue. But then there's been a strange feeling around recently. I keep wondering if I've done something wrong. People have been treating me like a leper, and Eric Johns has taken to giving me wise words from the Sun, or maybe it's the Daily Express or Daily Mail. Probably all three.'

'Really? I wonder why that would be.'

'Who knows? Who cares? They'll get over it, sooner or later.'

A thought appeared to strike him.

'This doesn't mean that I'll be posted, does it?' he asked anxiously. 'I'd rather like to stay in Wellbury. For personal reasons.'

'I'm aware of that, Inspector Summers. I've been fighting for the expansion of the force for some time now. There will be space for another Inspector. Two, possibly, in the near future.'

'Well, now thank we all our gods. Why don't we go for a drink to celebrate?'

Frieda sighed at the sound of the suggestion, a bell now tolling for her. Much as she wanted to avoid it, she had known all along that she could hardly refuse having a drink to celebrate his promotion. She could get out of the other, but not that, not his promotion, and the other would now inevitably come as night followed day.

'I suppose it's customary. Come on, let's get it over with.'

The young girl's jaw behind the bar at the Hangman's almost dropped beneath the counter. This was the fourth time she'd seen the young man enter, and each time he'd been accompanied by a different woman. She was rapidly revising her initial estimate of him. The woman definitely looked as if she were there under protest, a high class hooker regretfully doing her duty.

Having said that, and while she disapproved, of course, the barmaid could not but think that this latest woman had a certain something about her, something about the way she carried herself, a wounded dignity, but a dignity never the less. Women, she decided, were too noble to have to suffer the caprices of men like that one.

No, hold that, he appeared to be a decent sort of bloke – man. But, really, all these different women!

And that poor little kitten ... Just as well the cute little thing couldn't understand.

Frank and Frieda took their drinks to a table, totally unaware of the barmaid's disapproval.

'Frank, there's something I've been meaning to say to you,' Frieda said as they sat down together. 'Now, I don't want you to take this the wrong way, but, well – I don't want you rushing into something you might regret.'

'Marry in haste and repent at leisure, that sort of thing?'

'Well, yes, exactly.'

'Look before you leap?'

'Quite. Quite so.'

'A fool rushes in where angels dare to tread?'

'Exactly. Take time to think things over before you commit yourself. There's no need to rush your fences.'

'You really think I should do that?' he asked, taking a sip from his pint.

'I really do, Frank. I know you're engaged, but there's no need to rush to get married, you know. And I speak from experience.'

'Engaged? Who told you I was engaged? I'm not engaged – not yet, anyway.'

'You aren't?'

'No,' he said, checking his watch, 'but I hope to be so soon.'

'And are you going to tell me the name of the lucky young lady, or shall I guess?'

'I tell you what. I'll give you a clue,' he said, putting his hand into his pocket.

'Go on then, if you must. But I think I already know the answer. And I think you're making a bad mistake, Frank. I say that as a friend, not as – well, your former superior.'

Frank took out the engagement ring box and opened it facing

towards Frieda, going down on one knee.

The empty box.

'Frieda Garold, would you do me the honour of permitting me to become your husband?'


'Another bloody domestic,' Bobby Stang muttered in the radio room.

'You know Fabulous's orders, all domestics go to Frank,' Sidney Feeler replied. He had been about to go off duty when the call came through.

'Yeah, but he's knocked off for the day. I gave him one this morning, now I'm on evening shift and I have to give him another.'

'Only just. He's probably having his first pint now.'

'Seems a bit unfair. To both of us.'

'He deserves it after what he's done. Go on, give him a call on his radio.'

'Easy for you to say. I'm the one who's going to be crucified.'


The group in the members' only bar of the Blue Bliss had managed to get through two rounds without coming to any conclusions on what they might do.

'Right,' said Percy Hanson firmly, 'consider this a council of war.'

'A council of war?' asked Pete Phillips, pint in hand, puzzled frown on face. 'Who are we going to war with?'

'It's a metaphor,' Percy explained.

'Police forces can't go to war,' Eric Johns put in, 'only

countries can.'

'I think you'll find that it's actually nation states that can declare war,' Phil Walthers added helpfully.

'Look, it doesn't matter what you bloody call it,' Percy said. 'So long as we all agree that we're here to come up with a plan to help Frank.'

'Definitions are important,' Mrs Blower pointed out, joining the group. 'One must be clear and concise. Like Nelson. If we aren't sure of exactly what the plan is it will go wrong. Time for walkies. At the Battle of Trafalgar. England Expects and all that. Or is it din-dins? Take Churchill, for example. We wouldn't have defeated the Nazis if it wasn't for clear communication. Oh, thank you, Mr Walthers, just a small sherry. Then Nelson needs his din dins.'

Percy Hanson closed his eyes in disbelief. If there was ever a time he did not need Mrs Blower's random approach to conversation, this was it.

'Whose round is it?' asked Eric Johns, finishing his pint with a smack of his lips.

Pete Phillips checked his watch.

Yeah, just enough time for another.


The barmaid frowned her disapproval at the sound of a glass breaking. It was that young man. The tart he had brought in this time was obviously already drunk. And she had seemed so respectable.

That poor kitten looked frightened out of its wits.

'Frieda! Frieda, are you okay?' Frank asked, holding her as she sagged into his arms.

'Everything okay?' asked the barmaid, reluctantly coming up to see what the problem was.

'My, er, girlfriend seems to have fainted. It's very unlike her. Could you bring a glass of water?'

'Frank,' Frieda whispered in his ear, 'make that a double whiskey.'

'Er, forget the water, bring a double whiskey.'

'On the rocks.'

'On the rocks.'

The barmaid hurried away. Frank's radio beeped. He held Frieda with one arm and took the radio out with the other.

'Summers here.'

'Control here, Sarge. We've got another domestic, I'm afraid. Could you deal with it, we don't have anybody spare.'

'That's Bobby, isn't it?' Frank asked.

'Er, yes, Sarge. Over.'

'Bobby,' Frank whispered into his radio, turning his face away from Frieda, 'if you radio me once more tonight I will rip your balls off and make you eat them. Got that?'

He slipped the radio back into his pocket and turned back to Frieda.

'Frieda? Are you okay?'

'I'm fine, Frank,' she said, struggling to sit up. 'You just caught me by surprise there. And Bobby, by the sounds of it.'


'He said what?' asked Sid.

'That he'd rip my balls off and make me eat them if I radioed him again tonight.'

'Bit of a dilemma, that,' Sid said sympathetically. 'You get to choose; do you want your balls ripped off by Frank or by Fabulous?'

Bobby considered this point.

'Frank's a good bloke. He'd do it once and get it over with. Frigid would take her time about it. And if Frank knew we had our orders he'd probably understand. Wouldn't he?'

Sid considered the unlikelihood of this.

'What's this "we" business, paleface?' he asked.


'Okay, are we clear on this?' asked Percy Hanson, his hair adrift, his tie askew, standing unsteadily with the support of the bar.

'Very, er, clear,' replied Pete Phillips with slow deliberation. 'We're all going to phone Frank as often as we can to distract him.'

'Perhaps we should set up a rota,' suggested Phil Walthers.

'No, the plan is to keep him away from young Tricia,' interposed Mrs Blower. 'Distance makes the heart grow fonder of someone closer, as the saying goes. I must say I seem to have had a drink or two too many. Must take Nelson for his din-dins before I forget. She must be quite a girl, this Tricia. Are you sure we're doing the right thing? We'll fight them on the beaches, we will never surrender.'

'Keep his mind on other things,' said Eric Johns happily. 'As soon as he gets his mind on a case he forgets about everything else.'

'Good point, Eric,' Percy said. 'But we don't have anything at the moment, nothing that he'll find interesting.'

'Ah, so why don't we invent something?' suggested Pete Phillips.

'Such as what?' asked Eric Johns.

'Let's have a brain-storming session,' Percy decided. 'Whose round is it next?'

'Eric's, I think,' smiled Pete Phillips, somewhat crookedly.


Frieda took a deep sip of her whiskey. She grimaced as it burnt its way down her throat.

'Feeling better?'

She took another sip.

'Frank, did you – did you just ask me to marry you?'

'Well, I did try to put it more poetically than that, but, yes, in a nutshell, yes, I did ask you to marry me. You seem surprised. I thought you would have guessed. Didn't Gertie and Susan mention that I'd spoken to them? It wasn't them, so it had to be you. Who else could it have been?'

'Well, we thought … '

'Yes? You thought?'

'Oh, we can discuss it later, Frank. Frank, are you serious? About wanting to get married?'

'Well, now you come to mention it, I have been advised to look before I leap, that to marry in haste is to repent at leisure, that – '

'Stop it! Stop teasing! It's too late now. You've proposed. And I'm accepting. Oh, Frank!'

She threw her arms around him and hugged him. The barmaid, back behind the counter, shook her head. She didn't know what to make of it all.

'Careful, now,' Frank said, 'you're squeezing the breath out of me.'

'I'll squeeze you into little bits. Oh, Frank! I'm so happy.'

'Me too. But I'll be happier when I've put that little ring on your finger. Come on, let go now, just for a little bit.'

She let him go, but not before holding his face in her hands and kissing him.

'Now then, the ring.' He turned the little box around. 'That's strange, what's happened to it?'


'Okay, tails I call Frank, heads we give him a break,' Bobby Stang said.

He flipped a coin.

'Tails. Bugger.'

He paused for contemplation.

'I tell you what, let's make it six out of seven.'


'I have a plan,' declaimed Percy Hanson, one hand on his chest, the other swinging wide, just missing Eric Johns' head.

'Excellent!' cried Mrs Blower. 'Let's hear it. Nelson! Oooh, Nelssooon!'

'Well, I don't have a plan, as sush,' admitted Percy. 'I was just thinking of the shivil rightsh bloke in America, the one who kept on dreaming. Everybody remembers him. Now if we can shay "I wash there when shomebody shaid I have a dream", well, we're half way there, aren't we?'

'Calvin Klein,' said Pete Phillips.

'Who?'

'The bloke who said he had a dream. It was Calvin Klein.'

'No it washn't, Calvin Klein makes clothesh.' Percy paused. 'Hey, that almost rhymesh, that doesh.'

'I'm sure it was some bloke named after one of those blokes in the Reformation,' Pete insisted.

'Martin Luther King,' suggested Phil Walthers.

'Thash the one. Anyway, now we have a short of mishion statement. Onshe you got one of them you're halfway there.'

'I say we take the hull by the borns!' cried Mrs Blower. 'Grab the nettle! Stop fussing about footies and march on to the broad lit highlands. Action this day! Call Frank here this minute and demand to know just exactly what he thinks he's playing at!'

'I think you mean, "take the bull by the horns", my dear,' Phil Walthers said mildly.

'Good thinking!' exclaimed Pete Phillips. 'I'll give him a call right now! He has no option! He will come here right now and tell us just what he thinks he's doing.'

'What did you call me?' Mrs Blower asked Phil Walthers, batting her eyelids.

Pete Phillips pressed a button on his mobile phone.

'Hi, Frank? Hey, listen, Frank, me old mate, me old cobber, there's a group of us here at the Blue Bliss jush waiting for you to turn up. Whadya say, a couple of pintsh, eh, jush a few old matesh together?'

His face went suddenly white at the response he had received. He quickly switched the mobile off and looked at it as if it were an angry and very poisonous snake sitting in his palm.

'So, what did he say?' asked Percy Hanson.

'That wasn't Frank,' Pete whispered. 'I must have pressed the wrong button. It was the missus.'

'Well,' said Eric Johns philosophically, 'if you're in trouble, you're in trouble. Another pint won't make any difference.'


'It must have fallen out,' Frank said, groping on his knees on the floor. Frieda took the chance to slip it from her pocket and onto the table. What luck or intuition had caused her to decide against leaving it in her desk drawer she did not know or wish to think about. She was having sufficient problems trying to deal with the whirl her mind and emotions were in.

 'No, here it is, Frank, just next to the box.'

'Thank God for that,' he said sitting down again. 'Bad luck to lose your engagement ring on the night you propose.'

Frieda held out her hand and he slipped the ring on her finger. She looked down at the sparkling little diamond, and then up at Frank, her eyes moist. They sat looking into each other's eyes for some moments. The barmaid, now realising what had happened, began to cry.

Frank's radio beeped again. He took it out in a fury.

'I am going to kill Bobby Stang,' he muttered.

'Give it here, Frank,' Frieda said. He handed it over.

'Control to Sergeant Summers, Control to Sergeant Summers, over.'

'Control, this is Inspector Garold – for the moment, anyway. If you call Sergeant Summers' radio once more tonight I am going to tear your testicles off and make you eat them, understand? Oh, and it's Inspector Summers to you from now on.'

She smiled through her tears and handed the radio back to Frank.


Bobby Stang stared unseeingly ahead.

'Threatened to cut your balls off again?' asked Sid. 'He's coming around to do it right now?'

Bobby shook his head slowly and tried to say something. It came out as a croak.

'Rip your legs and arms off? Put your head through a meat grinder? Nail your toes to the notice board?'

Bobby shook his head again.

'It was – '

'Worse than that?'

'It was – '

'Can't imagine what can be worse than having your toes nailed to the notice board. You'd be hanging there all day. With everybody looking at you as they passed by.'

'It was the Inspector.'

There was a pause.

'Frigid?'

Bobby nodded.

'Oh, shit,' said his ex-friend. 'I mean, oh, damn. I mean ... I mean I'm going to have to go.'

'Wait a moment,' said Bobby as an idea struck him, 'if Frigid has the Sarge's radio, that means she's after him, doesn't it?'

'How do you mean?'

'Well, think about it. She must have gone looking for him, he saw her coming, legged it, and left his radio behind. Makes sense if you think about it.'

'You think about it. I'm off home before the missus starts wondering where I am. I don't need both her and Frigid coming after me. Enjoy the rest of your shift.'

'Cheers, mate.'


'Hello? Hello? Ish that the stashun?' asked Percy Hanson on his mobile. It was his third attempt to dial the right number.

'Yes, sir, this is Wellbury police station. How can I help you?'

'Thish is Inshpector Hanshon. Whoosh that?'

'It's Harry Wheatley, er, sir.'

'Ah, Harry, Harry, good lad, Harry. Now there'sh shomething I want you to do. You know old Frank Shummers, our mate Frank, like, well, well, I want you – I want you to call him on hish radio and tell him – tell him that there'sh a fra ... a fra ... a fight at the Blue Blish. Yesh. Have you got that, Harrysh?'

'With all due respect, sir, I think the only thing I can say to that is, not bloody likely. Sir.'

Percy looked at his mobile in amazement.

'Bloody Harry put the phone down on me,' he said. He looked around. Eric Johns was asleep. Mrs Blower had gone off for a lie-down. Pete Phillips was looking morosely into his beer glass. Phil Walthers was studying his whiskey with the attention of a connoisseur.

'Put the bloody phone down on me, can you believe it?'

'Sounds like an eminently intelligent young man to me,' suggested Phil Walthers. 'Interfering in young Frank's business is an undertaking not to be taken lightly. In fact I would suggest that the wisest move is not to contemplate it at all.'

Percy's shoulders slumped. Much as he hated to admit it, he could not help but feel that what Mr Walthers had said was a very good idea.

If only they could come up with a plan.


'I hope you aren't going to be using language like that once we're married,' Frank said, grinning. 'It could be very embarrassing.'

'No, I think that's the last time you'll hear that sort of thing.'

'So, shall we have a glass of champagne to celebrate? I've booked a table at Gino's, with champagne waiting, but we could have a glass here if you like.'

'Perhaps not. We'd have to finish the bottle, and I don't want to turn up at Gino's staggering around. I feel light-headed as it is. Pinch me, Frank, I think I'm dreaming.'

'Maybe we both are. But, what the hell, who cares? Who knows what dreams are and what's real? And I refuse to pinch my wife-to-be.'

She smiled.

'You don't know how good that word sounds, Frank. Say it as often as you want.'

'Sounds good to me too.'

'Compliments of the management,' a voice next to them said. They turned to find the young barmaid standing there, a bottle of champagne in one hand, two glasses in the other. She put the glasses on the table and began twisting the wire off the bottle.

'Oh, Frank, everyone's looking at us.'

'Come, now, Inspector, you should be used to that, a beautiful woman like you.'

For the first time since she had been a teenager Frieda actually blushed as the girl poured the champagne.

'Will you join us?' Frank asked the girl. 'It's supposed to be good luck, sharing champagne with a newly engaged couple.'

'Oh, would I!' she exclaimed and skipped off to get a glass. When she skipped back Frank poured for her.

'Important, that is,' he said. 'The man has to pour the drink. That way his luck rubs off on the other person. And I am the luckiest man in the world. Cheers.' He turned to Frieda. 'Here's to the most beautiful woman in the world, both in her looks and in her person.'

'To the most handsome, gallant, charming, loveliest man I have ever been lucky enough to meet,' Frieda said, smiling back, crying.

'To the lucky couple,' said the barmaid, sobbing.

'We're off to dinner, shortly,' Frank said. 'You might as well share the remainder of the champagne with anyone else you care to. We don't want to turn up at the restaurant tipsy.'

The other customers toasted the happy couple when they were offered champagne and told the reason for it. The landlord threw caution to the winds and opened another bottle to make sure that all who wanted had a glass. There was a general feeling that the happy occasion called for a quick finish of their current drink, a downing of the offered glass of champagne – after all, you could hardly sip the stuff on such a momentous moment – and, oh, what the hell, I was only going to have a couple/three/four pints, but go on, I'll have another, after all it's not everyday someone gets engaged in the Hangman's.

Frank and Frieda's departure was greeted with a cheer from the other customers. One fell slowly off his stool, waving.

Some might have called that a portent.

### Saturday and Sunday: The Chase Is On

'Have you heard the rumours?' Pete Phillips asked Percy Hanson, each wearing a matching hangover.

'I don't know. Maybe I have and maybe I haven't. What rumours were you thinking of?'

'Frank's eloped with Gertie.'

Percy's head shot back and he laughed uproariously. Then he winced as the pain in his head hit him.

'Don't be daft. How can they elope? They don't need their parents' consent. Anyway, he hasn't eloped with Gertie, he's run off with Tricia Leigh.'

'Run off with Tricia Leigh?'


'They hate me, I can feel it,' Tricia Leigh said. 'The worst is, I don't know why.'

'Come off it, nobody could hate you,' said the young man sitting next to her in her local pub. He was the young man she had mentioned to Frieda. They had met a few weeks before in the same pub, and he had instantly fallen head over heels for her. Tricia was slowly coming around to the idea that she might just like him enough to consider being in love herself.

He was still head over heels, but was getting a little tired of the fact that their relationship recently consisted entirely of her bewailing the treatment she was getting at work, interspersed with her over-the-top praise of two blokes, one called Frank Summers and one called Squishy.

What sort of bloke is called Squishy?

'You'll get to hate me as well. I'm a curse. I had this terrible job at an estate agents, and then I got the best job in the world, everybody was so nice, and now they all hate me, and I don't know why.'

'You're being silly. I could never hate you. No-one could. Bet you a fiver this is all a big mistake. Well, make it a quid, I'm a bit skint at the moment.'

'See? If you really believed it you wouldn't worry about losing money on it. You say you love me, but you don't really mean it.' She burst into tears.

The young man bristled. He wasn't experienced in love. He was experienced in romanticism. He had read Don Quixote and thought the man a noble fellow. Tricia Leigh was the first girl he had met who understood him. This Summers person was not a windmill. A man – a real man – could take a tilt at him. For Tricia's sake.


'I suppose I'll have to hang up the fishing rod,' Frank said, looking at the passing water of the river Wellbury as they walked along the riverbank.

'No, don't do that, Frank,' Frieda said, their hands entwined. 'We can come down together. Just sit peacefully watching the world go by. I'd like that.'

'You'll have to be careful you don't frighten the fish,' said a voice behind them.

They turned.

'I believe congratulations are in order, in more than one way. First, congratulations on your promotion, Frank. I put that first because I always reserve the greater pleasure for last. I might have been away for the station for a little while, but I haven't lost my powers of deduction, and I can recognise an engagement ring and a happy couple. Am I allowed to kiss the bride to be?'

'Of course you can, sir,' Frank said to the Chief Inspector. 'But only once, mind, I'm the jealous type.'

'Somehow I've always thought that,' the Chief Inspector said, smiling, giving Frieda a kiss on her cheek. 'But we're not at the station or on duty now, so why don't you call me by my nickname? Which happens to be Hal. It was originally Hell, but I've improved since those days. Come, Frank, let me shake the hand of the luckiest man I know.'


'The Inspector not in today?' asked Sam Nightingale.

'She called in. She'll be available if there's a major crisis, otherwise she's incommunicado.'

'Unusual for her.'

'Word is that she's gone to look for Frank with a butcher's knife in her hands.'

'Poor Frank.'

'Well, he did ask for it.'


'So, who are you going to share your good news with first?' asked the Chief Inspector. 'Accepting, of course, that, strictly speaking, I guessed rather than that you told me, my thus not being the first,' he added with a touch of pedantry.

Frieda looked at Frank.

'I thought – well, I thought, I might give tennis a miss tomorrow. But I'd still like to pop in and say hello to Aggie. She'll be delighted.'

'I agree,' said Frank. 'She'll be over the moon.'

'We'll make a party of it,' said the Chief Inspector. 'I haven't seen Aggie since Wednesday. And I want to see the smile on her face when she hears.'

'We'll have to do something about her before winter comes,' Frieda said.

'We'll see,' Frank replied. 'Though it might be a case of that old saying, if it ain't broke, don't break it.'


'Run off with Gertie,' Pete Phillips told Eric Johns. 'Percy reckons it's Tricia Leigh, but I know it's Gertie.'

'You sure?' asked Eric Johns. 'I heard it was Doctor Pleadle.'

'Nah, don't be daft. Why would he have run off with Doctor Pleadle?'

Eric Johns scratched his head. It was a good question. The only person Frank might have run away with had to be Tricia Leigh.

Despite his doubts Pete Phillips began to wonder if Eric Johns hadn't been right.

Or maybe he was wrong?


The young man sighed.

'Okay, okay. A tenner, how's that?'

'If you really believed it you'd put a million pounds on it.'

'Don't be daft. Why would I want you owing me a million quid?'

Tricia thought about the logic of this. And dismissed it.

'You'll hate me as well,' she repeated. 'You'll see. The only ones who care are Squishy and Frank and they'll end up hating me as well, I know it! I can't bear to think of Squishy hating me!'

She dissolved into tears again.

That was it, he had had enough. Anyone who made Tricia cry deserved – deserved something. He wasn't quite sure what, but he would teach this Frank and this Squishy a lesson.

'Are they at work now?' he asked.

'Who?'

'This Frank and Squishy?'

'They'll be in on Monday. I won't, though. I'll hand in my notice and take the week off sick.'

'But how will you live? You can't go straight on the dole if you hand in your notice.'

'I'll think of something.'


'Not a word of a lie,' said Harry Wheatley to Allison Hardbury. 'Frank's got engaged to his cleaning lady.'

'Don't be daft, Harry, Frank hasn't got a cleaning lady.'

'Well, it must be that student then, the one who he got to clean his flat up.'

'You sure? She seemed a bit young for him. She's only about seventeen.'

'Yeah. You think you know a person ...'

'Well, he won't last much longer in Wellbury, will he?'

Frank stood and looked down at the grave of Jean Candour. Frieda and the Chief Inspector stood a foot or so back, understanding that this was a personal moment for him. They did not know what had gone on between Frank and Jean, but it had, with the shock of her death and his almost-death, obviously been a traumatic experience.

'She says congratulations,' Frank said, looking at the gravestone. He chuckled. 'She also says that you should buy me a pair of slippers and a pipe, because I've become an old fogey.'

He paused for a moment.

'No, she says I've always been an old fogey. And now she's going off on a date with someone she's met, some handsome young fellow who doesn't act like he's sixty-four.'

He turned to them.

'Well, let's get on and see our Aggie, then.'

He took Frieda's hand and the three of them continued further into the cemetery in search of the reclusive Aggie.

Frieda had smiled at him when he turned around, but the smile had hid a worrying feeling that Frank should not be talking to the dead.

'Have you heard?' Pete Phillips asked Sam Nightingale.

'Heard? Heard what?'

'Frank's run off with Tricia Leigh.'

'Run off with Tricia Leigh? Maybe that explains why Inspector Garold has gone looking for him.'

'Fabulous has gone looking for him? Blimey.'

'Probably disappeared to somewhere large, like London.'


They eventually found Aggie sitting on an old wooden chair outside what looked like a garden shed at the back of the cemetery. There were allotments beyond the low cemetery wall, wearing the disused appearance of allotments worked on by those too serious about their vegetables to worry about looks. Separating the cemetery from the allotments was what had once been a sunken dirt road, now bumpy, potholed and with clumps of grass growing through. The back of the cemetery was an ideal place for someone who preferred to be alone.

Two cats were sitting in front of her, warming themselves in the sun. As the three approached the cats looked up, jumped up and fled. Squishy, looking out of Frank's pocket, watched them go as if wondering why they didn't want to stay and play.

'Hello, Squishy,' Aggie said. She always said hello and goodbye to the kitten rather than the people.

'Hello, Aggie,' Frank said, 'we've brought you some news – oh, and something for your friends.'

He held up a plastic bag full of pet food. Aggie tended to spend what little money she was given on food for what she called her pets, all strays like herself. She took the bag and looked inside. A little smile lit up her old face, whitening the scar on her forehead.

'People are so kind. They built this lovely shed for me in case it rains.'

'That's good news, Aggie. We also have some news – and the news is that Frieda and I are engaged. We wanted you to be the first to know.'

'Oh!' exclaimed Aggie, dropping the bag and clapping her hands together. 'That's wonderful! Squishy will have a father and a mother now.'

That was another strange thing about Aggie, her speech and mannerisms were exactly those of a well brought up twelve year-old of many years ago, and of an upper middle class family. No using "mum and dad", it had to be "mother and father".

'Yes, Squishy is a very lucky little kitten,' Frank said, putting his jacket on the ground for Squishy to get out and explore. Aggie immediately sat down and began stroking the kitten.

'You'll be invited to the wedding, of course,' Frieda said. 'When we've decided when that's going to be, September, probably.'

'Oh, I couldn't come,' Aggie said, looking down at Squishy, her thin grey hair hiding the expression on her face.

'Don't worry, Aggie,' Frank said, recognising a pointless, and for Aggie, painful, discussion. 'We'll make a plan when the time comes.'


'Hey, Sarge, have you heard?' Harry Wheatley asked Pete Phillips. 'Frank's run off with that student he got to clean his flat.'

'You what?'

'No word of a lie, Sarge. And she's only sixteen.'

'Blimey, that explains it all. I knew he wouldn't have done a runner with Gertie or Doctor Pleadle, but a sixteen year-old? Yeah, that makes sense. He wouldn't want to hang around if that was the case. The girl's parents will be after his blood in the first case. Can't see him walking back in here, ever.'

'Apparently he left word that they've gone to London.'

'Hah! That's classic, that is. Spread a few rumours that you're going to London and then disappear to Spain or somewhere. You'd be an idiot to believe a word of it.'


'Frank, you remember how surprised I was when you proposed?' asked Frieda. They were walking back through the cemetery, the Chief Inspector having decided to stay a little longer with Aggie, and to see if the stray cats would lose their fear if they became accustomed to his presence.

'Surprised is a bit of an understatement.'

'Well, it's just that – promise not to laugh at me.'

'Cross my heart.'

'Liar. Anyway, we all thought that you – that you'd already proposed to Tricia.'

'Tricia?' Frank asked, his face a picture of amazement. 'Well, there's no denying that she's extremely attractive, and an extremely nice person but – well, too late now, we're already engaged. What on earth made you think that, though?'

'Everybody thought it was a fact.'

'I smell the fertile and gossiping mind of a desk sergeant behind that, to whit one Eric Johns. At least it explains why everyone was giving me the cold shoulder, and why he was giving me his Daily Mail version of the Sermon on the Mount whenever he saw me.'

'Oh, Frank, I feel terrible about it. I treated poor Tricia ever so badly.'

'Everybody did. We'll have to make it up to her.'

'I'll have to make it up to her.'

'We'll do it together. It won't be difficult. She just wants people to like her. She doesn't have many friends, you know. She's an orphan. Parents died a couple of years ago, no close relatives left. I think the station is her family now.'

'Oh, Frank, I've been really awful. Really, really awful. I didn't even know she was an orphan. I should have. I should have. I really should have. Just because she was a civilian I never enquired into her background. Not the way I should have.'

'No, it's not that. Tricia's just one of those people we tend to forget. She's always so cheerful we forget that she too has problems.'

'You didn't forget. You took her out for drinks.'

'She needed a shoulder to cry on.'

'She should have been able to cry on my shoulder.'

'Now, Free, if you're not careful I'll get Eric to pass on bon mots such as the one about water under the bridge.'

'Free,' she said, smiling at his abbreviation of her name. 'I'll be Free for you, Frank.'

He chuckled.

'I suspect we might be hearing a few puns about Free and Frank.'

'I can't wait until Monday, to see their faces. I feel like a teenager again.'

'Not that bad, surely?'

'Done a runner with young Tricia to Spain,' Eric Johns said mournfully to Agnetha in the canteen. 'Lost a lot of money on Frank, I have. You think you can rely on a man and then he betrays your trust like that.'

'He hasn't done a runner with young Tricia,' Agnetha replied. 'I know what has happened, and you should be ashamed, spreading false gossip like that.'

Eric Johns rubbed his jaw thoughtfully. There was a certain confidence about Agnetha's statement which brooked no disagreement. And, if anyone was likely to know the truth it was the tight-lipped Agnetha.

'You do? Go on, Agnetha, what's happened then? Trust me, I shan't spread a word.'

If Agnetha had been capable of shrill laughter she would have burst Eric Johns' eardrums right then. Instead she merely gave a small, thin smile to show what she thought of that particular statement.

The young man rubbed his cheek, scratched his head, and wondered whether he should challenge this Frank and this Squishy to — well, a duel, perhaps. He had heard far too much of them from Tricia Leigh's lips. Squishy was obviously some limp-wristed gay, Tricia had always described Squishy as "adorable" and "sweet".

Yes, that was it. He'd take on this Squishy first. This Frank sounded more of a challenge, but once Squishy was out of the way maybe the big Frank Summers wouldn't be such of a problem after all?

Now, how was he going to do it?

Yes, that's an idea. No need to actually hurt the bloke, just threaten him a little.

Lean on him, as they said in a novel he had once read.

## Monday Morning: The Announcement

'Good morning, Tricia,' Frieda sparkled as she walked into the outer office that Tricia Leigh occupied, Frank Summers in tow. 'I'm afraid I've treated you rather badly, due to a misunderstanding on my part. So I've bought this to make amends.'

A miserable Tricia looked at the small box she was given. She had hardly slept the previous night, tormented by a battle within her as to whether or not she should go to work the following morning. Emotionally the answer was a definite no. Duty, on the other hand, told her that she should do what she was being paid for.

And she couldn't leave all her furry friends on her desk to the mercy of that lot.

But now, from what Frieda had said, she seemed to have been forgiven for whatever it was she had apparently done.

'I don't understand,' she managed to say.

'Oh, please, Tricia, open it and see if you like it.'

Tricia undid the wrapping paper to reveal a tiny, perfect, little furry teddy bear with bright black eyes, and a little pink bow around its neck.

'Oh, she's gorgeous,' she exclaimed. 'I love her already. But, why?'

Frieda smiled at her.

'We've all been acting very badly towards you, myself especially. Now I'm going to make amends. Frank and I are going to put up a notice in reception. We thought you might like to proof-read it for us before we do.'

A puzzled Tricia Leigh took the paper Frieda was holding and read it.

"Promotions

Detective Inspector Garold would like to announce the promotion of Detective Sergeant Frank Summers to the rank of Detective Inspector.

Detective Inspector Garold and Detective Inspector Summers would like to announce, following a proposal by Detective Inspector Summers, their own promotions vis-à-vis each other of fiancé and fiancée.

Detective Inspectors Summers and Summers-to-be would like to invite their fellow officers to celebrate this engagement with drinks this evening at the members-only bar at the Blue Bliss."

Tricia looked up, her mouth open.

'You mean you – ' she said to Frieda.

'You mean you – ' she said to Frank.

'You mean you both – ' she said to both of them.

Frank put his arm around Frieda's shoulders. She put her arm around his waist.

'We do,' he said.

'We do,' she said.

Tricia gasped, dropped the piece of paper and clasped her hands together.

'Oh!' she exclaimed. 'Oh! Oh! Oh!'

'Oh, indeed,' remarked Frank. 'Just what I've been thinking. Oh, and Oh again.'

'Oh!' repeated Tricia. She bounced out of her chair and around the desk and gave Frieda a hug. 'Oh!' she said, tears rolling down her face, 'Oh! I'm so happy for you. So happy. So happy! Happy! Happy! Happy!'

'You missed an Oh!' Frank pointed out.

'Oh! You teaser! Give me a kiss!'

Frank wasn't given the option of refusal.

'Well, once you've calmed down, Tricia,' asked Frieda, 'could you get me four drawing pins?'

'Oh! Oh! Oh!' said Tricia Leigh, apparently answering in the affirmative as she skipped around her desk to find the pins. 'Here you are. Oh! Oh! Oh!'

'Trish, you really are going to give the game away before we get the announcement up if you carry on like that,' Frank admonished, smiling. Tricia held a finger to her lips.

'I won't say a word,' she promised. 'Can I come along? Please? Please? Please? Pretty please with billions and zillions of cherries on top?'

'Of course you can, Trish. You can tell us what their faces look like when they read it.'

'I'm looking forward to having a word with some of them,' Frank said. 'I'll teach them to treat me like some type of outcast.'

'Frank, you are going to give me a wedding gift, aren't you?' Frieda asked him.

'Well, of course.'

'The wedding gift I want is for my husband not to take it out on his colleagues and friends. Will you give me that?'

Frank smiled.

'That isn't a wedding gift. That's a wish from my beloved, which I cannot refuse.'

'Oh! Oh! Oh!' exclaimed Tricia Leigh.

'Trish, if you don't stop that I will be forced to insert Squishy's football into your mouth to give us some peace.'

'Frank!' objected Frieda.

'Squishy!' exclaimed Tricia Leigh. As if on cue Squishy popped her head out of Frank's jacket pocket to demand to know what all this noise was about, and could they keep it down please, she was trying to sleep, having just beaten Italy twelve-nil in Frieda's car on the way to work, even with Frank's legs in the way.

'Come on, Squish, Trish wants to smother you with love,' Frank said, lifting Squishy gently out of the jacket pocket and handing her over to Tricia Leigh. 'Shall we go?' he asked Frieda.

They walked out together, Tricia Leigh bringing up the rear with Squishy cuddled in her arms. Tricia was tickling Squishy's stomach and whispering excitedly to the kitten.

Eric Johns was sitting on a stool in reception, scratching his head, slowly doing the quick crossword in the tabloid he had on the counter in front of him. He looked up in amazement as Frank, Frieda and Tricia Leigh walked in, Squishy in Tricia's arms giving him her usual look of "You're a strange man, aren't you?". His eyes opened wide and his scratching intensified at the sight of two people who were supposed to be in Spain, accompanied by another who should be chasing them with a butcher's knife.

157

To compound the confusion a young man wearing a leather jacket, a bad haircut, and large dark glasses, with his hands rammed into the jacket pockets, chose that moment to sidle into the reception area.

'I'm looking for an officer called Squishy,' the young man whispered out of the side of his mouth.

'Jeremy!' cried Tricia Leigh. 'What are you doing here?'

Jeremy turned and looked at Tricia in surprise, his oversized dark glasses slipping down his nose.

'You're spoiling everything! This is Squishy, you should know that! Oh! Oh! Oh!'

Jeremy had a lot of potential. He recognised immediately that taking out the expensive knuckle duster he had purchased from a side-street shop to threaten a little kitten would be a very, very bad idea.

Vastly a worse idea than using it to threaten the man standing in reception who he guessed was the mysterious Frank. Frank would merely crush him. Squishy would look on while everybody else ripped him slowly to pieces.

Never mind the other woman next to the presumed Frank who might look surprised at his entrance, but didn't look the type of person to stay surprised for long, about as long as his life would have lasted. She had that look about her which spoke of being in command. Of being in command of an entire police station. The type of police station that is filled with burly police officers who were there to follow her orders.

'Go away!' Tricia said, stamping her foot.

'Er ...'

'Go away!' Tricia repeated. 'I'll speak to you later.'

Jeremy slunk away, wondering whether the promise of later talks was a good thing or a bad thing.

'Who was that?' asked Frank.

'He's my boyfriend. He can be so tiresome.'

The announcement that she had a boyfriend surprised Frank and Frieda, and added, if possible, to the perplexity that had rendered Eric Johns speechless, a rare event in the annals of Wellbury police station.

He watched as, without a further word, Frank and Frieda together pinned a notice to the notice board.

Frank put his hand over the reception counter.

'Congratulate me,' he told an amazed Eric Johns.

'Er, congratulations, Frank,' Eric Johns said, shaking his hand. 'Any possibility you might tell me what it's all about?'

'Frank is now Inspector Summers,' Frieda told him. 'And I won't be Inspector Garold for very much longer.'

The three walked out of reception, leaving Eric Johns open-mouthed. Once through the doors Frank took Squishy from Tricia, winked at her, leaving her to listen while they retired to Frieda's office

Ah, thought Eric Johns, as he listened to the sound of disappearing voices singing "Let's do the time warp again", Frank and Fabulous had both been promoted.

He walked to the notice board to confirm his understanding.

After reading the notice he reeled back to his stool.

Sam Nightingale walked in wearing her motorbike leathers to find him almost prostrated on the reception counter, his face white.

'You okay, Sarge?' she asked in some concern.

He did not reply. He merely gestured at the notice board with his thumb. She walked over and read the note.

'Yes! That's wonderful!' she exclaimed. 'Wonderful! Oh! That's bloody wonderful!' She paused and walked back. 'You told us he was going to marry Tricia,' she accused.

'Fabulous was at four to one,' he groaned.

'I think you owe me eighty pounds, Sergeant Johns,' Tricia Leigh said, coming back into reception, the broadest of broad grins on her face.


'Stop it, Frank,' Frieda said in her office. 'Someone might walk in on us.'

'Oh, okay, if you insist.'

'Well, perhaps just a little bit longer,' she said, holding him and kissing him.

'Help! Help!' he cried softly, 'I'm in the hands of a maniac.'

'Shush! Idiot! Someone might hear you.'

'And? Who cares?'

'Well, there is that.'

A knock at the door caused them to part, adjusting their dress.

'Come in,' said Frieda.

'I'm not speaking to him,' Gertie said, entering. 'He isn't worth it. But, oh, Frieda! Congratulations!'

The two women embraced. Frank stood by, looking on, grinning. Frieda had convinced him that he should telephone Gertie and Susan on the Sunday evening to let them know, and he was now glad that he had taken her advice.

'Oh, okay, I forgive you, you bastard,' Gertie said, throwing herself into his arms. 'I'm just so happy for both of you.'

'Why do women always cry on happy occasions?' Frank asked himself, aloud, holding her tight.

'Mr Summers,' said Frieda, 'I am giving you fair notice not to question the motives or emotions of your wife-to-be or her friends or you shall regret it.'

Frank winked at her.

'I'm not interrupting, am I?' asked a voice at the door.

'Susan, come in,' said Frank.

'I got your message – I thought I'd come and wish you all the best. Frieda – ' She burst into tears.

'Come here,' said Frank, disentangling Gertie and taking Susan in his arms. Now, now, you're upsetting little Squish, dry your tears.'

'Ah, Squishy, how are you?' asked Susan, pulling herself from Frank and speaking to the puzzled kitten. She picked Squishy up and cuddled her. 'Dear little Squishy. Dear, dear little Squishy.'

'Why don't we all go for breakfast?' suggested Frieda.

'Good idea,' said Frank. I'm starving.

'You go on, I'll stay here and look after Squishy,' said Susan.

'We'll all go,' Frank said, taking her arm gently.

'Please do, Susan,' Frieda said. 'We do want you with us.'

Susan sniffed her tears back and rubbed her eyes with the back of her hand.

'Well, if you insist,' she said.

'I rather think we'll insist,' Frank said wryly. 'It's going to be strange speaking of "we" all the time, but I suspect I'll get used to it.'

And that was when, looking back on it, things began to go wrong.

## Interregnum: Engagement Breakfast

On their way to the restaurant Gertie excused herself, asked them to order scrambled eggs on toast for her, and popped into a newsagents. When she caught up with them in the restaurant a waitress was refusing to allow them in with a kitten.

'This is Squishy,' Frank said. 'The lady here and I have just got engaged, and Squishy is going to be one of the bridesmaids. You do allow bridesmaids in, don't you?'

The waitress looked at Squishy dubiously. Squishy looked back from Frank's pocket as if to say "How can you not let me in? Me? You strange human!"

'Well, so long as she behaves herself,' the waitress finally said, breaking into a smile and tickling Squishy under the chin.

'She is the best-behaved little kitten in the world,' Susan assured her.

'Well, okay, but sit in the corner, away from the window. If passers-by saw her someone might complain. You'd be surprised at what people complain about.'

They dutifully took their places in the corner seat away from their window and gave the waitress their orders.

'Ta-ra!' said Gertie, revealing her purchases. 'Wedding Day, and Bride and Groom,' she added, taking two magazines out of a packet.

'They have two magazines for weddings?' asked Frank in surprise.

'They had four in the newsagents,' Gertie said. 'And if you go to a larger shop you'll find at least ten.'

'Ten? Surely there can't be that much to say about getting

married?'

'There's Cosmopolitan Bride,' Susan said.

Frank blinked.

'Bliss for Brides,' added Gertie.

Frank blinked again.

'Wedding and Home.'

'You and Your Wedding.'

'The Wedding Directory.'

'Brides and Setting up Home.'

'For the Bride.'

'Perhaps we can look at them after we've eaten,' Frieda suggested, casting an anxious glance at Frank who appeared to have developed a permanent and rapidly repetitive twitch.

'Good idea,' said Gertie. 'Then we can really get stuck into them.'

'So, have you set a date yet?' asked Susan.

'Well, we were concerned about rushing in where angels dare to tread,' said Frank, his blinking rate slowing down. 'You know, marry in haste, repent at leisure. Look before you leap, that sort of thing. But, on the other hand, Carpe Diem. Strike while the iron is hot. They who hesitate are lost. In the end –'

'In the end we decided that September would be a good idea,' Frieda said before he could bore them all to death by cliché.

'A week after Harry and Allison tie the knot,' Frank said.

'So soon!' exclaimed Susan as their meals arrived. 'Will you be able to arrange everything in such a short time?'

'Plenty of time,' Frank replied, tucking into his fried eggs and bacon. 'Almost three months.'

'Seventy-five days,' Frieda corrected.

'Seventy-five?' asked Frank in surprise. 'You've counted them?'

'Of course she's counted them,' Susan said as Frieda blushed. 'Every girl counts the days until her wedding day. What colour wedding dress were you thinking of, Frieda?'

'Well, I think I might go for ivory.'

'Ivory?' asked Gertie. 'Surely it has to be white. Ah!' she exclaimed as Susan's heel came down on her foot.

'Sorry, Gertie, I think I caught your foot there. Ivory sounds wonderful.'

'And of course we want both of you to be bridesmaids,' Frank said, feeling that the conversation was leaving him behind, a long way behind.

'Ooh, yes please,' said Gertie. 'What colour should our dresses be? Orange is traditional, isn't it?'

'I thought that was pink,' Susan said.

'We'll find out just now,' Gertie replied, nodding at the magazines while she scraped the last of the scrambled egg onto her fork. 'Soon as the plates go and the coffee comes.'

'Anyway,' interjected Susan, 'we have to follow tradition to a certain extent, but if Frieda's going to be wearing ivory, we need something that doesn't clash. What about lilac, or lavender, Frieda?'

'We could all wear ivory. How about that?'

'That sounds wonderful,' sighed Gertie.

'I am not wearing ivory,' Frank said. 'I'd look silly.'

'Oh, shush, Frank,' Susan said. 'You'll be wearing top hat and tails, grey. Men are lucky, they have a standard outfit. See, even Squishy agrees.'

'Now, let's have a look,' Gertie said, taking out the magazines as the waitress came with coffee.

'Whatever you do, don't get married in green,' the waitress said as she took their plates.

'Green?' asked Frank, puzzled.

'Not unless you're Irish,' Susan said.

'Everybody knows that,' Gertie added.

'They do?' asked Frank. Gertie sighed.

'Marry in green, ashamed to be seen,' she said, shaking her head at Frank's appalling lack of knowledge. 'A green gown is supposed to be linked to having a roll in the fields – a woman's dress would be stained green from the grass, which showed her to be a trollop.'

'But it's okay for the Irish?'

'It's their national colour, dummy. They can do it because it shows patriotism.'

'Ah,' said a bemused Frank.

'When I get married I'm going to wear blue,' said the waitress, in no hurry to leave with the plates she was holding. 'Married in blue, your love will always be true. That's what they say.'

'They do?' asked Frank.

'Married in yellow, ashamed of your fellow,' added Susan.

'And ivory?' asked Frank weakly. 'Marry in ivory, your love will – what?'

'Don't be silly, Frank, there isn't one for ivory,' Susan said. 'Come on, Gertie, let's have a look at those magazines.'

'I'd better get back to work,' said the waitress sadly. 'Good luck.'

'Thanks,' Frank replied with a heartfelt voice.

'Ooh, look at this one on page three,' Gertie cooed.

'This one is gorgeous,' Susan sighed, having appropriated the second magazine.

'And another, page six.'

'These orange flowers really set this one off,' Susan noted on page seven. 'Oh, Frieda, there really isn't a lot of time left, is there? There's your bouquet, flowers for the church – you are going to have a church wedding, aren't you? Well, it doesn't have to be a church wedding, of course,' she added swiftly as she noticed Frieda looking down at the table. 'A bit old fashioned, in fact, probably better to hire somewhere, you can get married almost anywhere these days.'

'Photographers, catering, table decorations, speeches,' added Gertie, flipping a page.

'Your bouquet,' Susan pointed out, 'have you thought about that?'

'Well, I haven't had much time to think about it, but I've always thought Oriental Lilies would make an ideal choice.'

'What say we just nip into the register office, tie the knot, and then nip down the pub for a few pints?' Frank whispered to Frieda.

'Frank!' exclaimed Gertie. 'It isn't nice teasing Frieda like that.'

'I agree,' said Susan. 'You just keep quiet, Frank Summers. Be a good little boy, now.'

'Something old, something new,' said Gertie. 'Well, the new is easy, that's the dress. What about the old?'

'And something borrowed, something blue,' added Susan.

'And a silver sixpence in your shoe,' said Gertie, 'people tend to forget that.'

'I think I need a trip to the little boys' room,' Frank said, standing up and heading rapidly away, Frieda looking after him anxiously.

'What was all that about?' Gertie asked Susan. 'Kicking me when I asked Frieda what colour she was going to wear?'

'White signifies virginity,' Susan said. 'Frieda's already been married once. People would make some nasty comments, apart from it being bad luck. I almost screwed things up talking about a church wedding, some churches won't marry someone who's been divorced. And I don't think Frieda really wants Frank to be reminded of her ex-husband, do you Frieda?'

'No, I'd prefer to keep well away from that subject. If Frank doesn't mention it, I won't. It's fortunate that I kept my maiden name, at least there isn't that added complication. Though this time I think I will change my name to his.' She sighed. 'A church wedding would be nice, but it might be difficult, as you say.'

'Sod the other people,' Gertie insisted. 'I don't see any problem in wearing white.'

'Ivory's a nice compromise,' Susan said. 'Close enough to white without upsetting the traditionalists. And you don't want to risk tempting fate on your wedding day.'

'So, how did it feel when he popped the question?' Gertie asked, accepting that ivory would have to do. They leaned their heads together as if it were a secret conference. Even Squishy leant forward.

'You won't believe this,' Frieda said, 'but I actually fainted, more or less.'

'You fainted?' asked Susan in disbelief, with the emphasis on the "you".

'Well, I thought I was there for the "we can still be friends" routine. I'd been dreading that drink all week, thinking I knew what was coming. And then, instead of "we can still be friends" he was proposing to me! I thought it was a bad dream I was having.'

She was not going to mention the business with the ring. The other two had Oohed and Aahed over its perfection, determined to bury their sorrow in not being the bride by showing brave faces and taking a deep vicarious enjoyment with the one who was going to be. Their enthusiasm had reminded her of how bad she had felt when she had purloined the ring, and how much worse she had felt when Frank had proposed. She had vowed to herself that she would never, ever do that sort of thing again, no matter what the circumstances. Never again.

Definitely not.

'I suppose it would be a bad dream,' Gertie said. 'If it was a dream, that is. You'd feel awful when you woke up.'

'How did he propose? He didn't go down on his knee, did he?' asked Susan.

'Yes, he did. Thinking about it, I can't imagine him doing otherwise.'

'And then what happened?'

'Well, the landlord sent us some champagne, so we had that, or a glass each. And then we went to Gino's, and there was more champagne waiting, and the staff all knew about it, so we had the best service and the best meal I've ever had. Or at least, I think it was. I couldn't really eat much, I was still in a daze.'

'And then? Did you go back to his place?'

'No, he called a taxi and took me back to my house. We kissed outside the front door, he made sure I was in safely and told me he'd call first thing in the morning.'

'Aaah!' sighed the eternally romantic Gertie. 'And it was a full moon last night, a lovers' moon.'

'I know,' said Frieda. 'I stood watching it out of the window, trying to tell myself that what was happening was real. I couldn't sleep, I couldn't think of going to bed as if the day had ended just like any other day. In the end I must have fallen asleep on the couch, that's where I woke up.'

'How did you feel when you woke up?'

'I felt absolutely awful. The sun was streaming through the open curtains, and I knew I'd had too much to drink the previous evening – or that's what I thought. I presumed I'd dreamt it all and had to face another day and just slog on. It was very confusing – if I'd just dreamt it, how could I have had too much to drink the previous evening? What had I really done that made me feel that way? I was still three-quarters asleep. I couldn't make head or tail of it.'

'That's terrible,' empathised Gertie. 'What happened next?'

'Next,' Frieda said, sniffing and taking out a handkerchief, 'next I got up and found the rose he'd given me the night before, and the ring on my finger, and I knew it hadn't been a dream.'

The other two had their handkerchiefs out and an all-out sobbing session threatened.

'What's up with you lot?' asked Frank, sitting down again. 'This is supposed to be an engagement breakfast, not a wake.'

'You wouldn't understand,' sniffed Susan.

'No, he wouldn't,' sniffed Gertie. 'I don't know why you agreed to marry him, Frieda, he's about as useless as most men.'

'No, he isn't,' Frieda said, kissing him gently on his cheek. 'He's my knight in shining armour.'

'Can I skip the shining armour bit?' he asked. 'I hear it's very heavy, a bit of a pain to wear, and people with swords and lances keep trying to kill you. And it goes rusty in rain.'

'Silly,' Frieda admonished, squeezing his hand.

'So,' he asked, 'have you finally finished organising all the details of the wedding?'

'Finished?' cried Susan in disbelief. 'We haven't even started, and there's hardly any time left. The invitations will have to go out as soon as possible. And the gift list.'

'Who's going to give you away?' asked Gertie. 'You know, seeing as how ... '

Frieda smiled, somewhat sadly.

'Yes, I think my dad would have loved to be there. He died so terribly young. Funny how you always think of your parents as being old, and then, you grow up and realise how young they really were.' She paused. 'I was thinking of maybe asking the Chief Inspector.' She turned to Frank. 'You'll need a best man.'

'Best man? I hadn't thought about that. Can't my dad be my best man?'

'Of course not,' Susan said. 'Your best man is there to fight off your enemies, he has to be a comrade in arms, someone of your own age.'

'There you go, Frank,' Gertie said, 'that's something for you to do. Now, let's get down to business. Where are you going to get married, and where will the reception be? Have you told your parents?'

'Frank told his parents before he proposed,' Frieda said, smiling at him. 'I told my mother yesterday.'

'Oh, that's another point,' Susan said. 'Protocol. There'll have to be a main table for the bride, groom, parents and that, but how will you seat the rest?'

'You know, I think less planning went into the Normandy landings and the battle of Arnhem combined,' Frank said. 'And I think they were probably less worried about jumping than I'm beginning to be.'

'Stop being silly, Frank,' Gertie admonished. 'This is important. Frieda, it just has to be a church or chapel. You have to have an aisle to walk up.'

'A church would be better, if you can find one available,' Susan said, stressing the "if" as a hint to Gertie. 'Wherever it is, it has to be somewhere large enough for all the guests. Not too large, or it will look empty, but not too small or people will be cramped.'

'Everyone from the station will need an invite,' Gertie pointed out. 'And then there's relatives – Frank, you'd better make a list of all your relatives you need to invite.'

'Perhaps you should calculate how many thousands are likely to turn up,' suggested Frank. 'Then you have a base figure for working out what size church or cathedral we'll need. You never know, St Pauls might be available.'

'Really, Frank!' admonished Susan. 'You don't use the word "calculate" when planning a wedding. It sounds too brutal.'

'Diets,' said Gertie.

'Diets?' asked Frank. 'You don't need to go on a diet.'

'I meant what people will need special food, silly. Vegetarians, vegans, people with special requirements. But now you come to mention it, I will need to start dieting for the day.'

'Me too,' added Susan. 'I need to shed at least a few pounds.'

Frank gave up. It was obvious that, if he continued to put his oar in, he was likely to get hit over the head with it. He decided to play with Squishy instead. To his dismay Squishy was not interested in playing, and was following the discussion with great interest.

He might have expected it. Squishy was a she as well, after all.

'I suppose we should be heading back,' Frieda said eventually.

'I suppose so,' sighed Gertie.

They walked back to the station, Frieda with her arm in Frank's as if frightened that he might float off and disappear like an errant balloon. Susan and Gertie walked behind as if they were chaperones, chatting eagerly of invitations, flowers, gift lists, colour and style of dresses, getting their hair done, and the thousand other crucial requirements needing attention in the so short time left until the wonderful day.

'Don't worry, Frank, it will only happen once,' Frieda said. 'You're not regretting it, I hope?'

'Of course not, don't be silly. Everybody seems to be enjoying themselves, why should I complain?'

'Oh, please don't say it like that. You hate it, don't you? You do, I can tell.'

'Frieda, I promise you that I will be entirely honest and open with you. If I hated it I would have let you know.'

She smiled at him, but she had her reservations. He had been far too quiet, and they had excluded him far too much. She had sensed subtle signs of irritation, irritation suppressed, something far worse than open feelings. Men, Frank especially, bottled up their negative feelings. Eventually the bottle burst. There was still a long sail to the wedding altar, and Frank might suddenly decide to seek open waters. While he pretended to have fully recovered from his accident she knew there were still dark corners in his mind which he feared and would not let anyone else near.

And she had a distinct feeling that she would be "Free" when he was happy with her and "Frieda" when he wasn't. Exactly the same as her father had.

'Where would you like to go for our honeymoon?' he asked suddenly.

'Honeymoon? I hadn't really thought that far.' Hadn't hoped to think that far, she thought. 'What about Paris?'

'An excellent choice. Paris. I've never been there, you know. Roundabout France, yes, but not actually Paris, unless you count waiting in Charles de Gaulle airport a couple of times.'

'I spent five days there on an exchange course,' Frieda said. 'All I got to see was the inside of my hotel room and the insides of French police stations.'

'What, the charming, gallant Frenchmen didn't take you out to revues, to the theatre, to see the Champs-Elysées,?'

There it was again, that slight edge to his voice.

'When you're part of a group of Chief Inspectors, Superintendents, Chief Constables and other mighty ranks, you find that, in the real world out there an inspector doesn't rate very highly.'

She looked at him.

'Frank, I don't feel very much like work today. What say we take the day off? Percy's perfectly competent to run things as they stand. Come on, let's do it. We can go for a stroll along the riverbank. Go anywhere. Just have a nice quiet day away from everything.'

'Now that appeals,' Frank replied, grinning. 'I can't say I was overly looking forward to all the congratulations. They mean well, but it's all a little much. Especially after the way they've been treating me lately.'

She wondered whether he had known why he had been the subject of such treatment. Had he kept his secret in spite of it? The secret that he was going to propose to her?

But, then, as he had so artlessly said, she should have known that he was going to propose, having turned down Susan and Gertie.

Our fears fuel our worries, no matter how silly or illogical they might seem. Frieda was beginning to let hers breed and multiply. The shock and delight of Frank's proposal had now worn off, and she was beginning to doubt that Frank would go through with it.

No, not quite not go through with it. But he might be starting to have little doubts which might end up with him not going through with it.

Would she?

Yes, she would. She was in love with him, and she would go through fire and damnation so long as she was at his side. If he turned out to be, like her ex-husband, a wife beater, she would resign herself to her fate. This time there was no going back.

And, in the unlikely event that such turned out to be the case, this time she would take boxing lessons.

And make sure there was a heavy frying pan in the kitchen.

Susan left them at the station entrance, reluctantly, claiming the evil necessity of having to get some work done. The others entered the station reception area to find a revived Eric Johns. He had discovered that events had turned out in such a way that, despite the large pay-out to Tricia Leigh, he had come out with a profit, and, in a moment of goodwill which he might later regret, had decided to donate that profit to the start of a collection for the wedding, the second wedding, now, that the stretched purses and wallets of Wellbury's finest would be asked to contribute.

He beamed as Sam Nightingale, coming into reception at the same time as the happy couple entered the station, asked permission to kiss the bride and groom to be. Sam's being gay, he realised, did not mean that she did not feel the same emotions as most other women at the idea of a wedding. Indeed, her kiss and hug given to Frank was as ardent as any sister might give to her brother.

Sam Nightingale, at least, had nothing to bother her conscience. Everybody else was going around explaining that they had guessed all along, and never believed any of that nonsense about Tricia Leigh. Everybody apart from Agnetha, whose scornful looks were there to remind the miscreant gossipers of the evil they had done. But at least the pall of bad feeling which had hung over the station for the past week had disappeared.

Up in the outer office Tricia greeted them with an "Oh! Oh! Oh!"

'Careful, Trish,' Frank said, ruffling her hair, 'we'll make you into the town crier if you continue that.'

'Oh! Oh! Oh!' Tricia exclaimed, giving first him and then Frieda a hug.

'We're taking the rest of the day off,' Frieda told her. 'You can do the same if you want.'

'Oh! Oh! Oh!' cried Tricia Leigh.


'I get the feeling that you're finding things a little overwhelming,' Frieda said as they strolled along the river bank, hand in hand.

'I expected a little fuss,' he admitted, 'but all this planning an organising for the wedding? I thought I'd have you to myself, that we'd be married and settled down. We seem to have become public property all of a sudden.'

'I know. I'm sorry about that, Frank. I'm afraid it's a little to be expected. But I'll have a word with Susan and Gertie.'

'Does it matter?'

There it was again, that edge to his voice. As if he had done what he had to do, and now nothing mattered. All he wanted to do was get it over and done with. She knew she wasn't imagining things. Squishy had been regally surveying her queendom along the river from the comfort of Frank's pocket, now the kitten had turned to look up at him, a concerned look in her eyes. Frank might be able to disguise his feelings to other humans, but there was no way he could fool Squishy.

'Frank,' she said, turning him towards her, 'darling. I will call you that every day, because that is what you are to me. My darling. My one and only dearest. I will be a good wife to you, I promise. I will even do whatever you say, because you will be my husband.'

He grinned and the dark corners seemed to flee from his eyes.

'Promise me you won't, Free,' he said. 'Promise me we'll have arguments and disagreements and shouting matches. Promise me we'll get upset with each other, but never stop talking to each other.'

Squishy miaowed from his pocket as if she had decided he needed taking out of his thoughts.

'Hello, Squish, need to go?' he asked, lifting the kitten from his pocket and placing her gently on the grass. Squishy looked around inquisitively before ambling over to a small bush and going around it.

'I promise, Frank, my darling,' Frieda said. 'And whenever we have an argument or a disagreement we'll come down here to the river for a walk, to remember.'

He smiled at the passing water.

'Yes, the river. That's when I realised, you see.'

'Realised?'

'Well ... When I was in – out of sorts after the accident – and the Chief Inspector first spoke to me, he told me how he and his wife had stopped speaking to each other early on in their marriage. They had some silly spat and decided to act childishly. Then he was almost killed in a domestic that he was attending, and he realised how close he was to dying –'

He paused, as if searching for words, or an idea.

'It's the problem with the Enlightenment, you know.'

'The Enlightenment?' asked Frieda, blinking.

'Yes, the biggest fault line in the Enlightenment. Understandable, of course, when you look at the history. After all, they were moving from a culture dominated by religion to one of secular rationalism. The church – the Catholic church in France, for a good example – wouldn't tolerate this new way of thinking. So secular rationality became in itself a fundamentalist movement. Nothing mattered except for scientific rationalism. Proof. You had to be able to prove something before it could be believed in.'

Frieda nodded. She understood what Frank was saying. She just didn't understand why he was saying it.

'The problem was feeling,' he continued. 'Feelings exist, you can't ignore them. But they are unscientific, almost unmeasurable. Ironically the secularists were passionate about avoiding feeling and emotions. And then, of course, our culture, our identity, if you want, as opposed to the French or the Italians or the Spanish, helped muddy the pool with the idea of the stiff upper lip and all the rest. It's not surprising people grow up confused. Especially when you have satirists suggesting that that empty-stomach feeling someone gets when – I think "falling in love" is the phrase – is a result of eating something disagreeable rather than anything solid – if I can put it that way. But that also shows you the sort of problems we're faced with, that word "love". What does it mean? The extreme secularists would have it that it's merely some form of biological stimulus. I can't say I'm totally with them on that one.'

He pulled his earlobe thoughtfully.

'Playing that practical joke on me – the Curious Incident of Cleopatra's Clothes, as Phil Walthers put it. Well, that showed me you cared. But there was something else. Remember when Campbell and Hovis turned up?'

Frieda nodded. Jean Candour had turned up first, but that was probably best not mentioned.

'Remember how we were then? I'd invited Tricia to my place on my birthday thinking that no-one else was available, you turned up and ... Well, you were angry with me, and I was angry with you for being angry with me. And so we stopped speaking to each other. Or not more than was absolutely necessary.'

'I know, we were being childish. I'd prefer to forget it, to be honest.'

'Ah, but there's the thing, don't you see? That was my proof. I asked myself, how much did we really care for each other? And the answer was, enough to be absolutely childish about it. And, let's face it, we're at our most honest when we're being unconsciously childish. That was what proved to me that we really cared about each other. And the bonus was that it proved both sides, not just one.'

Frieda smiled. She liked the idea. Far too much to even think of applying any scientific method to test the logic.

'Proof of passion,' she said.

'In a way, I suppose, yes.' He smiled wryly. 'I've never been over fond of that word, "love". It always seems to mean too much or too little. But I've never been able to find a word that fits. "Fancy" sounds – well, it just doesn't sound right. Too short term. Same with infatuation. Longing, yearning, craving – there just doesn't seem to be a word that describes the feeling you have for someone who makes your life feel whole.'

Frieda nodded.

'Yes, I've often thought that.'

'Between them the media – advertising mainly, but the tabloids do their bit – and the politicians have pretty much ruined the English language. Everything has to be a crisis, a tragedy, brilliant, amazing, better than best. There's no place left for simple pleasures. A rose by any other name may still smell as sweet, but these days it has to have an aroma that will stun you at ten paces.'

She looked at him. He was looking at Squishy, toilet completed, sniffing around, exploring the area for any possible pals to play with. It reminded her of something she had being thinking about.

'We have an awful lot to discuss, you know, Frank.' She hesitated, not wishing to introduce any subject that might stampede him, but knowing that there were many things they would have to face up to sooner or later. 'For example, do you want children?'

He grinned.

'That good old saying, the more the merrier, comes to mind.'

She smiled in relief.

'I've always thought that I'd like a large family. Maybe it has something to do with being an only child.'

'Well, since we're  both only children we'll have to make up the numbers. And when they reach a certain age we'll have to get a puppy for them to look after. Something silly, a mongrel with long ears which it will keep tripping over. And then it

181

will grow up into the most idiotic and lovable dog in the neighbourhood and irritate them all.'

Squishy turned at this, sat down and looked up at them as if indignant.

"We don't need a puppy," she seemed to be saying. "By then I will be old enough to look after the children myself. Puppies are stupid things."

'There is one other thing, though,' Frank added.

'Anything, Frank, anything. What is it?'

He put his arms around her.

'When the first ankle-biters appear we're going to have a buggy with a see-through top so that we're sure the little buggers are where they should be. In fact, sod the buggy, we'll have an old-fashioned pram. With high sides no two-year-old can climb out of.'

She laughed and cried as she held him tight.

It was just as well that, while they were planning this happy future, she did not overhear a conversation between Eric Johns and Samantha Nightingale that lunchtime, a conversation that was going to put a spanner in the works.

Wellbury's finest could never be accused of a shortage in the spanners department.

**Monday Lunchtime: The Prophecy**

'I'll bet you he gets out of it,' Sam Nightingale said, sitting at a table in the canteen opposite Eric Johns, trying not to notice his approach to food, both in terms of quantity and speed of consumption.

'Gets out of it?' asked Eric in surprise.

'Frank. He won't get married.'

Eric Johns was so struck by this idea that he blinked twice before continuing demolition of the mountain of mashed potatoes, Scottish stew (Agnetha's interpretation) and spring peas in front of him.

'I thought you were the one who said all along that he hadn't got engaged to Tricia,' he pointed out.

Sam frowned. That wasn't quite what she had said. What she had said was that what Frank chose to do was his own business. But Eric Johns almost invariably had his own interpretation of events. Most of the time it was just easier to go along with his version, at least when speaking to him. She could return to reality once he was gone.

'And I was right, wasn't I?' she said.

'Well, then.'

'Well, then, what?'

'Well, then, why are you changing your mind now?'

Sam's forehead crinkled again. It made the freckles on her nose all appear puzzled.

'You've lost me,' she admitted. 'In what way have I changed my mind?'

'You said Frank would do the right thing. And you were right. Now you're saying he's going to break it off. Which isn't the right thing. So now you're saying he's going to do the wrong thing. And I reckon you're wrong.'

Eric Johns' mental processes, Sam decided, would be a good study for someone with a lot of time and headache tablets on their hands.

'I'm not saying he's going to do the wrong thing. It's just

karma. Fate. Some people are destined for matrimony. Frank just isn't one of them. He won't do anything intentionally. It will just happen.'

Eric Johns did not demur at the idea of something as fanciful as fate. In fact he had a healthy respect for fate.

And there could be no doubt that Frank was doing his best to avoid getting involved in the planning of the wedding.

Unlike the rest of the station, all of whom had a great deal to contribute. And they did, however uselessly. Harry Wheatley was privately pleased. It took some of the heat off of his own wedding preparations and fears.

'What is it, almost a hundred days left?' asked Sam rhetorically. 'Plenty of time for something to happen. Look at Napoleon. He had a hundred days after returning from Elba.'

'Ah, yes, he met his Waterloo,' Eric pointed out.

'Precisely,' replied Sam enigmatically.

Eric blinked. Sam had obviously made a point about something, but he wasn't quite sure what it had been.

'Less than a hundred days,' he said, deciding that ignorance was bliss. 'More like seventy.'

'Seventy-five, come to think about it. Seventy-five days to W-Day. And counting down. The way time passes these days it will gone before you know it. So will Frank, I bet you.'

Eric Johns rubbed his jaw. He had come out ahead on the book he had opened on who Frank would choose. He wondered if he should open a book on whether Frank would actually get married.

Almost everyone would put money on Frank marrying, especially if he could get them to bet before Sam

Nightingale's prophecy should become known. He'd make a right killing then.

The only problem was that he was likely to be the one killed if Fabulous ever got wind of it.

But it would hardly be his fault, would it? He wasn't responsible for Frank's karma, was he?

Sam excused herself, returning to duty without realising that she had made any prophecy whatsoever. It wasn't her fault. She was still relatively new, and had yet to learn the power of Eric Johns' imagination. Or the effect that that imagination could have on others in the station, other people who were, technically speaking, rational adults.

# Chapter Two – Counting Down Fast

## W-Day minus 74

'Come in,' Frieda said in response to a knock on her office door, hastily and guiltily shoving a number of wedding magazines into an anonymous folder, while Tricia did the same with several others. Apart from the fact that she and Tricia should have been concentrating on police business, the caller was likely to be Frank, and within twenty-four hours he was showing an ever-deepening allergy to magazines and periodicals devoted to the marriage trade. True to her expectations it was Frank who walked in.

'You desired my presence, oh master?' he asked.

'Erm, yes, yes, Frank. Okay, thank you, Tricia, that will be all for now.'

'Are you sure?' asked Tricia, a mischievous smile on her face. 'There's nothing else you want me for at the moment?'

A glare from Frieda sent her out of the office, giggling.

When the door had closed a smiling Frank leaned over her desk and kissed her. She had to stand up and lean over it to let him do so. Once this unusual method of two police officers greeting each other had been concluded she sat down while he put Squishy on the carpet with her tennis ball to play, and perched himself on the edge of her desk. He idly picked up a file to peruse, the same file Frieda had just stuffed with wedding magazines.

'Mail Order Bride Catalogue,' he quoted. 'Send off for your brand new bride today. Money back guarantee if not fully satisfied. Special offer of the week: ten day trial period for new subscribers.'

'Frank! There is no such thing, and you know it.'

'Tread softly, oh man who would take the Mickey out of marriage.'

Frieda frowned at him. She wanted to point out that marriage was a serious commitment, and things were not being helped by his flippant approach, but she was on very weak ground there. If he responded with a flippant comment she would only get irritated. If he responded seriously all he would need to point out was that some marriages lasted longer than others.

Her first, for instance. That hadn't survived many months.

'Stop looking so glum, Free,' he said. 'You have to admit that all this wedding day pressure is a little over the top. Let Tricia do the worrying. She's more than happy organising everything. Let's just enjoy ourselves.'

He leaned forward.

'I slipped a copy of Playboy inside one of the wedding magazines in her desk drawer,' he whispered. 'Maybe she'll find it when she takes it out to read on the bus on the way home.'

Frieda shook her head and frowned at him. At the same time she couldn't resist a smile. She could imagine Tricia taking out the wedding magazine on the bus going home, the copy of Playboy dropping onto the floor, and Tricia's face going beetroot-red as she tried to hide it. Tricia would be furious, but she'd see the funny side, and she was the type to pay Frank back in turn.

And she, Frieda, might well give Tricia a hand, just for the hell of it. No reason why Frank should have all the fun.

'There are one or two more serious things to be thinking

about,' she said, trying to remain poker faced. 'There's this ghost business for a start.'

Frank's eyebrows rose.

'You did say serious, didn't you?'

'It's become a high profile case. The media are demanding that we do something about it.'

Frank grinned.

'Zack the Prat, you mean.'

Frieda scowled.

'Yes, if you must insist. Unfortunately it's beginning to irritate the Chief Constable. He wants us to sort it out.'

'I thought it was Percy's case.'

'He said I was welcome to it if I wanted it. Pete Phillips has been complaining about spending time patrolling the cemetery for hours late at night. And he's started claiming overtime for it. That wasn't your doing, was it?'

'Moi?' asked Frank innocently. 'Would I?'

'Yes, you would. Anyway, Percy's attending a conference on how to handle sealing off towns in the event of an emergency security alert, so he won't have the time.'

'I thought we already had a plan for that?'

'We do, but no doubt they'll come up with a new one. Or new words to describe the same plan. For some reason Percy thinks that standing in front of a television camera explaining that he has had to take extreme measures in the face of an imminent security danger which will make everyone's lives intolerable – such as blocking off every entry and exit to Wellbury – will make him look important.'

'It will make him look a total idiot.'

'Precisely. People like Zack the prat might start off by congratulating him, but Wellburians aren't that daft. Anyway, there was another report of a sighting of our friend Caspar on Saturday night. Someone taking a short cut home claims that they were almost assaulted by the ghost – a Mr Samuel Harris. You wouldn't mind having a look into it, would you?'

'Okay,' said Frank, 'we still need to have a word with the Prat about his claims about paedophiles. I'll take Gertie with me, if that's okay.'

'Of course.'

They were being extra-polite to each other. Though now of the same rank Frieda was his senior by virtue of having been an inspector for longer. But their engagement made the relationship far more complex. It was one thing for Frieda to order him around at work as his boss. Doing so as his wife would contain any number of dangers. Doing so as his fiancée could well see the relationship end very quickly.

She had been honest with Frank about the ghost case becoming high profile. What she had failed to mention was that it was also something to keep Frank's attention occupied. With any luck he would be standing at the altar before he realised the time had passed. And it should keep him out of harm's way. After all, what danger was there from some imaginary ghost?

And since the ghost case wasn't going to take up all of his time she was looking for other safe tasks that might take up his time, and that was proving to be a problem. Ideally he should have a desk job, preferably chained to it, but he wouldn't fall for that one, and he wouldn't take kindly to being given all the security lectures to householders and talks to school classes about road safety or whatever else she could dream up.

He sure as hell wasn't going to attend any more domestics, she was going to make certain of that.

After he had left she took a calendar from her desk drawer and made a note in it: W-74. Seventy-four days to Wedding Day. Seventy-four days in which to make sure that nothing went wrong.

Which, with Frank, would be a miracle.

And Frieda, being a modern, intelligent, logical woman, did not believe in miracles.


'So, Sarge – I mean sir – nervous about September?' asked Gertie as she drove them towards the home of the latest "almost" victim of St Mary's ghost. Squishy had been left in the care of Tricia, to Frieda's concern. She wasn't sure that Tricia would get much work done with the kitten around. And she was pretty sure she wouldn't either.

'What's there to be nervous about?' Frank asked. 'I don't know why everybody's going on about it so much, it's just a simple wedding, that's all.'

Gertie grinned to herself. Normally Frank's fingers would be tapping the tune of some song. At the moment they were beating out a note of irritation. Frieda had warned her to keep away from the subject. She decided that that could well be a good idea.

'So, what do you reckon, Sarge, I mean sir. About the ghost, I mean.'

'Well, Gerts, there may be far more things in the world than dreamed of in thy philosophy, Horatio, but I somehow very much doubt that Wellbury has suddenly found itself a ghost. Might be good for the tourist trade, but this one sounds just a little too physical to me. Ghosts are supposed to appear at a distance, vaguely, not come flying into the attack at close quarters.'

'You think there's a physical explanation?'

'I'm willing to put good money on it, Gerts. The only question is whether we'll be able to find that explanation. But we'll give it a damn good try, whatever happens.'


Someone was already at the door to Mr Samuel Harris's house when they arrived, a man holding a camera.

'Mr Walthers,' greeted Frank, 'not here to track down our spectre, are you?'

'Indeed I am, Inspector. May I take it that that is also your errand?'

'Oh, no, Mr Walthers. Ghosts are not within the purview of the police. We are here to investigate an alleged attempted assault.'

Phil Walthers smiled.

'A very nice distinction, Inspector, you should have become a journalist.'

'I almost did. Then I saw the salary and terms and conditions. The police force paid a little more, and you wouldn't be expected to be the office tea-boy for your first two years. Apart from that, both jobs have similarities.'

'True, I was fortunate enough to inherit the Herald rather than having to go through an extended apprenticeship. Oh, congratulations on both your promotion and your engagement. I must warn you, however, that Mrs Blower is also awaiting your first call to the Blue Bliss to add her congratulations. She is most enthusiastic about the news.'

'Thanks for the warning. I think I might leave it for a few days, to let her get used to the idea. Shall we knock?'

'You don't mind my sharing your interview with Mr Harris?'

'Not at all, Mr Walthers.'

In fact you'll be doing most of the interview, he was tempted to add.

Mr Harris was physically an undistinctive man, apart from his wide, staring eyes, whether his normal mien or a result of his near-brush with the spirit world was a moot point. He invited them in, sat them down and offered tea, which his wife, with similarly wide eyes, rushed off to make so that she could return and share in her husband's adventure.

'It was that close, it was,' Mr Harris said, holding up a shaking finger and thumb close together, his eyes roving from their faces to Phil Walthers' camera, to their feet, their knees and then back to their faces before repeating the trip. 'If I hadn't moved as fast as I could it would have got me.'

'Perhaps we could start at the beginning, Mr Harris,' suggested Phil Walthers, with a sideways glance to Frank, who gave a brief nod. 'You were taking a short cut through the cemetery, I understand?'

'Yeah, that's right. I pop into the local for a couple of pints on a Friday, after work. Coming back through the cemetery is a short cut, and safer than walking along the road. The way some of these youngsters race around these days, sometimes you fear for your life.'

'What is it you do for a living?'

'I'm an undertaker. That's why the cemetery don't frighten me at night. Not until last Friday, anyway.'

'And whereabouts in the cemetery did the ghost attack you?'

'Close to the back, near where those allotments are. I was bleeding lucky, I was, I'd just stopped to check the time – because it was so dark I had to look down at me watch, closely. There was a sudden flash of light, shot past me, just missed me head, and the clanking of chains, it was obviously trying to wrap me in its coils. If I hadn't had me head bent down it would have got me, just like that! Scared the living daylights out of me, it did.'

'White as a sheet he was, when he got home,' agreed Mrs Harris, coming into the lounge with a tray of teacups. 'Gasping for breath as well.'

'I ran the whole way back, fast as I could.'

'Bad for him, at his stage of life.'

'I'm not that old. And it shows I can still run when I have to.'

'So that was that, you didn't see anything else?' asked Phil Walthers.

Samuel Harris paused before replying. "That was that" was far too brief a dismissal of the most important thing that had happened in his life, ever.

'It was, like all over, that light. Like everywhere, it just lit up the gravestones, the whole cemetery. And there was flapping. The wings of the Angel of Death, that's wot it sounded like, the wings of the Angel of Death.'

'Flapping?'

'And the cold, Samuel, tell em about the cold.'

'Yeah, there was also this weird cold wind shot through, froze me to me marrows, it did. I reckon the ghost was trying to paralyse me with cold, good thing I'm still fit enough to take it.'

'Freezing, he was, when he got home. Cold as ice to the touch. Cold as ice. Could have given him a heart attack.'

'What colour was this light?' asked Frank, speaking for the first time.

'Colour? Well … eerie, sorta. Yeah, an eerie, ghostly colour.'

'Pink?' suggested Frank.

'Pink? Nah, more, sorta … eerie. You know.'

'White as marble, his face, when he came through the front door.'

'Blue?'

'Blue?'

'The colour of the light.'

'Yeah, now you come to mention it, sort of white. Very white. I could see them gravestones like it was day. Could even read the inscriptions, I tell you.'

'But you weren't physically harmed?'

'Harmed? I almost killed myself, almost tripped over the graves as I was running.'

'He could have had a heart attack. Then it would have been murder. Wouldn't it, Samuel?'

Samuel Harris scowled at the thought.

'Almost killed me, it did, that ghost. If I weren't so fit I would have been done for.'

'Pushing up daisies, now, he would be, if he hadn't run so fast.'

'Anything else, Mr Walthers?' asked Frank.

'Just a shot or two, if you don't mind?' Phil Walthers asked Mr Harris, picking up his camera. Mr Harris did not mind at all.

'Right, well, thank you for your time, Mr and Mrs Harris,' Frank said, once the pictures had been taken. 'We'll let you know as soon as we discover anything.'

'You going to print this?' Samuel Harris asked Phil Walthers. 'Like, my name's gonna be in the paper? And me photograph?'

'We must act at the discretion of the police force,' Phil Walthers replied, giving Frank a wry smile. 'It very much depends on the delicacy of their investigations.'

'The discretion of the police force,' Frank quoted, once they were safely out of the house and back at their cars. 'Nice one, Mr Walthers. If you don't print anything he'll be telling his mates that the state security system has clamped down on the story.'

'Sorry about that. I have to avoid alienating the public. Much as I would like to print an article about the glorious imagination some Wellburians have, I'm afraid it will probably end up being a small article with much use of the words "alleged" and such phrases as "Mr Harris claimed". You could summarise the whole thing as "Man panics after seeing flash of light in cemetery". And the light sounds remarkably like a camera flash.'

'What do you think, sir?' asked Gertie as they watched Phil Walthers drive away. 'It does sound like it was a camera flash, doesn't it?'

'Very much so, Gerts. A little too much so. Notice how our

Mr Harris stared at Phil Walthers' camera while we were talking? Quite possibly a little mental association and invention'

'You don't believe him?'

'Let's just say I don't think his memory is entirely reliable.' He checked his watch. 'Come on, time for lunch, and then we'll go through the previous sightings of our spook, and see if we can identify any common points which might just turn out to be what you could call facts.'


They walked into reception to find a beaming Eric Johns awaiting them.

'Ah, Frank, there was something Tricia wanted to return to you. She wasn't sure when you'd get back, so she asked me to hand it over.' He produced the issue of Playboy. 'She asked me to tell you she'd already read this one, and could you let her have the latest when you'd finished with it.'

Frank smiled at him and took the magazine.

'Don't look too happy, Eric, you never know what the future holds.'

'Ah, now you can't get me for this one, Frank. Nothing to do with me.'

'Wrong on both accounts, Eric,' Frank replied gaily, heading towards the office he shared with Gertie.

'Well, he's got a point,' Gertie suggested once they were in the office.

'You know that, and I know that, Gerts, but there's no reason to leave Eric thinking he knows that, is there?'

Gertie frowned at him, a frown which gave way to an irritated smile.

'You have a really nasty sense of humour, sometimes, Frank Summers.'

He winked at her. She giggled.

'Aren't you supposed to act in a responsible way now that you're an inspector?' she asked.

'Responsible? Gertie, really, you shouldn't use nasty language like that in front of me.'

### Friday: W-71

'I do not believe this,' Frank muttered, staring at his computer screen.

'What's that, sir, another memo from on high?' asked Gertie, coming to his desk to look, tickling Squishy in her arms. Tricia had reluctantly ceded the kitten to her as it appeared that Squishy wanted some Frank time. 'Ah, that doesn't look like work. That looks like a holiday site on the Internet.'

'Honeymoon holidays in Paris. Have you seen how much they're charging? Who do they think they are, London?'

'Phew!' exclaimed Gertie, noticing the price tag on the page. 'That's a bit steep for a week.'

'That's the cost per night, Gerts.'

'You're joking!'

'Nope, afraid not. And I am certainly not paying that much. It's a rip-off. Call yourself the city of l'amour and then charge double.'

'I don't think I would want to have my honeymoon in a large city,' Gertie said, returning to her desk. 'Definitely not Paris or London or New York. They're great fun if you're just going for fun, but – well, I spent a week in London once. Felt like two seconds. We had a great time, but I can't remember much. I'd want to remember every second of my honeymoon.'

'You might well have a point, Gerts. Years ago I took a girlfriend out for a quiet romantic evening in London. We went to a play in the West End, which was okay, but expensive, and then to a restaurant which was expensive and awful. The waiters acted as if they were doing us a favour. The tables were tiny, probably so that you wouldn't realise how small the portions were. And the food was dire. Devilled asparagus and a peanut with pink sauce, or something. And then, when we left and were walking down Oxford Street – all the streets appeared to be full of drunken yobs, most of them wearing suits – some bloke puked all over my partner's shoes.'

Gertie laughed.

'Probably just bad luck,' Frank continued, 'or maybe Friday is a bad night for a romantic night out in the West End, but I think you're right, large cities these days are just too noisy for a quiet, romantic honeymoon. Hello, what's that?' he added as his computer made a pinging noise at him. He clicked on a button.

'Ah, an e-mail from Percy, this could be amusing.'

He scanned the screen quickly.

'Oh, dear, oh dear, dear, dear, Percy,' he said, shaking his head after he had read it.

'What's up?' asked Gertie.

'Dear old Percy has sent out an e-mail headed "Top Secret".'

'What's wrong with that?' she asked, coming back to his desk to read it.

'"Top Secret"? With "Highly Confidential" underneath in capitals? He must be daft. He might as well have printed it out and put it on the notice board in reception.'

'I'm not with you. Surely he'll only send it to the people who need to know?'

'Gerts, e-mail is the least secure method of communication since smoke signals. Didn't you see that article the other day about the bloke who sent a graphic description of his night of passion to a friend – that went around the world in about thirty seconds flat. Poor woman had to go into hiding.'

'Not much of a friend.'

'I don't think it's just a question of friendship, it's also remarkably easy to hit the wrong button and send your message to the entire world instead of just one person.'

'Mmm. "Operation Mackerel",' Gertie read. 'What's that?'

'From what he's written it sounds like whatever master-stroke they've come up with from that security conference he went on. "Officers will be briefed on the details over the coming days". Well, that's something to look forward to. I could do with a good laugh.'

'At least he hasn't given any details.'

'Just the code-name, Gerts. The Germans gave away a good deal during the Second World War by the code-names they used.'

He sighed and rubbed his jaw.

'I think Frieda's set on Paris. And I don't want to appear a cheapskate. And it is our honeymoon, after all.'

He drummed his fingers on his keyboard, causing Percy's e-mail to jump around on the screen and the machine to make pinging noises. Squishy looked at it and miaowed at Gertie to put her down on Frank's desk

'You know, this whole marriage business is far too much,' Frank said, watching Squishy pat the keys on his keyboard in curiosity, her head tilted to one side. 'I wonder if Frieda will agree to just living in sin.'

He didn't notice the wide-eyed look Gertie gave him which made it quite clear that that was never going to be an option.

Squishy also appeared to find his suggestion most alarming, turning her head to him with eyes wide. She turned back to the keyboard, almost appearing to shake her head in despair at Frank's suggestion. Then she hit the Delete key very hard.

**Monday Evening: W-68**

'A sudden light,' Frank said, sitting in Frieda's dining room as they finished the dessert of the dinner Frieda had prepared. 'That's the only common point in all the so-called sightings. Oh, and if you exclude the dafter ones, they all occurred on a Saturday.'

'So-called?' asked Frieda, Squishy curled up on her lap beneath the tablecloth, appearing happily content having had her dinner, plus the titbits Frieda had been surreptitiously feeding her.

'Everyone claims that they were almost assaulted by a ghost. Yet none of them actually saw this ghost. Oh, and that's another common point. None of them were actually injured. Not by the ghost. One of them cracked his shin against a gravestone as he ran, painful enough, no doubt, but our ghost appears to be remarkably incompetent at actually causing physical damage. Probably a case of mass hysteria – one report of a ghost been seen and suddenly there are five or six more. And I'd like to speak to that motorist who came up with the first one, I think he was making it up on the spur of the moment.' He put his spoon down. 'Yum, that was lovely. You'll have to give me the recipe sometime.'

'It came out of a packet,' Frieda replied, wondering why Frank would need the recipe when they were supposed to be getting married and living together in sixty-eight days, hardly more than a few weeks away. 'Do you think there is a danger that anyone could get hurt – assaulted?'

'Not in the slightest,' he said confidently. 'What we're dealing with is either someone playing silly buggers, or some natural phenomenon and people are letting their imaginations get the better of them.'

Frieda put her spoon down, linked her hands together underneath her chin and looked at him.

'Any ideas on how to solve this?'

'Ideally put up a couple of night-light cameras, but we'll need a few hundred to cover the whole cemetery.'

'You don't think maybe Aggie ... That she might have anything to do with it?'

'No, she tends to stick to her shed at nights these days. She's heard noises, she's frightened. She doesn't go listening to music anymore, she's too scared. Which is my main reason for wanting to nail whoever's causing this. I must pop in and see her soon.'

'What sort of noises?'

'Difficult to say. I don't think her hearing is that good any more. Whistling, whirring, clanking – that sort of thing.'

Frieda paused.

'Talking of going to see people, my mother wants to know when she's going to meet you.'

'Funny you should mention that, my mother wants to know when she's going to meet you.'

That was something that Frieda had been thinking about a lot. She had no doubt that Frank would have no problem in gaining her mother's approval. Whether his parents would like her was a totally different question.

And it was crucial that they did.

When Frank had been in intensive care after his accident his parents had been at his bedside almost every minute. At the time it had seemed a strange coincidence that she had managed to miss meeting them, since she herself had been at the hospital as often as she could.

Now she wondered if that had been a portent.

She told herself to stop being silly.

Something he had just said struck her. Or something he had not said, an omission.

'What about your father?' she asked.

'Oh, dad just takes things as they come. He's more interested in his history books than anything else.'

'Well, we're going to have to arrange a couple of weekends – one to visit your parents, another to see my mother.'

Frieda leant over to get her briefcase and took out her diary.

'What about the fifteenth of July? And then the nineteenth of August. We're both free those weekends.'

'Fine. Who are we going to see first?'

'I'll give my mother a call and see which date is best. And you can do the same with your parents. What's wrong, Squish?' she asked as the kitten miaowed.

'Needs to go to the loo.'

'I'll take her out the back.'

'Good training for having kids, I suppose,' Frank said, standing up and following her.

'Kittens are much less bother than children,' Frieda replied.

Outside, on the patio at the back, a cat sat waiting. It miaowed at Frieda as she stepped out, and then backed off as Frank joined her.

'Hello, Midnight,' Frieda said. 'I haven't fed you today, have I?'

'Midnight?'

'He turned up around midnight a few months ago. I don't know if you'd call him a stray, he seems to belong to all the houses around here. Here, Frank, you take Squish to the end of the garden, I'll get Midnight something to eat.'

When Frank returned after Squishy had finally decided that she had quite finished, thank you, Frieda was sitting at the patio table with their wine glasses in front of her, watching Midnight tucking into a bowl of sardines.

'Sometimes I think he spends his time deciding on what he fancies for his next meal, and then goes to whichever house he's most likely to get it,' she said. 'I always give him fish.'

'Looks like he's been through the wars.'

Midnight had one torn ear that drooped down, another alert as if aware that he was been talked about, a nose that had come into too close reach of several claws, and a thick coat which was suggestive of a man trying to grow his hair long to hide unsightly scars.

'I think of him as a retired roué,' said Frieda. 'A cat whose long career as Casanova and swordsman has come to an end, and has swapped it for a life of being fed and cosseted by humans.'

'Should call him the Colonel,' Frank suggested.

'You know, that's a good idea. I think I will. Colonel Midnight, villain of the Forty First Independent troop of buccaneers, pirates and basic outright brigands, retired.'

Squishy miaowed. The Colonel looked up and around, alarmed.

'Now, Squish, don't interrupt the Colonel while he's at dinner. Very bad manners. Behave yourself.'

Squishy struggled to get off Frank's knee and out of his hands. The Colonel finished his meal, and sat licking his paws appreciatively.

'Oh, go on, Squish, say hello if you must,' Frank said, putting Squishy down. 'But don't expect me to rescue you.'

'Frank, do you think that's a good idea?'

'No, but she's determined to say hello to him. I'll jump in when the fur starts flying. She has to learn that not all other cats are friendly.'

Squishy advanced on the Colonel with an interrogative miaow. The Colonel immediately sat bolt upright and looked around him for the source of this noise, the look on his face suggesting that he had repulsed many invaders before, often outnumbered ten to one, twenty to one, and, by Jove he could do it again.

Then he saw Squishy.

His eyes goggled at the impudence of the young kitten who was now sniffing at him. He spat at Squishy in a rather hopeless manner. Squishy miaowed again as if to say "Daddy!", and rubbed herself against the old tom-cat. The Colonel looked at Frieda and Frank in desperation.

To add further to the insult they chuckled at him.

The Colonel stalked off in high dudgeon to a part of the patio that was kitten-free, and lay down. Squishy followed him and curled up underneath his front paws.

'Bit of a bugger, that, Colonel,' Frank observed. 'Bet you wish you were younger and could run away from it like you used to.'

He missed the look that Frieda gave him.

"That's what you'd like to do, isn't it?" it said. 'Well, you can forget it, you are not going to. Not if I have anything to do with it, Frank Summers.'

## Friday: W-64

'Morning, Frank,' Eric Johns said breezily as Frank walked into reception. 'Oh, sorry, Inspector, sir.'

'Cut the carp, Eric,' Frank replied. 'Just because I've been made Inspector by some mistake doesn't change me. I'm still plain Frank, so stop trying to wind me up.'

'Okay, okay, Frank, just teasing,' Eric Johns said quickly, noticing a slight twitch in Frank's eye which matched the irritation in his voice. 'Listen, I'm not winding you up about this one – there's a bloke from the Wellbury Ghost Action Group in interview room two waiting to speak to you.'

'The Wellbury Ghost Action Group?'

'That's what he said they were.'

Frank shook his head in amazement. Then the look of irritation faded as he considered the possibilities of a Wellbury Ghost Action Group. They could turn out to be quite fun.

'I have a theory,' he said.

'No, please, Frank,' groaned Eric, 'not one of your theories, not this early in the morning.'

'There's nothing wrong with my theories, Eric. Anyway, this theory is that, in our modern society, we don't have enough causes to keep people's minds occupied. They can't go off and fight in some great cause – they'd have to join the army first. They can't organise marches to support their political party, because politics has become so bland. Even when they do get together for a demonstration, either the politicians ignore them or they get arrested – quite often both. But they need something to believe in. So you end up with fruitcakes believing in weird religious cults, followers of fashion, fanatics of football – and the Wellbury Ghost Action Group.'

'You might well be right, Frank. Just do us a favour, though: have a word with wonky-brain in the interview room and get rid of him, will you? I'm trying to keep this station tidy, makes it very messy having fruitcakes all over the place.'

'Will do, Eric. You know me. Dealing with fruitcakes is one of my specialities. I'll just take Squish up to Trish and get a cup of coffee first.'

Having left Squishy with an eager Tricia Frank fetched a coffee from the machine and went to his office. Gertie was sitting waiting for him.

'Good morning, Gerts, did you know that we have the leader of Wellbury's ghost-busters waiting to see us?'

'Yes, Sergeant Johns told me. Sounds like someone's lost some of their marbles.'

'Well, better not keep him waiting. He might lose all of them if we aren't quick. Eric would be most unpleased to find people tripping up on loose marbles all over the station.'

Frank sipped his coffee and smiled as they walked towards the interview room. He winked at Gertie and held up a finger to indicate silence. He took the handle gently and quietly opened the door, pushing it softly so that it creaked slowly open.

'Whooooh,' he called. 'Whooooooh.'

He then walked into the interview room, blowing on his coffee.

'Whoooh, too hot, this coffee. Morning,' he said to the man in the room, a man kneeling on the floor, peering wild-eyed at him over the top of the table, 'I'm Inspector Frank Summers. I believe you're from the Wellbury Group Ghost Action.' Behind him Gertie was struggling to contain her giggles.

'Er, it's the Wellbury Ghost Action Group,' the man replied, struggling to his feet. 'I'm Edward Boones, leader of the group.'

Frank paused.

'The Wellbury Ghost Action Group, I see. Well, Mr Bones, what can we do for you?'

Frank and Gertie sat down, Gertie with her head bent over her notebook, her shoulders shaking. Edward Boones sat down opposite, a look of disapproval on his face.

'I can see you aren't taking this seriously, Inspector. That is exactly why I have had to set up the action group. If the police will not carry out the action necessary to resolve this dangerous situation, then honest citizens like myself must take up arms.'

'And what sort of arms are you taking up, Mr Bones?'

'Sorry?'

'You said you were taking up arms. What sort of arms? Nothing illegal, I hope.'

'I meant that metaphorically, Inspector. I meant that we intend, if the police will not, to do something about the ghost.'

'I see. And what exactly is it that you intend to do?'

'We intend to take action. Direct action.'

'Such as?'

'The sort of action the police should be taking.'

'Which is?'

'I hope you do not expect me to tell you how you should be doing your job, Inspector.'

'What sort of action, Mr Bones?'

'That, I am not at liberty to reveal.'

'You can reveal it to me, Mr Bones, I'm a police officer. Go on, let me guess. You're going to hold a séance.'

'Certainly not. We do not believe in superstitious nonsense like that. However it's obvious that you have no intention of taking this seriously. I shall have to report that to my members.'

Frank stood up.

'You do that, Mr Bones. Gertie, show the chief spook hunter out.'

'Before I go, I demand to know what you have done to resolve this problem.'

'That, Mr Bones, I am not at liberty to reveal.'

The curt delivery and the way Frank left the interview room surprised Gertie. Something, she guessed as she escorted the leader of the Wellbury Ghost Action Group to reception, must be preying on his mind. She wondered if it was the wedding.


'The Wellbury Ghost Action Group?' asked Frieda in disbelief as she laid out the plates for dinner. 'Frank, we really need to get this nonsense sorted.'

'Oh, I don't know. It's fun. Maybe that's what I could go to the Policeman's Ball as, a ghost. What do you think, Squish?'

Squishy replied that he could go as whatever he pleased, so long as he hurried up with that tuna. There was a poor little kitten starving to death here.

'And how would you do that?' asked Frieda. 'Make yourself invisible?'

'Now there's a thought. If I announced that I was going as a ghost, and wasn't there, they'd have to award me the prize for best costume for being invisible, wouldn't they?'

Frieda gave him a look which told him what she thought of that idea.

'What about you? Had any ideas about what you'll go as?' he asked.

'I've already decided that. I'm going to go as Marie de Médicis. Susan knows someone in the Amateur Dramatic Society, they've promised to let me have a costume that could be adapted. But don't tell anyone.'

'Not a word. But why not someone better known – Marie Antoinette, for example. There you go, Squish. Now don't gobble, there's a good girl.'

'Because there'll probably be five Marie Antoinettes there at least. But seriously, Frank, you are going to get a decent costume, aren't you? I don't want to turn up all dressed up with you in a gorilla outfit or something equally silly.'

'Don't worry, I'll sort something out.'

Frieda frowned. Frank's easygoing approach to life was one of the things she had always found attractive in him. Ironically it was also the exact same thing that irritated her the most when she felt that he should be putting more effort in. Of course it could be argued that dressing up for a fancy dress ball was not quite the most important thing in life, but she had put a lot of thought and effort into it and she expected him to do the same.

They had to set an example, after all, being of inspector rank.

But belabouring the point would not be a good idea.

'Come, now, sit down before it gets cold,' she said instead.

'You know, we could just order a take-away every so often,' Frank said, sitting down as ordered. 'You don't have to go to all this trouble every night.'

'There's nothing wrong with the occasional take-away, but cooking doesn't take much longer than waiting for a pizza to arrive, and it's better for you. And it's a lot cheaper.'

'Ah, but you can have a couple of beers while waiting for the pizza to arrive,' Frank pointed out.

He received another look, one which told him that his days

drinking beer while waiting for a pizza delivery were numbered.

'Have you decided who will be your best man?' she asked casually.

'You know, I was thinking of asking Vic Brown.'

'Vic Brown! An ex-con? Are you mad?'

'Not at all. The Chief Inspector would be the ideal choice, but he's giving you away. Next in line is Pete Phillips, but he's likely to dream up something he thinks extremely funny to wind me up. Vic Brown, on the other hand, is so terrified of you he wouldn't dare put a foot wrong.'

'You aren't serious?'

'No, course not. I suppose it will have to be Pete Phillips.'

'You'd better ask him soon.'

'Plenty of time. I'll do it in the next day or so.'

'Frank, there are only sixty-four days to go.'

'Only sixty-four? Frieda, that's over two months. Plenty can go wrong in two months. No need to waste time over-planning. Now this, for example, is delicious. Let's rather enjoy ourselves now and let the future worry about itself.'

Frieda wanted to ask whether he was serious about the whole business, as he appeared to be treating it very lightly.

But that would be an excellent way of starting an argument, and that was not an option.

Definitely not.

### Tuesday: W-60

'Right,' said Edward Boones in the lounge of his and his wife's semi-detached house in Old Merrick, 'I hereby call this meeting to order.'

He wished he had a gavel that he could knock, authoritatively. And something to knock it on. As the other members of the Wellbury Ghost Action Group had fallen silent anyway it seemed a pointless wish.

'Doris, as the group secretary, you will take notes. For posterity, perhaps. Students of the spirit world in years to come may well find our meetings instructive, if not essential, in their work.'

Doris, a thin and greying spinster of about sixty, nodded enthusiastically. These days she worked on a till in a local supermarket. Prior to that she had indeed been a secretary, a valued position which the remorseless thrust of progress had made redundant. She still looked back to the glory days when Mr Peabody had opened the door to his office and called: "Miss Rubenstein, I need you to take a memo."

All gone now. Just the ghosts of memories in her mind.

'Present at this – what is it, the fifth meeting?'

'The fifth plenary meeting of the Wellbury Ghost Action Group, Mr Boones,' Doris prompted.

'Present at the fifth plenary meeting of the Wellbury Ghost Action Group are myself, Edward Boones, as leader, my wife, Muriel Boones as deputy leader, Doris Rubenstein, secretary of our group, our neighbours from number 50, Cecil Hedgewist and his wife Lorna Hedgewist, our neighbours from number 54, Mrs Edith Romerly and her son Wayne Romerly, and a representative of the media, Mr Phillip Walthers, editor of the Wellbury Herald.'

Approving glances went to Phil Walthers who was torn between incredulity and boredom. Wayne Romerly, a miserable-looking eighteen-year-old, looked at the carpet.

'Now,' continued Edward Boones, 'we are faced with a critical juncture. We have come to the point of no return. We are faced with the most extreme danger we have ever faced. It is a battle between good and evil. It is the battle between we, the righteous, and a most malevolent spirit. It is a battle which few are called to face, and those, such as ourselves, who are called to face it, should be truly grateful that we are given this chance to do the Lord's work. Oh, no, ladies and gentlemen, we are the few, the lucky band of brothers – and sisters – who will forever after thank the day we were given such a difficult, nay, impossible, task, and managed to survive – those of us who will survive.'

He turned to Phil Walthers.

'I have a copy of my speech in case you miss something,' he said.

'Obliged, I'm sure,' Phil Walthers replied, managing to stifle a yawn.

'We then, we lucky few, must go forward, accepting the perils and dangers of our calling, brave in heart and soul, and confront the terrible spectre. It is thus, therefore, that I am calling for volunteers.'

'Volunteers?' asked Cecil Hedgewist in an alarmed tone.

'Precisely, volunteers. While I as leader, and Mrs Boones as deputy leader, co-ordinate our strategy, we require volunteers to enter the very pit of danger, the very den of the devil, that most feared and accursed of places, the playpen of this evil spirit – the graveyard.'

The room was silent for a few seconds.

'Cecil will volunteer, won't you Cecil?' asked his wife.

'I'll miss Coronation Street,' he protested feebly.

'Well done, Cecil,' said Edward Boones. 'Who will follow Cecil's brave lead? Ah, yes, Wayne, I see you nodding.'

'Eh?' asked Wayne.

'And brave Miss Rubenstein.'

'Eh?'

'So gallant of you, as our secretary rather than as a woman, to volunteer. Thank you, brave volunteers, how readily you step forward even though your very lives are in peril! We who are likely to survive, salute you. Now, here is the plan.'


'Frank, will you put that down, you're frightening Squishy – and probably the neighbours,' Frieda called from her kitchen.

Frank put Frieda's violin back in its case and wandered into the kitchen. Squishy was backed up in a corner, hair on end, claws out, spitting at the terrible noise she had just heard.

'Must be something wrong with it,' Frank said, picking up Squishy and stroking her. 'After all, I can play my guitar without a problem.'

Frieda decided that it was best not to comment on that.

'Sure there's nothing I can do?' he asked. 'Squish, aren't you hungry? You haven't touched your tuna. Here you are.'

He put Squishy down in front of her bowl. She gave a final furious glare at the doorway just in case whatever had made that spine-chilling noise might still be out there, and took a dainty mouthful, one ear cocked just in case.

'Grab a cloth and take the macaroni out,' suggested Frieda. 'It'll be ready by now.'

'Yum, yum, ' he said, peering into the oven. 'One of my

favourites, 'Macaroni cheese.'

Frieda frowned at him. She had yet to hear him not describe any of her dishes as one of his favourites. It was becoming very irritating.

'So, when did you learn to play the violin?' he asked, putting the bubbling bowl on the kitchen table.

'At school. I really wanted to play the clarinet, but another girl was already quite advanced, and they didn't have a violin player, so I was delegated.'

'Mmmm,' he said, sitting down and sniffing the aroma of the macaroni cheese. 'Saxophonist, that's what I wanted to be.'

'Don't you think having a guitar and a piano is sufficient?'

'It's like books. You can never have enough musical instruments around the place. Our kids are going to grow up surrounded by books and musical instruments. I have decided.'

'Speaking of which, we need to start thinking about buying a house.'

'What's wrong with this place?' he asked, surprised.

She gave him another frown as she handed over a knife and fork and sat down.

'Rub-a-dub-dub, thanks for the grub,' he said. 'There, that's grace sorted.'

'It's all about a new start, Frank,' she said. 'I've always thought of this as my home. We want a new place we can call our home.'

'If you say so,' he said, tucking into the macaroni cheese. 'Oh, yes, that is nice!'

Frieda had to admit that it wasn't bad. Pretty good, really.

But she did wish that he would pay a little more attention to the requirements that marriage would bring. After all, there were only sixty days to go.

Perhaps best not to mention the figure.

But maybe just a small nudge?

'Frank, have you had a word with Pete Phillips?' she asked.

'Yes, I spoke to him at lunchtime. Why do you ask?'

'You didn't have a word with him, did you?'

'I've just told you I did, Free.'

'I meant about his being your best man.'

'Damn! I forgot all about that. I'll ask him first thing tomorrow.'

Frieda pursed her lips and made a note to have a word with Gertie the following morning.

### Friday: W-57

'Nervous about tomorrow?' asked Frieda.

'Tomorrow?'

'We're going to see my mother, remember? You hadn't forgotten, had you?'

'Ah, no, of course not. I just hadn't realised that it was tomorrow. The week seems to have flown by. Damn, I still have to organise someone to look after Squish.'

'I've already spoken to Tricia, she's more than happy to do so,' Frieda said, standing up as her phone rang in the hallway. 'All you have to do is pack some smart clothes.'

'Pack some smart clothes, eh, Squish?' Frank asked the kitten once Frieda had left the dining room. 'Why do I get the feeling that I'm going to be on display this weekend? Perhaps we should take you with us. It would give Frieda's mother something to coo over instead of me.'

Squishy did not appear to think this a good idea at all.

'Not to worry, Squish, I'm sure I'll find a way of turning invisible. Or something.'

'Well, you don't have to be nervous anymore,' Frieda said, coming back into the room. 'It's off.'

'Off?'

'One of my cousins went into labour prematurely. Her mother's not very well, so my mother's gone to give a hand.'

Gone to take over, she could have added, but that was something Frank did not need to know, not yet.

'That's a nuisance,' Frank said. 'We'll have to arrange another time.'

'Yes, but when? There are only fifty-seven days left.'

'Fifty-seven? Plenty. Hey, now there's a thought. Why don't we go to my folks this weekend instead, get that little duty out of the way.'

'Frank! I am not going to drop into your parents' home without any warning. What would they think of me?'

'They wouldn't mind. I used do it all the time. Mum never complained, she was always glad to see me.'

'Oh, yes, you could get away with it,' Frieda said bitterly. 'You could probably even get away with it with my mother. But your parents would think I was a right – flibbertigibbet. Your mother would go into a panic, worrying that the house wasn't in a pristine condition, that she didn't have enough food in, the rooms weren't ready, and everything else – and I'd get the blame. Women will excuse men almost anything, men don't spot things like specks of dust or unironed bed sheets, but women do.'

Frank blinked.

'They don't, do they?'

'Of course they do. Every last little speck.'

'No, I meant iron sheets.'

Frieda shook her head sadly.

'Frank, everything depends on the first meeting. Everything. Afterwards you can relax. But the first time everything must be absolutely perfect.'

Frank rubbed his jaw.

'Strange people,' he commented, frowning. 'I can quite happily say that you will never, ever catch me ironing sheets.'

Like most of his positive pronouncements that was going to prove to be wrong too.

## Monday: W-54

'I hear you've opened a book on whether or not I'm going to get married,' Frank said to Eric Johns in reception, placing Squishy on the counter.

'You're joking!' Eric replied, with the most honest look on his face he could make up, trying to ignore the look in Squishy's eyes that stated that she knew very well that the fat man was lying. 'That would be in terrible taste. Anyway, I wouldn't be that stupid. Everyone would bet on you, you'd get married, and I'd lose a fortune.'

'I tell you what, what if I put ten quid on this non-existent book?'

Eric pondered this for a few seconds.

'Well, on the understanding that I haven't opened a book on the betting whether you will get married, which way would you be laying your ten quid?'

'On my getting married, of course. I'd hardly bet any other way, would I?'

'Well, you could think of it as an even-way bet if you bet against. If you get married you lose a tenner, so what? If you don't get married, at least you get to win some pint money.'

'That is a very cynical view, Eric, I'm surprised at you.'

'Well, I would call it a practical view. But just one thing, Frank?'

'And what would that be?'

'Don't let Fabulous know anything about this book I haven't opened. Crucifixion would be a pleasant alternative to whatever she would dream up for me if she found out.'

'You're letting your imagination run away with you, Eric, she'd probably put a hundred quid on it. That would help defray the cost of the wedding. Come on, Squish.'

Eric Johns watched Frank walk away, wondering whether he should warn him about Sam's prophecy.

But no, better not. That would be interfering with fate.


'Let's go, Gerts,' Frank said, walking into his office. 'We have another ghost victim.'

'Another? When?'

'Friday evening. Usual thing, flash of light, sudden wind. Let's see what dippy imagination we have to deal with this time.'

'Are we taking Squishy?' asked Gertie, putting her jacket on, noticing that the kitten was missing.

'Nope, she's with Frieda. They're going through another wedding catalogue together. Squishy wants to wear pink, apparently.'

Gertie hid a smile. Frieda's office was beginning to resemble a major operations room, crammed with files and folders on every aspect of wedding plans. Anyone entering the office would almost invariably find Frieda and Tricia making notes on outstanding items, from cake (ordered) to wedding venue (desperately unresolved with only fifty-four days to go) and reception (thankfully Phil Walthers and Mrs Blower had offered the use of the Blue Bliss). Gertie and Susan could also be found there when they found the chance. Frank wasn't.

'Anyone we know – the victim of the ghost?' Gertie asked as they walked out.

'Nope. One Harold Godbeer. Probably more beer than god, I would imagine.'


Harold Godbeer had to admit that he had been imbibing that evening.

'Had a couple of drinks to see Pinky off,' he said as he sat in his lounge facing Frank.

'Pinky?'

'Pinky Edwards. Kenneth was his real name. We were in the desert together. North Africa. During the war. Called him Pinky. The sun made him go pink you see. Took ages to tan, poor bloke.'

'And where were you seeing him off to?'

Harold Godbeer glared back.

'Where do you think? At our age? Paradise, that's where.

Valhalla. Where all old soldiers go in the end.'

'Ah, yes, of course, sorry about that. So, how sober would you say you were?'

'Tipsy. Not quite drunk, but definitely tipsy. Seemed like a good idea. Everything had gone wrong. Pinky going, and he was the youngest of us. Caught a shell. Never the same afterward. Unscathed physically, but nervous as a cat afterwards. Then I find my blazer has moth holes in it. Had to go in black. Just not good enough. Car playing up so I caught a taxi. Pinky cremated instead of buried. Just not right. A few drinks seemed the right thing.'

'Blazer?'

'British Legion. Don't suppose you'd know anything about that. Too young. Feel sorry for you youngsters. At least my generation did something. Lived life. Passionately. Milksops these days.'

'You're probably right. Where was it that the ghost attacked you?'

'Ghost? What bloody ghost? That wasn't a ghost.'

'I'm sorry, I'm not with you. I was told that you were attacked by the St Mary's ghost.'

'St Mary's ghost? Surely you don't believe that nonsense, Inspector.'

Frank smiled.

'Not in the slightest,' he said. 'So, tell me what happened.'

'I was taking a short cut back through the cemetery. Just passed the mausoleum – should have a mausoleum for blokes like Pinky and the rest of us, but that's modern society for you – just passed the mausoleum. There was a rush of wind.

Burst of light. A sort of whoosh sound. Dropped to the ground. Thought I was back in the desert and Jerry was throwing eighty-eights over my head. Told myself to get a grip. Walked around the mausoleum to find the bugger who was playing silly buggers. Couldn't see anyone. Still, it was night. My eyes aren't what they used to be. But I tell you what, Inspector, it was human. These idiots who believe in ghosts – if they'd been through the war they wouldn't believe in such namby-pamby nonsense. Dead body is a dead body. I've seen enough, and none of them came back to haunt me.'

'What colour was the burst of light?'

'Colour? Hmm. Colour.' He thought for a few seconds. 'Can't tell you, really. I was thinking of having another beer when I got home – sort of final toast to Pinky and all the ones who didn't make it. I could see the golden colour of the beer – lager, I confess, shouldn't really, should drink good British ale, but I like the taste, reminds me of when we were in the desert. So if I said it was a golden light I'd be confusing the issue. See?'

'Yes, perfectly Mr Godbeer. I wish all our witnesses were as honest with their impressions.' He stood up and Harold Godbeer slowly followed suit, joints creaking.

'Good luck, Inspector. Hope you catch the bugger. Too much nonsense in the newspapers about ghosts.'

'It's good for the tourist industry, Mr Godbeer.'

For the first time Harold Godbeer chuckled.

'Good point. Silly Yanks will be lining up to hand over their money for a chance of seeing a ghost. Still, that's the Yanks of today. Knew some good Yanks during the war. Same thing. Back in those days you learned the hard way about being a man – or woman, come to it. Youngsters of today – excepting yourselves, but then you're doing your duty, aren't you? That's the point. Youngsters of today have it too easy. No idea of duty or responsibility.'

'And that,' Frank said once they were back in the car, 'is exactly what Socrates said two and a half thousand years ago.'

'Did he?'

'Well, I think it was Socrates. Could have been Plato. Could have been Plato quoting Socrates. Anyway, the point is that all generations think the younger generation have it easy. No doubt you and I, Gerts, when we're old and grey, will be muttering exactly the same thing. Just remind me when that happens, and I'll shut up.'

'Will do, sir. Where to now?'

'Let's pop in to St Mary's and have a word with the vicar. Maybe he's seen Caspar.'


'I have taken your advice, Inspector,' the vicar said in the vestry, a broad smile on his face.

'Advice?' asked Frank, alarmed. 'I didn't give you any advice, did I? I don't, if I can avoid it. Too often people blame me when it all goes wrong.'

'Now, now, my boy, don't be so self-deprecating. I have taken your advice and married my divorcee. Snap wedding! The bishop will probably have a few words to say, but I've done it! What do you say to that, eh?'

I'd say that you were barking mad, thought Frank.

'Er, how has Mrs Barton taken it?'

The vicar rubbed his hands in delight.

'It's stymied her. Spiked her guns. Caught her broadsides. She's speechless. It's a victory, I tell you, a triumphant victory.'

'Right,' said Frank slowly. 'By the way, we had another sighting of that ghost of yours last Saturday. Didn't see anything did you?'

'Well, no,' the vicar replied, twisting his hands nervously. He looked at Gertie and leaned towards Frank. 'As a matter of fact my bride and I were celebrating our nuptials on Friday evening,' he whispered.

'Ah, I see. Talking about nuptials, I'm getting married in September. Any chance of getting married here?'

The vicar blinked, surprised.

'Well, er, well, er, let's see, I have the appointments book somewhere, yes, here it is.'

He leafed quickly through it.

'Saturday the ninth appears to be free. The parties cancelled a few days ago, something to do with the mother running off with the boyfriend. Will that do?'

'Saturday the ninth sounds excellent, vicar. You couldn't read the banns and all that sort of thing, could you?'

'Well, um, certainly. If you give me the details, yes, certainly. Your full name, your wife to-be's full name?'

'That's very kind of you, vicar. I'll write them down for you.'

'Um, just a little bit of admin,' the vicar said nervously as Frank wrote. 'Um, you aren't Roman Catholic or anything like that, are you?'

'Not that I'm aware of, vicar.'

'Ah, excellent. Not that I mind marrying Roman Catholics, or any religion, really, it's just that I married two members of the Jewish faith once, and their rabbi took the greatest exception. Never crossed my mind to ask them what faith they were.' He sighed at the memory. 'And it didn't stop there. Oh, dear Lord, no. I was hauled before a board of the rabbi, the local Catholic priest, an Imam and someone from the Hindu temple. I can't repeat the language the priest used. Apparently I was trespassing, and they did not like that. Just fortunate the Greek Orthodox chappie was on holiday in Las Vegas at the time.'

'Don't worry, vicar,' Frank said, handing over the paper. 'You can marry myself and my fiancée with a free heart. September the ninth it is. See you then.'

'See, Gerts,' Frank said once they were back in the car, 'see how simple that was? Two minutes and I've arranged the wedding venue. I really don't know why everyone is running around chasing their tails and getting stressed out about how little time is left.'

Gertie shook her head in amazement.

'Frank, has anyone told you what a jammy bastard you are?'

'Plenty of times. I don't know why. People just tend to create problems for themselves so that they have something to complain about.'

Concentrating on the road, Gertie did not notice Frank look out of his window, twisting his face in a mixture of relief and the knowledge that he was having difficulty in keeping it straight.

'I wouldn't tell Frieda that,' she said. 'Or Tricia. It's supposed to be a special day. And a special day can't be special if everything just falls into your lap, now can it?'

'Of course it can, Gerts,' he replied, having recovered from his facial contractions. 'Now, more importantly, back to business. Harold Godbeer said something important. What was it?'

Gertie frowned at him. It was a bad habit he occasionally had. He would refer to something that had happened a few hours before, sometimes even weeks before, and expect you to guess what he was thinking about.

Or was he just changing the subject?

'You are taking this wedding seriously, aren't you, Frank?' she asked.

'Course I am.' He chuckled. 'Did you know that Eric Johns hasn't opened a book on whether I'll get married? He can be a daft pillock at times. I've even put down a tenner on myself.'

Gertie did not reply. She knew about the "non-book" herself, but had refused to take part in case it tempted fate. But almost everyone else had put money down. And they'd put their money on Sam Nightingale's prophecy.

Gertie actually liked Sam Nightingale. But she should have kept her premonitions to herself.


'All on your own, Frank?' asked the Chief Inspector. Frank started. He had been gazing at the river, lost in thought.

'Ah, hello, sir. Yes, I thought a few quiet moments on my own might do some good.'

'Far from the madding crowd and anyone mentioning the W word?'

'Precisely.'

He turned back to the river.

'Apparently,' he said after a pause, 'Sam Nightingale has made a prophecy that I won't get married. I hope Frieda doesn't get to hear about it.'

'A prophecy? Frank, surely you of all people don't believe that sort of nonsense.'

Frank smiled.

'Macbeth never believed the prophecies of the witches,' he said. 'Otherwise he wouldn't have murdered Duncan. Why commit murder for something that's going to fall into your own lap?' He shook his head. 'No, I don't believe in prophecies. The problem is that, when you're under pressure, you start to believe in things you wouldn't normally do. You do things which lead directly to what you fear – like people dying because the juju man has cast a spell on them.' He chuckled. 'I organised St Mary's for our wedding. I've been worried that we wouldn't find a church to get married in, and Frieda's set on the idea for some reason. I didn't think there was a hope in hell of the vicar agreeing, but for some reason he did, straight away – only because he was embarrassed, I think. I'd been around the vicarage a couple of times because of domestics, maybe he thought he owed me.'

'Obviously a sign from the gods,' chuckled the Chief Inspector. 'They want you to get married.'

'The last people I want involved are the gods,' Frank replied with deep feeling. 'From what I recall from my Greek mythology they weren't the most competent of people.'

'You're worried, aren't you? That something will happen?'

Frank took a few moments to reply.

'Yes, I am,' he said finally, slowly. 'I've been trying to work it out rationally – the thing is – well, I don't believe Sam Nightingale made any such sort of prophecy, she's far too sensible. But once again it's the old story of the dead man and the witchdoctor. A man from a tribal village believes a witchdoctor has put a curse on him, so he dies because he believes he's going to die.'

'You think people will make the prophecy come true because they believe it – however inadvertently?'

'That's what worries me. Logically it's simple: all I have to do is make sure the wedding happens. Unfortunately it's not a very powerful weapon to use against people who are determined to prevent the prophecy from coming true, while at the same time managing to believe that whatever they do the prophecy will come true.'

The Chief Inspector nodded as if he understood what Frank was on about.

'Still, only fifty-four days to go,' he said.

'You haven't been counting as well, have you, sir?'


The Wellbury Ghost Action Group Volunteers stood outside the darkened cemetery in a nervous group.

'Well,' said Cecil Hedgewist.

'Well,' agreed Doris Rubenstein.

Wayne Romerly stayed silent. He didn't like the idea of spending the night in a cemetery waiting for a ghost. There wasn't likely to be anywhere he could play computer games while waiting. His latest gadget needed a plug socket, and from what he had heard there wasn't likely to be one. Still, he had brought the game along just in case.

'Are you going in?' asked Phil Walthers. He had decided to accompany the group more out of a sense of amusement than duty.

'Well, there's a question,' said Cecil Hedgewist.

'There's a question,' echoed Doris Rubenstein. She was beginning to look up to Cecil. He spoke just as Mr Peabody used to speak.

Especially just before the business went bust. So resourcefully.

'Wot's in the cemetery?' asked Wayne Romerly.

'Graves, tombstones, normal things you would find in a cemetery, I would imagine,' suggested Phil Walters.

'The question is, what is our aim?' asked Cecil Hedgewist. 'What are we here to do? That is the question.'

Doris Rubenstein almost sighed in admiration. That was exactly how Mr Peabody would have put the issue.

'To catch a ghost?' suggested Phil Walters.

'Well, precisely, that's the question.'

Phil Walthers shifted the camera in his hand as if weighing it to test the merits of applying it to Cecil Hedgewist's head.

'You see,' continued Cecil, 'to my mind we are not here to catch a ghost, we are here to monitor the ghost – what one might describe as objective observers carrying out a reconnaissance mission, as it were.'

'A reconnaissance mission,' breathed Doris Rubenstein.

'Now the important point is the question of the Heisenberg principle – that the observer affects the behaviour of the observed. In this situation it is crucial that the ghost should not know that we are here. Otherwise it will not appear at all.'

'Very true, Mr Hedgewist,' agreed Doris Rubenstein, 'how very true.'

'We come, therefore, to the question of how to carry out our mission. To my mind there is only one manner in which we can be successful.'

'And that is?' prompted Phil Walthers.

'We cannot enter the cemetery until we receive a report of the sighting of the ghost. In fact we must remain out of sight of the cemetery entirely until that happens. Of course, the minute such a sighting is reported we will go into action immediately.'

'So where do you propose waiting for this sighting?' asked Phil Walthers, looking at his watch.

'Well, that is the question, isn't it? As it happens there is a rather welcoming hostelry not too far from here, the Woodman, one in which we can act in such a manner that the ghost will never suspect us. And, to make things perfect, it is a place to which anyone, catching a glimpse of the ghost, will retire immediately, in order to brace their shattered nerves. We will be in precisely the right place at precisely the right time.'

'Oh, Mr Hedgewist, what a perfect solution,' sighed Doris Rubenstein.

'Will they have a plug-point?' asked Wayne Romerly.

### Wednesday: W-52

'Mind if I join you?' Pete Phillips asked, sitting down at the table Frank and Gertie were occupying.

'Be our guest, Pete.'

'There's something you wanted to ask Sergeant Phillips,'

Gertie prompted.

'Is there? Oh, yes, thanks for reminding me. That bloke you nicked last week, the tall one with the moustache – '

'No, Frank, no,' Gertie said. She whispered something into his ear.

'Oh, yes, of course. Here, Pete, I need a best man for the wedding. Fancy having a crack at it? All you have to do is hand over the ring at the right moment.'

'It would be – an honour, Frank, I – '

'Great. That's that sorted. See, Gertie, how simple that was? I don't know why Frieda gets herself in such a tizz over these little things.'

Gertie did not notice his mouth twitch as he spoke.

## Monday: W-47

'Here, Frank, Eric Johns said in the canteen at lunchtime, 'what's this about you going around giving bad advice to vicars? About getting married?'

Frank shook his head slowly, his mouth pursing.

'Eric, I did not give the vicar any advice. Or, at least, not about getting married. I would never advise anyone to get married. Or not. Anyway, where did you hear about it?'

'He was in this morning asking for advice on how to deal with his cleaning woman.'

'Mrs Haggerty? What has she done?'

'No, not a Miss Haggerty, a Mrs Barton.'

'Ah, she's not his cleaning woman. She organises – how did he describe it? The secular side of things. She hasn't been having a go at him again, has she?'

232

'More than a go, Frank. Apparently she's been trying to kill him – loosened a tread of the steps leading up to the lectern so that he fell off just before giving the sermon last Sunday. Left vases of flowers just around corners for him to walk into. Loosened all the pages in his bible – they dropped out in the middle of Sunday service. Put something nasty on his vestments, itching powder or something. Wrote a rude message on the back, just to make sure nobody missed her point.'

'She has a point?'

'Something to the effect that men who marry divorcees are the spawn of Satan and should be burnt at the stake.'

'Poor bloke. I told him to get a restraining order on that woman.'

'Well, that's what he's going to do. Women like that are well dangerous. Oh, by the way, there was another sighting of the ghost last night.'

Frank groaned.

'Not another one. I suppose that's another nutter I'm going to have to interview.'

'Well, Frank, apparently this one was sheltering from the rain inside the cemetery when there was a bolt of lightning that lit up the entire area. He could clearly see a man with no head on his shoulders, looking at him. From what he says the man's head was tucked underneath his arm.'

'Well, that's a relief. I think we can ignore that one.'

'Ignore him? The Prat has already interviewed him. We can hardly ignore him.'

'I think we can, Eric. For a very simple reason. It hasn't

rained for weeks, and the last time there was a bolt of lightning anywhere close was months ago.' He sighed. 'Why people let their imaginations run away from them instead of looking at the obvious facts I have never understood.'

## Wednesday: W-45

'Here, Pete,' Eric Johns said as Pete Phillips walked into reception, 'what's this I hear about you being Frank's best man?'

'Yes, I was quite chuffed when he asked. I know it's just having to stand there and hand over the ring at the right moment, but it feels kind of special to be asked.'

Eric Johns shook his head sadly at the naiveté of the other man.

'Pete, don't you know what the best man has to do? It's not just a case of handing over the ring. Listen, you know what the best man was there for in the first place, years ago? He was a swordsman. His duty was to fight off any enemies and make sure that the groom got married and not killed.'

'Don't be silly, Eric, I'm hardly likely to have to carry a sword around, now am I?'

'I didn't mean that. He also has to make sure the groom turns up. The point is, if the groom doesn't make it to the church and get married, the best man takes the rap.'

'And?'

'Listen,' Eric said, leaning over and whispering, 'you remember how Sam Nightingale prophesied that Frank would propose to Fabulous?'

'Yeah?' answered Pete, his brow wrinkling, wondering if that was what had really happened.

'Well, I reckon she's, not a psychic, of course, that would be daft, but I reckon she kind of knows what's going to happen. Sort of subconsciously predicts things, you know?'

Pete Phillips rubbed his jaw thoughtfully.

'You know, there might be something in that. I've always thought there was a strange look in her eyes.'

'And she's lesbian, it stands to reason.'

'How do you mean?'

'Well, most witches are lesbian – I was reading something only the other day where this bloke was explaining that the reason people burnt witches in the old days wasn't just because they were witches, but because they were gay. Very intolerant society was, then. But it proves the point, doesn't it? Sam's got the second sight.'

Pete Phillips blinked a few times. He hadn't quite followed the logic, but it seemed to make sense. And Sam Nightingale had predicted that Frank would propose to Fabulous. So the facts supported it.

He blinked again and scratched his head.

'Here, Pete,' Eric Johns added, confidentially, 'you know what she's got down as her religion? On her personnel file? Pagan, that's what. Pagan. Think about it.'

Pete Phillips' eyebrows rose.

'Pagan? That sounds a bit dodgy.'

'It's Celtic, that's what it is. You know, people think that we're a quiet little Christian island. But they forget about the Celts. They never disappeared, the Celts. And the Gauls.'

'Gauls?'

'You know, the Gaelic lot. All dark haired and dark faced,

brooding eyes.'

'But Sam has red hair.'

'Ah, they're the worst. They're the ones with real second sight. Even other Pagans are wary of them lot. They're known as the Wickers, cause they used to make big wicker baskets and burn people in them.'

'Burn people in them?'

'Well, in the old days. Course now they just put a curse on people. And they're good at it. People might scoff, but you know what Shakespeare said about the mysteries of the universe.'

Pete Phillips ran a finger around his collar. It wasn't that he believed in this witch nonsense. He just didn't want to get on the wrong side of someone who might be a witch.

'I'd never thought of it that way,' he admitted, 'though I've always thought she looked Scottish.'

'Anyway,' said Eric, frowning slightly and wondering what looking Scottish had to do with it, but feeling that he had carried his argument, 'now she's prophesied that Frank won't get married.'

That was too much for Pete Phillips. He had heard about the prophecy, but had disregarded it as the usual rumour and gossip that floated around the station. Now it seemed as if it might have some substance. And it was aimed right in his direction.

'Now hold on a minute, Eric, hold on a minute. I thought you just said she was the one who said that Frank was going to marry Fabulous.'

Eric Johns smiled the smile of a man who knows what he is

talking about.

'Ah, no, you see this prophecy business is subtle,' he explained. 'She said he was going to propose to her, not marry her, and she was right.'

Pete Phillips nodded slowly at this subtle distinction. He did not like subtle distinctions. He had faced too many lawyers in court who played with subtle distinctions. They should be made illegal.

'Wait a minute,' he said as the next logical thought arrived in his mind, 'if Frank doesn't marry Fabulous, and I'm the best man, I'm going to end up in deep trouble with her.'

'Not just her, Pete, I doubt if there's anyone here who will forgive you. And I don't reckon "deep" is the right word. I reckon you'd have to apply for a posting to somewhere far, far away. New Zealand would be too close.' He licked his lips with the enjoyment a certain type of person might have at the thought of someone else's problems. 'Imagine the scene, Pete. Frieda is standing inside the church, all decked out in her wedding finery, and you have to take this long walk up to her to explain that everything's off because you failed to make sure that Frank made it to the altar.'

Pete swallowed hard. He could imagine the scene only too well. In it Frieda was looking directly at him, and she wasn't happy at all, no matter how her bridal dress sparkled.

'That's bloody unfair!' he snapped. 'It's not my fault he isn't going to marry her, it's Sam's bloody fault, going around making predictions like that.'

'Calm down, Pete, calm down. It might not happen. You know that play by Shakespeare, Macduff?'

'You mean Macbeth?'

'Yeah, that's the one. Anyway, those prophecies the witches made. Now if Macduff had left it alone, if he hadn't done anything, he wouldn't have come cropper. That's the thing about prophecies. They only come true if you act on them. Ignore them and you'll be fine.'

'You mean I shouldn't do anything?'

'No, no, it's Frank who mustn't do anything. You have to do everything you can to make sure he gets to the church on time. So long as you make sure that Frank does nothing to make the prophecy come true you should be okay.'

'I don't see what I can do to beat a prophecy, Eric. You can't just lock it up in the cells for a weekend.'

'Now, Pete, don't be defeatist. Use the power of reason. We live in a modern age, reason will always beat the dark side. Be prepared, that's the main thing.'

'Be prepared? What, to leave town, you mean?'

'Nah, Pete, don't be silly. I reckon what you want to do is write out a list of all the things that could go wrong, and what you can do to prevent them going wrong.'

'I see what you mean,' Pete replied, relieved at the thought of a physical plan. 'Make sure he doesn't get injured on his stag night, that sort of thing?'

'Well, not just his stag night, Pete. Oh, and you're supposed to be arranging that, that's another duty of the best man.'

'Well, now that's definitely something I reckon I'll be good at.'

'Just remember, Pete, don't let Frank do anything that might jeopardise things. Do all you can to prevent that.'

'I bloody well, will, Eric. I bloody well will.'

238

## Thursday: W-44

'Good morning, Wellbury!' cried the voice of Zack the Prat over the radio. 'Welcome back to the only show in town worth listening to, the show that brings you all the news you need to know. And a fine start to the morning it is. We already have a number of callers waiting. Julia, who do we have on line one?'

'Someone either insane or brain-dead,' muttered Frank as Gertie drove them to the station. Squishy paused in her contemplation of the outside world to look at the radio, as if to say "What a strange person".

'It's a Mr Pettigrew, who claims to have seen a light in the cemetery last night,' came Julia's neutral voice.

'Well, well! Things are hotting up. Good morning, Mr Pedigree.'

'Ah, um, Pettigrew, yes, good morning.'

'Now I understand that you saw a ghostly light floating around the cemetery last night.'

'No, no, it was just the light from a torch. Someone was walking around there.'

'Ah, come now, Mr Pedigree, surely you're being too modest. After all, how can you be sure that it was torchlight? Did you see the torch?'

'Well, no –'

'Did you see anyone carrying a torch?'

'Well, no –'

'There you go then. Well, folks, you heard it here first. A weird light was seen in the cemetery last night by an honest, upright, sober man of the parish. Not, as some people claim, a weirdo. Now, don't go away, I'll be right back after this commercial break.'

'You have to hand it to the Prat,' Frank said, turning the volume down as the commercials began. 'He can twist the most innocuous situation into the coming of Armageddon.'

'We still have to interview him about those claims he made – about paedophiles.'

'True,' sighed Frank. 'It's not something I'm looking forward to. Listening to him on the radio is bad enough. Facing him across a desk in an interview room – well, I can think of much more fun things to do.'

He smiled suddenly.

'I know what. I'll get Pete Phillips to take it on.'

'How will you do that?'

'Oh, I'll think of something. Pete's a good bloke, but it's so easy to con him into doing something it's almost unfair.'

'Have you always been good at getting out of things, or did you train hard?' asked Gertie. 'If there's a course on it I'd like to take it.'

'Just natural instinct, Gerts, isn't it, Squish?' he replied, gently scratching Squishy's chin, making her purr. 'Right, adverts are over, let's see what drivel the Prat has for us today.'

'Welcome back, folks. Now I see the switchboard is lighting up like a Christmas tree. Just how many callers do we have waiting, Julia?'

'Three, Z – '

'Thirty three! Well, we'll have to get ourselves moving and grooving if we want to let everybody have their say, and that's always been my motto as you great folks out there know.

Who's on line one, Jules?'

'It's a Mr Doug Tidsell.'

'And good morning to you, Don Tonsil! So, tell me, Don, what's your take on this ghost business?'

'Er, Doug. Ah, well, that's the thing, you see. I reckon they've got it all wrong. It's not a ghost.'

'Not a ghost? But, Don, everybody knows it's a ghost.'

'Er, Doug. Ah, no, they might think it's a ghost, but it ain't. And how I come to realise that is a story in itself. Quite a weird one, and the truth, in this case, is even stranger than fiction, as they say.'

'Well, go on Don, but you'll have to have a good explanation to convince the listeners that it isn't a ghost.'

'Er, Doug. Ah, well, I have. You see, last night the missus is putting out the rubbish – our collection day is Thursday, see – when she saw this eerie glow in the sky.'

'An eerie glow in the sky! What time was that, Dave?'

'Don. I mean Doug. Well, just about sunset, it was. Anyway, I was flipping through the channels on the telly, and, just by coincidence I saw a programme on the Rosswell case – you know, where they dissected them aliens. And all of a sudden, it comes to me like a blinding vision. What we got here ain't a ghost, it's aliens. Think about it. Sudden flashes of light, rushing wind, and something goes flying past, leaving a cold air behind it. That's their propulsion system they use, nitrogen, doesn't harm the environment like. Very green they are, these aliens.'

'Well, well, now that's an interesting theory, Don. Let's go to the next caller, Jules. Who do I have waiting for me?'

'A Miss Letitia Fullblind. She's a psychic.'

'A bit early in the morning for a psychic, who's next?'

'Mr Arthur Pengon.'

'Let's have Archie! Now, Archie, what's your take on this alien business?'

'Er, that's Arthur. But definitely aliens, Zack. I've actually seen them.'

'You've seen them, Archie?'

'Er, Arthur. Yes, I've seen them. In the cemetery. About a week ago, two weeks, perhaps, on my way home after a quiet pint. I didn't realise what I had seen at the time, but now it all makes sense. And it proves they're aliens. They're very good at not being seen.'

'Wow! What did they look like, Don?'

'Arthur. They had on shiny, sort of silvery, clothes, to protect themselves from pollution. They had these sort of long faces, fat stomachs, and eyes like large pools of black.'

'Eye-witness evidence! This will make the sceptics sit up and take notice! How did you feel at the time, Alfie? They might have kidnapped you.'

'Er, Arthur. Well, that's the thing. That's what had me really worried. Shivering in my boots, I was. If I hadn't been so careful I could have ended up in their spacecraft being cut into little pieces. But that's another thing. It's something I've noticed what's common to all these sightings.'

'And what's that?'

'Well, all the people who've seen them, and not been kidnapped, they've all been on their way home after a pint or two. Now the people who've been kidnapped, they haven't.

You see, the aliens don't kidnap anyone who's had a jar or two, it interferes with their experiments.'

'Well, folks, there you go, it's official. And we have the witnesses to confirm it. Not only do we have a ghost roaming Wellbury, but aliens are using the cemetery as a base to kidnap innocent young girls to perform experiments on them. Don't forget, you heard it here first, on Radio Pithead, the only station with yours truly, Zack the Man. And I'll be back after this short break.'

'Oh dear sweet Jesus, Mary and all the saints,' muttered Frank. 'All the weirdos of Wellbury are climbing out of the woodwork. I think I'll emigrate.'

'Is that before or after you get married, sir?' asked Gertie.

Frank rubbed his jaw.

'Good point, Gerts, good point. Unless we get this ghost nonsense sorted soon, I'm not sure I can hang in there that long.'


'And may we be truly grateful for this short break,' Eric Johns said as he placed his meal on the canteen table and sank into the chair with a sigh of relief.

'Busy morning, Eric?' asked Frank with a smile.

'Busy? Bloody hectic, it's been.'

'What, two lost dogs today?'

Eric gave him a dirty look.

'Aliens,' he said. 'Nine people reporting lost animals stolen by the aliens, four cats, three dogs, a duck and a gerbil. Eleven people reporting sightings of aliens, one on a night bus. That bloke claimed he was lucky he was pissed otherwise he might have been abducted. As it was the alien asked to see his ticket.'

He looked at his meal, shook his head and began eating. The busy morning had increased his appetite.

'Two lots claimed that they knew someone who had been abducted,' he continued as he ate. 'One, it turns out, was a kid who had gone off on holiday to her nan's in Portsmouth. The neighbours spotted she was missing and called us. Didn't bother to ask their neighbours, of course. The other one was a fifteen year-old who had run away from home. Only thing is, she'd run away all of half a mile, to her boyfriend's folks' place. So my uniforms have to waste their time running around looking for her, when all was needed was for her boyfriend's folks to call her folks and tell them she was okay.'

'No little green men popping in to ask for directions?' asked Frank, trying to hide a smile. Gertie giggled. Eric Johns gave him another foul look.

'By rights this should be your case, Frank. You're the one investigating the ghost.'

'Ah, Eric, that's just the point. I'm the ghost expert. I haven't had alien training. Be more than me job was worth if I began investigating aliens without proper training, now wouldn't it?'

Phil Walthers, not to be outdone, printed a picture from the Rosswell case on the front page of the Herald, only explaining inside, for those who did not remember, the commonly held view that the Roswell case was a hoax. Unfortunately many readers did not manage to get as far as that explanation.

## Monday: W-40

Frieda crossed off the Saturday and Sunday on her calendar.

She looked up at Tricia.

'And don't let Frank know I'm doing that,' she said.

'Secrets already? And you aren't even married yet,' teased Tricia.

'Yes, well, some things a spouse does not need to know.' She put the calendar in a drawer and closed it. 'You know,' she sighed, 'I'm wondering about the honeymoon. Frank thinks I'm set on Paris, but I think I'd prefer somewhere quieter.'

'You do?'

'Yes, why the surprise?'

'Well, problem solved. He told Gertie he'd like somewhere quieter himself.'

'Ah.'

'So, why don't you just tell him?'

'I can't do that. He'll think that I really do want to go to Paris, but I'm just saying I don't because I've found out that he doesn't want to go there.'

Tricia nodded. She could understand that sort of thing.

'And Frank being Frank, he'll insist that it has to be Paris,' she suggested.

'Precisely. Oh, well, I'll have to think of some way of getting around that. Now, have you found any other safe jobs for Frank to do?'

'I've booked him into eleven meetings so far for this week.'

'Ten of which he'll miss, you know him.'

'We could always invent something – another sighting of a ghost, or something?'

'No, Tricia, definitely not. If he found out I'd really be in it.'

'I know – did you read that story in the Herald about the grave they're digging up? The one they suspect doesn't contain a body. They think it was an insurance fraud.'

'Yes, I saw that. One Godfrey Uriah Tumbledown, a made-up name if ever I heard one. But that's more of an archaeological dig. The burial took place in 1895.'

'Well, if it was an insurance fraud, that's a crime, isn't it?'

'Mmm. A possibility I suppose.'

'What about this thing Percy's working on? Operation Mackerel? From the sounds of it it's mostly paperwork – planning and that sort of stuff.'

'Yes, it's certainly keeping Percy and Pete Phillips busy. But I can't see Frank falling for that. No, we'll just have to make sure that he spends all his time on this ghost nonsense. And the aliens. After all, the Chief Constable is most insistent that we get it sorted.'

'He is?'

'He will be once I've had a word with him.'

She tapped her fingers on her desk.

'Just keep Frank busy, Tricia. But make sure he doesn't actually do anything.'

Frank's face was a picture of amazement when Frieda asked him to investigate the burial of Godfrey Uriah Tumbledown.

'One of my very first cases in Wellbury was to investigate a philanderer who had been dead for forty years. Now you want me to look into someone who hasn't been dead for over a hundred years?'

**Tuesday: W-39**

'Right,' said Percy Hanson, 'everybody here?'

Those present looked at each other in perplexity. They had been individually instructed that the meeting was top secret, and that they should discuss it with no one, not even their colleagues. If they hadn't discussed it there was no way for them to know whether anyone was missing, since they did not know who else had been invited. And to mention that someone was missing would reveal that they had discussed it. Since they had all discussed it, they were not about to reveal to Percy that they had by pointing out that everyone was there.

Percy was the sort of man who had that effect on people.

'Good,' he said. 'Pete, you take care of the door.'

Pete Phillips, a pained look on his face, left the room, closed the door, and stood outside to make sure nobody could eavesdrop.

'Well,' continued Percy, 'you're probably all wondering what this is about.'

They looked at him poker-faced. Everyone knew what it was all about.

'This,' Percy said, throwing a switch connected to a laptop computer which projected the outline of a map of Wellbury onto a whiteboard, 'is Wellbury.'

'Damn,' whispered Frank to Gertie, 'I thought it looked more like a teapot.'

'And our meeting today is to outline the top-secret plan for sealing Wellbury off in the event of an unexpected emergency.'

'Ask him what sort of unexpected emergency,' Frank

whispered to Eric Johns.

'Not bloody likely, Frank.'

'Excuse me, sir, what sort of unexpected emergency?' asked Sid Feeler from the other side of the room.

'Well,' replied Percy, confused, 'the unexpected sort. You know – the sort we don't expect.'

'Ah,' replied Sid Feeler.

'Good, now that we've sorted that out, let's continue. Now, most of you are familiar with the physical aspects of the plan, so I won't go into those – those are listed in the printouts I'll be handing out later – which must be signed for and treated as top secret.'

'And if anyone loses their copy they can get a spare from Phil Walthers,' muttered Frank.

'The major change in our long term strategy is that of visibility. Now we have to presume that the bad guys will be monitoring our frequencies. There are longer-term plans to provide a solution to that, but at the moment our equipment isn't sophisticated enough to handle such things. So we will be using code words. These sheets I'm handing out now are those code words. Guard them with your life.'

'Memorise this and then eat yourself,' murmured Frank, taking a sheet and passing the bundle on.

'Now these code words have been randomly assigned,' Percy continued, 'so they have no reflection on the individual to whom they been given.'

Frank chuckled.

'Eric, I see you're Moby Dick. The great white whale.'

'Very funny, Frank.'

'Is there a problem, Inspector Summers?' asked Percy, an eyebrow raised.

'Eric here was wondering if he could have his code name changed to Aberdeen.'

'Aberdeen? All these code words are related to fish. Aberdeen isn't a fish.'

'Well, it is a place.'

There was a pause before the groans broke out.

'Thank you for that, Frank,' Percy said. 'I don't suppose there's any chance of you taking this seriously, is there?'

'Of course. My mind just seems to be on other matters these days.'

There was a chorus of cheers from those who had bet on Frank's getting married. All those who had bet against suddenly developed a deep interest in their fingernails.

## Thursday: W-37

'You're going to love this one, Frank,' Phil Walthers chuckled over the phone. 'A certain Mr Graham Meedles came to see me. I've pointed him in your direction. He has some photographs to show you.'

'Photographs? Anything interesting?'

'Enjoyable rather than interesting, I would say. Good luck, Inspector.'

There was another chuckle as Phil Walthers put his phone down.

'I wonder about our Phil sometimes,' Frank said, putting his own phone down. Squishy lay curled up in his in-tray. She had opened one eye when the telephone rang, and then gone back to sleep, having decided that it wasn't the tuna-delivery man calling to announce his imminent arrival.

'Our Phil?' asked Gertie.

'Phil Walthers. I think looking after both the Herald and trying to stop Mrs Blower re-inventing the Blue Bliss has been too much for him.'

'What did he say?'

'Someone by the name of Meedles is bringing us some photographs. Phil Walthers thinks they will prove to be enjoyable rather than interesting. At least he seemed to find it enjoyable, he was certainly having a good chuckle about it.' He frowned. 'I'm not sure I share Phil Walthers' sense of humour.'

Gertie hid a grin. The reason Frank did not share Phil Walthers' sense of humour was probably because it was so similar to Frank's, and at that moment was headed in his direction.

'Ah, Frank,' said Eric Johns from the doorway, 'I have a Mr Grey-ham Meedles awaiting your presence in interview room two, if you could spare the time. Asked for you personally.'

'Grey-ham? Sounds like dead meat to me. What does he want to speak to me about?'

'He wouldn't say. Claims it's top secret, and that Phil Walthers sent him here.'

'We don't have any urgent security lectures at the moment, do we, Gertie?'

Gertie shook her head.

'No bored housewives wanting their locks checked out?'

This time Gertie grinned as she shook her head.

'Ah, well, we'd better have a word with Mr Grey-ham Meedles then.'

'Looks like it's unavoidable,' agreed Gertie. 'Want to come along, Squish, or would you prefer to stay here?'

Squishy miaowed to state that she was definitely coming along if there was ham to be had.

'I bet you I can get the phrase "dead meat" into the conversation at least five times,' Frank said as they walked to the interview room.

'No chance, you always win that sort of bet. And you'd have me giggling the whole time.'

Frank smiled as he opened the door. He wasn't sure he would have won that bet. But it would have been an interesting challenge.

'Mr Grey-ham Meedles?' he asked of a small, portly gentleman who stood up as they entered. The man was wearing thick glasses which made him look as if he were peering at the world through two goldfish bowls. If he was surprised to find a kitten brought into the interview room he showed no sign of it. Squishy looked at his glasses in fascination, possibly wondering where the fish were hiding.

'Er, Gray-hem,' he corrected. 'The second a is an e.'

'Ah, important, that,' Frank said as they all sat down, Squishy on Gertie's lap. 'Gray hem. Different.'

'It was my father's eyes,' Grahem Meedles explained. 'He could never read his own writing.'

'Well, well. Such are the accidents of history. So, Mr Meedles, you wished to speak to me?'

Grahem Meedles looked around the room to make sure there

was no one else to overhear and leaned forward. Squishy leaned forward too, peeking at him over the top of the table.

'What is vital is that you understand that I do not believe in ghosts,' he whispered.

'What about the tooth-fairy?'

'Sorry?'

'Do you believe in the tooth-fairy?'

'Inspector, I don't think you're taking this seriously.'

'I am sorry, Mr Meedles, please continue.'

'Yes, well, where was I?'

'You were saying that you don't believe in ghosts.'

'Ah, yes. Ghosts. And it's vital that you understand that, until last night, I did not believe in aliens.'

He nodded several times to emphasise the importance of this.

'In fact, it was entirely because of this that I was in the cemetery last night.'

He nodded several times to emphasise the importance of that.

'You see, I took my camera with me to take photographs of the cemetery at regular intervals to prove that there were no aliens infesting the cemetery.'

He nodded again. Gertie noticed that Frank had started nodding in unison and tried to kick him under the table to make him stop.

'Proof, you see,' Grahem Meedles continued, 'if I could produce photographs taken at regular intervals showing absolutely no trace of aliens then that would be emphatic proof that they did not exist.'

He and Frank nodded at each other.

'It's always a problem, Frank agreed, 'proving the negative.'

'Precisely.'

Gertie stuffed a handkerchief in her mouth.

'And then I saw them.'

With this statement Grahem Meedles' goldfish-bowl eyes grew even wider.

'At first I could not believe it. I was absolutely stunned. I could not move. There I was, an impartial – even biased – observer, and I was looking at two aliens. Two aliens hovering above the ground outside the mausoleum. And, Inspector, I have the proof!'

Frank was genuinely impressed.

'What proof is that?'

'Well, the thing is, as soon as I had recovered from the shock, I knew that I must immediately photograph them. Nothing else would do. And I had to act fast. From what I have read – and previously refused to believe – these aliens can move at the speed of light. So, without any thought for my personal safety, I immediately brought up my camera and took as many shots as possible.'

'You have the photographs?'

Grahem Meedles took a pack of photographs from his pocket, hesitated, and then handed them reverentially to Frank. Frank opened the pack and began laying the photographs on the table, Gertie leaning forward in fascination. Squishy miaowed and put a paw up to the desk to drag herself onto the desk so that she too could view the photographs or at least find out if they were edible.

The first photograph was a brilliantly flash-lit shot of the mausoleum.

So was the second.

And the third.

And the fourth.

All of them in fact.

And not a hint of an alien.

'I took the roll of film around to the chemist's as soon as they opened,' Grahem Meedles said. 'I made sure that the person doing the developing did not get so much as a glance at them. I told him to stand twenty paces away once he had put the roll in the machine and started the process. Though we had to compromise, as the shop was not large enough. I made him stand ten paces away instead, and turn his back. You can rest assured that no-one else, apart from Mr Walthers and us, knows about this. And I have sworn him to secrecy until the time is right. Only when you give the go-ahead will I allow him to print these photographs.'

Frank and Gertie looked at each other, eyebrows raised. Frank turned back to Grahem Meedles.

'Um, Mr Meedles, I don't know how to put this, they are very good photographs, lots of flash, you might even think it daylight, and the clarity of the stonework is perfect, you can see every individual grain. But – and I'm not sure how to put this – but, well, they appear to be lacking something.'

Grahem Meedles studied the photographs with a puzzled air.

'I don't follow, Inspector.'

'Well, Mr Meedles, they appear to be lacking in the alien department. No aliens, Mr Meedles, no aliens.'

'But that's just it! That is it, Inspector! Don't you see? This proves how fast they really do move. As soon as they noticed me – and what incredible senses they must have – they shot into the mausoleum even before I managed to press the button, and I was fast, I can tell you!'

Once again Frank and Gertie exchanged another raised-eyebrows glance. Frank turned back to Grahem Meedles, rubbing his jaw.

'Right,' he said slowly. 'Well, I tell you what, Mr Meedles, why don't you go back to Mr Walthers and tell him that we have no problems with these photographs being published.'

'Are you sure? Isn't it a matter of national security?'

'Well, Mr Meedles, the safety of the population is more important than national security, is it not? No, no, I can honestly state that we will not repress publication of these rather interesting, and very well taken, photographs. In fact perhaps sooner rather than later, don't you think?'

'I am most impressed, Inspector,' Grahem Meedles said, standing up. 'I had thought that the police would prefer to keep this under wraps, as it were, and I, as a responsible citizen, should co-operate no matter how much I might initially feel that the public should be informed. Oh, you may keep that set of photographs, I had two copies made.'

'All part of the service, Mr Meedles,' Frank replied. 'Gertie, show Mr Meedles out. And thank you for sharing those fascinating photographs with us, Mr Meedles. Come on, Squish.'

Having showed Grahem Meedles out Gertie returned to their office to find a thoughtful Frank watching Squishy play with Grahem Meedles' photographs lying across his desk. Squishy had discovered that, if she pounced onto one of them, she could slide almost the length of the desk.

'He's even more barmy than the others,' Gertie said, dropping into her chair. 'I hope there aren't more like him waiting to crawl out of the woodwork.'

Frank rubbed his chin.

'Interesting, though.'

'In what way?'

'He was convinced that he had seen aliens. But he hadn't expected to see any. So what was it that he really saw?'

'You think he did see something?'

'Oh, he saw something alright. But was it something unusual, or did his imagination just interpret a branch moving in the wind or something similar as an alien?'

'I thought you weren't going to get involved in this alien nonsense?' Gertie asked.

'I'm not. Not officially. Phil Walthers asked me to speak to someone, which I did. If anything else comes up I think Pete Phillips can handle it.'

'Still, I wouldn't trust his sight – Grahem Meedles, that is. Not with those glasses.'

'Ah, but that's the point, Gerts. People think that people who wear glasses have bad sight. But it's precisely because he was wearing glasses that I think we should trust his sight – up to a point, anyway.'

He looked down at the photographs and tapped one of them. Squishy took this to mean it was a special one, pounced extra hard and went sailing off the end of the desk, miaowing frantically as she fell into the waste-paper basket, little paws flailing. There was a scrunching sound as she churned up the remnants of notes and memos in the basket, disappearing into the bits and pieces of paper before her head re-appeared with a most indignant look on her face.

'You okay, Squish?' asked Frank, lifting her gently out of the basket. She looked up at him, and then back towards the treacherous basket. Then she looked back at him and miaouwed in a pleased way. "That was fun," she seemed to be saying. "Let's do it again."

'The problem,' Frank continued, putting Squishy back on his desk, 'is that the flash has wiped out any shadows that might have been falling on the mausoleum. But even then, Meedles claimed that he didn't believe in aliens, so surely he wouldn't have been taken in by a mere shadow?'

'Trick of the light, I reckon.'

'What's a trick of the light?' asked Frieda, entering the office.

'We've just had a visit from a Mr Meedles who claims he went to the cemetery to take photographs which would prove, by their absence, that aliens did not exist. This morning he brought us photographs without any aliens in them, to prove they did.'

Frieda cocked her head as if trying to understand the logic of this.

'He sounds like another weirdo from the woodwork,' she decided.

'Mmm. I'm not so sure. You know, I think I might have my own little stake-out next Wednesday evening. I'm convinced that our Grahem Meedles did see something. I don't believe it was aliens, but it was something unusual, something strange.'

Frieda cocked her head again, this time to the other side, and looked at him.

'Frank, you have a terrible habit of making strange things happen yourself. I think perhaps I should come with you, if only to protect innocent civilians.'

'Right,' he said, smiling, 'it's a date. Who said the age of romanticism was dead?'

Frieda wasn't thinking about innocent civilians or romanticism.

## Sunday: W-34

'We'll have to book the honeymoon soon,' Frieda said as she ironed sheets in her living room.

'Oodles of time,' Frank replied, sitting in an armchair with the Observer, Squishy curled up on his lap.

'Frank, there are only thirty-four days to go, you know.'

'Oodles of time,' Frank repeated. Frieda put the iron down and looked at him.

'Frank, you are taking this seriously, aren't you? You do realise just how much organisation is required?'

'Of course I'm taking it seriously, Free. Tell you what, I'll check the Internet tomorrow, how about that?'

'No, I'll check the Internet now. And, if you want to make yourself useful, you can finish off these sheets. I don't see why I should slave over them while you sit doing nothing.'

Frank watched her go. He looked at Squishy.

'Well, don't look at me like that, Squish, I don't see why the damn things need ironing in the first place.'

Squishy tossed her head, jumped off his lap and went off to see what Frieda was doing in case it involved tuna.

'Bloody women,' grumbled Frank, putting the newspaper

down and starting on the sheets.

He had just finished the last one and was packing the ironing board away when Frieda returned.

'Nothing,' she said. 'We've left it too late. The whole of Paris is blocked solid for those weeks.'

'Everything?'

'Not even a broom closet.'

'Oh, hell, I'm sorry, Free. I should have looked sooner. I know how much you really wanted Paris.'

'It's my fault, really. I've been concentrating on the wedding, I forgot about the honeymoon. And I know you had your heart set on Paris.'

He looked at her, a smile hovering on his lips.

'You didn't really want Paris, did you?'

'Of course I did. Why shouldn't I? After all you were set on it.'

'No I wasn't. It was just an idea. When I got to thinking about it I decided somewhere quieter would be much better for a honeymoon. We can always have a holiday in Paris some other time.'

'Well, now you come to mention it, I was thinking the same thing.' She gave him a suspicious look. 'How did you know?'

'Well, I just realised it now,' he said, edging towards the door. 'When you said Paris was booked solid. I was on the Internet yesterday and there were loads of places available.'

Before she could reply he had disappeared towards the kitchen.

'Frank Summers! Why you deceitful little – Come back here right now!'

'I'm going to stay locked up in the kitchen with the beers until you say you forgive me,' he called. 'Oh, and by the way, pots and kettles, na-na-na-naa.'

She shook her head angrily. Really, did he have to act like a child?

And pots and kettles?

Really.

Well, perhaps a touch. Just a touch, though.

'Okay, Frank Summers, you're forgiven. You can bring me a glass of wine, it's almost lunchtime.'

He appeared in the doorway almost immediately, beer in one hand, glass of wine in the other.

'You knew I was going to forgive you,' she accused.

'Of course. Why else would I be marrying you?' he asked, giving her the glass and a kiss.

Why else? she wondered.

'Normandy,' he said, dropping into an armchair. 'I was having a look yesterday. Loads of lovely-looking places.'

'Oh, so you've already arranged an alternative to Paris, then?'

'Now, now, Free. I was just surfing the net and thought I'd look up other places, maybe for a holiday next year. But Normandy looks ideal for a honeymoon. Lovely countryside, quiet little towns and villages, and chock-full of history.'

She took a sip of wine and looked at him over the rim of the glass.

'Anything else you've been concealing from me?'

'Me, Free? As if I would.'

He grinned.

He was definitely concealing something. Definitely.

## Monday: W-33

'You're looking rather cheerful, Pete,' Frank noted as Pete Phillips joined him and Gertie in the canteen at lunchtime.

'I'm feeling rather cheerful. Percy and I are on something a little more interesting than usual. Cannabis farms.'

'Cannabis farms? In Wellbury?'

'Aye. Word's come from London that they've been moving them away from there. They reckon a couple might have started up around here.'

'Not real farms?' asked Gertie. 'Not in London?'

'It's a bit of a misnomer, Gerts,' Frank said. 'What they do is they rent a house for about three months. They fill it with cannabis plants, install arc-lights and turn on the radiators full blast – effectively turning it into a hot-house. They also bypass the electric and gas meters, not only because they don't want to pay for them, but also because they don't want the electricity or gas companies noticing that a quiet suburban house is suddenly using up so much.'

'Is that why we're going after them?' asked Gertie. 'I thought cannabis was pretty much ignored these days.'

'Not the amount we're talking about,' Frank explained. 'Apart from that, the people behind this sort of thing aren't university students growing the stuff for themselves or trying to make a few spare bob, they're normally from the nastier areas – Russian mafia, that sort of thing. Find the farm and you'll find a whole lot of other nasty things going on, drugs, people trafficking, money laundering. A couple of farms they found in London had illegal Vietnamese boys being forced to look after them.'

'You seem to know a lot about the subject,' Pete said. 'I'm surprised it wasn't given to you.'

'I'm on special assignment,' Frank said with a touch of bitterness. 'Ghosts and talks on security to bored housewives, that's me. When you get promoted to Inspector they don't allow you to take risks anymore.' He sighed. 'Still, at least I don't have to worry about the aliens, someone else will get that one. Though I could do with an interesting case. You know, one of the things I read about as far as cannabis farms go, they drove down the streets with a heat-detecting camera. Because of the arc-lights and radiators it's easy to spot – unless the house is on fire, of course, which would give the same effect, but I'd imagine your average copper could spot the difference. I can see myself with some fancy gadget checking the temperatures of the houses of the good citizens of Wellbury.'

'Can't win them all, Frank,' Pete said.

'No, but I wouldn't mind a little chase now and again. Even going after some spotty-faced shop-lifter would give me a little exercise and a soupcon of excitement.'

'Hey, whoa, Frank,' Pete said nervously as he realised the import of what Frank was saying. 'You don't want to take any chances, not with only thirty-three days to go.'

'Thirty-three days to go? What's happening in thirty-three days?'

Pete Phillips blinked his eyes. Surely Frank must know what he was talking about?

'I seem to recall that you're getting married in thirty-three days,' he said. 'You haven't forgotten, have you?'

'Oh, that. Of course I haven't forgotten. You seem to be more worried about it than I am. Don't tell me you're also counting down the days?'

'Of course not,' lied Pete. 'And I am the best man, you know. It is my responsibility to see that you make it to the altar. If anything happens I'll be the one who gets the blame.'

Frank's mouth twitched slightly and his eyes twinkled. Had Pete Phillips not been looking down at his lunch he would have recognised the signs of someone thinking about a wind-up.

'That is true, Pete,' he said. 'Awful lot of responsibility. Frieda wouldn't be happy with you if anything went wrong and I didn't turn up on time.'

Pete gave him a sour look.

'By the way,' he said casually, 'organised a costume for the fancy dress ball?'

Frank's mouth twitched again. He knew where that question had come from. Frieda had obviously somehow leant on him to bring the subject up.

'Plenty of time, Pete. Plenty of places to pick up a gorilla costume or something.'

'You can't go as a gorilla, Frank! It would – well, it would look stupid.'

'I'll sort something out, Pete. You just concentrate on making sure you get your duties as best man right.'

'Which reminds me,' Pete Phillips said, 'I have to organise your stag night.

'Pete, I am not going to have a stag night. You can forget about that totally. Especially any ideas about getting me blind drunk, strippograms or anything of that ilk.'

This time it was Pete Phillips' mouth that twitched. He hadn't thought about the requirements for a stag night in detail, but a strippogram sounded like a must.

One dressed up as a woman police officer would be ideal.

Frank would not need to know about it until she walked into whatever pub they chose.

### Tuesday: W-32

'Good morning, Frank, Gertie,' Eric Johns said with far too much enthusiasm as they entered reception. Both gave him a suspicious look. Squishy, riding in the pocket of Frank's old leather jacket cocked her head at him as if to ask, "What's the fat one up to this time? And where's the cream cake he normally gives me to taste?"

'You have something to tell us that we aren't going to like,' Frank said.

'Now, Frank, would I take any malicious delight while purely carrying out orders?'

'All the time, Eric, all the time. Come on, out with it.'

'Ah, well, as it happens you have a delegation awaiting your presence in interview room two. The Wellbury Alien Action Group.'

'The Wellbury Alien Action Group? Well, not my job, you know that, Eric. Ghosts, yes, aliens, no.'

'Ah, well, as it happens, they've asked for you personally. And Fabulous has politely requested that you have a word with them.'

Frank groaned.

'How many?'

'Oh, just two of them. Two, upright, staid, conscientious citizens giving up their spare time to assist the local police force in their never-ending battle against alien invaders.'

'Very funny, Eric. Come one, Gertie. Let's grab a cup of coffee and then hear what our alien activists have to say.'

'Shall I leave little Squish with Tricia?'

'Well, Squish? Tricia time or interview time?'

Squishy decided that she would rather like to meet these alien people. They sounded interesting.


'Biddy, biddy-biddy-biddy,' Frank said, advancing on the interview room in a robotic motion. 'Quark. Quark. Smell human blood. Must abduct. Dissect. Dissect. Biddy-biddy-biddy.'

'Stop it, Frank,' Gertie said, giggling, 'you'll give me a fit of the giggles.'

'Human giggle. Must investigate. Quark. Biddy-biddy. Investigate.'

He shook his shoulders before he entered the room and assumed a more official pose. Inside two men rose from their seats. Two short men, both with large eyebrows, flickering eyes, and a resemblance which announced that they were related.

'I'm Detective Inspector Summers and this is Detective Constable Gregson,' Frank said, sitting down, Squishy sitting on Gertie's lap. 'Oh, and this is special constable Squishy. How may we be of assistance to you?'

'Er, Gerald Green,' introduced the slightly taller man, at five-foot-one about half an inch taller than his companion. Both seemed slightly disconcerted at the sight of Squishy's eyes peering at them from just above the desk. 'This is my cousin, ah, Reginald Green.'

'Ah, I was told the green men were here,' Frank commented. Gertie almost choked on her coffee. The two Greens looked at her in surprise, heads cocked to the same side. Squishy cocked her head back at them. 'So, what can we do for you?'

'Er, ah, yes. We have formed a group, the Wellbury Alien Action Group, to, ah, protect – to protect – innocent young women of Wellbury from being abducted by aliens.'

'I see. You don't offer the same protection for innocent young men?'

The Greens blinked, swivelled their heads and looked at each other. Then they swivelled them back to Frank.

'Well, ah, of course,' said Gerald.

'And gerbils?'

The two Greens swivelled their heads and looked at each other again. Then they swivelled them back to Frank again.

'Gerbils?'

'Someone reported a gerbil abducted by aliens the other day.'

'Ah, well, naturally, we, er, we, er try, er to protect all species, er, all human, er, well, all earth species. Yes, of course.'

They looked nervously at Squishy. Squishy returned their gazes as if to say "Oh, don't worry about me. I don't need looking after by you. If anything it's you who need looking after."

'Ah, naturally,' agreed his cousin.

'But, ah, much as we are, ah, gaining new members on an

hourly basis – '

'Hourly, ah.'

'We, ah, cannot, naturally, ah, be everywhere at once.'

'Everywhere, ah.'

'Which, ah, is where you, er, come in.'

'Is it? My goodness. Where?'

Another swivel, puzzled look, and then return swivel.

'Ah, where?'

'Where, ah?'

'Where do we come in?'

'Ah, yes, er, that's just it. We, ah, need police, er, protection, ah.'

'Protection, ah.'

'Not, ah, for our main, er, tasks, er. But as, ah, cover, er, just in case.'

'Just in case, ah.'

Frank blinked.

'Just in case what?'

Swivel, puzzled look, and then return swivel.

'Ah, in case, while, er, leading our, ah, group, the, ah, we should, er, suffer the, er, ultimate, er, sacrifice.'

'Ah, ultimate sacrifice.'

'Which would be?' asked Frank.

Another swivel.

'Well, ah, abduction, of course, er. Abduction and, er, dissection.'

'Ah, dissection.'

Frank nodded, a serious look on her face.

'Yes,' he said, 'I would imagine you would be quite cut up if that happened.'

The Greens gave Gertie another strange look as she stuffed a handkerchief into her mouth.

'However, I'm afraid we don't have the resources to give you the close protection you would need carrying out such potentially lethal work. I can only advise you to take all possible precautions.'

'We, ah, are already doing that,' Gerald Green said.

'We, ah, only, er, approach the cemetery from the far side, never the, ah, entrance.'

'Camouflaged, of course,' suggested Frank. 'You know, the way soldiers do. Face paint, bits of grass and twigs in your clothing, that sort of thing.'

Swivel. Nod of agreement. Swivel back.

'Ah, an excellent, er, idea, Inspector.'

Gertie sat shaking, making the table vibrate, trying to kick Frank's leg.

'And we go, ah, equipped,' added Reginald.

'Equipped?'

Swivel. Look. Nod. Swivel again. Each took a can from an inner pocket, cans of Carlsberg Special Brew.

'We are, ah, normally against the, ah, consumption of alcohol,' Gerald said, 'but under the circumstances we feel, er, that, should such action be necessary, we have no option but to imbibe. It is a, er, well known fact that the aliens avoid those under the influence.'

'The, ah, shop assistant, assured, er, us that this brand was one of the most potent they, er, had.'

Frank nodded.

'Even so, you'd have to down the whole can in seconds,' he pointed out. 'And if you aren't used to alcohol it could take too long. Before you could get half-way through they'd have you by the bowels.'

Gertie resumed her choking into her handkerchief.

'The – ah – what?'

'Bowels. Intestines.'

Swivel. Look. Nod. Swivel.

'Under extreme, ah, circumstances the average, er, humans can carry out the most incredible actions, ah, when required.'

'Look, you'd have to finish the can, not so? How long do you think you would have? Five seconds? Less?'

'Oh, ah, yes, in imminent danger, er, five seconds at the, ah, most.'

'Ah, most.'

'There you go. You couldn't down a can of that stuff in less than twenty seconds.'

'In the, ah, circumstances we would have to.'

'Ah, would have to.'

'I'd like to see you try.'

Swivel. Nod. Swivel.

'Pull the, ah, pin, Reginald,' Gerald said.

Each took the ring-pull on his can and opened it. As one they lifted the cans to their mouths and began gulping the beer down before an increasingly wide-eyed Frank and Gertie. About a quarter of the way down they came up for breath before continuing. Another quarter, another breath. The final two quarters required three breaks for air. Finally both slammed their cans on the table and sat looking at Frank as if to say "Told you so".

Then each burped mildly.

'You see,' said Frank, 'twenty-two seconds. Seventeen seconds ago the aliens would have had your guts for garters. Literally.'

Swivel. Burp. Swivel.

'Perhaps, ah, we need to, er practise.'

'If I were you, totally off the record,' Frank said confidentially, leaning forward, 'I'd also think about getting hold of a couple of cans of Old Stoat. But if anyone asks, I never suggested that.'

Gertie gasped. Old Stoat was a local brew sold to unwary tourists as a "full ale". One pint was the equivalent of about ten pints of lager.

Or a pint of extremely powerful brandy, which was what the stuff really was when it came down to it.

'We, ah, we, ah, we ah ...' Gerald Green began.

Swivel. Shaky nod. Shwivel back.

'Had, er, contem ... contemp ... thought about that, er, posshibility.'

'Posshibility,' agreed Reginald, spitting spume.

'Well, I'd better not take up any more of your time,' Frank said, standing up. 'If you'll just wait here I'll get the duty sergeant to let you out.'

Gertie hurriedly followed Frank in his exit, Squishy in her arms craning her head for a final look at the two strange men.

To Frank's delight Eric Johns was just passing.

'Eric, could you let the alien abduction squad out? Gertie and I have to see Frieda urgently. Thanks.'

A puzzled Eric Johns watched them leave. He shrugged his shoulders and entered the interview room.

'Oh, dear god, no,' he muttered as two heads swivelled in his direction, struggling to keep him in focus, going too far in one direction, before changing swivel and over-accommodating.

'Very helpful,' said the one head.

'A tribute to the polishe forsh,' said the other.

'Very nishe person, your Inshpector Shummers.'

'And the conshtable ... very nishe ... very nishe.'

'Ansh the little kitten. The shpeshul conshtable.'

Eric Johns, had he been able to speak, might have put forward a different point of view.

**Wednesday: W-31**

'Ah, Autumn, season of mists and fruitfulness,' Frank said as he and Frieda huddled together in St Mary's cemetery with what would have been a clear view of the mausoleum if it weren't for eddies of mist occasionally interrupting their view.

'Mellow fruitfulness,' Frieda corrected.

'Where are the songs of spring? Think not of them, you have your music too.'

'Thou hast.'

'Well, something like that. Though I think this mist is a little early. And it should be warmer.'

'It's that time of year. One cool day and people will complain that winter's early, then we'll have two months of sunshine and they'll be talking of an Indian summer.'

'Ah, but you will always have your favourite season, Free.'

'Oh, and what's that?'

'Summers.'

She smiled and looked at his shadowed face.

'Do you mean that?'

'Of course. Why shouldn't I?'

She nestled her head against his shoulder.

'Let me know when the aliens come,' she said.

'I have the feeling they won't be coming here tonight.'

'Why's that, darling?'

'Oh, I don't know. It doesn't feel right. Call it intuition if you like.'

'I thought you didn't believe in intuition.'

'Well, intuition is probably a sloppy word to use. Perhaps precognition is better. Experience tells you that something is wrong, though you can't verbalise why.'

Frieda understood and agreed. What worried her was that her intuition – or precognition – was telling her that not being able to see Frank's face clearly was an omen, as if he was receding from her. She shivered.

'Cold, Free?'

'Just a little. This cemetery's giving me goose-bumps too. It looks strange with the mist swirling around.'

'Too many ghost movies,' he chuckled. 'A Pavlonian reaction.'

He chuckled again.

'You know what would be fun?'

'No, what?' she asked, snuggling deeper into his arms. She liked the sound of his chuckle.

'If the Wellbury Ghost Action Group volunteers turned up. We could creep up on them and make ghostly noises. Even better, we could hide in Godfrey Uriah Tumbledown's grave – they've got down to five feet, no sign of a coffin. We could hide in it and jump out at them.'

'Frank Summers, you do have an evil sense of humour.'

'There's another kind?'

'So long as you don't practise it on me.'

'Of course not, Free,' he said, kissing the top of her head. 'Tell you what, another half an hour and we'll call it a day, what do you say? Go for a quick pint at the pub down the road. The Woodman, I think it's called.'

'Now that sounds like a good idea. Make mine a gin and tonic, though.'

'Now, Squish, you don't want to go, do you?' Frank asked as Squishy made noises from his pocket.

Squishy popped her head out, looked at him, looked around the dark and misty cemetery and retreated back into the pocket. If she had wanted to go she had obviously decided that it could wait until they were in more salubrious surroundings.

'Frank, do you really think it's a good idea taking little Squish into interviews with you? We don't want her getting into bad company.'

'Squish likes it. I think she's got over her fear of people, she's becoming quite sociable. And she'd make an excellent police feline.'

'Police feline?'

'Well, we have police dogs. Why not police felines? Only in the detective division, of course. I'll bet you Squish could detect a baddie at a hundred paces. And she probably wouldn't need to. Anyone objecting to having Squishy join an interview must be guilty.'

'Unless they have an allergy to cats.'

'Well, then they're guilty of allergy.'

'Be serious, Frank.'

'Well, okay, we'll excuse the allergists. But you know how gullible most of the petty-criminals we have to deal with are. I'll put Squishy somewhere behind them in the interview room, tell them that Squishy can instinctively tell when they're lying, and that she'll let me know.'

'And how will she do that?'

'Oh, Squish is a very intelligent kitten, aren't you, Squish? Tuna?'

Squishy head popped out from Frank's pocket, miaowing. Frieda could not help but smile.

'She'll have to be a Special Constable then – a Very Special Constable, aren't you, Squish?' she asked, gently stroking the kitten. Squish looked back with eyes that said "Yes, I am, but what about this tuna that someone mentioned?"

'When we get home, darling,' Frieda assured her.

Squishy retired back into the pocket with a delicate snort. Honestly! Talking of tuna and then not producing any. Well, really!

'Moody bugger, wasn't he?' remarked Frank.

'Who, darling?'

'Keats. All death and woe and doom and gloom. And, oh, all those poems that start "O". O thou who has faced winter's wind, or however it goes. And the lady without mercy. I don't think he trusted women much.'

'To sleep, perchance to dream.'

'That was Hamlet.'

'I know. I just feel like falling asleep, that's all.'

'Okay, I can take a hint. Let's call it a day. Or even an evening.'

'No, Frank, we can stay if you want.'

'Waste of time. Come on, sleepy-head, I'll drive. A drink at the Woodman and then homeward bound.'

They walked back to the entrance, hand in hand, unaware that they were being observed. Aggie stood in the shadows, stroking Blackie in her arms. A tear ran down her cheek.

'Silly girl,' she whispered. 'Feeling sorry for yourself is a sin, isn't it, Blackie? It's right that they should be happy. That is the way God has planned it, so it has to be right, not so? And I've got you, and you purr so nicely, don't you, Blackie?'

She wiped away the tear.

'And you need your dinner now, don't you? Let's go and see what we have for dinner.'


'Well, well,' said Frank, reaching the bar of the pub while Frieda took a seat near the open fire, the first of the year. 'If it isn't one of the tricky twins. Hello, Rachael.'

The girl in front of him spun around.

'Sergeant Summers! What are you doing here?' she asked.

Rachael and Richard were twins studying journalism at the university who had taken Frank on in a game of practical tricks. They had lost.

'Having a quiet pint. What about you?'

'Ah, we're doing an article on the pubs of Wellbury. We're hoping to sell it to a national magazine.'

'Having your pint and drinking it, as it were.'

Rachael smiled.

'Yes, I suppose you could call it that. Are you on your own? You can join us if you want.'

'Thanks, but I'm with my fiancée, over there.'

'You're engaged?' she asked in a surprised and disappointed voice.

'Absolutely. You don't recognise Inspector Garold? Oh, and I've been promoted to Inspector too.'

'Congratulations,' Rachael said with a distinctive lack of enthusiasm.

'Thank you. Well, good to see you in honest endeavour. I'd better get back to Frieda before she wonders whether I've disappeared. See you around.'

Frank chuckled as he brought the drinks to their table and slid in next to Frieda.

'How people change at a certain age,' he said. 'Recognise those two over there, Rachel and Richard, the tricky twins? They're doing an article on the pubs of Wellbury, hoping to sell it to a national magazine. They'll probably be lucky if Phil Walthers pays a nominal sum for it, but it shows they're working hard – and they've picked up the lure of mammon. Pity, really. Money, money, money.'

'Have to pay for their studies somehow. It's expensive these days. We were lucky, at least we had almost everything paid for.'

Frank made a face.

'Sounds too much of the "when I was young" approach. Not that many years between us and them.'

'Quite a few years between us and the couple in the corner canoodling,' Frieda noted.

Frank looked in that direction and choked on his pint. The couple in the corner, mostly hidden from view by a brick pillar and semi-darkness were more than canoodling. Their hands were making a search of each other's body better suited to a room containing a bed. Or at least somewhere out of the public gaze.

'Bloody hell!' Frank whispered, wiping his mouth with a handkerchief. 'You know who those two are? Cecil Hedgewist and Doris Rubenstein. She's the secretary of the Wellbury Ghost Action Group, he's one of the members. I wonder if his wife knows what he's doing.'

'I doubt it.'

'Well, there you go. The rich tapestry of life. Amazing what people get up to when they should be doing something else.'

'I think it's inexcusable. Carrying on like that when he's married.'

'Come on, Free, be fair, we don't know the reasons. Perhaps his wife's a total harridan.'

Frieda was tempted to suggest that it was typical that a man should find reasons to excuse the infidelity of another man, and also immediately condemn any woman who might indulge in such behaviour, but the drink had woken her up sufficiently to realise that that would be a good way to start an argument.

And that was something she was going to avoid at all costs. She was not going to give him the slightest excuse to call things off.

'Anyway,' she said instead, 'That's definitely the last time I sit in a cold cemetery waiting for aliens.'

Frank chuckled again.

'I don't know. I think we're quite lucky. After all, imagine being at a party with other engaged couples discussing what you'd done recently. They would all be yakking on about dinner at a restaurant, films, wedding preparations, that sort of thing. At least we'd have something interesting to contribute.'

Frieda would have been more than happy to be at home with Frank discussing wedding preparations. There were still hundreds of requirements to be resolved.

But there was no way she was going to mention it.

## Thursday: W-30

'And now, exclusive to Radio Pithead,' Zack the Prat announced, 'an interview with Gyant Pickle, an expert on the supernatural. Now, Mr Gyant – that's a strange name, isn't it?'

'It is a name I received while studying the ancient arts in India,' Gyant Pickle replied solemnly.

'Ah, I see. There you go, folks, a real expert. Now, Mr Pickle, you studied for a long time in India, not so?'

'Indeed. I have just recently achieved one of my life's ambitions, a week-long study in the country of ancient and honoured tradition.'

'Hotter than Wellbury, hey? But a lovely place, I must go there sometime. I used to know someone from there. Very into their ghosts, they are.'

'One of the last sources on earth for true believers and students of the paranormal. But, as you say, a trying climate. Indeed, it was when I retired to the more amenable air-conditioning of my hotel room that I made the discovery. I was surfing the Indian Internet when I came across an article on the BBC website. It should have been obvious, but you miss these essential details when you are forced to live in a Westernised society.'

'The discovery? What was that, then?'

There was a pause, as if someone were leaning forward before whispering an answer.

'Spirits need propitiation. Just as gods require regular sacrifices, spirits need little gifts left at their abode.'

'You're saying we should leave pressies for the poltergeist?'

'I'm saying more than that. I have gone further. I have proved it. I asked myself, "what would be the most appropriate propitiation for a ghost in an English country cemetery?"'

'And the answer was?'

'Tea.'

'Tea?'

'A Thermos of hot tea, milk, one sugar. Each evening at ten o'clock I put on my kaftan – it is important to dress properly, of course, and I keep a careful eye on my cleaning lady while she irons it – and I leave the gift in the centre of the cemetery, and then retire humbly, walking backwards in honour and respect, clapping my hands softly twice. And each morning when I return to collect the Thermos it is empty, spotlessly clean – and there is always a little posy of flowers next to it.'

'That's fascinating. Just one last question.'

'Of course.'

'Do you walk backwards into the cemetery when collecting it?'

## Saturday: W-28

'Locked solid,' Frank said, tapping the door to the mausoleum in St Mary's cemetery. 'And even if it weren't locked, it hasn't been opened in decades, not if this dirt is anything to go by.'

'Which means?' prompted Gertie, Squishy in her arms.

'Something Meedles said. I should have picked up on it at the time. That's the problem with dealing with half the fruitcakes in town. You tend to ignore even the important bits.'

'What was it he said?'

'He said the aliens disappeared into the mausoleum. This door's the only way in. There's no way that whatever he saw did disappear into this lot.'

'What about that grave over there? The one that's been dug up.'

'Ah, our good old friend Godfrey Uriah Tumbledown, the man who never was. They're down to eight feet and still no sign, no coffin, no body, nothing. Maybe the grave robbers got there first. But it's too far away. If someone was dressed up as an alien they couldn't have got there without been seen.'

'Maybe Squish can sniff them out,' Gertie said, putting Squishy down. 'Go on, Squish, sniff out the aliens.'

Squishy yawned and rolled over to have her tummy tickled.

'Well, Squishy doesn't seem too concerned,' noted Gertie. 'And cats know when there's danger around.'

'Hello, Squishy,' said a voice from behind the mausoleum. 'She wants her stomach tickled.'

'Hello, Aggie,' Frank replied. 'Go on, Squish, go to Auntie Aggie, she'll tickle your stomach for you.'

Squishy looked up at him as if to say "Me? I will have my stomach tickled right here, thank you."

Aggie slipped between them, sat down and tickled Squishy.

'You're spoiling her, Aggie,' Frank said. 'She's got to learn that not everything is going to come to her.'

'Cats have their special places,' Aggie said.

Frank smiled grimly and looked around.

'Any ghosts recently, Aggie?' he asked. 'Aliens, spectres, wraiths, little green men or other assorted apparitions?'

'There are no such things as ghosts. But there have been lights. I stay in my shed when the lights come. I pray for protection. The Lord looks over me if I pray. But it's safe when everyone's gone.'

Frank grimaced.

'When everyone's gone? What time would that be?'

'I don't know. I don't have a clock or a watch. Time is not important.'

'About eight? Nine? Midnight?'

'I don't know.'

Frank rubbed his jaw.

'Lights,' he said thoughtfully. 'Smoke and mirrors. Shadows.'

He sighed and shoved his hands into his trouser pockets. 'Sounds like people letting their imaginations run away.

'Could you do something for me?' asked Aggie.

'Of course, Aggie. What is it?'

'Could you thank the nice lady who leaves the tea for me each evening. It's very kind of her.'

She paused.

'But she does have a very strange way of walking.'

'Did I detect a little note of irritation back there?' asked Gertie as they drove away. Frank pursed his lips and stopped scratching Squishy under her chin. He looked at the road ahead of them. Squishy miaowed up at him and put a claw into his hand as if to say, "Oi! I didn't say you could stop."

'Gently, now, Squish,' Frank said, resuming his scratching duty, making Squishy purr. 'I think it was Bomber Harris who said "There's always a bloody something". It was when he had been told for the umpteenth time that there were various reasons he couldn't get a thousand of his toys to send over to say hello to Brlin. He was right. There always is a bloody something to go wrong. The trick is to watch and wait until you know where it's coming from.'

Gertie guessed that he was talking about the wedding.

'And you think it might be coming from this nonsense about ghosts and aliens?' she suggested.

He nodded.

'That's the feeling I'm getting. It's all pure nonsense. That doesn't mean it can't have a real effect. It doesn't mean it can't interfere with our plans.'

He drummed his non-scratching hand on the window sill.'

'Just twenty eight days to go,' he said. 'I ask myself, what can go wrong in twenty-eight days? The trouble is that the answer is, almost anything.'

Gertie didn't reply. But she did think that it would be ironic if the very plans Frieda had come up with to keep Frank safely and harmlessly occupied turned out to be the cause of anything going wrong.

## Monday: W-26

'Good morning, Wellbury!' Zack the Prat's voice assaulted the good citizens of the town. 'And do I have a treat in store for you this morning! With me today are representatives of both the Wellbury Ghost Action Group and the Wellbury Alien Action Group. Now, starting off with the Wellbury Ghost Action Group, Mr Edward Boones. Now, Eddy, I understand that you have received absolutely no co-operation from the police force?'

'None whatsoever,' replied Edward Boones.

'None, none at all,' agreed his wife

'Absolutely disgraceful,' Boones added. 'We spoke to an Inspector Summers, and his response was less than helpful.'

'But I understand he was very helpful to the Wellbury Alien Action Group,' Zack said. 'Not so, Mr Gerald Green?'

'Very much so. But, ah, perhaps that is because, ah, Inspector Summers realises that ghosts do not exist, but aliens do.'

'Ah, aliens do.'

'What utter rubbish!' exclaimed Edward Boones. 'Aliens are entirely imaginary, a figment of an overworked imagination!'

'Imagination! Exactly!' declared Muriel Boones.

'There is, ah, scientific proof for the existence of aliens.'

'Scientific proof.'

'Poppycock!' declared Edward Boones.

'Poppycock!' agreed his wife.

'Ah, yes, well, perhaps we could move on,' Zack interrupted hastily. 'I understand that both groups have armed themselves against the, er, potential dangers of their pursuits. Eddy, care to say a word about that?'

'Of course. Naturally we aim for the highest levels of protection, as would any group concerned with health and safety. Our reconnaissance group never go out without their ghost-deterrent.'

'Ghost deterrent,' echoed his wife.

'Which is?'

'I have it here. As you can see, it is a metal device designed to emit a concentrated stream of electricity. It is a well-known fact that ghosts react negatively to electricity.'

'Ah, that wouldn't be a cattle prod, would it? Would you mind not waving it around like that?'

'Not in its current insubstantiation. It is now a ghost deterrent.'

'Well! Fascinating stuff! And the Alien Wellbury Group Action, Gerry? What do you do to protect yourselves?'

'Ah, Wellbury Alien Action Group. Well, as is well documented from several alien encounters around the, er, world, aliens do not abduct those under the, ah, influence.'

'Ah, influence.'

'Naturally, as, ah, committed Christians we are entirely against imbibing under normal circumstances. However, should the need arise we will drink these as fast as possible.'

'As possible.'

'Well, listeners, you can't see it, but I can tell you that the Wellbury Action Aliens Group are showing me two cans of Old Stoat. Er, if you wouldn't mind not shaking those.'

'Drunkards!' declared Edward Boones.

'Drunkards!' echoed his wife.

'No wonder they see little green men everywhere. Look at that stuff, disgusting!'

'Disgusting!'

'Er, Eddy, could you not point that cattle prod around like that? This radio equipment is quite sensitive.'

'Our, ah, research has been most intensive. We do not, er, like the idea of imbibing, but it is a scientific necessity. Far more so than a, ah, cattle prod.'

'Cattle prod.'

'Ha-ha-ha,' said Zack weakly. 'Let's not get excited now, please stop waving those cans around, that stuff is bloody dangerous.'

'Ghosts do not like electricity, that is a well-known fact,' said Edward Boones. 'And we have trained with our ghost-deterrent to the point where we could use it in our sleep.'

'Show him, Edward.'

'No, please don't – '

'We, ah, have trained ourselves down to five seconds,' pointed out Gerald Green. 'Watch.'

'Noooo,' cried out Zack.

A sound of two cans being opened came over the radio. Followed by the sound of what happens when said cans have been shaken too much. And then the sound of what happens when the liquid in the cans connects with a ghost-deterrent device which has been switched on.

Several screams, electricity arcing between humans, cans, ghost-deterrent device and a host of modern electronic radio equipment.

Then silence.

'Well,' said Frank, 'Zack the Prat always said his show would shock.'

Gertie groaned. Even Squishy gave Frank a look which clearly stated that she thought that the best place for that pun was the litter tray.

### Tuesday Evening: W-25

Frank and the vicar sat in a pew at the back of the church, watching Frieda and Tricia make notes about who would sit where, flower arrangements, and all the million other necessities of a wedding. Squishy patrolled the pews, looking for a church mouse to play with.

'I should never have done it,' said the vicar.

'What, take out a restraining order on Mrs Barton?'

'No, that was a mistake, but worse was marrying the divorcee, Mrs Galapogos. I thought Mrs Barton got carried away with zeal on the odd occasion, but Lucy is even worse. She actually tries to write my sermons, would you believe. All hellfire and damnation. The sin of drinking alcohol is one of her favourite topics. Believe me, Mrs Barton is a kind and gentle Christian compared to that divorcee. I wish I had never married her.'

'Right,' said Frank. 'I'll bear that in mind.'

'Oh, no, my boy, don't let me put you off. I'm sure yours will be a very happy marriage. But take my advice and make sure that you have somewhere to go to when you need to get away from the wife. A bolt-hole, as it were. A room of your own.'

Frank wondered how the vicar could be so sure that he and Frieda would have a very happy marriage when the vicar's experience was totally the opposite. A holding on to some idea of what things should be like, he decided, in the face of experience which proved the exact opposite.

'My only consolation is that Mrs Galapogos has the same dislike of sick people that Mrs Barton has. It's about the only time I have to myself. And the only time I have a chance to have a drink. She refuses to allow me anywhere near alcohol. After visiting hours I slip into a pub close to the hospital. You have no idea how good a pint can taste.'

Frank could empathise. Right at that moment he would much have preferred to be sitting in a pub having a pint. Optimistically he held up his hand and waggled it at Frieda, suggesting a drink. The scowl she gave him said no.

'And then I have to slip in the back way and pretend to be working in the vestry in case she gets a sniff of anything,' continued the vicar. 'Who would have thought that marriage would force men into being so devious?'

He stood up.

'I'd better get back,' he said. 'It's dinner time, and Lucy insists on punctuality. Let me know when you're finished so I can lock up.'

Frank watched him go. He came to a decision. He stood up

and strolled along the aisle to Frieda and the others. Squishy scampered after him.

'You don't need me for anything, do you?' he asked. Frieda looked at him.

'Let me guess. If we say no, your next statement will be along the lines of, well, in that case I might as well pop down the pub for a pint.'

'No sense in my just sitting around doing nothing.'

Frieda nodded.

'We're more or less finished here. We might as well all go for a drink.'

There, thought Frank. That wasn't difficult. You just have to be firm.

## Friday: W-22

'We have a slight problem, Frank,' Frieda said, coming into his office.

'We? A problem? That doesn't sound good. It sounds as if we might have a problem.'

'Frank! Would you mind being serious for just a few minutes?'

'Sorry. Okay, but can I go back to being Frank afterwards?'

Frieda sighed.

'Frank, Percy's been called away. His mother was taken to hospital last night.'

'Ah. Not too serious, is it?'

'Hopefully not. A mild heart attack, according to the doctors. But it means that Percy will be away for at least the next few days.'

Frank nodded.

'Which means that one of us will have to be on duty over the weekend.'

'Precisely.'

'The weekend we're supposed to be going to my folks' place.'

'Exactly.'

'So only one of us can go. Tell you what, why don't you go? After all, I've already met my folks.'

'Frank! You cannot be serious.'

Frank grinned.

'Thought you might not go for that one. But with only three weeks to go it doesn't leave an awful lot of time to go visiting parents.'

'We're just going to have to find the time, Frank. I have no intention of meeting my parents-in-law on the day I get married.'

'Well, why don't we make like Mohammed.'

'Mohammed? That wouldn't be some witty allusion, by any chance?'

'No, Mohammed and the mountain. If we can't get to see our folks, let them come to see us. I could let my folks have my bedroom and I'll kip on the sofa-bed in the lounge. And you've got oodles of spare room in your house for your mom.'

Frieda considered this. It was a reasonable solution, and she did have two large spare bedrooms.

But could she cope with her mother almost twenty-four hours a day for any lengthy period?

'I tell you what,' she said, seeing an answer to that possible problem, 'why don't we have them all stay at my house? It wouldn't be fair on your parents to have them cramped up in your flat. And they could get to know each other.'

And Frank's flat would be a refuge if they needed one.

'Well, I suppose we could. Let's just hope they get on with each other.'

'I'm sure they will. Why shouldn't they?' asked Frieda, who could think of a million reasons their parents might not get on, and not a single one why they would. Not with her mother.

'What do you think?' she asked. 'A week before?'

'Two weeks, I reckon. The last week is going to be hectic. We don't want to be looking after our folks and running around sorting out last minute problems. Give them a week to settle down, then leave them to look after themselves. If your mum's anything like mine that won't be a problem.'

Frieda was not sure whether or not she could share Frank's confidence. The problem with Frank was that he was always confident. Even when it was obvious that things were going terribly wrong he was confident. If the word hubris had not existed it would have been invented just for him.

And two weeks of having her mother around? Her mother had been known to destroy long and carefully laid plans within seconds. God knew what she would do with two weeks to play with.

## Monday: W-19

'Well I've played the Wild Rover, no never, no more,' sang Eric Johns as a blushing Harry Wheatley entered reception.

'Morning, Sarge,' he said weakly.

'Morning, Harry. If I were you I'd get to my pre-shift meeting and then get on the beat as soon as possible. And keep out of Fabulous's way as if your life depended on it. Which it does, as it happens.'

'Er, why's that, Sarge?'

Eric gestured towards the notice board to which was pinned the fax of Harry sitting in a Dublin jail wearing only a hangover and a blanket.

'Oh, god,' Harry muttered.

'I doubt that all the gods in the world could save you if Fabulous gets hold of you, Harry.'

'Nothing to do with her, Sarge, is it, really?'

Eric leaned over the reception counter, a smile on his lips, always a bad sign for the person it was aimed at.

'Whether it falls within her purview as a professional matter is a subject for debate, possibly, Harry. However, in terms of private, personal matters, as it were, the man who organised your piss-up in Dublin also happens to be the best man of the man she is supposed to be marrying a week after you tie the knot, to whit Sergeant Pete Phillips and Inspector Frank Summers respectively, my son.'

'Oh, god,' repeated Harry Wheatley.

'Precisely, my lad. She wasn't too pleased when she found out what you and Pete and the others had been up to. She's worried Pete Phillips might pull the same stunt with Frank, and she would not be at all happy if that should happen.'

'Oh, god.'

Wellbury police officers have a strong sense of humour. Harry was paired with Allison Hardy for his beat. It gave the word a whole new meaning.

'You're not looking very happy, Pete,' Eric Johns noted later at lunch as he sat down opposite Pete Phillips in the canteen. 'Not recovered from the weekend yet?'

'I thought I had,' Pete Phillips replied. 'Until Frigid invited me into her office for a quiet chat.'

'Oh, dear.'

'You can say that again. I tell you something, Eric, Frank can organise his own stag night if he wants one.'

'I thought he didn't?'

'Good. Because I'm keeping well clear of that sort of thing from now on. Apart from Frigid's quiet chat, Allison's giving me looks of daggers, and the missus found out about it from somewhere. She says she wouldn't blame Allison if she called it off, and it would be my fault. Everything's my bloody fault these days.'

Eric chewed on a slice of tart and thought about that.

'Yes, you wouldn't want to be the cause of Fabulous and Frank splitting up, would you? You'd have to emigrate.'

Pete Philips groaned.

'I'm not going to do anything apart from get him to the altar. After that it's up to him.'

Eric finished off the slice of tart and looked at his plate as if hoping to discover another hiding somewhere.

'And the fates are already against you on that one,' he said comfortingly, thinking of a certain prophecy.

Inside her office Frieda looked at Frank with a certain hint of irritation in her eyes. He was slumped in a chair fashioning a paper plane out of one of her memos.

'You've heard about Harry Wheatley and Pete Phillips and their trip to Dublin?' she asked.

'Yup. Everyone's heard about it. Poor Harry's getting stick from Allison.'

'Richly deserved, I think.'

'Oh, I don't know. I'm sure they'll get over it.'

'I suppose you'll be having a stag night. Just don't overdo it, Frank, I don't want to find that you've been handcuffed naked to a lamppost in the Old Town.'

Frank chuckled.

'I think I'll give it a miss. Not my cup of tea, really. Though I have heard of some pretty good tricks being played on stag nights, especially on those silly enough to have theirs the night before the wedding. One was a medical student. His pals got him stinking drunk. When he woke up the next morning he had a plaster cast on his leg from the toes to the hips. They told him that he'd fallen down and broken the leg in several places. He went through the wedding and the honeymoon before they revealed that it was a joke.'

'That does not sound very funny to me.'

'Lighten up, Free. It was probably funny to them. And then there was the Australian bloke who worked for an airline, had his stag do in Sydney. He woke up in London wearing nothing but a nappy – apparently the stewards and stewardesses had slipped him on board somehow. Customs were not at all amused, not to mention his wife-to-be – and the in-laws-to-be. I think he only just made it back in time for his wedding.'

He threw the paper plane he had made.

'And that sort of thing is not going to happen to me,' he stated confidently.

The plane crashed.

### Wednesday: W-17

Frieda was beginning to be a little irritated about Frank's reaction to her cooking. She had wanted to find out what his favourite meal was, but, while he praised all her preparations, there was no single dish she could identify as that special one.

'Oh, by the way,' he said as he peeled potatoes in the kitchen, Squishy sitting on a chair while keeping an eye on the peels in case they turned into something edible, 'mum said ta very much for the invitation. She'll be coming by train on the 26th, Saturday. She said she'd get a taxi from the station. I did offer to pick her up, but she said she didn't want to put us out, there was no guarantee that the train would arrive on time, and she didn't want me waiting around just for her to turn up. She's like that.'

That could be the case, thought Frieda. On the other hand Frank should have insisted on picking his mother up. But then his mother undoubtedly knew him well enough to know that he wouldn't insist.

Perhaps his mother expected her daughter-in-law-to-be to do the right thing and convince her son that she should be met at the station? Was this one of the trials she would have to endure to prove herself?

She looked at Squishy, who looked back as if to say, "I think you're right, you know". Or possibly "Where's my dinner, then?"

'Saturday. I could pick her up, Frank. After all, we can't leave her at the mercy of some taxi driver she's never met.'

'No, she'll be fine. She's used to it, she goes almost everywhere by train and taxi. The folks only use their car when absolutely necessary, dad's never liked the infernal combustion engine as he calls it, and mum hates driving.'

Frieda realised that Frank hadn't included his father in his original statement.

'What about your father? He'll be with your mom, won't he?'

'Oh, no. Apparently he's got a seminar he can't miss. He'll be here the Friday before. Sometime in the afternoon.'

'The Friday before? The first?'

'No, the eighth. The Friday immediately before the wedding.'

'But, Frank, that means I only get to meet him less than twenty-four hours before we get married.'

'Don't worry about dad. You and he will get along fine.'

He chuckled.

'Of course, if you really want to get in his good books you should get him one he hasn't already read – a history book I mean. Not that it would be easy, mind.'

'He'll have to come to dinner on the Friday,' Frieda decided. 'I'll cook him his favourite meal. What is his favourite meal?'

'Now, Free, don't be silly. You won't have time. And anyway, you don't like his favourite meal.'

'I'm sure I will. What is it?'

'Take-away pizza,' Frank answered with a grin.

Frieda glowered at him.

**Friday: W-15**

Frieda looked at her calendar. She stared at the entry for some time. It was an entry she had been dreading. 'M & M' it read.

Whenever she saw it she had an almost uncontrollable urge to rush out and buy as much chocolate as she could find and gorge herself. Except she couldn't. She was on a diet.

Tomorrow afternoon her mother would be arriving to help (interfere?) with whatever preparations remained to be seen to.

The same afternoon Frank's mother would be arriving, also to help (interfere?).

The question was: would Frank's mother like her?

The other question was: would Frank's mother like her mother?

The other other question was: would her mother like Frank's mother?

She had this horrible feeling that her house could resemble a very unstable dynamite factory over the next two weeks.

'Godfrey Uriah Tumbledown. What a name.'

Frank was so startled at the voice behind him he almost jumped into the deep pit that was supposed to have contained the earthly remains of Mr Godfrey Uriah Tumbledown. Squishy, nosing around on the ground, was also startled, enough to spring into the air and fall indelicately into a tall clump of grass.

'Sorry, Frank,' said the Chief Inspector, 'I didn't mean to surprise you like that. Or little Squish.'

'Oh, it's okay, sir, just a little lost in reflection.'

Squishy accepted his apologies with a sniff and went back to nosing.

'Reflecting on our Mr Tumbledown?'

'No, not really.'

'On Mr and Mrs Summers, then.'

'You could put it that way.'

'You're not still worried, are you? Frank, two weeks tomorrow and you'll be a married man.'

Frank folded his arms, still intent on the hole.

'I've been thinking, recently.'

'You do too much of that, Frank. Too much of the wrong sort of thinking, any road.'

'I've always been lucky. Everybody says so. As an only child – an only son – my mother doted on me. My father, being an academic, always treated me as an equal. I never had to work hard at school, I was always good at understanding things, and good at sport too. Finding a girlfriend was never a problem.'

He paused and a wry smile crossed his face.

'Keeping them was another question, though. They always seemed to think they could change me – get me to study harder, change the way I dressed, whatever.'

The Chief Inspector knew far more about Frank Summers than Frank realised. He could have pointed out the unhappy years Frank had spent at an all-boys boarding school. Or his previous posting where his Inspector had disliked him intensely, and had gone out of his way to make his life hell. Or the death of his girlfriend, Jean. And the death of a second Jean, whose grave lay not too far away. But if Frank wanted to believe that life had been unstintingly good to him, it was not up to the Chief Inspector to point out the flaws in his thinking.

'The point is, I've never wanted anything so much as this,' Frank continued. 'And I – well, the thought keeps cropping up in my mind that perhaps this is payback time for all the times when I should have tried harder. Now, when I really, really want something, Lady Luck is going to present her bill for payment. One short, sharp dose of bad luck to balance out the other.'

'Frank, you're being silly. And you know it.'

'Ah, yes, the big question. Intellectually I know I'm being silly. The other – well, I don't know.'

'You surprise me. Everything I've heard made me think that you're sailing through, not a care in the world.'

'Well, you have to put up a pretence, don't you? No reason to make anyone else nervous. In fact, every reason to – to put on a blasé appearance. What with all this nonsense about prophecies! Bloody prophecies! In this day and age!'

The Chief Inspector gave him a few seconds to cool down. Squishy looked up as if to say, "Now, now, Frank, I'm here, you'll be okay".

'It's your mother arriving that's worrying you – and Frieda's mother, of course,' suggested the Chief Inspector.

'Not at all. They'll get on like a house on fire. I'm sure of it.'

The Chief Inspector smiled.

'That's your answer to Frieda, Frank, not to me.'

'Okay, okay, I admit it. I'm terrified that something's going to go wrong, but I've got to pretend that everything's going to come out roses, if only for Frieda's sake. I've got to beat this nonsense!'

The Chief Inspector wanted to advise him to share his worries with Frieda, but he knew that was the sort of lesson they both had to learn.

He wondered if part of the attraction between the two was their pig-headedness. Neither was the impetuous type, yet this sudden rush to get married ... Whatever he did, he wasn't going to mention any phrases such as "marry in haste". There were enough people willing to throw out advice without request, he wasn't going to be one of them. He decided to change the subject.

'I'll tell you what, though, Frank. That hole that supposedly contained Godfrey Uriah Tumbledown is an accident looking to happen, if ever I saw one. Now, come, let's go for a drink. I need to go through this business of giving Frieda away again. I keep having these nightmares where I trip and fall over as we walk up the aisle. And there's the one where I accidentally stand on her train and her wedding dress comes right off. Not to mention the one where I've lost my glasses and can't see a foot in front of me – which is a particularly strange one, as I only wear glasses for reading. If I'm not careful I'll become a nervous wreck.'

Frank smiled. He could no more imagine the Chief Inspector being a nervous wreck than he could imagine ... Well, the Chief Inspector was right. He was being silly. A drink sounded like a good idea. And forgetting all this nonsense sounded like a better idea.

'Come on, Squish,' let's go for a drink.

Squishy scrambled eagerly up to him. Going for a drink was fun. Humans did funny thinks when they had a drink. And it was easier to convince them that she was a poor little, orphaned, starving kitten desperately in need of tuna.

**Saturday: W-14**

'Weetabix,' Frank said as he pushed the packed trolley along in the supermarket, Squishy happily asleep in his jacket pocket. 'My mum insists on having two for breakfast every day without sugar, even though she doesn't like the stuff without sugar. She thinks it's good for her.'

'That's a good start,' Frieda commented, putting a box in the trolley. 'My mother prefers muesli with Demerara sugar.' She added a bag of muesli to the trolley and another item to the two pages of notes in her hand. 'I'd forgotten about the Demerara.'

'I read an article a couple of weeks ago about an East German woman making it across to West Germany shortly after the wall came down. She couldn't understand why the West Germans insisted on eating muesli when they could afford something better. To the East Germans muesli was food for poor people.'

'Thanks for the insight, Frank. If you have any more, please let me know before our mothers turn up. I would rather not have your mother think that I stock my shelves with whatever cheap foodstuffs I can find.'

'It's going to be fun watching them. I bet they'll be falling all over themselves for the first two days, trying to be extra polite to each other.'

'Easy for you to say, you can always disappear to your flat if things start going wrong.'

'We can disappear to my place,' he corrected, trying to stand on the back wheels of the trolley. 'Anyway, I'm sure they'll be fine.'

Frieda looked at him.

'Will you stop doing that on that trolley? It's likely to fall over and tip everything out.'

'Sorry, mum.'

Frieda tried not to glare at him. The white quiff in his hair was a daily reminder of just how Frank Summers could endanger his own life. There was the solid floor beneath him, he could slip off the trolley and bang his head, badly. And there were shelves groaning with bottles. What if he fell into them and they shattered?

'Any chance of picking up a couple of beers?' he asked. 'I fancy sitting out in the garden with a beer.'

She frowned at him.

'Just a liddle-liddle beer?' he pleaded.

She shook her head and smiled.

'Okay, Frank, we'll pick up some beers.' She paused. 'Your mother doesn't mind you drinking beer, does she?'

'She hates it,' grinned Frank.


'And they're off,' said Frank as they sat on the back patio at Frieda's house, lounging in a deckchair, a beer in his hand, Frieda sitting at the patio table trying to concentrate on notes about the imminent nuptials. Frank's comment was a response to the sound of the front door bell. 'Wonder which one will be first. My mum, at a guess. She always gets anywhere early just in case. Apart from when she's late. Drives my dad bonkers.'

'Nice of you to mention it,' Frieda replied. 'Well, here goes, wish me luck.'

'She's a silly fusspot, isn't she?' Frank asked the Colonel and Squishy, lying in the sun, looking at Frank as if to say "isn't it time for dinner yet?". The Colonel eyed Frank's beer and licked his lips. Since Frank and Squishy had turned up he appeared to have decided that Frieda's patio and back garden were his real home.

'No, Colonel, you can't have any,' Frank said. 'Apart from setting little Squish a bad example, I don't want my mother and mother-in-law-to-be to turn up and find I got a cat pissed.'

The look on the Colonel's face suggested that he did not have a very high regard for mothers-in-law. Certainly none of the ones he had ever had.

Frieda walked along the passage to the front door, smoothing her skirt. Normally on a Saturday off work she would have dressed very casually, wearing something such as jeans and an old polo-shirt, but for this occasion she had chosen her smartest casual blouse and skirt, and just sufficient make-up without overdoing things. She checked her hair in the hall mirror, took a deep breath, composed herself, put a welcoming smile on, and opened the door to greet Frank's mother.

'Frieda, darling!' exclaimed one of two smartly-dressed women on the front step, both wearing hats. 'It's been ages! Give me a kiss.'

Frieda did so, wondering who her mother's friend was.

'This is Mrs Summers,' explained her mother. 'We met at the station and decided to share a taxi.'

'How do you do, Frieda?' Frank's mother said, holding out a hand for her to shake. 'Frank said you were pretty, but, as usual, he didn't say just how beautiful you are.'

Frieda blushed at the compliment, wondering at the same time why Mrs Summers felt a handshake rather than a kiss sufficient, and whether she should read anything into that.

'Now, now, Frances,' her mother said, 'don't overdo it, she's not bad looking, I grant you, but she never really puts enough effort into it. Your hair, darling, you really should have popped into the hairdresser, you know, if only to impress Frances here. After all, she is going to be your mother-in-law.'

With a sinking feeling Frieda recognised the hectoring tone her mother had always used when any of her boyfriends had been around.

'Come in,' she said, 'Frank's at the back.'

'Well, Katherine, I think she looks delightful,' Frances Summers said as they stepped inside. 'And if we're talking about putting an effort in, I'm afraid you will find that Frank is a total loss as far as that sort of thing goes. I'll bet he's lounging around in a chair with a beer in his hand, enjoying the sun.'

Frieda winced.

'And why not?' asked Katherine Garold. 'Just the right weather for a young man to relax in. After all, from what Frieda's told me Frank needs to relax as often as he can. You have been looking after him properly, haven't you, Frieda?'

'Frank is a lovely boy,' Frances Summers put in before Frieda could make a reply she didn't have. 'But he can be very lazy, I'm afraid. He's always been far too happy to let others do everything for him. I suppose I have only myself to blame, I let him get away with too much when he was little.'

'I'm sure you exaggerate, Frances. From what Frieda's told me he's a lovely boy.'

The "lovely boy" was no longer lounging, but rather sitting up straight listening to see if he could tell who had arrived. As the voices announced the imminent arrival of both mothers a twitch passed across his face and he stood up to meet them. The Colonel and Squishy promptly fled to the cover of a bush, the Colonel in front. There was a time for a strategic retreat, and a time for just running away, and he knew the difference.

'Frank! Darling!' Frank's mother gushed, almost running to him and throwing her arms around him. 'Give your mother a kiss my darling boy. Now, how are you keeping? Have you been looking after yourself? I hope you haven't been letting Frieda do everything for you.'

'Hello, mum. No, I – '

'She's a lovely looking girl, Frank, you're a very lucky boy.'

'Yes, mum, I – '

'Frank! Oh, Frieda, he's gorgeous! You are so lucky. How do you do, Frank, come, give your mother-in-law-to-be a kiss.'

'Hello, Mrs Garold, I – '

His mother released him to Katherine Garold. An enthusiastic hug and kiss killed anything he was about to say. Then Katherine Garold leaned back, holding his hands.

'You know, that quiff of white in your hair really does suit you,' she said.

'Mother!' Frieda exclaimed in a warning tone.

'Oh, yes, yes, I know it's a result of that dreadful accident you had, but it still suits you. You look extremely handsome. Now, you really should be resting, Frank, sit down, sit down, no need to stand on ceremony. Frieda! You haven't even offered Mrs Summers a cup of tea, and here we are both parched.'

'No hurry, Frieda,' Frances Summers said, 'we agreed on the way over that we wouldn't be a burden on you. Why don't you sit down and I'll make some tea? Oh, that reminds me, our luggage is still in the taxi.'

'I'll put the kettle on,' Frieda said, heading rapidly towards the kitchen.

'I'll sort out the luggage,' Frank said, racing after her.

'He is such a charming boy,' Katherine Garold said.

'Such a lovely girl,' replied Frances Summers. She looked around the garden. 'Well, I suppose we should try not to get under their feet. Isn't this a lovely garden?'

'It isn't bad for Frieda, but I think it could do with some tidying up. Now I'd put a honeysuckle in the corner over there, it would catch the morning sun.'

Inside the kitchen Frank and Frieda looked at each other with raised eyebrows and worried faces.

'I think I might be doing a bit of overtime over the next two weeks,' Frank said.

'Yes,' agreed Frieda, 'I have this feeling I'm going to be very busy too.'

'I'd better get their luggage,' Frank said, shaking his head. 'If your mother's anything like mine there should only be about fifty cases to carry.'

Outside the taxi-driver was waiting, leaning against the car with an irritated look on his face, chewing on a matchstick. Seeing Frank come out he went to open the back hatch.

'You must be the poor sod getting married,' he commented.

'I have this suspicion that that is going to turn out to be an accurate description,' Frank replied.

'You should have eloped, mate. Much less hassle. And cheaper. It was bad enough just having to listen to those two driving here, I'd hate to think of what it's going to be like as a lifetime attachment.'

'I'm keeping it as a reserve option just in case. Is this all their luggage?'

The taxi was a large people-carrier. The capacious rear was crammed with suitcases.

'No such luck, mate. The smaller stuff's on the front passenger seat and the rear seats. Good thing the coppers didn't spot me, I'd have got a ticket for having me view obscured.'

'Yes,' said Frank, picking up two suitcases, 'you have to be careful of those coppers, they can be nasty buggers.'

'Thought you was a copper,' the driver noted as he picked up two cases and carried them to the front door.

'Ah, yes, I am. I guess you heard that on the way here.'

'Mate, I heard so much I probably know more about you than you do. And I could tell you some things about your wife-to-be that you didn't know.'

'Such as?'

'Well, she was a girly swot at school and you were forever getting into trouble as a kid. Oh, and she can be a right little bossy Miss Prim and Proper when she wants, which apparently is most of the time.'

'Thanks for the insight.'

'Oh, don't worry about it, mate, I'm just repeating what those two were saying. I wouldn't take any notice of it. My missus is just the same about our kids.'

Once all the luggage was on the front doorstep Frank handed the driver a tip.

'Have a pint on me.'

'Cheers, mate, I'll do that. Good luck, you're going to need it.'

Frank watched the car leave, thinking that a quiet pint sounded like an excellent idea.

But that, he told himself, will be an occasional pleasure in future, rather than an ever-available option.

Then he began lugging the many suitcases indoors.

'I've put their stuff into their rooms,' he told Frieda in the kitchen when he had finished. 'Fortunately they each have matching sets, bought, I would guess, about a week ago. Just for the occasion.'

He grimaced.

'How do you fancy eloping?' he asked.

'Frieda!' called Katherine Garold from outside the patio door. 'You didn't make poor Frank carry all that luggage by himself, did you? In his condition? Come, Frank, come sit down my dear, you must be exhausted.'

'Let me give you a hand with the tea, dear,' Frances Summers said to Frieda as her mother dragged a protesting Frank outside.

'I'm okay, Mrs Summers, it's all ready.'

'Call me Frances, dear. Just like Frank to leave everything up to you. I hope you'll have better luck in training him than I did. Still, he was such a sweet little boy, it was hard not to forgive him anything.'

Outside Frieda began pouring the tea while Frank was forced by her mother to relax and enjoy the afternoon sun. She had just finished when she heard her mother say:

'Oh! I almost forgot.'

This was followed by the ominous sound of a handbag being opened.

'My little album of my dear little girl,' Katherine Garold said taking out a small photograph album. 'I picked out the best ones especially.'

Frieda closed her eyes.

'You've just reminded me,' Frances Summers said, reaching for her handbag. 'I've got my own little album of little Frankie.'

Frank closed his eyes.

Underneath a bush Squishy and the Colonel looked on as the two mothers began a description of their dear little ones' formative years. Squishy miaowed plaintively. The Colonel gave her a lick on the forehead and then lay down and composed himself for a nap. He had plenty of experience, and recognised a long wait when he saw one.

He just hoped it would be sardines for supper. The last time he had encountered human females like those two he had been offered some rubbish called muesli.

**Wednesday: W-10**

'Another autumn fruitful night,' Frank noted as he and Frieda sat cuddled together in the cemetery. 'Even got the mist again.'

Frieda did not reply. She was thinking that the weather had been particularly warm and sunny – until they had decided that duty required them to stake out the aliens, whereupon it had immediately turned cold and misty. She was beginning to wonder if someone wasn't trying to tell her something.

And explaining to their mothers why they had to carry out this particular duty rather than assigning it to subordinates had not been easy.

The truth being, of course, that this was one way she could be alone with Frank for a few hours without being criticised by her mother and consoled by Frank's mother.

Squishy, on being asked whether she would like to come along, had been quite emphatic that she would. Especially if the alternative was to be cosseted by Frank's mother. There was only so much cosseting a kitten could take, especially if it came with a distinct lack of tuna. At the moment she was lying on the ground in the folds of Frank's jacket, looking out at the whirls of mist, trying to decide whether she was going to enjoy the approaching first winter of her little life. On the one hand it got cold, and she did not like being cold. On the other hand she could stay indoors in the warmth, sit on the windowsill, and look at the cold outside, which, it had to be said, was rather nice.

'You okay, sweetness?' asked Frank. 'You're very quiet tonight.'

'I'm fine, darling. Just a little tired, that's all.'

'We can go home if you want. I can't see anything happening tonight.'

'No, no, I told you, I'm fine.'

Frank left it at that. Frieda would tell him what was worrying her when she was ready.

Frieda wished she could explain her fears to Frank. But that would be interfering with fate. And if you didn't interfere with fate it might just not notice you slipping past it.

'Why did you say you didn't think anything would happen tonight?' she asked.

'I don't know. Something to do with this mist, I think. All the other sightings have been on clear nights. Whatever it is that people have seen has to be a result of certain conditions – the way the light falls, shadows, that sort of thing. And that won't happen while it's misty.'

'If that's the case it might not happen again until next spring or summer.'

'I know. I think it might be a case of packing it up and forgetting about it. Pity, I was hoping to work this one out before we got married – tie it up, as it were. Oh, well, what say we go for a drink and then on home? Mum's making steak and kidney pie for dinner. Yum, yum.'

That was another thing. Both their mothers had insisted on taking their part of the domestic chores. Which, since both Frank and Frieda were at work during the day, had been a reasonable suggestion. But she still felt that she was losing part of Frank to his mother.

She might have felt some jealousy of Frank's appreciation of his mother's cooking, but it was the same reaction he gave to her cooking, and his mother had told her that Frank had told her that her – Frieda's – cooking was fabulous.

Of course his mother had then ruined it by remembering that

cooking for Frank had been such a pleasure, as he had always been more than happy with whatever was placed in front of him, scoffing everything with enthusiasm. Unlike his father who you could serve boiled coal which he would consume as he did anything, without the slightest appearance of enjoyment or otherwise, and afterwards compliment her on a "very tasty meal".

How strange it was that she, a modern, well-educated, professional, intelligent, logical woman, should still feel that cooking for her husband – or husband-to-be – should be her prerogative.

However strange it might be, if that was what it was going to take, that was what she was going to do.

Ten days to go. Just ten days.

### Thursday Evening: W-9

'To Saturday,' proposed Susan in the Hangman.

'To Saturday,' echoed Gertie.

'Cheer up, Frieda,' Susan said. 'This is more or less your hen night. Why the miserable face?'

'Oh, just a little tired,' Frieda said, taking a sip of wine. 'Having your mother and mother-in-law-to-be staying can be a little trying at times. During the day you have to be a mature, grown up police officer trying to run the station, then, as soon as you get home again, you're treated like a twelve-year-old.'

'His mother doesn't treat you like a twelve-year-old, does she?'

'No. It's – oh, it's so many things.'

Frieda paused.

'Gertie, my guess is that you were with the bike-shed gang at school. And Susan, you were one of the swots.'

'Well – yes, okay, I was a back-of-the-bike-shed girl. Once. Having a fag, playing truant, nothing serious. I never – well, I didn't.'

'If I'm going to be honest,' said Susan, 'yes, I suppose I was the school swot. So what?'

'My father was one of the biggest feminists I've known,' Frieda replied. 'Okay, I know it sounds silly, but he was. I was an only daughter, and he wanted me to succeed. If I'd had a brother – well, who knows? Anyway, top of the class, head prefect, captain of the hockey team … I remember seeing footage of the Nazi youth movement once. I thought, my god, that's me and every boyfriend I've ever had. Okay, perhaps not that bad, but clean, crew-cut and ever so pompously correct. I – well, I wanted to have time out, I wanted to slip behind the bike shed and have a fag, I wanted romance, the thought of lying in a strong man's arms, just once … '

'To read Georgette Heyer in public and not be embarrassed,' suggested Susan.

'Yes. Yes, I think that puts it rather well. And then my father died, and … my ex-husband turned up. I mean, that was the first time I met him. I think I overdosed on the romantic bit. I should have known … Anyway … anyway … Oh, I'm being silly.'

'You're allowed to be silly, Frieda,' Susan said. 'It is your hen night, after all.'

'It's a question of wanting,' Frieda pursued her thoughts. 'I didn't really want to marry – that person. I was in love with the idea of being in love. But now ... I really do want to be married to Frank. I know he's not perfect, I know ... I know ... Oh, god, I think I'm a little drunk.' She looked at her glass of wine. 'This is the first time I've really, really wanted something – something for me, not to make others, my father, happy. I just have this horrible feeling that it isn't going to happen. Just for once in my life I want something for me. And I'm going to be punished – punished for being a divorcee!'

'Frieda, Frieda,' said Susan, holding her arm, 'stop talking nonsense. You're just tired and emotional. It has been very trying for all of us, and you especially. It will all turn out fine, trust me. I'm a doctor.'

Frieda tried to laugh through her tears, and blew her nose on a handkerchief.

'How is Frank taking it?' asked Gertie, changing the subject. 'With his mother and your mum both there?'

'Oh, Frank, it doesn't bother him. His mother's used to him disappearing on any excuse. What would his mother think of me if I tried that?'

'Must be a bit claustrophobic,' Susan said. 'What's Frank's mother like? I've always presumed she must dote on him.'

'That's the ironic part. Yes, she does dote on him, but she also keeps telling him he's lucky to have found me. And then my mother tells me I'm lucky to have found Frank. And then they get out their photographs of us when we were babies. It's a little embarrassing.'

'I'll bet Frank was a cute little baby,' said Gertie.

Frieda chuckled.

'He certainly looked cute on his potty,' she said.

'You're joking!' exclaimed Susan. 'His mother showed you a photograph of Frank on his potty?'

'Oh, yes. That was cute. The ones my mother was handing around of me on my potty weren't that funny though.'

The other two giggled.

'It's a pity it's already Frank's stag night tonight,' Gertie noted. 'The blokes would have paid good money for copies of those photographs for tonight.'

'Just as well they haven't got them,' said Frieda. 'Frank seems to be getting more jittery as the days go by.'

'He wasn't going to have a stag night,' Gertie explained to Susan. 'Pete Phillips was trying to organise one, and Frank told him where to put it. Pete was going to go ahead anyway, until Harry Wheatley's stag night in Dublin. After that Pete decided he wasn't cut out for such things.'

'So what made Frank change his mind – about a stag night?'

'I think he decided that an evening out drinking with the boys meant one less evening of listening to his mother reminisce about his schooldays,' said Frieda, checking her watch. 'He said he'd be here at ten. We told our mothers that I'd stay at his place tonight, to save on having to catch taxis all over the place. He'd better – he'd just better be on time.'


'Cheer up, Frank,' said Pete Philips in the members-only bar at the Blue Bliss. 'Less than a fortnight and you'll be a happily married man.'

'Thank you for reminding me of the time left, Pete,' Frank replied. 'I hadn't quite noticed.'

'Not getting nervous, are you?'

'Well, Pete, is it worth it? That's the question I ask myself. Don't I, Squish?' he asked the little kitten playing with a piece of string on the bar counter. 'Squish, doesn't think so, tuna, Squish?'

Squishy miaowed in apparent agreement and looked around for the tuna. She turned back to the piece of string just in case it was hidden under it.

'Of course it's worth it, Frank,' an alarmed Pete Phillips replied, staring at the kitten in amazed fear. It was bad enough having to face the prophecies of a witch, a talking kitten was far more than he needed.

'A fine institution, young Frank,' said the Chief Inspector.

'What do you say to that, Mr Walthers?' Frank asked Phil Walthers.

'Sorry, Frank, I'm not falling for that one,' Phil Walthers replied. 'As it happens I think it can be a marvellous experience, but, as a bachelor myself, arguing the point might be a little like the Pope laying down the rules on sexual congress.'

'I've always wondered if men were really designed to get married,' Frank said thoughtfully. 'After all, many men are described as being confirmed bachelors. Maybe men only get married because of societal pressure. Originally, back in the hunter-gatherer days there was no concept of marriage.'

'That's nonsense, Frank,' Pete Phillips said. 'I mean, yes, okay, some men aren't made for marriage, but, I mean, you aren't one of them.'

'Well, I can speak from experience,' Eric Johns put in, 'and I think the two of you will have a wonderful marriage.'

'Ah, that's the point,' Frank replied, speaking Pete's unspoken thoughts. 'To have a wonderful marriage you have to have a wedding first, wonderful or otherwise. There's over a week until that happens, and a week can be a long time outside of politics as well as in.'

Pete Phillips and Eric Johns exchanged a glance. Eric raised his eyebrows as if to say "remember the prophecy".

Squishy looked up at them from the piece of string as if to say, "Strange people!".

'Well, we have another wedding before that,' the Chief Inspector said. 'If Harry and Allison manage to tie the knot on Saturday, there's hope for even you, young Frank.'

Frank chuckled in the taxi on the way home, Frieda nuzzled into his shoulder, Squishy snoozing on her lap.

'What's funny, darling?'

'Pete Phillips. He's so easy to wind up it's almost cruel. I spent the evening telling him I was having second thoughts. Silly bugger was panicking that I wouldn't go through with it and he'd get the blame.'

'Frank! That isn't funny!'

'Course it is, Free. You don't think I'm about to change my mind now, do you?'

'Are you?'

'Don't be silly, Free. Don't you trust me?'

'Well, yes, of course, but you don't want to tempt fate like that.'

'Tempt fate? Free, what are you on about?'

'I just think – well, it's not superstition or anything, just – well, there are enough things that could go wrong without –

tempting fate like that.'

'Bloke I used to know did the same thing,' offered the taxi driver. 'Joked about not getting to the altar. He never made it. He was dead three days later. A day before the wedding.'

Both Frank and Frieda glared at the back of his head.

'Why don't you concentrate on the road,' suggested Frank. 'Otherwise I might have to nick you for negligent driving.'

'Keep your shirt on, mate, I was just trying to be helpful.'


'God protect us from the helpful,' Frank said as they walked up the stairs to his flat.

'Sergeant Summers!' exclaimed a voice as they reached the flat door.

'Oh, cobblers,' muttered Frank. He turned and smiled at the source of the voice, one of his neighbours. 'Mrs Jones! How delightful to see you. This is Inspector Garold. I do hope you'll excuse us, but we have some urgent police matters to discuss.'

'Oh! You're always working, you never stop, Sergeant Summers. It's dreadful, the crime rate, why, I was saying only the other day – '

'Quite, quite, Mrs Jones,' Frank replied, hastily unlocking his door and steering Frieda in. 'We'd love to chat, but, as you say, work, work, work, it never ends. And little Squish here needs the bathroom urgently.'

He sighed in relief as he closed the door on a Mrs Jones praising his dedication in the face of a world gone crime-mad.

'That's last thing I need at the moment,' he said.

'Inspector Garold?' asked Frieda, wondering why Frank had

chosen that title rather than, for example, to take a random pick, "my fiancée".

'Mrs Jones is a lovely person,' he replied, leading her to the kitchen, Squishy racing ahead, 'just a little talkative. A lot talkative, to be more accurate. If there's anything you want to tell her you have to be prepared to listen to her gab on for half an hour, then you might be able to slip five seconds' worth of what you want to say before she's off again – and even then she doesn't listen. I don't even dare mention that I'm an inspector now. And she has a very good imagination. I always tell her I'm off on some urgent police business, it's the only way I know to get away from her.'

He chuckled.

'She firmly believes that I'm the most dedicated and over-worked copper on the planet.

He put his arms around her and kissed her.

'Now, Inspector, let's get down to this urgent police work.'

It would have taken him a second to say "my fiancée", thought Frieda.

Only one week to go, thought Frank.

A week can be a long time outside of politics as well as in, a voice in his head echoed.

# Chapter Three – Seven Days, Seven Prophecies

## Saturday: W-7: Assaulted By A Ghost?

After cheering Harry and Allison Wheatley off most of the guests returned to their celebrations. Eric Johns and Pete Phillips sat down together at a table, jackets off, ties loose.

'So, you reckon Frank's actually going to go through with it?' asked Eric Johns.

'Course he will,' Pete Phillips replied. 'Can't back out it now, can he?'

Eric morosely watched the dancers back on the dance floor. The "non-book" he had on Frank's getting married – or the book he didn't have on Frank's not getting married – had not gone down well. People seemed to think that he was casting a hex on the whole business. Not that it stopped the betting, though. And so far the vast majority, having heard about Sam's prophecy, had laid money on Frank escaping matrimony.

'Your turn,' Sam Nightingale said to Pete Phillips, coming up to their table.

'My turn?' he asked fearfully, sitting up straight and wondering whether it was his turn to be turned into a frog.

'To dance, of course. You men are so useless. Make yourself useful for a change, come on.'

Pete Phillips reluctantly got to his feet as Eric Johns smiled.

'Doesn't your partner dance?' asked Pete Phillips as he was led to the dance floor.

'She's got a broken ankle, dummy, haven't you noticed?'

Pete Phillips had indeed not noticed. All he had seen was a

full-length dress and a limp.

Another thing about weddings, he decided, was that it was one occasion when a uniform constable could call a detective sergeant a dummy and get away with it. He wasn't overly sure that that was a good thing.

But since she was also a witch he was not about to protest.

'Haven't had this much exercise for years,' the Chief Inspector said, mopping his brow as he and Frieda returned to their table. Frank had been dancing with a six year-old girl named Bonny, who had demanded that he stay with her for the next dance.

'He's good with kids, isn't he?' the Chief Inspector said as they sat down.

'Yes, he is.'

'Looks very smart with that bow tie and black jacket. Not many people can get away with wearing bow ties.'

'Yes, he does.'

The Chief Inspector glanced at her.

'You sound a bit worried about something, Frieda.'

'Oh, just pre-wedding nerves, I guess.'

'Perfectly understandable, everyone gets them. I'll bet even Frank has the butterflies when he stops to think about it. In fact I'd go so far as to say that I know he does.'

This less-than-subtle hint was lost on Frieda.

'I suppose that's partly it. I'm worried about Frank. Every so often he seems to be so distant. He goes into himself, as if I'm not there.'

'You're imagining things, Frieda. Everything will turn out just fine.'

Frieda wasn't so sure.

'I just know that something's going to go wrong,' she said grimly 'I keep having this dream where I'm standing at the altar and he doesn't turn up.'

'That can't happen,' the Chief Inspector pointed out, not very helpfully, 'you don't walk up the aisle until he's already at the altar.'

'That is comforting. That means I'll just be standing outside waiting for him not to turn up.'

'Frieda, have you ever heard the phrase "self-fulfilling prophecy"?'

The band chose that moment to begin a rendition of "Fifty Ways to Leave Your Lover".

'Not quite the most appropriate song,' noted the Chief Inspector.

'Frank doesn't need fifty ways,' said Frieda, 'only one.'

The Chief Inspector sighed deeply and melodramatically. This was a side of Frieda he had never come across before. He was not given to blasphemy, but even so had a deep urge to suddenly cry out, "Jaysus, woman! Will you stop your nonsense!".

'Seven days to go,' he said instead. 'Give me seven ways Frank would even try to get out of it.'

'He could get himself attacked and badly injured. Then we'd have to postpone everything. And he'd put it off again and again.'

'Well, I grant you that he does manage to get himself in some tight corners from time to time, but I can't see him taking chances this week.'

'He wouldn't take chances. It would just happen naturally. It could be something simple like being hit by a bus.'

'I can't say I've ever thought of being hit by a bus as being something simple,' mused the Chief Inspector. 'Anyway, the way they've cut back bus services recently I wouldn't worry too much about that.'

'Food poisoning. He'll have one of those terrible take-aways and come down with food poisoning.'

'It would have to be quite a remarkable case of food poisoning to make him unwell for so long – unless this food poisoning is going to take place the night before the wedding?'

'He could be attacked by a rabid dog and have to be quarantined for a month.'

'That would be unusual. The last known case of rabies in Wellbury was the year of the Restoration, 1662.'

'You've just made that up, haven't you?'

'My imagination must be working overtime. Perhaps I picked it up from you.'

'Knowing Frank, he could be abducted by aliens.'

The Chief Inspector sighed again and rubbed his forehead.

'You're not honestly going to tell me you believe in aliens, are you, Frieda?'

'Maybe he'll get religion. Decide to become a priest or monk.'

'Frieda – '

'Most likely he'll just disappear, leaving a note saying that he'll be gone some time.'

'You're imagining things, Frieda. One week from now you'll be Mrs Summers. A week and a day and you'll be on your honeymoon.'

This failed to make an impression on Frieda's gloom.

'Mind you,' noted the Chief Inspector, 'it's going to be a little confusing, having Inspector Summers and Inspector Summers. We'll have to call you Mr Inspector and Mrs Inspector.'

'You won't have to call us anything. It isn't going to happen.'

The Chief Inspector gave up. It was the gin. Frieda had been drinking gin and tonics. He had heard that gin could make a woman depressed. He hadn't believed that until now.

He looked across the room and noticed Eric Johns. He knew about Eric Johns and the book he had on whether or not Frank would marry Frieda. The Chief Inspector was not a betting man. And right then, even if he had been, he wouldn't have put a tenner either way.


'Does he always cry at weddings?' Gertie asked Susan. "He" was one of Susan's single brothers who had been press-ganged into service as a partner for Gertie, the idea of attending a wedding without a partner being unthinkable. Susan herself was nominally with one of Gertie's brothers for the same purpose.

'Oh, Wilf cries at almost anything,' Susan replied. 'He claims it's his artistic side.'

'I'm surprised that he and Tom seem to be hitting it off so well,' Gertie said, referring to her elder brother, Susan's partner. 'Tom's very much a down-to-earth sort, if I can put it that way.'

'They both support Arsenal. They've probably disappeared somewhere to discuss whether Henri was their greatest player ever.'

'What?' exclaimed Gertie. 'While they should be here dancing with us? I could understand if it was a decent team like Man United, but Arsenal? Come on, Sue, let's go find them and remind them why they're here.'

'It's been such a wonderful day,' Tricia said, elbows on the table, chin in hand, looking dreamily on at the dancers. 'Don't you think?'

'Absolutely,' replied Jeremy, who had hated most of it. He had spent the entire day being dragged around behind her. She had been asked to look after the organisation required, and had spent most of the day making sure little problems did not become big ones. He could not help but feel that he was just a useful pair of hands to her, and could be replaced with any other arbitrary male, or possibly just a well-made hat stand. One with wheels.

'Don't sound so down in the dumps, Jeremy, it's all over now, we can relax.'

'Oh, great. I'll start relaxing, then, shall I?'

'Jeremy! Stop spoiling everything. You're acting like a spoilt little child. And spoilt little children do not get a kiss.'

'I'm going to get a kiss, am I?'

'Only if you behave yourself.'

'Very well, then, I shall behave myself.'

Tricia leaned towards him and gave him a decorous kiss on his cheek. The day, he suddenly decided, had not been so bad after all.

'Time to go pick Squish up, I reckon,' Frank said, sitting down. 'Aggie probably wouldn't mind if we left her there overnight, but I doubt if she'd be able to get any sleep for worrying that Squish might wander off.'

'I'll come with you,' Frieda said.

'No, that's okay, I'll just shoot off and be straight back.'

'Frank Summers, I will not let you go visiting another woman on your own.'

Frank frowned.

'I'm hardly likely to run off with Aggie, Frieda.'

'I'm sorry, Frank, I was only teasing. I just wanted to come with you, that's all.

'It'll only take twenty minutes, I'll be back in a tick.'

He leaned over and kissed her, and left.

The Chief Inspector rubbed his jaw thoughtfully as he watched Frank go. Perhaps Frieda did have something to worry about after all.

'Can we have our ball back?' asked a little boy, wearing the remains of a suit. Behind him were a group of children whose clothing, in the lights outside the Blue Bliss, little resembled the smart outfits they had been some hours before.

'Just a second, kid,' Tom said. 'I just want to show Wilf here a trick I learned from a bloke in Italy.'

'Tom Gregson, give that ball back to the children right now,' Gertie said, taking Tom's ear as if he were a recalcitrant child himself. Since he stood six inches taller than her he had to stoop as she pulled his ear down.

'And you, Wilf Pleadle, can come along now,' Susan said, taking his ear, much to the great amusement of the watching children. 'You're embarrassing me. You're supposed to be dancing with Gertie.'

'And you're supposed to be dancing with Susan,' Gertie told her brother. 'Instead you leave her inside sitting on her own with me like two aged spinsters. Some older brother you are. I'm ashamed of you.'

'Okay, okay,' he pleaded, 'we'll come in and dance, just let go of my ear. Please?'

Gertie and Susan released their respective ears and the two men stood looking like a couple of guilty schoolboys.

'Inside, now!' Gertie said, jerking a thumb in the direction. They duly made their way with the two women close behind to make sure they did not get lost or try to make a run for it.

'You let your sister get away with that sort of thing?' Wilf asked Tom in a whisper.

'Well, you let yours do the same thing,' Tom pointed out.

'It's bloody weddings,' Wilf said. 'Women think they can get away with anything during a wedding.'

'Know what?'

'What?'

'They just have and all.'

Frank walked swiftly passed the serried ranks of tombstones in the low moonlight, irritated that he hadn't brought a torch. The cemetery at night held no fears for him, but it was darker than he had expected. He had meant what he had said to Frieda. Pick up Squishy and get back. There would be no shortage of volunteers to look after Squish once he had got back, and the night was as yet young. He was looking forward to dancing with Frieda into the early hours.

He stopped suddenly as he came close to where he knew the grave of the non-existent Godfrey Uriah Tumbledown was. He had no wish to fall in. The men digging it up needed a ladder to get out.

Something leapt up behind him. There was a sudden rush of wind and a flash of light. His head felt like it had exploded, and he fell into what should have been the final resting place of Godfrey Uriah Tumbledown.


'Man United?' asked Wilf in disbelief on the dance floor. 'Anybody but Man United. I could never sully my soul by going out with anyone who supported Man United.'

'A good thing we aren't going out, then,' replied Gertie. 'I could never, even for a split second, consider going out with an Arsenal supporter. Thugs, every one. I'm never happier than when I throw an Arsenal supporter into the cells.'

'Thugs? How dare you? We are not thugs. And, anyway, your brother's an Arsenal supporter.'

'Well, he's always been a bit soft in the head. I think he was dropped on it when he was a baby.'


'You play badminton?' Susan asked in surprise. Badminton was the last sport she would have associated with the solidly built young man.

'I cracked my neck playing rugby once, when the scrum collapsed on me,' he replied. 'Doctor told me I could never play again. I needed something to keep me fit, and badminton is great for that. If you can find decent opposition, that is.'

'Well, while you're here, there's a social club I belong to. You could come along for a game, if you like. When do you go back to Portsmouth?'

'Next Sunday. A week from tomorrow.'

'Well, we play Thursdays. Are you free on Thursday? I can lend you a racket.'

'Thursday sounds great.'

'Oh, damn, I've just remembered, it's the fancy dress ball on Thursday. I don't know if Gertie mentioned it?'

'Yes, she's told me I have to go. Er – will you be there?'

'Of course, I've been looking forward to it for ages.'

'Excellent. Excellent.'

They danced in silence for a while.

'Um, you work at the university,' Tom said. 'Gertie says there are some great walks around there.'

'Yes, it's called University Heights.'

Another silence.

'I could show you around, if you want,' offered Susan.

'I'd like that.'

'And the university is arranging a display of exhibits representing Medieval England. They even have mechanical models of people, cows, that sort of thing.'

'Wow! That sounds neat.'

'I thought you might like that.'

Frank groaned. Something had clipped his head, stunning him briefly. The fall into the grave had winded him. What was slowly seeping into his consciousness that he was in a sheer-sided grave with no way out.

A young couple who had slipped into the cemetery for a quick cuddle and perhaps more stopped their exploration of each other's body as they heard something groan.

'It's the ghost,' the girl whispered.

'Don't be silly, ghosts don't exist.'

'It's coming from that open grave. Let's get out of here before it finds us.'

'Don't be – '

Frank gasped for breath, deeply, painfully and very audibly.

The girl was on her feet, running.

Her boyfriend beat her out of the cemetery by five yards.


Jeremy could hardly breathe. He had gone to the gents and encountered Tricia Leigh on the way back. She had dragged him into a dark corner in the corridor, and was now apparently attempting to discover the location of his tonsils with her tongue. Sheer surprise was getting in his way of enjoying the experience.


Aggie came across the grave, approaching it carefully. She had thought she heard that strange noise she had heard before, and had picked up Squishy to keep her safe, retreating into her shed. Eventually her curiosity had overcome her, and, armed with the knowledge that she knew the cemetery like the back of her hand and could flit through it without being seen, had gone to investigate.

'Aggie?' called Frank.

'Who is it? Who's there?'

'It's me, Frank Summers. You don't have a ladder with you by any chance?'

'No.'

'Be a good girl and find me one, would you? Someone clobbered me over the head and now I can't get out of this bl ... blasted grave.'


'I want a dance,' the young girl said defiantly to Eric Johns. Eric started. He had just reached the stage of relaxation in which he was confident no-one else would force him onto the dance floor.

'Er, you want to dance? With me?'

'Yes. Like with Uncle Frank. With my feet on his shoes.'

Eric Johns had noticed that, Frank whirling around with little Bonny standing on his shoes.

He sighed.

'You don't half get me into trouble sometimes, Frank,' he said to himself as he stood up.


'Ah, Chief Inspector,' Phil Walthers said in an unusually effusive tone, 'I wonder if I might borrow a little of your time for the opinion of an expert, something I'd like to show you.'

'An expert? I can hardly claim such an attribute, Mr Walters, but if you want my opinion on something, well, sir, you shall have it. Back in a second, Frieda.'

Frieda hardly noticed him go. She was checking her watch for the fifth time in thirty seconds.

'A subterfuge, I'm afraid, Chief Inspector,' Phil Walthers said in a soft voice as they walked out of the bar. 'I didn't want to alarm the Inspector – Frieda. I'm afraid Frank has been found unconscious in the cemetery. From the sounds of it he's been hit over the head. The caretaker found him. Unfortunately she doesn't have a phone, so she went to a house to get help. An ambulance has been sent for. The woman who called the ambulance, on the advice of the caretaker, then telephoned here. That's all I know so far.'

For caretaker, thought the Chief Inspector, read Aggie. The woman she went to for help would be Mrs Fuller, the woman who had first found her sleeping in her garden shed just before Christmas of the previous year.

'I need to use your telephone, Mr Walthers,' he said. 'I left my mobile phone at home. It seemed impolite to bring one to a wedding.'

'I fully agree, Chief Inspector. Come through to my office.'


'Do you play front and back, or side to side?' asked Tom, a question which any non-badminton player might have misconstrued.

'Normally front and back,' Susan replied, 'but it depends on the opposition and the play. If I find myself coming back for a shot I expect my partner to take the front.'

Tom nodded agreement. He was discovering that this doctor, while obviously a woman of character, was not the harridan that he had expected. Perhaps he had let his imagination run too freely over the word Gerts had used to describe her – "forceful".

'There's a French film on at the Arts Theatre,' Wilf said. 'Naturally I could never go with a Man United supporter, but we could go separately together, if you see what I mean.'

'I would never lower myself to be seen in public with an Arsenal supporter.'

'I suppose that's it, then. My heart is broken. I fear I shall never recover.'

'Anyway, I have a TMA – an assignment – to finish, and I don't have the time.'

Wilf stopped in surprise.

'What course are you doing?' he asked.

'Law, with the Open University. W200.'

'I'm doing AA309, Culture, Identity and Power in the Roman Empire,' he said.

'You're an OU student as well?'

'Yes. Well, there's hardly any reason to be surprised, there are something like two hundred thousand of us around the world.'

'Well, if you're an OU student – is it a good film?'

'I haven't a clue. The critics all disagree. For all I know it could be the crappiest thing the French have come up with since Louis the Crapulent.'

'Well, if you're an OU student, and it might be a crappy film, what girl could refuse?'

'Frieda,' the Chief Inspector said softly, leaning over Frieda's shoulder, 'Frank's had an accident. They're taking him to hospital. I've got my car out front, I'll give you a lift there.'

'Oh my god! What's happened to him? Is it serious?'

'I don't know much at this stage, but as far as I can gather he was attacked in the cemetery. From the sounds of it he received a blow to the head, but how bad it is I don't know.'

Frieda stood up, picked up her handbag and followed the Chief Inspector.

'You have to hand it to him,' the Chief Inspector noted as they walked into the front lobby, 'he has a habit of getting into trouble in the most unexpected of places.'

'Who else would be in a cemetery at this time of night? Apart from Frank?'

'Unlikely to be anyone up to any good, I would imagine.'

They were about to get into his car when an ambulance drove up the driveway leading to the entrance of the nightclub.

'Either of you a copper?' asked the driver, pulling up next to them.

'We both are,' the Chief Inspector answered.

'Ah, I've got a delivery for you.' He turned and spoke into the back of the ambulance. 'We're at your destination, Inspector, we do hope you enjoyed your ride. Please call us again whenever you require a taxi.'

The back doors of the ambulance opened and Frank stepped out, the leather jacket with Squishy in draped over his shoulder, a white patch on the right side of his forehead.

'Frank!' cried Frieda. She hurried to him and took his arm, scanning his eyes.

'Told him he needs to get it seen to,' the driver told the Chief Inspector. 'Wasn't having it. Said there was no way he was going to sit in A and E for four hours waiting to be looked at when all it was was a little clip on his head. Mind you, I'm not saying he's wrong. This is about the time we start bringing in the survivors from the pubs. Unless you're dead it can take a long time to get seen too.'

'How bad is it – his head, I mean?'

'Officially, he should have an X-ray just to make sure he's okay. Unofficially, he'll probably be fine, whatever it was just clipped him, nasty, but probably not life-threatening. Doesn't look whoever did it got a really good shot in, just enough to make him a bit woozy for a few minutes.'

'See?' said Frank. 'Nothing wrong with me that a stiff drink won't sort out.'

'Yeah, well, I'd go easy on that if I were you, mate,' said the driver. 'You're going to have a headache in the morning as it is. Anyway, time I was getting on with me job. Take it easy, mate.'

'Thanks, I will,' said Frank. 'And thanks for the lift.'

'Darling, what happened?' asked Frieda as the ambulance left.

'I haven't a clue. One minute I was walking towards Aggie's shed, the next I'm lying in Godfrey Uriah Tumbledown's grave. Fortunately Aggie turned up and went to get Mrs Fuller. She telephoned the paramedics, I think she misunderstood what Aggie told her. They arrived, followed by one of our patrol cars. Apparently someone telephoned the station and told them that a police officer had been injured in the cemetery. They thought it was a wind-up until Mrs Fuller telephoned with the same message.'

'Someone else phoned the station?'

'Yes, a man. I'm guessing that it was the same bloke who clocked me in the cemetery. Come on, I need that drink.'

'Frank, are you sure you're okay? Perhaps it would be better if I took you back to my place, you need some rest.'

Frank laughed as he led them back into the Blue Bliss.

'You must be joking, Free. Having my mother mothering me would be bad enough. Having both her and your mother at it – I'd be digging an escape tunnel within half an hour. Without the regulation teaspoon.'

'Frank, you can't just act as if nothing's happened. You should have gone to hospital. They would at least have kept you under observation overnight, just in case it's worse than you think.'

'Free, I'm fine, I really am, just a bit of a throbbing in my head. You can come back to my place and observe me, if you're that worried I might suddenly keel over.'

'I'll do that,' she said determinedly. 'I'll phone my mum and let her know I won't be back tonight.'

'While you're doing that I'm going to get myself a drink.'

The Chief Inspector followed him to the bar as Frieda went to their table, mobile phone pressed against her ear.

'Well I've decided on the wedding present I'm going to give you, Frank,' the Chief Inspector said.

'What's that?'

'A large, professional First Aid kit. With extra bandages.'

Frank chuckled.

'Best give it to Frieda,' he said. 'For use on me.'

'Seriously, Frank, you aren't going to ignore this? An assault on a police officer?'

'No, of course not. But the area's been taped off, it's too dark at the moment to see much, and we're too short on the ground to start bringing in teams with arc lights and all the rest. I'll go there at first light tomorrow, see if I can find anything. Right now, we have a wedding to celebrate. And in a week we'll have another wedding to celebrate, and nothing, repeat nothing, is going to get in the way of that. I don't care if Downing Street decide they want to invade Iran, they'll just have to wait. There is important and there is important.'

'Your mother wanted to speak to you,' Frieda said when they returned to their table. There was an admonishing tone to her voice that suggested that Frank had known this would be the case, and had deliberately made sure he was not there when Frieda made the call.

Which was exactly what he had done.

'And you told her I was so busy partying you might not get a chance to pass the message on,' he said, giving her a kiss as he sat down.

'No, I told her you'd be afraid she'd want to fuss over you, so you'd find any excuse not to call her. And she said she was glad to hear that I knew you so well, it would save a lot of heartbreak later,' Frieda said bitterly.

Frank was saved from having to reply by the appearance of Sam Nightingale.

'Someone told me you'd been in a bit of bother,' she said. 'A knock on the head?'

Prior to becoming a police officer she had been a nurse. She now took Frank's head in her hands and examined it as if it were a rather uninteresting specimen.

'Just a lucky shot that caught me in the wrong spot.'

'You'll be fine,' she said. 'Apart from possibly a bit of a headache and a rather nasty bruise.'

'That's what I've been telling everyone. See, Free?'

'Frank, are you okay?' asked Susan, appearing at his left shoulder. 'I heard you'd had an accident.'

'I –'

'Frank, what's this I hear about you being attacked?' asked Gertie, appearing at his right shoulder.


'Run this one by me again,' Wilf said. 'They dragged us in to dance, and now they're fussing over that bloke with the quiff of white hair. What's his name again?'

'Summers,' replied Tom. 'Frank Summers. He's the one getting married next week.'

'Susan seems to fancy him,' Wilf said in an offhand fashion.

'I think Gertie fancies him more,' Tom said, more hopeful than sure.

'No, I'd say Susan's after him more than Gertie.'

They watched in silence for a few seconds.

'Well, if Gertie fancies him,' Wilf said, 'what do I care?'

'Exactly what I was thinking. If Susan fancies him, that's her choice.'

A third person looked disconsolately on as his partner joined Susan and Gertie. Jeremy had been deserted. Tricia Leigh had heard the news and wanted to make sure that both Frank and Squishy were okay.

'Is that a kitten he's got with him?' asked Wilf in disbelief.

'Ah, so that's the reason,' Tom replied. 'Women fall over themselves for a man with a kitten.'

'Cats give me hay fever,' Wilf said, sneezing to prove the point.

'I'm more of a dog person, myself,' Tom noted.

'You know, Free,' Frank said, 'I'm beginning to wonder if you weren't right. Maybe our mothers would be the lesser fusspots.' He sighed. 'Still, in just over a week you'll be the only one with legal rights to fuss over me.'

## Sunday: W-6: Hit By A Bus

Frank and Frieda scanned the cordoned-off area around Jean's grave from behind the tape. Squishy, with less respect for the cordon and more interest in chasing butterflies had wandered into it.

Gertie, since she reported to Frank, was also there. As was Susan, as forensic expert. And since Gertie and Susan were there, Tom and Wilf had tagged along to experience police work at first hand.

Or that was their excuse.

'Looks like someone was waiting just behind that gravestone,' Frank said, nodding at the sight of two depressions in the otherwise dry and hard earth.

'Flat shoes,' agreed Frieda. 'Probably a man's.'

'Either a woman with large feet or a man with medium sized feet,' said Frank.

'They don't look fresh,' noted Susan, dubiously.

'If someone were hiding behind the gravestone they'd be on their haunches, wouldn't they?' asked Gertie. 'The impression of the front of the shoe would be deep, with little of the heel. Those indentations don't look like that.'

Tom and Wilf looked at each other with raised eyebrows. They had hoped to witness the brilliant unfolding of a crime scene. This was hardly what they had expected.

Squishy pounced on something in a tussock of grass, batted it, and then, as it showed no response, ignored it and wandered on.

'Come here, Squish, that's a crime scene you're interfering with,' Frank ordered, with little expectation that the kitten would obey.

'She's found something,' said Frieda, stepping underneath the tape. 'It's a wedding ring,' she added, taking out a pencil and using  it to pick up the object. 'No, not a wedding ring. A brass curtain ring.'

'A curtain ring?' asked Frank, looking at it. 'Reminds me of the joke: what's the most important invention of all time?'

Frieda gave him a look which suggested she knew she shouldn't respond.

'Go on, then, what is the most important invention of all time?'

'Venetian blinds.'

'Venetian blinds?'

'Otherwise it would be curtains for all of us.'

Frieda groaned. Susan and Gertie smiled. Tom and Wilf chortled quietly.

'You aren't taking this business seriously, are you, Frank

Summers?' Frieda accused.

'Well, yes and no. Yes, I want to catch the person who clobbered me last night, but I haven't any intention of letting them spoil my day. The sun is shining, the sky is blue, and I'm with you.'

The others groaned.

'Give the curtain ring to me,' said Susan, holding out a handkerchief. 'I'll run some tests on it, see if there's part of a fingerprint on it. Perhaps find some DNA on it.'

'You don't think our mystery mugger dropped it, do you?' asked Gertie. 'A curtain ring?'

'It's the clue that will lay this case wide open,' Frank said, poker-faced.

Tom and Wilf looked impressed. They were the only ones that did.

'Has to be done, you know that, Frank,' Susan said.

'Just teasing,' he replied, grinning. 'Well, since we've crossed the tape we might as well see if we can find anything else. Come on, Squish, pay attention, watch how the professionals do it.'

The professionals searched the area in vain. Squishy found a dead mouse.


'Why don't we go have a word with Aggie, see if she saw or heard anything? Then we'd better get on to the Grove if we're going to get a table.'

'Good point, Frank, replied Frieda. 'Best if just the two of us go, Aggie's shy of strangers. We'll meet the rest of you back at the cars.'

'Who's Aggie?' asked Wilf as they began walking back.

'She's an old bag woman who looks after the graves,' replied Gertie. 'Except she thinks she's twelve years old.'

Tom looked surprised.

'Strange sort of town, this,' he noted.

'I'd forgotten how strange,' replied Wilf. 'You never know what can happen around here.'

'Indeed, you don't,' said Tom, glancing at Susan. He took her hand.

Noticing this Wilf took Gertie's hand.

'I'm never going to support Arsenal whatever you say,' she whispered.

But she allowed him to keep her hand.


'Hello, Squishy,' said Aggie. She looked at Frank. 'Are you better?'

'I'm fine, Aggie, just a slight bruise. You didn't happen to see anyone last night?'

'No. I heard something. But I didn't see anyone.'

'What did you hear?'

'It sounded – like a sudden rush of wind. Almost as if someone were moaning. Or whistling in a strange way. That sound I told you about.'

Frank rubbed his chin and looked at Frieda.

'I seem to remember something like that. A sudden rush of wind. And a flash of light. Something shiny.'

'You don't think – could it have something to do with this alien nonsense?'

'It's possible, but I doubt it. Have you noticed that the aliens mostly appear on Wednesday nights?'

'You think that's significant?'

'The Herald normally comes out on Thursdays. The reports of aliens occur with just enough time to get into the newspaper, but not enough time to be investigated properly. Fortunately Phil Walthers is too experienced to fall for that one.'

'Good point. But it means that it's unlikely to have been someone involved with the alien hoax that attacked you last night.'

'No, I rather think it wasn't.' He checked his watch. 'We'd better get moving if we're going to get to the Grove for lunch. Come on Squish, say goodbye to Aggie.'

Aggie picked up the kitten and gave her to Frank. She looked at him, and then down at the ground again.

'I got hurt once,' she said. 'But I'm better now. And when October gets here it won't matter anymore.'

Frank exchanged a glance with Frieda.

'We'll pop in and see you later in the week, Aggie,' he said.

'Bye bye, Squishy,' Aggie replied.

'We'll have to do something about Aggie before winter arrives,' Frank noted as they walked back to the cars.

'The vicar said that they were arranging to supply her with warm clothing and blankets,' Frieda replied. 'They'll also make sure she gets at least one hot meal a day.'

'Well, I suppose there is something closer to hand we should be concentrating on. What you might call a special occasion. And we don't want anything to interfere with that, now do we?'

'No, we certainly do not.'


The Grove was a pub-cum-restaurant on the side of University Hill. It was renowned for its Sunday lunches and only the fact that the rest of the diners appeared to prefer eating indoors allowed them to find a couple of tables outside, pre-emptively occupied by their mothers and the Chief Inspector.

'Frank!' exclaimed his mother as they walked into the beer garden. 'Are you okay?'

Frank winced as both women stood up and came towards him to indulge in their share of fussing over him.

'I'm fine, mum, really. It was just a little bump, that's all.'

'Just a little bump?' said Frieda's mother in disbelief. 'Frieda, you really should take more care of Frank. You don't want to lose him before you even get married.'

It was Frieda's turn to wince, both at being chastised like the child her mother seemed to think she still was, and at how her mother had identified her own, internal, fears.

'Come sit down, Frank,' said his mother, leading him to the table. 'Here, you and Frieda sit here, opposite Hal and the two of us. The others can take the table alongside.'

Wilf and Tom exchanged grins at Frank's discomfort.

'Something you find amusing, Wilf?' asked Susan.

'So does Tom,' said Gertie. 'Care to share the joke, you two?'

The two looked at each other and rolled their eyes.

Fortunately for Frank discussion on the state of his health was rapidly displaced by discussion of the next Saturday. The mothers would inspect the church last thing on Friday evening to make sure everything was ready for the next day. Frank managed to smother a smile over that. Mrs Haggerty and the vicar's wife were unlikely to take kindly to doubts about their ability to get the church ready. Then there were questions about the weather. Thunderstorms were forecast for the middle of the week, following which a warm and sunny period was expected, the sunniest since 1940.

Just as well. Their mothers might well have had something to say to the weather forecasters had it been otherwise.

Frank was happy enough to relax and enjoy a couple of glasses of wine with the meal while their mothers went through their check lists of what was outstanding. They even missed him glancing at Frieda and winking. The Chief Inspector noticed the look, and also Frieda's return glance, and how it had something of relief in it.

After dessert Frank left to visit the little boys' room.

'Frieda, you look worried about something, pet,' said her mother.

'Oh, it's nothing really, mum. Just nerves, I suppose.'

'He's a fine catch. You should be ecstatic. I know I would be. You must be very proud of your son, Frances,' she said to Frank's mother.

'Oh, I am, Katherine, I am. And he's very lucky to have Frieda. They'll make a lovely couple.'

Frieda had heard the same statements every day since their mothers had met. Far from encouraging her it made her even more nervous. It put more pressure on both her and Frank, and she knew he was not taking it well.

Another thing that concerned her was that Frank's father was not going to arrive until the Friday afternoon. "He knows my mother too well," Frank had said, only half-joking. "If he got here any earlier he'd be used as a skivvy to run any and every errand they decided they needed him to."

What if Frank's father did not like her? They would be meeting for the first time of Friday afternoon. What if he took a sudden dislike to her? She knew Frank had a great deal of respect for his father. If his father took against her ...

She had mentioned this to Frank one evening at his flat. His response had been to tell her to stop being silly.

Thanks very much for the support, Frank.

But she dearly wanted him with her now. If she could have she would have him under her own surveillance twenty-four hours a day until Saturday.

'Frieda? You aren't listening, are you?' asked her mother. Her mother turned to Frank's mother. 'Don't worry, she's normally very down to earth, it's just waiting for the wedding that's getting her down.'

To Frieda's relief Frank now re-appeared, walking back from the pub. To her dismay he was rubbing his chest and grimacing.

'What's wrong, darling?' asked Frieda, standing up in alarm. 'Indigestion?'

'No, I got hit by a bus.'

The group paused at hearing this information.

'You got hit by a what?' asked Frieda.

'I told you,' Frank said, sitting down. 'A bus.'

'This is some convoluted word play, is it, Frank?' Frieda demanded. 'Something that will make sense when you finally explain it and show how clever you are.'

Frank looked at her, puzzled.

'No, it's pretty straightforward. I got hit by a bus. That group inside. One of their kids was playing with a toy bus. For some reason he thought it would be funny to throw it at me. Caught me just between my ribs.'

'Oh, a toy bus!' exclaimed Frieda.

'Of course a toy bus, you didn't think I meant a red double-decker taking a right past the gents, do you?'

'Well, you made it sound melodramatic. I thought it was much more serious than just a toy bus.'

'Just a toy bus? It wasn't one of these modern plastic ones, Free, it was an old metal one, a large Dinky toy or something, the edges were sharp as hell. The father was worried that I'd damaged it, he reckons it could be worth a fortune in a couple of years as an antique. I almost damaged him when he said that.'

'If he's so worried about it, what was his child doing playing with it?'

'Apparently he didn't know the boy had it. And the brat, and I quote, "will get a right thumping when we get home".'

The Chief Inspector smiled as something struck him. He picked up a napkin, took a pen from his pocket and made a few notes. When he had finished he waited until Frank was assuring his mother that he was perfectly okay, and slid the napkin to Frieda. She picked it up, eyebrows raised, and read the few lines.

"Attacked and injured.

Something simple like being hit by a bus.

Food poisoning. He'll have one of those terrible take-aways and come down with food poisoning.

Attacked by a rabid dog and have to be quarantined for a month.

Abducted by aliens.

He'll get religion.

He'll just disappear."

She turned her head inquisitively towards the Chief Inspector.

'Your predictions from last night,' he said softly, out of Frank's hearing. 'You seem to have got two out of two so far.'

She gave him a look which showed how much she thought of that.

It wasn't much.

She wasn't so silly as to take such things seriously.

Was she?

## Monday Morning: W-5: Food Poisoning?

Frieda looked at her watch. Frank had complained of tiredness the previous evening and had gone back to his flat early. She had felt worn-out herself, and had also had an early evening, leaving their mothers watching television and swapping stories. Early to bed, early to rise, early in the office. She had expected Frank to be the same, but he wasn't in yet. Her telephone rang.

'Hello, Free, it's Frank here.'

'Frank? Where are you?'

'I'm at home. I'm afraid I must have eaten something that didn't agree with me. You're okay, are you?'

'Yes, yes, I'm fine. Frank, you mustn't come in if you're not feeling well. How bad is it?'

'Not too good. I woke up halfway through the night and haven't been back to sleep since. I think I might go back to bed now and see if I can't sleep it off.'

'You do that, Frank. I'll give you a call this evening.'

'Yes, I'm sure I'll feel better this evening.'

In her office Frieda took out the napkin the Chief Inspector had given her. Third on the list was the phrase "food poisoning".

Don't be silly, she told herself. It's pure coincidence.


In his flat Frank rubbed his hands.

'Much as I'd love to take you to London, Squish, I somehow don't think you'd appreciate it at your age. Far too noisy and bustling. Instead  I think I'll leave you with Auntie Aggie. What do you say to that?'

Squishy looked back with eyes that stated quite clearly that Frank was doing something very naughty.

'Just the once, Squishy. When we're married I won't ever tell any white lies again. Probably.'


In her office Frieda tried to concentrate on work, but failed. Logically it was foolish to even think that the list was somehow some form of ordained trial that Frank would go through, with the ultimate result that he would just disappear. It was just the Chief Inspector's way of showing her how foolish she was being.

And he was right.

She stood up and opened her office door.

'I don't have any important meetings today, do I, Tricia?' she asked Tricia Leigh.

Tricia looked back in surprise.

'But of course you do!' she exclaimed. 'Two o'clock. You can't have forgotten!'

Two o'clock was her appointment for the final fitting of her wedding dress.

'No, of course not. I meant anything to do with work.'

'Oh, no,' replied Tricia dismissively. 'I've kept the week as free as possible. And remember, you must not wear the full outfit. That's terribly bad luck.'

'I'll remember,' Frieda replied. 'Leave a shoe off, isn't it? Or a glove, or something?'

'Yes, that should do it, I think. I'll remind you when we get there.'

'Okay. Well, if there's nothing pressing, I think I'll go for a drive. I'll have another look at the cemetery. There might be something we missed yesterday.'

And, she thought to herself, I'll look in on Aggie.

The thing about Aggie was that, if you ever felt miserable or depressed, she was an instructive lesson in teaching you not to let the minor problems of life affect you.


'Lovely,' said Frank to the proprietor, an ancient man wearing a threadbare cardigan in the musty shop. 'Do you take credit cards, or will a cheque do?'

'Well, er, if you have some form of identity, a cheque would, er, be most acceptable.'

'Will this do?' asked Frank, showing his warrant card.

The old man peered at it.

'Most eminently, Inspector Summers, most eminently. One can hardly doubt the trustworthiness of our brave men in the police force, er, now can we?'

Frank decided not to answer that question.


'What's Squishy doing here?' asked Frieda in amazement as the kitten came to her to rub itself against her legs.

'I can't tell,' replied an unhappy Aggie. 'I promised not to. I was supposed to keep her out of sight.'

Frieda gritted her teeth.

Frank had betrayed her on two counts. Firstly by lying about being ill. Secondly, by involving Aggie. Aggie had the mental simplicity of a child of twelve, a protected and innocent child of twelve. Putting her in a position whereby she might have to lie to one of them was not just unacceptable, it was unthinkable.

For the first time the thought that it might be her who broke off the engagement crossed her mind.

'Don't worry, Aggie,' she said, thinking desperately. 'It's probably just a surprise he's planning. He's like that.'

Aggie grinned conspiratorially.

'I thought it was something like that.' She looked nervously at Frieda. 'Can I tell you a secret?'

Please don't, thought Frieda.

'If you want to,' she said.

'Do you know that tomb, just outside the church? I hide

behind it when they have choir practice, so that I can listen. And when they have mass I creep up to the side of the church. I was there when they had that wedding on Saturday. I hope you don't mind. I saw you there.'

'Of course not, Aggie.'

'Can I be there when you get married?'

'Of course you can, Aggie.'

If I get married.

Later that day Frank attended another appointment. This time his interlocutor was not as easygoing.

'Inspector Summers, you appear to have the idea that we doctors are here merely to hand out prescriptions on request.'

'It's just to get through the next couple of weeks. If they happen again after that I promise I'll come back to you. I probably won't need anything anyway. It's just a little insurance, just in case.'

The difference between the look on the doctor's face and the look on Frank's face when a suspect told him blatant lies was that Frank's face showed some amusement.

'Two months since you last had a serious headache,' the doctor said. 'I'll translate that as six weeks. Before that?'

'Oh, ages. A couple of months.'

'Four weeks, then. And before that? About four weeks too, I would guess.'

Frank waved a hand to indicate "more or less".

'And you wouldn't be here if the stuff you can buy over the counter was powerful enough.'

Frank gave a half nod, half shrug to indicate that this was unfortunately the way things were.

'So, that rumour is true, is it?' the doctor asked after a few moments of silence.

'Which rumour?'

'That you're getting married.'

'Absolutely. And if you don't believe me – about coming back if the headaches don't go – I'm sure my wife will drag me back.'

'That much I do believe.' He rapped a pen on his desk. 'Inspector, I want you to understand something. The headaches you've been getting recently could be a result of stress – a stress related migraine. What makes me wonder is that you have no record of having them before you were shot. It's a difficult area. But, something you must understand: if they are a result of your accident, you need to have some tests done. Right now you say they're just the occasional blinding headache. Well, if it isn't looked at properly you could end up passing out just like that.' He snapped his fingers. 'And one day you might not wake up afterwards.'

Then he frowned at Frank before turning towards the keyboard next to him.

'Only this once, Inspector. I'll give you a prescription for some rather powerful tablets. But I'm warning you, Inspector, treat them with respect. Only take one if absolutely necessary. And never take them if you've been drinking, never drink after you've taken one, at least not for eight hours. And if you feel any side effects, come to me immediately. In fact, get straight to the nearest hospital and show them the tablets.'

He printed out the prescription and read it before signing it.

'Congratulations on your forthcoming nuptials, Inspector,' he said, handing it over and looking Frank in the eye. 'I just want you to understand that, if you don't take care of yourself, you might never be able to make that particular appointment.'

He watched Frank leave. The world, it seemed to him, was divided into those who couldn't live without taking vast amounts of medicine they didn't need, and those who tried to avoid the little attention they did need.

And then he smiled. Inspector Frank Summers was right about one thing. If he did manage to get married to Inspector Frieda Garold, the woman wouldn't hesitate to drag him off to a doctor when she found out about his headaches. In fact, he'd have a headache of a totally different kind, one which did not fall under the auspices of medical science.


'Perfect,' said the dressmaker in the bridal shop.

Frieda smiled nervously. She had to admit that the wedding dress wasn't bad. And the diet she had been on – which Frank, of course, hadn't even noticed – had worked.

'You look absolutely gorgeous,' Tricia said, clasping her hands together.

Then her eyes opened wide.

'Frieda – you've got it all on, take something off, quickly!'

Frieda looked at her image in dismay. She had forgotten to leave off a shoe or glove. She quickly flipped off a shoe.

'That didn't happen, Tricia.'

Tricia looked back, wide eyed.

The dressmaker made herself as invisible as possible. She had seen this sort of thing happen before. Getting involved was a bad idea.

'Tricia,' Frieda said carefully, 'it's just tradition not to wear the entire outfit. Let's not make tradition into superstition. Okay?'

'Errm, okay,' replied Tricia, slowly, in a small voice which said she was doing her best to believe it but not quite succeeding.

Frieda did not believe any of that superstitious nonsense. What worried her was that Tricia might. And Tricia was in charge of co-ordinating everything. If anyone was in a position to accidentally derail things it was Tricia. It wouldn't be deliberate. Tricia would do her best, but at the back of her mind would be that little voice saying "It's going to go wrong". And so it would.

The worst of it was that she couldn't blame Frank for this one. The only thing everyone would remember is that she, Frieda, was the one who had cast an evil spell on the whole business by failing to remember not to put on the entire outfit. Frank could be as guilty as sin, but it was going to be herself getting the blame.

'Not a whisper about this,' she told Tricia. 'Not a word. To anyone. Not even Jeremy. Okay?'

Tricia nodded, a finger against her lips.

The dressmaker made a note to get payment before the planned date.

### Tuesday: W-4: Attacked By A Rabid Dog

For the second morning in a row Frieda checked her watch. Frank was late again. She hoped he wasn't going to pull the "something I ate disagreed with me trick". The previous evening, apart from a solicitous enquiry about his health – to which he had replied that he was now famished and could eat several horses – she had not pursued the topic. Pretending that she suspected nothing had exhausted all her self control. She had none left if he came up with any more tall stories.

Although she had enjoyed a little revenge. That of making sure their mothers knew all about his indisposition. It had been hard keeping a straight face as each prescribed their own cures for such a malady. His dinner had been continually interrupted by debates about whether he should be adding salt, whether milk would be better than the beer he was drinking, or perhaps a small glass of wine?

Especially good was Frank's mother's memory of the stories of feeding charcoal to children with upset stomachs.

Her telephone rang, interrupting her thoughts.

'Hello, Free? I'll be a little late in to work. You're not going to believe this one.'

'I suppose you were attacked by a rabid dog?' suggested Frieda, looking at the list.

There was a pause.

'How did you know that?'

'Oh, Frank, please. If this is a joke I don't think it's very funny. And you can tell that to the Chief Inspector too.'

There was another pause.

'Free, what are you talking about?'

I'm talking about you lying to me, thought Frieda. I'm talking about becoming your wife, someone you should trust implicitly.

She sighed.

'Very well, Frank, tell me about this rabid dog. Please, go ahead, I can't wait to hear this one.'

'Well, it wasn't a real rabid dog, of course. Otherwise I'd be in quarantine. You remember the university are doing an exhibition on Medieval England? They have an exhibit of a rabid dog, a mechanical thing. Susan and Tracey were trying it out when I dropped in on my way to work to find out if Susan had any further information on that curtain ring. You won't believe this, but the damn thing had a go at my leg. Fell over next to me, rattling like crazy, next thing I knew was that I had a mechanical limpet locked onto my leg. I don't think they programmed it to answer commands such as "sit" or "get off my bloody leg".'

Frieda's suspicions disappeared. If anyone was likely to be attacked by a mechanical rabid dog it would be Frank.

'Frank, are you okay? How bad is it?'

'Well, I'll be limping for a couple of days. It was like having a hyena attach itself to my shin.'

She smiled.

'Frank, you will be a good boy and get it checked out, won't you? You don't want it turning septic, do you?'

'Of course not, Free. You forget, Susan's a doctor. She's spoken to her boss and they've both decided that I have to go to hospital to have it checked out. Not much use arguing. I'll be in before lunch.'

'Look after yourself, Frank. See you later.'

Frieda put the telephone down and tapped the desk with her fingers.

'Frank back in the wars again?' asked Tricia, bringing in a cup of tea.

'He managed to get bitten by a mechanical rabid dog this

time. I'm beginning to wonder whether I should put a twenty-four hour watch on him.'

'I'd volunteer but I'm going to with you to see the Chief Constable tomorrow,' Tricia said with a melodramatic cough as she said "Chief Constable".

'That's one thing we can all rely on Frank for,' Frieda noted with a wry smile, 'his allergy to senior officers. I did invite him along. Fortunately he declined.'

'You have a wicked sense of humour,' Tricia said with a grin.

'Can't have Frank the only person around here with one.'

'What's next on the list?'

Frieda tapped a pen on the list. The next prophecy was that Frank would be abducted by aliens.

'Abduction by aliens,' she said. 'Not even Frank could manage that.'

And that, she thought to herself, would be the end of this superstitious nonsense.


'Ghosts,' Frank said, drumming his fingers on his desk that afternoon. Gertie looked up.

'Funny you should say that, sir,' she said, 'I had a look at the original report – the bloke who was done for drunken driving. There's something funny about it.'

She had been unsure of whether or not to mention it. On the one hand there was Frieda's injunction to keep Frank occupied. On the other Frank's leg had obviously taken a beating, and he should rest as much as he could.

If only he would. Knowing that he should be taking things easy appeared to be making him restless.

'Old Merrick,' she said, standing up and tapping the map of Wellbury on the wall. 'That's where he lives and was on his way to. But he'd been drinking in the Old Town. So how did he end up at the cemetery? It's way out of his way.'

'Gerts, my sweet, you've got it. The son of a sod was lying. Now if we can prove it we can show that this whole ghost business is a nonsense. Come on, get your jacket. We're going to get this idiot to confess. What's his name?'

'A Mr Kevin Morton.'

'Right, Mr Kevin Morton, you're history. Come along, Squish, we're going to lay a ghost.'

Kevin Morton looked ill at ease as he sat in his lounge with his wife. Having the police turn up was bad enough. The kitten made things far worse. He could swear it could read his thoughts.

'So, Mr Morton, you popped into the cemetery to relieve yourself while on your way home?' asked Frank.

'It's just as I explained to the policemen who arrested me,' replied Kevin Morton.

'Yet the cemetery was totally out of your way. Care to explain how you found yourself there?'

'I took a wrong turning. Yes, I know, I've lived in Wellbury all my life, but business is going through a bad patch. I was too lost in thought to notice.'

'And your business is?'

'I'm a salesman. In the funerary line.'

Try as he could Frank could not shake his story. Morton's recollection was a bit hazy, and he contradicted some of the things he had previously said in his statement, but that wasn't unusual. He still stuck to the core of the story: a sudden flashing light, a whirring, clanking noise, a cold wind. And if something had happened, something unusual – such as being attacked by a ghost – then it wasn't surprising that Morton might have been a little confused.

He began to wonder if the man wasn't telling the truth after all.

'Black,' he said as Gertie drove them back.

'Black?'

'Morton is a funerary salesman, so he wears black. Godbeer was wearing black when he was attacked, he'd just been at a funeral. So was I, though I was wearing it for Allison and Harry's wedding. There has to be a link there.'

He sighed and rubbed his chin.

'Frieda's got an all-day meeting with the Chief Constable tomorrow,' he said. 'It would have been nice to hand over the ghost case, closed.'

'Chief Constable? Shouldn't you be going? Now that you're an inspector?'

'God, no, Gertie. Spend almost an entire day discussing statistics? That is just not my forte. I might not be the best copper in the world, but I'd make a much worse statistician.'

Squishy had fallen asleep in his lap. She chose that moment to wake up, roll over and yawn, stretching.

'So what do you think, Squish?' he asked her, tickling her stomach. 'Was Morton lying, or did he really see something?'

Squish grabbed his finger, gave a soft miaow and another yawn. To Gertie she seemed to be saying "Of course he was lying. Isn't it time for tuna?"

'I agree, Squish,' said Frank. 'He definitely saw something. What, though?'


'You think he believed you?' asked Mrs Morton.

'I bloody well hope so. Six points off my licence. I was lucky to keep the job.'

'But you weren't anywhere close to the cemetery. At least that's what you told me.'

'Of course I wasn't. The story just popped into my head. I knew I was over the limit. I was hoping they'd think I was a bit doolally, leave me alone, forget to do the breathalyser.'

'But they didn't.'

'No, they didn't. And now half of Wellbury think there's a ghost in the cemetery.'

'If they want to be silly that's up to them. I mean, after all, what sort of a person believes in ghosts?'


**Wednesday Afternoon: W-3: Abducted By Aliens**

'Ah, you're back,' Frank said to Tricia as he limped into the outer office of Frieda's eyrie in the late afternoon. He had just spent one of the most boring days of his life, clearing paperwork so that he could get married and go on honeymoon leaving a clean desk behind him. He had also gone through the files Tricia had prepared outlining the details of W-Day, hoping to find some little thing he could do, without luck. Tricia had everything nailed down to the last little pin and needle.

That made him nervous. His approach to plans was to

presume that something would go unexpectedly wrong somewhere. He wouldn't have a plan to handle whatever it was, since you couldn't plan for the unexpected. But you would be expecting it.

If that made any sense.

But he couldn't spot any possible flaw in Tricia's detailed notes. Normally he could sense where something was likely to go wrong, even if only through a gut feeling. There was something definitely wrong if he couldn't do that with a wedding, an occasion just begging for a visit from the gods of disasters.

What was even worse was that Frieda had been away almost the whole day, and Percy had been off, which left him the senior officer. He believed that his forte was in pushing awkward decisions upstairs. He wasn't used to being at the top of the stairs himself.

And Gertie had been in mothering mode. And Frieda had telephoned every second hour until the early afternoon to make sure that he hadn't managed to harm himself. Tricia had called every other hour on behalf of Frieda to do the same.

And his mother and Frieda's mother had decided that cooing over him and making him relax the previous evening had not been enough. They had decided to interrupt their shopping to pop into the police station to make sure that he wasn't over-exerting himself. Eric Johns had telephoned to warn him that they were about to enter the station, whereupon Frank had taken the easiest option, that of escape, and climbed out of his ground-floor office window, only to discover that the two mothers had missed the front entrance by taking a wrong turning, and were now staring at him in some amazement. Fortunately they appeared to believe his story that he was testing fire drill procedures, but it had also meant that his mother-in-law-to-be had loudly protested to all who would listen that "poor Frank" should not be expected to have to climb out windows in his state, especially now that he was an inspector.

After that every officer in the station had tried to hide a smirk whenever he passed. There had also been one or two muttered puns about "windows of opportunity" and "the flying detective".

That should just not happen. He was, as Frieda's mother had noted, an inspector after all.

And above all he still didn't have a clue on what next approach he could take with the ghost and alien cases. That was the most infuriating bit. It was undoubtedly just people's imaginations running away, but something must have happened to spark off those imaginations, and he was convinced that he could identify that something if only he applied himself properly. A day of going through all the notes again with Gertie, tossing ideas back and forth, coming up with more and more ludicrous scenarios had resulted in nothing. Apart from the feeling of a headache coming on. So he had decided it was time for an early end to the day and a quiet drink with Frieda before facing the combined onslaught of the felicity of their mothers.

'Frieda busy?' he now asked Tricia. He had just heard that they had returned and had gone to Frieda's office looking for company.

'She's, er, on the phone to the, er, Chief Constable,' replied Tricia. 'How's the leg?'

'Feeling a lot better, thanks. I thought you'd just come back from there?'

'Er, yes, we did, about five minutes ago. Um, I think there were some figures he wanted that we didn't have. She promised to telephone them through. Um, don't you want to sit down? Rest the leg?'

Frank looked at her. He could have sworn that she was flustered for some reason. Most unlike the eternally unflappable Tricia he knew.

'You're sounding puzzled, Trish,' he said, 'anything wrong?'

'Oh, er, not really. I'm, er, just trying to work out what to do with all these – these boxes of plastic sheets.'

'My goodness,' he replied, noticing the three boxes that had come out of Frieda's office. 'Overhead transparencies. Haven't seen those used for a while.'

'Overhead transparencies? What were they used for?'

'Surely you've seen overhead transparencies before, Trish?'

'Um, they ring a vague bell. I think I've seen them before. Tell me about them.'

'Ah, Trish, back in the old days, the dim and distant past, aeons, aeons ago before laptops and other computers became ubiquitous – about five years ago, probably – people, lecturers, that sort of thing, would print notes on these pieces of plastic and display them on a white-board or other suitable surface via means of what was called an overhead projector. It had a large base with a powerful light on which you placed the piece of plastic. The light shone the text or diagram up to some sort of prism or mirror, which then projected the image onto the whiteboard. These days, of course, you just hook up a laptop to what they now call overhead projectors.'

'Hey, I remember! They used to use one at school once. A supply teacher. All of the permanent teachers hated the thing.' Frank chuckled.

'I was at a police lecture once when I was still a trainee constable. The lecturer was quite an old chap who seemed to think an overhead projector was some malignant modern device. God knows how he would have coped with computers. Anyway, one day he was giving a lecture and the fan in the projector was playing up. It was fine so long as he held onto it, but as soon as he moved away it would start vibrating – and he had this habit of walking up and down as it was. So there he was, strolling up and down, gabbing away, and the fan motor was vibrating, making the transparency move until it was upside down. He turned around to look at the whiteboard and his notes were the wrong way up. So, you know what he does? He turns the overhead projector around, the daft sod. Of course that meant that the notes were still upside down, but projecting onto the back wall. We were killing ourselves laughing.'

'I don't suppose you thought of helping him?' asked Tricia, giggling.

'Well, yes, we did think about it. For about two seconds.' He chuckled again. 'And then, later, after he'd worked it out and had got going again, he was talking to one of the side walls when one nasty constable-in-training leaned forward and nicked the transparency as it was about to drop off. The poor old duffer couldn't work out what had happened. He even got an engineer in to take the thing apart, thinking it might have slipped inside.'

'And that constable-in-training wouldn't have been one Frank Summers by any chance, would he?'

'Moi? Course not, Trish, you don't think I'd be sitting at the front of a lecture room, do you? I always made sure that I was hidden at the back.'

'Well,' Tricia agreed, smiling, 'I have to admit you do have a point there.'

'Still, thinking of the funding for schools these days they might well still use overhead projectors. Maybe you should have a word with Sue. Even the university might not have completely converted to computers.'

'Mmmm, there's a thought. If someone does still use them I can give them these. Maybe a primary school can find a use for them, to draw on or something. I really don't want to just throw them away, it would just add to the greenhouse effect.'

'Wouldn't be much use for drawing on. You'd have to project them onto ... '

'Have to what?'

'Trish, my sweet, my love, you've done it. And it's Wednesday.'

He gave her a hug and a kiss on the cheek.

'Done what?'

'Cleared the fog of my confusion, the mists of my mind. Here, I'll find a use for one of these sheets. No, make it two in case I mess up with the first one. Let's just hope the photocopier's working properly.'

'Done what, Frank?'

'I'll tell you later, if what I think is going on is going on.' He checked his watch. 'An hour or so before darkness. I should just have about enough time. Tell Free I'll be home a little late tonight, probably about nine.'

'Done what, Frank?' Trish asked again as Frank disappeared, limping away as fast as he could.

'Who has done what, Frank?' asked Frieda, coming out of her office.

'Frank said that I'd done it, and gave me a great big kiss,' Tricia replied. 'Only I don't know what it is I've done. And if I don't know what it is I've done, I don't know what to do to get another kiss like that.'

'Tricia, I asked you to keep him occupied for a few minutes, not get into a kissing competition.' She paused. 'Still, if you find out let me know.'

'Oh, and he said not to wait up for him because he'd be home late.'

Frieda looked at her.

'Did he really? The cheek of the man.'

She thought for a few moments.

'Tricia, do me a favour. Tell whoever's on reception that I want to know immediately Frank gets back from wherever he's gone.'

'You're working late?'

'I'm staying late. The first thing my mother and his mother will want to know when I get home is where Frank is. I don't think either will appreciate the answer "I don't know".'


Frank limped through the cemetery in the twilight humming a tune to himself, a small rucksack over his shoulder. Aggie sat outside her shed, watching him. The two cats which had been lying next to her skulked off into the undergrowth.

'Well, that is an improvement, isn't it, Aggie?'

'What is?'

'Whackey and Blackie didn't race away like scalded cats when they saw me coming. Maybe one day they'll even trust me enough to stick around.'

'They're afraid of strangers. It isn't their fault.' She paused. 'Have you hurt your leg?'

Frank smiled.

'It's nothing serious. Aggie, would you mind looking after Squish for me for the evening?'

'Oh, yes, I'd love to! Come here Squishy.'

'I'm going to arrest two aliens tonight.'

'You're teasing me again,' Aggie said. nestling her cheek against Squishy.

'You see those two bushes over there? The ones that are moving towards the mausoleum?'

Aggie squinted in the half-light. She could just make out what appeared to be two bushes which were moving erratically towards the entrance to the cemetery.

'Bushes can't walk,' she said, confused.

'Ah, those aren't bushes, those are the little green men, Aggie.'

'You're teasing me again! There are no such thing as little green men.'

'Well, yes and no. Those two bushes are two men named Green, and they're quite short, so they are two little green men.'

'Why are they wearing bushes?'

'It's a disguise. They don't want the aliens to see them.'

'But there aren't any aliens.'

'Perhaps not in the usual sense, but tonight we're going to catch them.'

He checked his watch.

'Another fifteen minutes to darkness. What do you say to a cup of tea, Aggie?' he asked, taking a thermos from his rucksack.


Gerald and Reginald Green, wearing camouflage jackets, shirts and trousers, green camouflage paint, and half an oak tree each finally made it to their vantage point fifty yards away from the mausoleum. Reginald eased a pair of binoculars from his satchel.

'Ah, that's strange. It's black as anything. Do you think the aliens are using some kind of rays to block our sight?'

'Ah, I think you, need to, er, take the caps off, ah, you pillock.'

'Ah.'

Reginald took the caps off and peered through the wrong end of the binoculars. Instead of bringing the mausoleum closer it seemed take it so much further away.

He wasn't going to mention that to Gerald, though. He'd already been insulted enough for one evening.


'Lively little cemetery, isn't it?' said Frank.

'I preferred it when it was quiet,' Aggie replied, playing with Squishy.

'Don't worry, Aggie, if everything goes according to plan we should be able to lay the aliens to rest tonight. You stay here and I'll be back in a short while.'

He left her at her shed and crept as stealthily as he could with a bandaged leg towards the mausoleum, taking a wide arc. It took him fifteen minutes before he found the spot he was looking for. He lay down flat and took a powerful torch from his rucksack.

Gerald squinted through the leaves he was wearing. The camouflage paint was beginning to dribble down his perspiring brow. All in all he did not have a very good view of the mausoleum. By rights he should have the binoculars, he thought. After all, he was the eldest. But, no, they were Reginald's, given to him as a birthday party when he was ten. Typical, Reginald was always getting the better presents. And he never used them. He could remember when …

'Ah!' he exclaimed at the sudden appearance of two glowing aliens hovering in front of the mausoleum wall, silver-bodied with large black, oval eyes. 'Ah!'

'Ah!' echoed Reginald, desperately trying to focus the blasted binoculars so that the wall came closer instead of receding fuzzily away.

'Aliens!'

'Ah! Aliens!'

'Ah?'

'Ah? Inspector Summers?'

The two stood up in wooden amazement as Frank Summers' smiling face appeared alongside the aliens, the same face which normally adorned his warrant card.

'Oh, shit!' said a quiet male voice some forty yards away from the Greens and about ten yards in front and two to the right of Frank Summers.

'Oh, dear,' said a quiet female voice from about five yards to the right of the male voice.

'Time to go,' said the first voice.

'Absolutely! Outta here!'

'I'm right behind you,' Frank called softly. 'Switch those torches off and don't move until I say you can.'

Reginald Green took a few tentative steps forward, adjusting the binoculars, trying to bring the image of the aliens and the Inspector closer. He tripped over a tuft of grass. Gerald Green, wiping the camouflage paint across his eyes, looked down at him and then immediately back up.

'Ah! Ah! Gone!' he cried. Reginald Green got to his feet and looked. There was nothing to be seen.

'Ah! Aliens! Gone!'

They looked at each other. Each swung around to look behind himself. And then back again, twisting their heads feverishly in a search for the missing aliens, until they finally backed into each other and fell over.

'They're after us!'

'They're behind us!'

'Pull the pin, Gerald.'

The two men feverishly pulled cans of Old Stoat from the pockets on their camouflage trousers and pulled the ring tops. A sound of desperate glugging followed. Eight seconds later they had finished and looked at each other, eyes wide, breathing deeply.

'We've survived, Reginald!'

'Yes, ah, we've survived, Gerald.'

'I, ah, knew it would work.'

There was a pause.

'But what, ah, about Inspector, ah, Summers? They've kidnapped him.'

There was silence while they contemplated this.

'We must, ah, warn the police station.'

'The police station.'

'Hurry.'

The two men scrambled back the way they had come, occasionally tripping over graves and other obstacles as the Old Stoat kicked in. Aggie and Squishy both watched in bemusement as they stumbled past.


'Right, you can stand up now,' Frank called softly.

Two sheepish shadows stood up slowly. Frank switched his torch on again.

'The tricky twins,' he noted as Rachael and Richard tried to shield their eyes from the beam, a distorted smiling face of Frank Summers playing across them.

'How did you guess?' asked Rachael.

'You wait here while I collect Squish,' said Frank. 'And then you and I are going to have a little chat.'


Eric Johns had volunteered to do some evening overtime in the belief that it would be a quiet night. He wasn't quite expecting two green bushes to stumble into reception, even less that they should evidently be quite drunk. On what he didn't want to know.

'Inshpector Shummers hash been kidnapped,' gasped Gerald, 'by, ah, aliensh!'

'Aliensh!'

'You have to, ah, reschue him, immed-ah-iately!'

'Ah.'

Eric Johns blinked. He leaned forward slowly, put his elbow on the counter, and rested his chin in his hand.

'Aliens,' he said slowly.

'Thatsh, ah, it. Emergenshy.'

'Emergenshy.'

'Kidnapped,' noted Eric.

'Esh.'

'By aliens.'

'Esh.'

Eric nodded slowly. There were a number of ways to handle this. Normally chucking these two drunk madmen in the cells to sleep it off would be the first option. But he had no wish to have to listen to them calling out how Frank had been abducted by aliens for the rest of his shift, and he had no doubt that that was what would happen. These weren't your normal drunks who would fall peacefully asleep after fifteen minutes of loud complaint.

He reached for the internal phone.

'Inspector Garold? I have two civilians in reception who claim that Inspector Summers has been abducted by aliens.'

In her office Frieda had the list of prophecies in front of her. Somehow she was surprised at how little she was surprised.

The only question was what to do next.

Of course.

There was that pub close to the cemetery. If Frank had been abducted by aliens the first suggestion he would make is that they all go for a quiet pint.

At least there were some things in this life you could rely on.


'I should have twigged that it was you two when we met here a few weeks ago,' Frank said as he and the twins sat in the Woodman, each with a pint in front of them. Frank was sitting quite comfortably. The twins weren't.

'How did you guess?' asked Rachael sulkily.

'Well, let's rather start with why you were doing it.'

They looked at each other before looking back to Frank.

'We're doing psychology along with journalism,' Richard explained. 'We heard about the radio interview where someone said the ghost in the cemetery was an alien. We wanted to see how credulous people could be.'

'You saw how silly the images looked,' Rachael said. 'To us it was quite obvious they were just projections someone was shining on the mausoleum wall. But, given the context of the cemetery, and the fact that we showed them for only short bursts we thought that maybe, just maybe, people wouldn't believe what they were seeing.'

'And you chose your victims carefully.'

'Well, that too,' admitted Richard. 'Anyone who appeared to be a couple of sheets to the wind. Or a little soft in the head.'

'So?' asked Rachel. 'How did you work it out?'

'Trade secret, I'm afraid.'

'Oh, come on, that's not fair.'

'Okay,' Frank smiled. 'At first I thought it was the result of over-active imaginations and a couple of pints too many. Then I realised that the people who reported seeing aliens must have seen something, even if it wasn't really aliens. So Frieda – Inspector Garold – and I staked out the cemetery on a Wednesday – all the sightings had been on a Wednesday. Coincidentally, the day before the Herald comes out.'

'It's the only week-night we both have free. Other nights we have to work to pay for our books and stuff.'

'Ah, so that's it. Anyway, it was a misty night, and I had a feeling that nothing would happen, though I didn't know why. So Frieda and I gave it up and had a pint in here. And came across you two. I should have put two and two together and come up with you two, but I fell for your story about writing an article about the pubs of Wellbury.'

'That wasn't a story. We are writing an article. It's almost finished.'

Frank nodded.

'Maybe that's why I didn't suspect you at the time. Anyway, a week later and Frieda and I are again on stake-out, and again it's a misty night and nothing's happening. It was only late this afternoon that the pennies began dropping. Frieda's secretary had a few boxes of overhead transparencies she had to get rid of, which first gave me the idea that maybe someone could be projecting images around the cemetery. One of your victims, Grahem Meedle, swore blind that he'd seen the aliens. He immediately took a picture. But he was using a flash, which would have wiped out any images, no matter how strong the torches that were being used. So he thought the aliens had fled. And then another suspect claimed that the aliens had slipped into the mausoleum. Now when a projection moves off a solid surface it might appear to slip away because there's nothing to reflect the light.'

'The mist,' Richard said, 'you guessed that the mist had something to do with the aliens not appearing – the night you were on stakeout.'

'Exactly. You couldn't use your torches because the beam of light would reflect in the mist, just as a car's headlights do. A bit of a dead give-away. Even a drunken idiot would have noticed and tracked the beams back to you two.'

'But how did you know it was us?' asked Rachel.

'I told Tricia, Frieda's secretary, to ask Doctor Pleadle whether the university still used overhead projectors. And lo, it all became clear. Someone was obviously playing tricks, and you have form for that. You were in here that misty Wednesday night because you never expected the mist. You decided to give it up for the night and have a pint in here.'

'We had to hide in the loo last week when we saw you coming in,' Rachael said. 'We knew you wouldn't believe it a coincidence if we met again on a Wednesday in the same pub.'

Frank laughed.

'No, I don't think I would have.'

'So, what are you going to do with us?' she asked. Frank smiled.

'I bet you two have got that off pat.'

'Got what off pat?'

'If you two are in trouble with a woman, it'll be Richard doing his innocent, small-boy apology. With men it's you that takes a turn.'

Rachael scowled at him.

'So? What's next?' asked Richard.

Frank looked at each in turn.

'I could have you for wasting police time, but a good lawyer would argue that it was us wasting our own time. After all, aliens?'

'That's a point,' noted Richard.

'I tell you what, no more aliens, and I'll drop it, okay? I'm getting married on Saturday – I don't have time to run about kicking your two backsides.'

'Deal,' said Richard.

'You're not seriously getting married to that thing, are you?' asked Rachel.

Frank leaned forward and took a card out of his pocket.

'I am, god willing. Here's an invitation for you two. And I'll tell you something in confidence which may help you live a little longer.'

'What's that?' asked Rachael, taking the invitation and looking at it unwillingly.

'That thing, as you call her, my wife-to-be, Inspector Garold of the Wellbury police force, a woman who could eat you two for breakfast, looks like she's quite happy to have you for dinner instead.'

'What do you mean?' asked a puzzled Rachael.

'She's just walked in the door.'

The twins looked around. Frieda had just spotted the twins

and Frank and was bearing down upon them.

'Oh, shit,' said Richard.

'We're outta here,' said Rachael. She stood up and gave Frank a kiss on the cheek. 'Good luck, see ya later.'

Frieda hardly paused in her stride as the twins swept past her like a tide looking for another place to be.

'Would you care to tell me what exactly has been going on, Inspector Summers?' she asked, standing, looking down at him.

He looked at his empty pint glass and stood up slowly, giving his gammy leg the full works.

'Let me get a round of drinks in first,' he said, kissing her on the cheek. 'Oh, and you'll have to drive me home then, I don't want to be nicked for being over the limit three days before we get married. I've always thought the limit way too low.'

'I'll get the drinks, you sit down,' Frieda replied. 'You need to rest that leg.'

When she returned with their drinks he gave her the same explanation he had given the twins.

'What really irritates me,' he concluded, 'is that I should have twigged long ago. When there's some funny business going on, and the twins appear, they have to be involved in one way or another.'

Frieda's anger had subsided somewhat. Subsided, but not completely gone. Part of it was that she agreed with Frank's estimation. She should have concentrated on the alien case. Instead she had treated it as some local stupidity. But then she had had her mind on more important things at the time.

'You should have charged them,' she said. 'Wasting police time at the very least.'

'I considered the option,' he replied, grinning, 'but the paperwork put me off.'

She scowled and took a sip of her drink.

'Come on, Free, lighten up. It was just a silly joke. And do we really want to get bogged down by something like that three days before we get married?'

She smiled.

'No, of course we don't, darling,' she said. 'I think I'm just letting my nerves get to me.'

'Nerves? You, Frieda Garold? There's nothing to be nervous about. You say "I do", I say "I do", that's it.'

He was right, she thought. She was letting coincidences get to her. Okay, he had been attacked on the Saturday night, but it hadn't been that serious. Yes, he had been hit by a bus, but it had been a toy bus. What he hadn't had was food poisoning – but he was going to explain that one sooner or later, she was quite determined that he would – nor had he been ravaged by a real rabid dog, nor been abducted by real aliens.

If there was such a concept.

The next thing on the list was that Frank would get religion. She looked forward to seeing how her imagination came up with something that would fulfil that prediction.

She avoided thinking about the final prophecy. You wouldn't need any imagination to work out how that one could be fulfilled.

## Thursday: W-2: Frank Gets Religion

'You all ready for tonight, Frank?' Pete Phillips asked as he passed Frank in the corridor.

'Tonight? What's happening tonight?'

Pete's eyes widened.

'The Policeman's ball. You haven't forgotten, have you? You can't have forgotten. Tell me you haven't forgotten.'

'Oh, bollocks. I had, you know. I suppose I'd better get a costume from somewhere.'

Pete's eyes had reached the bulging stage.

'You won't find anything in Wellbury, or even close by, Frank. People have been planning for ages.'

'Oh, I'll think of something.'

'What's Fabulous going as?' Pete asked, hoping not to find out that Frieda had spent a lot of time and energy on a costume, and was going to be very unimpressed with Frank and his best man. Especially his best man.

'Can't tell you, Pete, it's a surprise, I'm sworn to secrecy. But it's really good, I'll say that.'

'Frank,' Pete said, grabbing Frank's arm desperately, 'you've got to get something decent. Frigid won't take kindly to your turning up in something like a gorilla costume, you know.'

'Oh, I'll come up with something, Pete, don't you worry. A gorilla costume will do just the trick. Must be one somewhere for hire.'

He left an anxious Pete Phillips who was opening and closing his mouth in a desperate attempt to make words form, but failing. In his mind Pete Phillips was thinking: 'No, please, Frank, Frigid will crucify me.'

Followed by: 'It isn't bloody fair. It's not my fault. Blame

Frank, not me.'

And the worst thing was that he couldn't even take the coward's way out and not go to the ball. His wife had been looking forward to it for ages. A thought which only added to his misery. Frank would turn up dressed as something silly like a gorilla, and his wife would want to know why he – Pete Phillips – hadn't done something about it. Arguing that the ball had nothing to do with the wedding would be a waste of time. With two days to go the best man would get the blame for anything, he was sure of it. After all, Eric Johns said so, and he knew what he was talking about.

'That'll be Frank,' Frieda said at the sound of the doorbell. She did not add "and he'd better be wearing a proper costume". He had assured her that he had everything in hand, but his reactions to her questions on what he was coming as had been far too off-hand. She went to the door, carefully holding the long skirts which showed her to be Marie de Médicis. She opened the door and gasped as she saw the sight in front of her.

'Bon soir, Madame,' Frank said in the best French accent he could manage, taking a cardinal's hat off and bowing deeply. 'Allow me to present my deepest regards.'

'Cardinal Richelieu,' she whispered, taking in the moustache, goatee, flowing purple cape, large white collar, sword, ruffed knee-length boots, and a blue band holding a cross that declared him to be without doubt Louis XIII's most senior minister.

'After all, Cardinal Richelieu and Marie de Médicis were as thick as thieves.'

'Frank, you had this all planned, didn't you?'

'Of course, I told you I'd sorted it out. Didn't you trust me?' he replied, giving her a kiss. 'But it was fun winding Pete up. You know, there's nothing to prove that Richelieu and Marie ever had anything going between them,' he whispered into her ear, 'but we can test whether it might have.'

'Frank! Stop it!' she giggled.

'Frank! My goodness, you do look handsome,' Katherine Garold said, appearing in the passage dressed as Madame de Pompadour. 'Come, a kiss from the handsome – who is it you're meant to be?'


'So, Madame de Médicis,' said Oliver Cromwell, also known in normal life as the Chief Inspector, sitting down next to Frieda in the main bar of the Blue Bliss, 'I think you and the Cardinal are bound to win first prize. Where is he, by the way?'

'Oh, hello, sir, he's getting another round,' Frieda replied, blushing and hoping the strobe lights hid it. 'But I'm sure someone else will win first prize,' she said. 'Everyone has gone to such an effort. Anyway, who cares? Everyone is having a great time, the prizes don't matter. After all, the charity is the main thing.'

'Please, on such a night let us not stand on ceremony, madame. You may call me Oliver tonight – or Ollie for short.'

Frieda laughed.

'Where on earth did you get such a realistic costume – er, Oliver?'

'I'm a member of the Sealed Knot – the organisation which

re-enacts battles of the civil wars, as you no doubt know.'

'I'd heard of them. I've never seen one.'

'Ah, yes, well, I can get you tickets to the next one if you want. Generally I keep quiet about it. There's always the fear that people will think it's just an excuse for grown men to get dressed up and act like little boys. Fortunately most people who come are schoolchildren. They find it all fascinating.'

'The Cardinal and I would love to come to the next event, Oliver.'

'Ah, yes, the Cardinal. He does look the part, doesn't he?' The Chief Inspector glanced at her briefly. 'Of course, you realise that this makes it, what, six out of seven?' he chuckled.

'Six out of seven? I'm not with you, sir – Oliver.'

'Your sixth prediction was that he'd turn to religion – become a priest. Being our Frank a priest wasn't sufficient. I'm surprised he didn't opt for Pope Gregory – I think it was Pope Gregory at the time. Can't remember the number, though.'

Frieda should have been relieved. Just as with all the other prophecies Frank's "getting religion" was stretching the imagination to fit a coincidence into superstitious nonsense. The trouble was, she knew what the last prophecy was. Frank would just disappear. And there was no way you could confuse that with coincidence.

'Just shows you how silly it is,' Oliver Cromwell said. 'Now why don't you relax and enjoy the evening. Only a day and a bit to go.'

He took a sip of his drink and then destroyed everything.

'Of course, what most people don't realise, is that Marie and the Cardinal were at loggerheads for most of the time. Started off great chums, but it didn't last very long.'

'Loggerheads?'

'Well, worse than that, really. They hated each other's guts.'

'Frank, you weren't trying to tell me something, were you?' Frieda asked when Frank returned from the bar. 'Coming as Cardinal Richelieu?'

'Tell you something, Free? Such as what?'

'Cardinal Richelieu and Marie de Médicis had a great falling out. She tried to get Louis XIII to dismiss him. Instead she was exiled.'

'Was she? Well, there you go, I never knew that. I know they were great pals at one stage, and I thought people were more likely to remember the name of Cardinal Richelieu. I doubt if anyone knows a great deal about either. For example, did you know that the Cardinal kissed Marie just like this?'

He put words to action, putting both his hat and her headdress at peril.

'Frank! Stop it! People are watching!' she exclaimed once he released her mouth.

'Oh, I'm terribly sorry. I wasn't aware I needed everyone's permission to kiss the woman who is supposed to become my wife in two days' time,' he replied bitterly. 'If madame will excuse me, I need a leak.'

'The Cardinal and Madame de Médicis appear to be somewhat closer than propriety expects,' said Romeo, standing with Juliet next to the corridor.

'I hope they aren't giving you ideas,' replied Susan.

'Ah, but are we not star-crossed lovers?' asked Tom, kissing her hand. 'Juliet, Juliet, you make my heart sing. Come, let me clutch thee.'

'Tom!' protested Susan, giggling, giving in to his caresses.

'Enjoy it while you can, Tom,' said Cardinal Richelieu as he passed on his way to the gents. 'Once they've got you they think they can order you around as they like.'

'Blimey, he's not a happy man,' Tom commented, watching Cardinal Richelieu's angry cape disappear. Susan's mouth twisted.

'You know, I think he might just be letting his nerves get to him,' she said.

'Frank Summers? I thought he was the king of cool.'

'I think he'd like to be – the king of cool. Which makes it more difficult when he finds things getting on top of him. Anyway, how would you feel two days before your wedding day?'

Tom developed a coughing fit. That question had come out of nowhere. And was best sent back there.

'Oh, dear,' he said, recovering quickly. 'Bit of dust floating around. Hey, they're starting an Abba tune. Come on, let's go dance.'


'I'm going to have three babies,' a shepherdess called Gertie said, rather tipsily, 'a girl, a boy, and I don't mind what the third is. What would you like?'

'Well, I don't know,' replied a bemused Byron, also known as Wilf. He was trying to work out whether Gertie was telling him this as a matter of her preferences, or whether she had already decided that he was to be the father concerned. He didn't quite object to either, but would have liked to have known when the latter had occurred.

And whether or not he was going to have a say in it.

'Hey,' he said, 'they're starting an Abba song. Come on, let's go dance.'

'Frieda!' exclaimed The Wife of Bath in the Ladies'. 'You've been crying. What's wrong, my pet?'

'Oh, nothing, Mrs Blower.'

'Call me Cornelia, Frieda. Now, what's wrong?'

'Oh, I've been such a fool! I keep thinking Frank won't marry me in the end, so I keep being short with him.'

'Sounds like one of those self-fulfilling prophecies to me. And silly, too. Even if the idea ever entered Frank's mind, which I'm sure it would never, he wouldn't be allowed to get away with it.'

'It's not Frank's fault. It's – fate. Destiny. Call it what you will.'

'What I'd call it, my dear, is total and utter bollocks, if you'll excuse the phrase. If it is destiny, which I doubt, you might as well enjoy yourself while you can. Now dry those tears and go out and make Frank deliriously lustful. Which is what I intend to do to Philip.'

'Philip' asked Frieda in surprise. 'Phil Walthers?'

'Precisely, my dear. The one area in which my late, unlamented husband was proficient was in the bedroom. I might not be a svelte eighteen year-old, but, at our stage of life companionship and the odd bonk every other night are more important to us. Now go to, young lady, go to!'

Frieda watched the Wife of Bath bustle out. Mrs Blower – Cornelia – had a point. If fate so decreed she had only a little time left with Frank.

So why not enjoy it?

'Hand the camera to dear Mr Cromwell,' the Wife of Bath ordered Frank Capra. 'We are going to dance.'

Frieda returned to the main bar where the dancing was picking up tempo to find that her mother and Frank's mother had cornered Oliver Cromwell. He was trying to appear relaxed but she could see a hunted look in his eyes, the hunted look of a Puritan surrounded by Madame de Pompadour on one side and Miss Marple on the other, each with a hand on one of his arms.

'Ah, Frieda,' he said, relief flooding from his face, 'we were just discussing some of Frank's cases.'

'Yes, my dear,' said Madame de Pompadour. 'Hal here was just telling us the various measures he's looking at for ensuring the safety of his officers. After all, we don't want a repeat of that nasty business when Frank was hurt.'

'Frank really shouldn't associate with criminals,' said Miss Marple, 'but he's such a sociable boy he tends to get on with everyone.'

Ah, thought Frieda. Their mothers had been demanding – politely, no doubt – what he was doing to look after their respective son and son-in-law to be. It was the first time she had ever seen him look nervous.

'Where is Frank?' asked Madame de Pompadour, looking around, maintaining her grip on the captive Cromwell. 'He does look so elegant in that costume.'

'He's probably got himself entangled in a long conversation with someone,' Frieda said. 'Or someone challenged him to a game of snooker or something like that. I'll go find him.' She left quickly before either mother could say anything. Much as she liked and respected the Chief Inspector it was everyone for their selves as far as Madame de Pompadour and Miss Marple went.

To her dismay Frieda discovered that Frank had apparently disappeared. Two gorillas in the snooker room, in normal life constables Ken Edgars and Steve Right, denied having seen him.

'Maybe he's in the members-only bar, ma'am,' suggested Ken.

'Robin Hood's in there,' Steve offered, 'maybe Inspector Summers is having a word with him.'

'Robin Hood?' asked Frieda.

'Sergeant Phillips, ma'am.'

'Ah, yes, you're probably right, I'll have a look in there.'

After she had left Ken Edgars looked at Steve Right and sniggered.

'Unless the Wicked Witch has turned him into a frog,' he commented with some enjoyment.

Frieda hurried to the members-only bar. At the bar Marie Antoinette – Mrs Phillips – was chatting excitedly with a witch dressed in black – Sam Nightingale, in black boots, tight black trousers, black shirt, long black cape and what might have been a pointy hat had it not flopped down beside her long red hair. She looked like a witch for the modern era. Robin Hood was standing miserably next to his wife with the look of a man who wants to be somewhere else but doesn't dare leave. When Sam had walked in she had been wearing reflective sun glasses. They were on her witch's hat now, but he couldn't get rid of the memory of seeing his little reflection in them, as if he were a trapped little insect under her control.

'Hello, Sam, Pete, Mrs Phillips,' Frieda said, trying to give an outward appearance of unconcern. 'Having a good time?'

'Oh, yes,' Marie Antoinette said, 'it's great, Inspector. I don't think I've had this much fun in years. Sam here has been telling me what it's like to be a real witch, I didn't know there were such things.' Pete Phillips' face twitched.

'Of course we don't turn men into frogs or frogs into princes these days,' Sam said. 'Well, not very often,' she added with the giggle of a woman who has had a few drinks and is enjoying having a chat with another woman while winding up the sole male present.

'Frank's, er, costume is pretty good,' Pete Phillips put in, to change the conversation, tugging at the collar of his outfit.

'Yes,' said Frieda, 'he really put a lot of effort into it. Er, I don't suppose any of you has seen him recently?'

The others shook their heads.

'Last I saw him was in the main bar with you, Inspector,' Sam said.

'Yes, he's probably back there. Well, must carry on, make sure everyone is enjoying themselves, that sort of thing, see you later.'

'Oh, oh,' Sam said as they watched Frieda's skirts sweep out,

'I think she's lost him.'

'Lost him?' enquired Mrs Phillips.

'She looks flustered,' Sam explained. 'And Inspector Garold does not do flustered. She's the type who runs things with an iron fist. Apart from Inspector Summers, that is. He's the only one who can get away with anything. I wonder where he is.'

'Probably with his drinking buddies,' Mrs Phillips said. 'Men do that, you know.' She turned an accusing eye on her husband. 'I hope you haven't anything to do with it.'

'Me?' asked a wide-eyed Pete Phillips. 'How can I have anything to do with it? I've been standing right next to you all evening.'

'Hmmm,' Marie Antoinette replied slowly.

Frieda returned to the corridor where the gents was and waited until someone came out. It turned out to be Eric Johns, dressed as Friar Tuck.

'Frank isn't in there is he, Eric?' Frieda asked casually.

'No, ma'am, it's empty,' replied a puzzled Friar Tuck.

'Ah. You haven't seen him recently, have you, in the last ten minutes or so?'

'Last I saw him was in the main bar, Inspector. About half an hour ago.'

'Yes, he's probably back there. Thanks, Eric.' Friar Tuck scratched his head as Marie de Médicis headed off in the direction of the Blue Bliss's offices. He was pretty sure that they hadn't moved the main bar there recently.

Frieda checked all the offices, including anywhere where a Cardinal Richelieu might, for some strange reason, have fallen asleep. Frank might well have returned to the main bar, but if he hadn't Madame de Pompadour and Miss Marple would be extremely upset if Marie de Médicis returned without the Cardinal. Madame de Pompadour would almost certainly do something silly such as demanding that Oliver Cromwell begin an immediate search, just in case Frank had had another accident. That was the last thing Frieda needed. Having made doubly sure that none of the rooms contained any suggestion of Frank she hurried off to the last place she could think of that he might, for some impossible reason, be, the kitchen.

'Um, has anyone seen Cardinal Richelieu?' she asked a group of bemused waiters taking a ten minute break. They looked at each other blankly. 'He's wearing a long purple cape, almost maroon, boots, sword, goatee?'

'Ah,' said one waiter, 'you mean someone in fancy-dress. No, miss, no-one's been in here like that. This is the kitchen,' he added, just in case she'd mistaken it for something else.

'Yes, thank you. Never mind, I'm sure he'll be in the main bar.' She hurried back along the corridor until she found a spot where she could peek into the main bar without being seen. She scanned the area. There was a distinct lack of Cardinal Richelieu. Through the gaps between the dancers she could see that Madame de Pompadour and Miss Marple still had Oliver Cromwell captive.

'Something wrong, Frieda?' asked someone at her side. She turned to find Peter Pan – Tricia – holding Charlie Chaplin's – Jeremy's – hand.

'Frank's gone missing, Tricia. I've looked for him everywhere. Absolutely everywhere, including the kitchen. He's just disappeared.'

'Oh, I think he's out in the back garden,' Tricia replied airily. 'I saw him heading that way about twenty minutes ago. Getting a breath of fresh air, I expect.'

'Thanks, Tricia, you're an angel.' Frieda immediately turned and rushed towards the back garden.

'No I'm not, I'm Peter Pan,' Tricia said. She shrugged. 'You think I look like Peter Pan, don't you, Charlie.'

'Absolutely,' replied Charlie Chaplin with little enthusiasm. Tricia in the tight green outfit with long flowing blonde hair looked dead gorgeous. He just wasn't sure about her being called Peter.

Frieda opened the door to the back garden and saw Frank sitting on a swing, swigging at a bottle.

'Frank!' she cried, hurrying over to him, her skirts rustling along the lawn. 'I've been looking for you everywhere. What are you doing here?'

'Just getting some fresh air,' he replied, with just a suggestion of a beer too many. Frieda recognised the tone. It was one he used when he was withdrawing into himself, pushing the world, and her, away.

It was because she had pushed him away when he had tried to kiss her, she knew that. But he was over-reacting, after all it wasn't that big a deal, was it? She had to retain some propriety in her position, didn't she?

For a moment she was close to losing her temper. While she and Tricia had worn themselves out with getting every detail of the wedding just right, Frank had acted as if it were a mere bagatelle, as if he just had to click his fingers and it would be done. Now he was acting like a sulking schoolboy.

She thought of all the hard work she and Tricia had put in,

and Gertie, and Susan, who was obviously still hiding her feelings at Frank's rejection of her in favour of herself. It seemed to her that it was all the women who had to shoulder the burden while the men just stood around in the pub drinking.

It was that image that stopped her. While she and the others could exchange girlie gossip, fears and worries, she couldn't imagine Frank doing that with Pete Phillips or, god forbid, Eric Johns. The Chief Inspector, perhaps, but he had been monopolised by their mothers. And however much he might pretend to be unconcerned, even Frank must surely have his private fears and worries. And while he might not be a posturing, macho man, even he would be bound by the "boys don't cry" culture.

She looked at the elegant costume he had obviously gone to so much pain to organise, no doubt shrugging his shoulders at the time as if it were nothing.

And he had done it just for her.

Perhaps she should be giving her husband to be a little more TLC. After all, much as she loved him, he was still a man, and men got upset over the silliest little things, didn't they?

She lifted her skirts slightly and sat gently on his lap.

'I love you, my darling,' she said. 'I'm grateful that you took so much trouble. And you can kiss me as much as you like.'

Frank blinked.

'I can?'

'As much as you like my sweet.'

Frank did so. It was probably some minutes before they realised they had an audience.

'Oy, Romeo!' Frank called. 'Give us a push.'

Frieda nestled into his shoulder as Tom unwillingly obeyed orders, Susan watching and giggling. Cornelia was right. She was being absolutely silly. Letting all this nonsense about prophecies get to her. And she could hardly blame Frank for getting upset. Everyone was allowed to let their emotions get a little carried away.

In fact, if you thought about it, it would be a bad sign if Frank hadn't got a little upset sooner or later. It showed that he really did care.

She put the final prophecy out of her mind.

For a while she even managed to forget that Frank's father was arriving the following day.

### Friday: W-1: The Simple Solution: Just Disappear

Frieda watched in apprehension as the train pulled slowly in. The doors opened with a mechanical sigh.

'There he is,' said Frank, pulling her along, 'let's catch him before he disappears.'

'Before he disappears?' she asked, struggling to identify Frank's father and struggling not to fall over as Frank dragged her along.

'Bad habit of his,' Frank replied breathlessly. 'He's a bit absent-minded. Or at least he pretends to be.'

You're telling me that now? thought Frieda.

'Hi, dad,' Frank said as they pulled up in front of a man with greying hair looking at his suitcase as if unsure where it came from. If you saw a snapshot of him for a second you would swear afterwards that he was wearing glasses and a waistcoat and looked like a bemused Frank Sinatra.

'Frank, my boy!' the man exclaimed, throwing his arms open and giving Frank a hug. He then held himself at arm's length and peered at him. 'You are looking well, Frank, very well.'

He suddenly seemed to realise that Frieda was part of the party.

'Oh, dear,' he said, 'thoughtless of me. Your secretary, no doubt.'

Frieda bristled.

'No, dad, this is Frieda. My bride to be. Remember? Dad, allow me to introduce you to Frieda. Frieda, this is my dad, Professor Frank Summers.'

Frieda's knees went weak. Professor? Why hadn't Frank told her that his father was a professor? "Dad's a historian" did not equal "Dad's a professor". When she had been at university professors had been the equivalent of unapproachable Greek gods, and as intelligible. Suddenly she was about to marry the son of an unintelligible Greek god! And Frank hadn't even mentioned it!

She had a horrible feeling that he had, once, years before, before she had fallen in love with him, when it wasn't that important.

It was, now.

'How do you do?' she managed to say.

'Charmed, I'm sure,' replied the professor, looking anything but. And looking everywhere but at her, as if the sight were distasteful. He blinked several times and looked around, presumably surprised at having discovered that he was not, actually, on Mount Olympus and wondering where here was.

'Would you like me to carry your case for you?' asked Frieda, making a move towards the suitcase. Apart from the fact that Frank's father was an unintelligible Greek god, he also had a strangely vulnerable air about him. Normally she would have dismissed such a man as a harmless eccentric, but, after all, he was an unintelligible Greek god and Frank's father. She was more than willing to be his humble suitcase bearer.

'No, no, I am quite alright,' replied the professor, snatching at the item before she could get there. She winced and cursed herself. It had been exactly the wrong thing to do. Had the professor needed help it was up to his strong son to provide that help. All she had managed to do was imply that she thought the professor a feeble old man.

'Come on, dad,' said Frank, 'let's get you to my flat. You'll be staying there until the wedding's over.'

'Capital,' remarked the professor automatically. In a whisper he added, 'Will your, er, fiancée be staying with us?'

'No, she's looking after mum and her mum. Come on, let's get you to the flat.'

Frieda drove them back to Frank's flat in a less than happy mood. What she had feared had come true. While Frank tried to keep the atmosphere lively by asking his father questions, they were met by monosyllabic responses as he peered out of the window at the passing streets. It was quite clear the Frank's father totally disapproved of her.

'I'll take dad up to my flat,' Frank said when they arrived. 'You get back and assure our mums that everything is going according to plan.'

Whose plan? Frieda wanted to ask. And why wasn't she invited up to his flat?

Because it was obvious that his father did not think her worthy of his son. And Frank had realised that straight away. She cried on the way home. It wasn't going to happen. She knew it wasn't.

You're being silly, she told herself. You're nervous and you're over-reacting. Just because you made a few silly suggestions which could, if you really stretched the imagination, be called prophecies that came true. It's nonsense. Buck up and stop being a feeble-minded old woman.

She didn't need to look at the list on the napkin. She knew the last prophecy. Frank would just disappear. Along with his father, the professor.

### Friday Evening: Activating Mackerel

Your mother wants new curtains,' Frank's father told him, sipping a cup of tea in the kitchen of Frank's flat.

'And she wants you to go with her to choose them,' suggested Frank.

'Precisely, my boy. Or, to be more precise, I have already been taken around every available furnishing shop within a twenty-mile radius, and she has yet to find the pattern she wants.' He peered around the kitchen. 'Nice little flat you have. Just right for a bachelor. Just the sort of flat I always thought I would end up having before I met your mother.'

'Which I won't be, by this time tomorrow.'

'Doubt everything, my boy, as I've often told you. Doubt everything. Is that a kitten?' He got down on his hands and knees to inspect Squishy. Squishy looked back with a similar curiosity.

'That's Squish,' Frank said. 'She was in the car with us,

remember?'

'Ah, yes, of course, I was a little pre-occupied, I'm afraid. Hello, Squish,' the professor said, tickling her under her chin. 'She'll get them from John Lewis in the end. Or Marks. She always does. Who's a cute little kitten, then, Squish? And what do you want to be when you grow up?'

Frank smiled. It had taken him a long time to realise that his father's role-playing of the absent-minded academic had also been a means of allowing his son to grow up thinking for himself. Other fathers ordered their children, shouted at them, threatened them. His father had always treated him as a small version of a grown-up. He had just looked puzzled, scratched his head and asked, "Do you really think that's a good idea, Frank?" as if genuinely wishing to find out the answer.

That is, on the occasions when he hadn't said, "Well, why don't we have a go and find out, eh, Frank?"

'Frank was never intentionally naughty as a child,' said Frances Summers. 'But he did get into such terrible scrapes.'

'Frieda was never like that, were you, Free?' countered Katherine Garold. 'She was always top of her class – head prefect in her final year. The perfect student.'

The perfect student did not respond. She had an incredible urge to go out into the garden and light a joint. She could obtain the necessary ingredients from the evidence room at the station. At least it would get her out of the house.

'Oh, Frank was almost always top of his class – well, when he applied himself. But I can't imagine him ever being a prefect. I'm afraid responsibility isn't his forte.'

The perfect student wondered if turning up for her wedding with a couple of glasses of wine inside her, and a reefer in her hand, would be considered acceptable. It would certainly present the police officers at the wedding with a dilemma. Should they arrest her, pretend it wasn't happening, or join in?

Join in, she decided.

'He was always disappearing on important occasions. But then I blame his father for that. You know, there was one time when we were on holiday, staying with some friends along the coast. We'd arranged to go to a recital at eight, with dinner before at a highly recommended restaurant. Frank and his father had gone for a walk along the beach in the afternoon. When it got to six o'clock I began worrying. In the end they got back about ten in the evening. Extremely embarrassing.'

'My goodness. What happened?'

'Typical of his father. Neither of them had ever been fishing, so they decided to have a go, as they put it. Frank was always trying anything and everything, I think he believed there was nothing he couldn't do if he tried. And his father looks at everything as some form of academic exercise. Anyway, they found a couple of poles, bought some string and hooks, and borrowed a boat lying on the shore. Of course they didn't have the first idea. The coast guard rescued them three miles out at sea.'

'Heavens! That sounds extremely dangerous.'

'Oh, that wasn't the worst by any manner of means.'

As Frances Summers began a recital of Frank's, and his father's, ability to disappear into thin air the perfect student closed her eyes. Please let this be over, she prayed. Please let this be over and I'll believe in anything you want me to.


'Right,' said Frank, emptying his pockets. 'Wallet. I'd better have that with me tomorrow. Just in case.'

'You must buy something as soon as you are married,' his father said, on his hands and knees, dragging a piece of string for Squishy to attack.

'Why's that, Dad?'

'Apparently whoever buys the first thing ends up controlling the finances. Superstitious nonsense, of course. Though I wish I'd listened to it when I married your mother.'

'In that case I think I'll let Frieda do that. I'm no good with money. What's this? Ah, a curtain ring from one of my cases.' His father stood up and peered at the object in its plastic wallet.

'That's not a curtain ring,' he said. 'Believe me, Frank, I've seen all sorts of curtain rings in the past couple of months, and that isn't one.'

'What would you say it is, then?'

'You know, it rather reminds me of an artefact I saw on a television programme the other day. Roman, I think they claimed it was. I wasn't paying much attention, these television people come up with the most absurd conclusions. Anyway, it was a lamp of sorts, in a bowl, hanging by three chains, with a ring at the top linking the three chains. Very similar to this. You can see the markings where the chains have dragged. That wouldn't happen with a curtain ring. A curtain ring would only have one indent. You can see your ring is scarred in – hmm, could be three places. Three somethings, possibly four.'

Frank looked at him.

'Or perhaps a ring on a thurible?' he suggested.

'A censer? Possibly. A thurible – or censer – normally has a ring rather like this holding the chains together. Four chains. The priest would push it down to hold the lid of the bowl in place.'

'And the lid would have perforations in it to allow the smoke out. And if you swung it around it would make a whirring noise. And they're normally brass. If you swung it across someone's face very quickly it would leave the impression of a bright light having just passed.' He nodded as another thought struck home. 'And if someone is dressed in black they could just be mistaken for a vicar from behind.'

'If you say so, my boy. Not a new game, is it? Some new television show?'

'Not quite. Dad, I need to pop out for a short while. Could you look after Squishy for me?'

'But of course, my boy. Police work, is it?'

'Partly. I'll be back in an hour or so. There's one last loose end I need to tie up.'

Frank opened his front door to find his neighbour Mrs Jones on her doorstep.

'Hello, Mrs Jones,' he said, recognising in the woman's face the hope of spending an enjoyable half hour safely complaining of the dangers of living in the modern world. 'I'd love to stay and chat, but I have to go out. I might be gone some time,' he added over his shoulder as he tripped down the stairs, gammy leg forgotten.

'And then there was the time the circus ran away with Frank, as I like to put it,' Frances Summers said.

'You mean he ran away with the circus?'

'Oh, no, that would be what a normal boy would do. No, Frank was certain that the fortune teller had rigged up her caravan to produce special effects for séances and the like. Heaven knows. So, being Frank, he hid himself in the caravan. Again, being Frank, he hadn't noticed that it was their last day, and that they were leaving that evening. So there he was, stuck in the caravan, and, of course, keeping hidden in case someone discovered him. He managed to get out when they stopped about a hundred miles away, and then he hitched a lift back home. I can't tell you how furious I was with him.'

I can feel your pain, thought the perfect student as she inhaled an imaginary spliff.

'Of course he didn't understand why I was so cross. And his father was never much help, all he wanted to know was whether or not Frank had found anything in the caravan.'

She sighed.

'But you could never stay angry with Frank for long.'

'I can well imagine,' replied Katherine Garold.

I can't, thought the perfect student.

Pete Phillips was about to knock on Frank's door when Frank's neighbour came up the stairs.

'He's not in,' said Mrs Jones.

'Not in?'

'He said he was going away for a few days. I passed him as I was going out to get some milk.'

'A few days?'

'Said he was taking a holiday,' the woman continued, making up a conversation that had never occurred, apart from in her fertile imagination. 'He confides in me, you know. He certainly needs a holiday. He works so hard, you know. But what with the state of things these days, it's hardly any wonder, is it? Why, only the other day I read in the newspaper about that man who had broken into over three hundred houses in less than two years.'

'Er, let me get this straight,' Pete said, blinking at the flow. 'You say Frank – Inspector Summers – has gone away?'

'Oh, yes, I saw him go. He was quite definite about it. Cornwall, I think he said. Or was it Portugal? They sound so similar, don't they? Though anywhere these days is dangerous. I was speaking to someone I know only yesterday – '

'Are you sure he's gone away?' Pete interrupted desperately.

'Quite sure, young man. Why shouldn't he go away? He does need a good holiday. And I could see he was under such pressure from that Inspector of his, the woman Inspector. You know, they're quite often the worst, these so-called –'

'Thanks,' Pete replied, going down the stairs two at a time. As he ran to his car he pulled his mobile phone from his pocket. He knew all about these "so-called – ". Right then he could see her face. And she wasn't smiling. 'Hello, Inspector Hanson? I think we might have a little problem on our hands.'

Behind him Mrs Jones scratched her head. Now why had that strange man referred to Sergeant Summers as "Inspector

Summers"?

She would ask Sergeant Summers when he came back from holiday. When he was rested.

Frank smiled as he entered the vestry. The vicar sat at a desk, writing out notes. His wife sat next to him, sewing a hem on a piece of brightly-coloured material.

'Evening vicar, Mrs Cringely.'

'Good evening, Inspector,' the vicar said, a broad smile on his face. 'Say hello to the Inspector, my dear.'

'Evening,' she muttered, her head down.

'I think you know why I'm here, don't you, Mrs Cringely?'

She failed to respond.

'You were the one who clobbered me with a thurible last Saturday, weren't you?'

'I thought you were him coming back from the pub,' she muttered. 'I didn't mean to hit you, you just stopped so suddenly.'

'What you meant to do is irrelevant. Let's see, an assault on a police officer. Leaving the scene of a crime. And all the other times you were chasing the vicar with a thurible – the time you almost hit Harold Godbeer. Kevin Morton. Oh, yes, I could throw the book at you.'

'I did warn her,' the vicar said, obviously enjoying himself. 'Thirty years, I told her, that's what you get for attacking a police officer in this country. Not to mention the shame and disgrace. The tabloids would have a field day. I can see the headlines now.'

'I'm sorry, I told you, I never meant it,' she repeated, still looking down. Frank guessed that the vicar had finally found a way to control her, and had grasped it with both hands.

'Normally I'd arrest you on the spot,' he said. 'Fortunately for you I have something more important to do at the moment. I'm getting married tomorrow. If I arrested you I'd have to take the vicar down the station for a statement, and that could throw a spanner in the works. So I'm going to let you off on the proviso that you make damn sure that everything runs like clockwork. Nothing is going to interfere with tomorrow, understand? Nothing. Got it?'

'You aren't going to arrest her?' asked the vicar.

'So long as there aren't any more problems, and so long as it never happens again. I've had enough of this ghost nonsense. And you aren't going to put a spanner into the works either, vicar, understand?'

'There won't be any problems,' she assured him. She looked up at him. 'How did you know it was me?'

He smiled.

'I'd like to see that famous thurible if you don't mind.'

'It's in the cupboard,' she said, standing up, putting down the material she was working on. She opened the cupboard and took the thurible out.

'You see,' he said, taking it from her, 'thuribles have this ring that holds the chains together.'

He paused. The thurible had a ring where one should be missing.

Mrs Cringely sat down, dislodging her work. A number of curtain rings fell onto the floor.

At Frank's flat Professor Summers sat on the lounge carpet playing football with Squishy.

'This is fun, isn't it, Squishy?' he asked. 'But I think we both need something to drink. Some milk for you and something cold for me. Let's see what Frank has in his fridge.'

Squishy followed him to the kitchen.

'My goodness,' he said, peering into the fridge. 'He has stocked up well on beer. You know, Mrs Summers hardly ever lets me drink beer. She claims wine is far healthier.'

He pursed his lips.

'It's not quite the same as a good old-fashioned pint, but ... You won't tell Mrs Summers, will you Squishy? And look, there's some kitty tuna for you.'

Squishy miaowed as if to say a saucer of kitty tuna would buy her silence very nicely.


'We're going to have to act fast,' Percy Hanson said. 'If we're lucky Frank won't have got out of Wellbury yet. We can stop him before he leaves.'

'How are we going to do that?' asked a desperate Pete Phillips.

'The Mackerel Plan.'

Pete gasped at the idea.

'But that's for extreme emergencies. Terrorism. Assassinations. International plots. Disasters.'

'Pete, think of it this way. Frank is your responsibility. If he isn't at the altar tomorrow you won't live very long. Now personally I think I would consider that an emergency, don't you?'

Pete Phillips had to admit that Percy had somewhat of a point.

'But even if we find him – we can't take him to the altar in handcuffs.'

'Yes we can, Pete. That is one thing we can do. We might not be able to argue him into doing the right thing, but we can hand him to Frieda as a ritual sacrifice. To save you being the ritual sacrifice.'

He picked up his police radio.

'Inspector Hanson to Control, come in Control.'

'Control here, Inspector, over.'

'Bobby, activate the Mackerel Plan. Immediately.'

There was a pause.

'Repeat, please.'

'I said, activate the Mackerel Plan, Bobby. Now.'

'Er, right, Inspector. Um, who is it we're looking for?'

'Someone known as Inspector Frank Summers. He's gone AWOL.'

Bobby paused for less than a second. If Inspector Frank Summers had done a runner then Inspector Frieda Garold would be furious, to say the least. And if Inspector Frieda Garold was furious, everyone else at the station would share in her pain.


'All thuribles have a ring like that as far as I know,' said the vicar. 'Is that relevant?'

'Ah, no, I just wanted to confirm something I heard the other day, er, something about how thuribles worked. Right, yes, good, so that's all clear then. Wedding tomorrow, no problems, and no more running around the cemetery. Okay?'

'You haven't answered my wife's question, Inspector. How did you work out that she was the one responsible?'

Frank smiled knowingly. Rather feebly, but knowingly.

Remember, he told himself, there is only one important thing at the moment. What people think is irrelevant. It's what they believe is important. After tomorrow they can think whatever the hell they want to.

There was going to be a wedding tomorrow, even if he had to raid the armoury and take people there at gunpoint. Including the vicar. Perhaps especially the vicar.


'You know what, Squishy,' Professor Summers said, having finished a second beer, 'I'm feeling a little peckish. What say we order a pizza? That's another thing Mrs Summers never allows me. You won't tell, will you? I'm sure Frank will have the number of the local pizza place, his mother is always complaining about him living on take-aways. They do that, mothers.'

Squishy watched as he riffled through the papers on the coffee table, finding the one he wanted.

'Here we go. Now, how does this phone work? One of these strange modern ones. Mobile phones, I believe they're called.' He sighed. 'I really do not understand this strange modern urge to be in contact the whole time. I'd never get any work done if I had one of these things.'

Squishy looked on in interest as Professor Summers studied Frank's police radio with some bemusement.

'I'm just going to check the radio quickly,' Frieda said to her mother and Mrs Summers.

'Your police radio? Darling, you work too hard. Tomorrow's your wedding day. You should be thinking of that, not about work.'

'I think Frieda is trying not to think of tomorrow,' Frances Summers said, smiling at Frieda. 'Everything's ready, there's nothing left to do but worry. I think having something else to do is probably a good thing.'

'I'll only be away a few minutes,' Frieda said, smiling her thanks at Frances Summers for her understanding. In her bedroom she lay down on her bed and stretched her neck muscles. Apart from giving her something to do checking the radio gave her an excuse to be on her own for a few minutes.

She switched the radio on.

'Cape Cod to Red Herring, come in, over,' Bobby Stang was saying.

'Red Herring to Cape Cod, over,' came Percy Hanson's voice.

'The trawlers are in position, Red Herring, over.'

Frieda sat up, staring at the radio. Someone, she realised, had activated the Mackerel Plan. Without telling her. She leaned over for her briefcase to find out what her code name was.

Tiger Shark.

Tiger Shark?

Well, really.

'Tiger Shark to Red Herring, over,' Frieda called over her radio.

There was a pause before Percy replied.

'Red Herring to Tiger Shark, come in.'

'What's going on, Per – er, Red Herring? Why has Mackerel been activated, and why wasn't I told? Over.'

'Ah, er, the thing is, um, you see, well … er, it's a trial run, that's it, Tiger Shark, a sort of practice, you could say. An impromptu one, as it were. Over.'

'An impromptu practice run, Red Herring?'

'Yes. We thought it best not to disturb you.'

Frieda smiled. Typical Percy. Like a little boy with a new train set.

'I see. Well, have fun, Red Herring. Out.'

She looked at the radio and shook her head.

'Cape Cod to trawlerman one. Come in, Piranha,' she heard the radio say.

'Piranha here, over,' came Sam Nightingale's voice.

'Any sign of Swordfish, over?'

'Negative, Cape Cod.'

Frieda switched her radio off. She had no urge to listen to various varieties of fish reporting in. She lay back and decided to have a five minute snooze, wondering who was code-named Swordfish, which poor constable was playing the part of the fleeing suspect.

Silly nonsense.


'Trade secret, I'm afraid, vicar,' Frank said, putting the thurible down. 'I'll see you tomorrow.' He left quickly before they could say anything else.

'What did he mean, "all the other times"?' asked Mrs

Cringely. 'It was only once.'

'I don't know, my dear. He appears to think that you are the source of all these ghost stories. If I were you I wouldn't ask any questions. You're very lucky not to be in prison.'

He stood up.

'And now, my dear, I am going down to the pub. Whether you like it or not it's an ancient English tradition, so you're just going to have to get used to it.'

She scowled at him.

'Thirty years, my dear, thirty years. And you wouldn't like the porridge.' He paused. 'You know there was a politician who claimed he used to be able to drink eight pints at a sitting. I might see what that feels like.'


'Ah, here we go, Squishy,' Professor Summers said, pressing a button on Frank's radio.

'Red Herring to Halibut, come in, Halibut, over.'

'Halibut here, Red Herring, over.'

'Anything to report, over.'

'Cars are backing up, Red Herring.'

'My goodness, Squishy, we seem to have a crossed line,' Professor Summers said, pressing another button. 'I didn't know you could still get them.'

The radio fell silent for a few seconds.

'Identify yourself, the person who spoke last,' Red Herring ordered.

Professor Summers looked at the radio in astonishment.

'Er, do you mean me?' he asked. 'Er, over?'

'Yes, you. Identify yourself.'

'Well, I'm Frank Summers, if you really need to know.'

'Swordfish? Where the hell are you, Swordfish?'

'Swordfish?'

'Stop pissing around, Swordfish, where are you? Over?'

'Well, there's no need to be rude. Really,' Professor Summers said, switching off the radio. 'People can be terribly rude these days, Squishy. I think you should be covering your ears, don't you?'

Squishy's ears remained solidly at attention. This was much more fun than attacking string.

And all those names of fish ...


Constable Ken Edgars held up a hand to stop a small, pop-popping delivery motorbike coming towards him, ridden by a gangly youth with his head crouched down almost at the level of his knees, a black half-face helmet on his head which might just once have been a horse rider's helmet, a tattered black plastic raincoat streaming behind.

'Why are you stopping that?' asked his colleague Steve Right. 'That's coming into town. We're looking for something going out of town.'

'Ah, it could be a double-bluff. Maybe Swordfish has got out and is coming back in.'

'Yeah, right.'

'Anyway, I'm bored. Everyone else is complaining about traffic backing up, and we get this poxy back lane with about a car every hour.'

The motorcyclist brought his machine to a halt in front of

them. His long legs spread out in front of him, and he looked nervously at them through thick goggles. With his thin caved-in cheeks and goggle eyes it was difficult to tell where the goggle eyes ended and the goggles began. He was of the age when a sudden spurt of growth had got bored with waiting for the nutrition to fill the body out. The only difference between him and a skeleton was a covering of skin.

'We're looking for a swordfish,' Ken said. Steve sniggered behind him. 'What's in the back?'

'You polis?' asked the rider.

'Yeah, mate, we polis. We'd like to know what you've got in that box behind you.'

'Polis?' asked the youth again. 'No problem. Licence is okay. Is good licence.'

'I'm sure it's a lovely licence, mate, we still want to have a look in your delivery box.'

'He can hardly be hiding the Inspector in there, Ken,' pointed out Steve Right. 'Anyway, I think he must be one of those East European blokes come over here to find some work.'

'Polish?'

'Polska,' agreed the youth, grinning insanely, his white teeth an advert for toothpaste, his face an advert for simplicity. 'Polska.'

'Great, all we need, a Polish idiot who can't speak English. Open the box,' Ken said loudly, pointing at the white box and miming the actions. The driver shrugged his shoulders, scratched his helmet, and turned and opened the box. Ken switched his torch on and he and Steve peered in.

'Some sort of plants,' Ken noted. 'Who the hell rides around at this time of night delivering plants?' He looked up at the rider. 'Where you go with these plants?' he asked loudly.

The driver shrugged again. He took a piece of paper from one of the raincoat pockets and handed it to Ken.

'Nussry,' he said.

'Old Merrick Nursery,' Ken read. 'Bit late to be delivering stuff to the nursery, innit?'

The rider grinned and shrugged again, either because the time was not his concern or because he hadn't the faintest clue what the police officer was saying.

'Okay, my Polish friend, you get on then,' Ken said, returning the piece of paper.

'Is okay?'

'Is bloody marvellous, mate. Go on, get on with you.'

A wave of Ken's hand convinced the rider that Ken was dismissing him. He gave them a final insane grin before pop-popping off into the night.

'Poor bugger,' said Steve. 'Having to make a delivery this time of night. Bet you he gets paid peanuts, too. They get these foreign workers over, pay them nothing, and treat them like rubbish. And that one looked a bit simple, too.'

'Tell you what, though, I wouldn't pay peanuts for those plants. Looked like weeds to me.'

'They did, didn't they?'

There was a silence.

'Steve, you thinking what I'm thinking?'

'You mean, as in, weedy-looking plants, and, shall we say, something called cannabis?'

'That is, sort of, roughly, in the direction my thoughts were, kind of, moving, as it were.'

'And remember what Inspector Summers saying about how they used illegal Koreans?'

'He wasn't Korean, he was Polish.'

'How do you know? He was foreign, wasn't he? He was probably just pretending to be Polish.'

'Oh, bloody hell!' exclaimed Ken, racing for the car. 'If old Percy founds out we've let him through we'll be dead meat. Come on, we can still catch him.'

Frieda gave up trying to get a few minutes' snooze. She picked up the notes marked "Mackerel – Top Secret". She flipped through the code names.

A puzzled look came into her eyes. Swordfish was Frank.

What was Frank doing taking part in an impromptu test run of Mackerel the night before his wedding? She reached for her radio and switched it back on.

'Red Herring to Cape Cod,' the radio said, 'the next time Swordfish uses his radio try to get a fix on its position.'

'Roger, Red Herring.'

'Tiger Shark to Red Herring, over.'

There was a slight pause.

'Red Herring here, Tiger Shark. Shouldn't you be getting some rest?'

'What is Frank doing taking part in the operation, Percy?'

'Tiger Shark please remember security. Use the correct call signs.'

Frieda glared at the radio.

'Very well, Red Herring, just answer my question. What is the hell is Fr – Swordfish doing gallivanting around town tonight?'

'Er, well the thing is … Kipper, come in, Kipper.'

'Kipper here, over,' said a very reluctant Pete Phillips.

'Perhaps you could answer the question, Kipper.'

'Do I have to?'

'I think it would be a good idea.'

'Pete – Kipper, what is going on?' asked Frieda.

'Er, well, the thing is, Ins – er, Tiger Shark, well, um, how can I put this … '

'Piranha to Tiger Shark, over.'

'Yes, Sam – Piranha?'

'Swordfish wanted some distraction, so we thought this one up.'

'Ah, I see. That makes sense. Just don't keep him up too late.'

'We won't, Tiger Shark.'

'See you all tomorrow, out,' said Frieda. She switched the radio off, a relieved smile on her lips. Frank had probably agreed to it to give his father an idea of his work. And what a good idea it was. Perhaps if he understood their work better he might feel more fondly towards his daughter-in-law.


'Tiger Shark, come in Tiger Shark, over.'

There was no response.

'No, I think she's gone. Phew, that was close. I owe you a pint, Piranha.'

'Make it a double gin-and-tonic, Kipper,' said Sam Nightingale.

'Okay, that's enough, now,' said Red Herring. 'If we don't find Swordfish we'll need more than a double gin and tonic.'

'Turbot to Red Herring, Turbot to Red Herring, over.'

'Come in, Turbot, over.'

'Red Herring, we're pursuing a motorbike believed to be carrying – Steve, what's the code for cannabis?'

'Just a second – here it is. Whitebait.'

'A motorbike believed to be carrying whitebait.'

Percy Hanson closed his eyes. If they really, really had to discover the cannabis gang at this particular moment, could they not use the code properly and not announce it in clear? He sighed.

'Report your position, Turbot, I'll get someone to cut him off.'


The rider of the pop-popping motorbike smiled toothfully as he turned into the sunken old dirt road between the cemetery and the allotments. Steve Right had been accurate in his assessment that the youth was somewhat simple-minded. The youth's employer had taken a while to realise it, thinking that it was a problem of communication, that the boy had yet to learn to speak English. By the time he had realised that the boy was not of the brightest he had also realised another thing: the boy might be simple, but he was a genius at finding a place on a map. Unlike some other delivery drivers the employer had taken on, who couldn't find Nelson's column if they were leaning against it, the boy only had to be shown an address, the spot pointed out on a map, and it was as good as delivered. Not only that, he was more than happy with the little motorbike, with his low wage, and he also seemed to use less petrol than anyone else.

In truth the boy was happy. He had no urge to ride some monster motorbike. His was the type to make schoolchildren laugh at him – especially when he passed, pop-popping with his head almost between his knees and his old raincoat trailing behind – and then wave when he became a familiar sight. Schoolchildren might admire big men on powerful monster motorbikes, but they never waved at them and laughed with them.

But otherwise there was not much fun in his job, so he invented some when he found the chance. Such as this short cut. Over the months he had almost perfected the art of speeding up just enough to allow him to put the little bike into neutral and coast almost the entire length, holding the handles tightly as the wheels bucked from pothole to pothole. To increase the excitement he did most of it without lights. In the beginning he had to switch them on and off a couple of times on the darker nights, but by now he knew the track almost blindfold.

The one time he had got to the end and scared the daylights out of someone walking their dog, not expecting a ghostlike flying raincoat to suddenly shoot out. He wondered if that would happen again tonight. It would be fun.


'He's bloody disappeared,' said Ken Edgar.

'Can't have,' replied Steve Right. 'He must have turned somewhere.'

'Hey, there's an old track between the cemetery and the allotments – I'll bet that's where he's gone.'

'Won't be able to go very fast on that. Let's get around the other side. We'll block off the exit. Like a cork in a bottle. We'll have him before he knows it.'


'Hi, dad,' Frank said, coming into the lounge. 'Sorry I was gone so long. Have you had anything to eat?'

'Well, I tried to order a pizza, but I'm afraid I couldn't get the hang of your mobile phone here,' his father replied, tickling a delighted Squishy's stomach while ignoring a programme on the television. Frank chuckled.

'That's not a mobile phone, dad, that's a police radio.'

'Ah. I wondered why they were speaking in some form of code.'

'Code?' asked Frank, picking up the pizzeria leaflet. 'What do you fancy, dad? I normally get the extra large with pepperoni and olives.'

'I'll have pepperoni and extra cheese without the olives. They were using names of fish. Red Herring, Halibut, that sort of thing.'

Frank shook his head in wonderment.

'Daft sods. It's a top secret plan. Percy – Inspector Hanson – was probably doing a dry run.'

'Whoever it was was incredibly rude.'

'Were they, now?'

'Told me – and I quote, naturally – to "stop pissing around". Really, language like that from what should be responsible adults? Tsk, tsk.'

'I agree, dad. Especially since they are supposed to be police officers,' Frank replied with his tongue in his cheek. He picked up his radio and pressed the on-switch.

'Cape Cod to Sprat, over,' Control was saying.

'Sprat here, over.'

'Report on situation, over.'

'Things are calming down, Cape Cod. Traffic's much lighter. Over.'

'Hey,' said Frank into his radio, putting on a breathless voice, 'two parrots are sitting on a perch. One says, can you smell fish?'

There was a silence.

'Swordfish?' asked an anxious Kipper.

'You lot are barking mad,' Frank said. 'Why don't you give up, go home and get some sleep.'

He switched the radio off and dropped it onto the coffee table.

'That should confuse them for a while. Right, now for the important stuff. A beer and a pizza.'

'Your mother never lets me have take-away pizza,' his father said mournfully. 'I don't want to alarm you, my boy, but I rather fancy that your Frieda won't allow you to have any either.'

'Dad, I will have a take-away pizza whenever I want one.'

'That's what I thought when I married your mother. Not pizza in those days, fish and chips, wrapped in newspaper.'

'I'll train her, dad. Frieda, I mean.'

'She's a very forceful looking woman, isn't she? Very

attractive, but very forceful.'

'She's a softie, dad.'

'So was your mother, my boy, so was your mother.'


'Cape Cod, did you get a direction on that call?' asked Percy.

'Negative, Red Herring. Too short.'

'Bugger's laughing at us,' said Pete Phillips. 'Did you hear what he said? We might as well pack up and go home, because we'll never find him.'

'We'll carry on for another hour,' decided Percy. 'If we haven't found him by then we'll give it up and start again at first light. Cape Cod, keep trying Swordfish's radio every fifteen minutes. Maybe we can irritate him into revealing his position.

'Um, Turbot to Red Herring, over,' came Ken Edgar's voice.

'Come in, Turbot. Have you caught that motorbike? Over.'

'Um, sort of, Red Herring. Well, it crashed, anyway.'

'Ah, so there is some good news.'

'Not as such, Red Herring.'

'Not as such?'

'Well, he sort of, er, crashed into our patrol car.'

'Well, at least you caught him.'

'Er, there's a little problem with that, just a little hitch, you might say.'

'A little problem?'

'Apparently it was sage plants in the box.'

Percy Hanson took a deep breath.

'Sage plants? Turbot, how can you not tell the difference between cannabis and sage plants?'

'I grew up in the city, sir.'

'Wish you'd bloody stayed there,' muttered Percy Hanson to himself. Then he sighed. 'Okay, Pete, let's call it a night. We'll start again first thing in the morning.'

Pete Phillips did not quite agree with giving up. But he couldn't think of anything else he could do that would make a difference. All he knew was that the sun was going to rise in a few hours, and that if he couldn't find Frank he was going to be in many people's bad books. He wasn't too worried about what Frieda would say. All she would be able to do was to walk over whatever remains his own wife left. She was very particular about weddings, his wife was.

And she seemed to have a perverse enjoyment of funerals.

He had never been a hundred-percent convinced of the power of Sam Nightingale's prophecy. But now he was. And now he had to do something to prevent it coming true. But he didn't know what.

## Saturday: W-Day?

It was noon. The sun was shining. It was a heavenly summer day tinged with autumnal tints. Most Wellburians had finished their weekly domestic chores and shopping, and were settling down to an old-fashioned Saturday afternoon of relaxing in the garden, watching sport on the telly, going for a ramble along the river, or sitting in the pub garden catching up with the newspaper. Most of them.

'We can't just drive around all day,' Percy Hanson said. 'Apart from the fact that we keep getting strange looks from people

– which is understandable, I'd be suspicious of two men dressed for a wedding cruising the streets – we'll have to tell Frieda at some stage.'

"We" meaning me, Pete Phillips thought to himself.

'Better leave it until the latest,' he said. 'We might still be lucky and find him. He's got to be somewhere.'

Someone else was also feeling sorry for himself. In the vicarage at St Mary's Vicar Cringely was sucking on his fifth aspirin of the day and earnestly praying for the Good Lord to smite his wife with something, anything, anything that might stop her banging pots and pans around, a noise that was rapidly driving him insane. That bloody politician must have been lying about the eight pints.

'I'm going to have to call it off,' he moaned, 'I've come down with a bad case of twenty-four hour flu.'

'The wages of sin are death,' boomed his wife with great pleasure. 'Woe unto him who falls under the power of the devil's drink.'

She smacked another empty pot onto the heavy stove just in case he had missed her point.


'Oh, darling, you look gorgeous!' exclaimed Katherine Garold, looking at Frieda checking her appearance in a mirror.

Frieda smiled. She had woken up to sunshine, butterflies in her stomach. She had managed a little breakfast. As the day wore on without any bad news she had become more and more optimistic. Now there was not long to go. She could barely believe that it was actually going to happen.

And, while she wouldn't have said so publicly, she thought she looked pretty good in the ivory wedding dress.

'What's wrong, Gertie?' she asked. 'You've been looking miserable ever since you got here.'

Gertie looked down at the floor.

'They've lost Frank,' she said.

'They've what?'

'They've lost Frank. That's what the Mackerel thing was about last night. They were trying to find him.'

'How do you mean lost?'

'Pete Phillips went around to his flat last night. He says Frank's done a runner. I don't believe him.'

Frieda sat down abruptly.

'Careful, my dear, you'll crease the train,' her mother said.

'Oh, rubbermats to the train! Who cares about the train? I knew this would happen. I knew he'd get out of it. I knew it.'

She detached the train and flung it on the floor.

'He will not get out of it,' Frances Summers said with some force. 'I will not allow my son to jilt you at the altar.'

'He won't jilt me at the altar. I'm not going anywhere near the altar unless he's there already.'

Tricia looked at her and bit her nails. She knew it was a result of Frieda putting everything on when she had had the last fitting. But she wasn't going to say so.


'Well, well, my boy, we do look a pair, don't we?' asked Professor Summers. 'A long time since I wore top hat and tails. Or had a good fry-up for breakfast.'

They had had a late breakfast consisting of everything Frank could think of to fry – eggs, bacon, sausages, mushrooms, tomatoes with side helpings of baked beans and butter-drenched toast – based on the theory that they weren't likely to have lunch, and needed something which would sustain them until at least the evening.

'I wonder where Pete Phillips has got to,' Frank said, checking his watch. 'He should have been here an hour ago.'

'Have you tried calling him?'

'Three times. I left a message on his mobile answering service.'

'Does he have the rings?'

'No, I've got them. He's a good bloke, but I didn't want to give him the chance to wind me up by pretending to have lost it. Not today.'

'Well, shall we be on our way? You have the rings, now all you need is the bride.'

'That is something. At least Frieda will be on time. Pete will just have to turn up when he turns up. If he doesn't you can be best man.'

'If she's like your mother, it will be the first and last time she'll be on time, ever. Either early or late, no compromise.'

'Dad, you can be cynical at times, you know. Come on, Squish, hop into your jacket pocket, you're going to a wedding today.'


'I don't suppose you've tried calling him?' asked Percy Hanson.

'He doesn't have a mobile.'

'Well, try his landline.'

'What for? His landline goes to his flat, and we know he isn't there.'

'Oh, for God's sake, Pete, at least try. After all, you have nothing to lose apart from your life.'

Pete reluctantly took his mobile phone out. He looked at it and shook it.

'That's all I need. The bloody battery's gone dead. I forgot to recharge it overnight.'

He looked at Percy.

'Er, could I borrow yours, sir?'

'My mobile phone? I don't have it on me. Bad manners to take a mobile phone to a wedding, didn't you know that? The Chief Inspector said so only last week.'

'What bloody wedding?' asked Pete Phillips morosely. 'It's going to be a funeral. Mine. Bloody Frank.' His head sank against the steering wheel. 'Never again,' he muttered, 'never again will I be a best man.'

'You haven't been particularly good at this one,' Percy replied without any sympathy.


'He'll just disappear,' Frieda said, reading the last prophecy. 'I was right, he has just disappeared.'

'Oh, don't be silly, darling,' wailed her mother. 'Now stand up and we'll get the creases out of your dress. It's almost time to leave for the church.'

'I am not going to the church. Not until I have proof that that – man – is standing in front of the altar waiting for me. If he wants to get divorced two seconds later, fine, I'll agree. But he is not going to humiliate me like this. I am not going to the church, and that's final.'

'Darling, the chauffeur's waiting outside.'

'Let him wait. Send him away if you want. I'm not going.'

Gertie slipped out of the room into the passageway and took out her radio.

'Sergeant Phillips? Have you found Frank?'

'No, Gertie,' Pete Phillips replied in a tired voice. 'He's probably miles away by now.'

'Okay, Sarge, out.'

Gertie switched her radio off and leant against the wall, looking up at the ceiling. She was convinced that Pete Phillips was wrong. Frank would never just up and leave like that. But it did feel as if the fates were somehow conspiring against them.


'Let's go around to his flat,' said Percy Hanson. 'This could all be just something trivial, some silly misunderstanding.'

'I suppose we might as well,' replied Pete Phillips. 'I can't see it making a difference, though. You can't fight fate.'

Percy did not reply. He did not believe in such things as omens or fate. But he did know that when things are not meant to be, they are not meant to be.


'I can't believe Frank would do that,' Susan said, coming up next to Gertie. 'I'm sure it's all a big mistake.'

'I agree. I think we should get Frieda to the church on time and just see what happens, leave the rest in the laps of the gods of love, as it were.'

'But how?'

'What about operation Mackerel?'

'Operation Mackerel?'

'It's a plan designed to cope with an emergency. If we can get someone to put Frieda in charge she won't have time to get changed. All we have to do is get her to St Mary's. Tell her that it's going to be the control room.'

'There's only one person Frieda would listen to – apart from Frank.'

The doorbell rang.

'And I think he's just arrived.

The Chief Inspector wasn't quite expecting to be dragged into the lounge by the bridesmaids, with the door firmly closed behind them.

'You have to activate Operation Mackerel,' Gertie told him.

'It's an emergency,' Susan put in.

'Frieda's refusing to go to the church.'

'She thinks Frank's done a runner.'

'But we're sure he hasn't.'

'And we have to get her to the church on time.'

'She mustn't know you're here.'

'You'll have to slip out into the garden.'

'You can borrow my radio.'

'There's a bush you can hide behind.'

The Chief Inspector looked from one to the other.

'I rather think you're right,' he said. 'Just one question – what is Operation Mackerel?'

'Bugger,' said Frank, 'just what we don't need, a traffic accident.'

The road ahead was completely blocked by a jack-knifed lorry and trailer. There was only a small gap between the cab and a front wall, far too small to let a car through. A traffic jam was building up nicely, with even the side roads beginning to clog up.

'You do seem to lead an interesting life,' his father said. 'When your mother and I were married everything went off without a hitch.'

A traffic officer was contemplating the scene, his motor-bike to one side, apparently awaiting reinforcements and a very large crane. He turned around, looked at them and came over.

'Geoff!' said Frank with some relief. 'Listen, we need to get through. I'm supposed to be getting married in about half an hour. At St Mary's.'

'With all due respect, sir – and congratulations on the promotion – and your wedding day, sir – but I think you'd be better off doing a U-turn and taking the long way around. You should still have just enough time. Maybe a few minutes late, but you'll never get through this way. Not for a couple of hours at least.'

'Cheers, Geoff, I suppose we'll have to.'

Geoff Keene smiled and returned to his duties. He was glad to have been able to help the Inspector. Inspector Frank Summers. His mates looked at him with some respect when he spoke of Frank Summers as a mate. No-one else in traffic could do so.

'Just enough time,' Frank muttered, tapping the steering

wheel, staring at the blocked road. 'Or maybe just not enough time, and then what?'

'Cutting it awfully fine, Frank,' his father noted, checking his watch.

'Dad,' said Frank, looking from the gap between the lorry and the front wall to  Geoff Keene's motorbike, 'how do you fancy a ride on the pillion of a motorbike?'

'An excellent idea, my boy. I haven't ridden a motorbike since before you were born. Your mother disapproves of them, you know.'

'I'll have to put my leather jacket on. Come on, Squish, you're in for a treat, your first motorbike ride.'

Of course, the first time he had met Frank Summers, Geoff Keene remembered as he looked at the overturned truck and trailer, the man had nicked his motorbike. He had been very polite about it, but he, Geoff Keene, had got an awful lot of stick about it.

'Sorry, Geoff, it's an emergency,' said Frank Summers appearing at his side, gunning the motorbike, his father behind him, his arms around Frank's chest, clutching their top hats, 'I'll get her back to you as soon as possible.'


'Frieda, I switched your radio on by accident,' Susan said. 'It sounds urgent.'

'Angler One to Tiger Shark, come in please, Angler One to Tiger Shark, come in please, over,' said the Chief Inspector, squatting uncomfortably in his suit, tails and top hat underneath a bush in Frieda's back garden. The Colonel looked at him with some curiosity, head cocked to one side.

'Who the hell is Angler One?' asked Frieda.

'It's the Chief Inspector,' said Gertie.

'Oh, great. The man I'm supposed to be marrying in less than an hour has disappeared, and the man who is supposed to be giving me away is calling himself Angler One. Give me that radio.'

Susan handed the radio over.

'Well, Angler One, this is Tiger Shark. Over.'

'Sorry, Tiger Shark, I realise how important today is for you, but we have a crisis on our hands. I need you to co-ordinate operation Mackerel. Over.'

'Angler One, I might as well, it doesn't look like this wedding is going to take place. What's the situation, over.'

'Tiger Shark, proceed immediately to the fishmongers and set up a control post. Over.'

'I'll be there as soon as I've had a chance to change, Angler One.'

'No time for changing, Tiger Shark. You must get there as soon as possible.'

'Very well, Angler One, I'm on my way. Come along, Gertie. Bring my briefcase, you can look up the fishmongers. Must be the code for the station, but we'd better check.'

'I know where the fishmongers is,' Gertie sang.

'Right,' said Susan to the two mothers as Frieda and Gertie ran out to her Range Rover, 'veil, train, bouquet, all the rest. You take them in the chauffeured car, I'll follow in my MG. Just don't have an accident on the way, we've enough problems as it is.'

'What about Hal?' asked Katherine Garold. 'Where is he?'

'Oh, hell! He's still hiding in the garden. I'll go get him.'

'Hiding in the garden? Whatever for?'

'Oh, dear, I hope this isn't an omen,' sighed Frances Summers.

'Not at all, Mrs Summers,' said Susan. 'In Wellbury we call this normal.'


Another motorbike pulled up alongside Frank and his father at a traffic light. A woman without crash helmet, but holding a pair of crutches held onto the black-clad driver.

'With all due respect, sir,' said Sam Nightingale, 'you are absolutely mad.'

'Hiya, Sam,' grinned Frank. 'Sam, this is my dad. Dad, this is Sam Nightingale.'

'How do you do?' said Frank's dad. 'I would offer to shake hands, but I can't let go of these.' He indicated the two top hats he was holding around Frank's chest.

'Pleased to meet you, sir,' said Sam. 'This is Martin, my partner, short for Martinique. Um, I don't wish to be forward, but are you as mad as your son?'

'I trained him, my dear, I trained him.'

'Oh, just one thing, Sam,' Frank said as the light turned green and he revved the engine.

'What's that, sir?'

'It's illegal for a passenger not to be wearing a crash helmet,' he replied, dropping the clutch.

'The strap broke,' Sam called after him. 'And with all due respects neither of you – '

'The strap broke, my arse,' said Frank as they roared away.

'That will be police terminology,' commented his father.

'Come on, after them!' cried Sam's passenger.

Sam dropped the clutch and took off after the groom and his father, her passenger waving her crutches with one hand.


'Just our sodding luck to be on patrol today,' Constable Ken Edgars said, sitting in a patrol car with Constable Steve Right. 'Up half the night, that bloody Pole screaming at us, and now patrol.'

'I don't know what he was saying, but I'm pretty sure most of it wasn't very polite.'

'At least if we were on radio duty we could have a quiet snooze without anyone saying anything.'

'Quiet is the word. Saturday afternoon and Wellbury United playing away – this is going to be the most boring afternoon of the year.'

They watched as Frank and his father raced past.

Then they watched as Sam Nightingale and Martinique raced past.

'Yup, bugger-all happening,' Ken Edgars said, tipping his cap over his eyes.

'Bugger-all,' agreed Steve Right, doing the same.

After a few moments Ken scratched his cheek.

'I wonder what the Inspector was doing not riding past on a motorbike at about twice the speed limit.'

'What I want to know was why that Sam Nightingale wasn't chasing him with someone on the pillion waving a pair of crutches.'

'Amazing what doesn't happen on a Saturday afternoon.'

Steve Right checked his watch.

'Oh, well, at least we'll finish up in time for the reception.'

'Inspector Garold to Control, over.'

'Control here, er, ma'am. Over.'

'Control, activate plan Mackerel, immediately.'

'Repeat, please.'

'Activate plan Mackerel. Now!'

'Yes, ma'am. I mean Tiger Shark. Cape Cod to all trawlers. Operation Mackerel has been re-activated.'

'One small change, Cape Cod. All trawlermen are to meet at the fishmongers. Understand?'

'Understood, Tiger Shark.'

Bobby Stang consulted his reference book.

'Bloody hell,' he said, 'the fishmongers is the cemetery at St Mary's. Strange place to meet.'

'All trawlermen,' Ken Edgars said slowly. 'Do you suppose that includes us?'

Steve Right scratched his chin and debated this one internally.

'W-e-ll, technically speaking, I suppose it might.'

'Only thing is, Tiger Shark didn't sound too happy.'

'Not surprising, really, she's supposed to be getting married to Inspector Summers in an hour or so.'

Both men nodded slowly. They didn't understand what was

going on. They did understand that Frigid was well pissed off. Under such circumstances a police officer used his own initiative.

'We'll have to go, Constable Edgars,' Steve Right decided. 'But drive with due caution.'

'Good point, Constable Right. I shall drive with due caution. First of all I'll reverse very slowly for about a mile just in case we might accidentally appear to shoot out into the road and surprise a passing motorist. You never can be too careful.'


'Tiger Shark to Angler One, I'm in position, over,' Frieda said, standing next to her Range Rover just inside the cemetery. Several people paused on their way to the church at the sight of the veil-less bride speaking into her radio, with one of her bridesmaids alongside.

'I'll just pop into the church,' Gertie said.

'I wouldn't bother, Gertie. Come in, Angler One, over.'

'Angler One to Tiger Shark,' came the Chief Inspector's breathless voice. 'Susan, do you have to drive so fast? Sorry, Frieda, we should be with you in a few minutes, if Susan's driving doesn't kill us first.'

'Oh, you look beautiful,' said a voice from next to the mausoleum.

Frieda turned to find Aggie hiding behind a tombstone.

'And he looks so handsome,' Aggie added.

Frieda smiled weakly. How was she going to explain to poor Aggie that it was all off?


'So, that's it,' Percy said as they stood outside of Frank's flat.

'It's obviously empty, quiet as the grave. And it's too late now. Time to tell Frieda, I'm afraid.'

Pete Phillips did not reply immediately. He was trying not to face the inevitable. An idea came into his mind.

'But, sir, if operation Mackerel has been activated, shouldn't we get into position?'

'Hmm. I suppose you're right. I haven't got the plan with me. Where are we supposed to be?'

'As far away from the fishmongers as possible.'


Gertie came skipping back, a broad grin on her face.

'There's a fish in the church,' she said.

'Gertie, do you mind? We have an emergency on our hands.'

'Not any more, we don't. Don't you want to know what type of fish?'

'Gertie! I couldn't care less if there was an entire school of performing dolphins floating around the font.'

'It's a swordfish.'

'Really? Well, good luck to it.'

'The Swordfish, in fact.'

Frieda's eyes widened.

'Frank? Frank's in the church?'

'Standing at the altar, checking his watch.'

'He looks so handsome,' Aggie repeated. 'Though the vicar looks a little ill. And he seems to be wearing dark glasses.'

'You've seen him? Frank?' asked Frieda, suddenly noticing Squishy in Aggie's arms, Frank's leather jacket next to her, and the import of her earlier statement.

'He arrived on a motorbike. With an older man.'

'A motorbike?'

'And then another motorbike came. With two women on.'

'Two women?'

'Frieda,' said Gertie, 'I hate to ask this, but you do intend getting married in – what is it, about ten minutes?'

'Oh, my god! My god, Gertie! I haven't got my veil! Or my bouquet! I look a mess!'

'Don't be silly, now. You look gorgeous. And here come your mother and Frank's mum. And there's the Chief Inspector in Susan's car, though he isn't looking very well.'

'I'm going to be late! I'm going to be late for my own wedding! Frank will never forgive me!'

'Now, Frieda, you still have ten minutes. I can think of some other people who are going to be late, though. Here, give me your radio.'

A feverish Frieda let Gertie take her radio.

'Stingray to all trawlers, Stingray to all trawlers,' Gertie called. 'Swordfish is at the fishmongers, Tiger Shark is in position, and you have ten minutes to get there or you'll all be kippered. Out.'


Percy Hanson and Pete Phillips looked at each other aghast.

'Frank's at the church?' asked Percy. 'How the hell did he manage that?'

'Ten minutes?' said Pete. 'We'll never make it.'

'I suggest you use your siren, Kipper.'

'We'd better go in, now,' Katherine Garold said, having tweaked Frieda's train and adjusted her veil until everything was as perfect as possible.

'You do look gorgeous, my dear,' said a tearful Frances Summers.

A car sounding a siren came around the corner and pulled up with a screech of brakes.

'Isn't that the best man?' asked Katherine Garold as Pete Phillips raced past them, terror in his eyes.

'He looks more nervous than Frank,' noted Susan. 'Shall we go in? I think I can hear the organ starting.'


'Nervous, my boy?' asked Professor Summers, standing next to Frank at the altar.

'Terrified, dad. Still, not long now, eh?'

'That's the spirit, my boy. Speaking of which, have a drop of this.'

'Thanks, dad,' Frank said, taking the offered hip-flask. 'Oh, look, Pete's finally turned up.'

He took a mouthful as the congregation turned around to watch Pete Phillips rush up the aisle, coat tails flapping.

'I'd better take my seat. Keep the flask just in case. Good luck, my boy.'

'Thanks, dad.'

'Sorry, Frank, got caught up,' a breathless Pete muttered as he joined Frank.

'Have a drop of this,' Frank offered the hip flask.

'With everyone watching?'

'Quick, now, they're turning to see Frieda enter.'

The organ began the Wedding March, and heads craned to have a glimpse of the veiled bride entering the church, the Chief Inspector at her side. Pete took the chance to take a generous gulp and returned the flask. Frank took another mouthful and slipped the flask into his pocket.

'You know what's ironic, Pete?' Frank whispered.

'Everything, when you're around, Frank. Anything special this time?'

'I think Frieda looks more beautiful than she ever did, even though I can't see her face.'

'Could you two face the front?' croaked the vicar.

'You sound a bit under the weather, vicar,' noted Frank. 'Try a sip of this.'

Vicar Cringely looked at the proffered hip-flask, glanced guiltily around, and took a long pull.

'Thank you, my son. I feel much better. God bless us all.'

Then he hiccoughed quietly.

Frieda walked slowly, holding the Chief Inspector's arm, her heart beating so loudly she was sure everyone could hear it. Each step was an agony, another chance to trip and fall over. She wondered whether she shouldn't do so deliberately and get it over with. It was the longest walk she had ever done. She wondered what lunatic of an architect could have designed a church like this.

'Nothing can go wrong now,' Frank whispered.

'Shut up, Frank,' Pete whispered back. 'Knowing you I wouldn't be surprised if the fire alarm went off and we had to evacuate the church before you get around to saying yes.'

'They haven't got a fire alarm.'

'Are you sure about that? Isn't that illegal? Against health and safety regulations?'

'You can nick them afterwards if you want, Pete. But only afterwards, okay? Try it before and they won't find the little bits that constitute your remains.'

Frieda, coming up next to Frank, wondered why on earth he and Pete Phillips were discussing fire alarms. Trying not to show her nervousness, she raised her veil.

'Dearly beloved,' began the vicar, a huge smile on his face, 'we are gathered here in the sight of God to join together in holy matrimony ...'

Frank turned slightly and winked at Frieda. Frieda wondered why Frank had a twitch in his left eye. And why the vicar was droning on and on and on ... And why he sounded so unnaturally cheerful ... And why he was swaying ever so slightly ...

'So, if any now here know any just  cause or impediment why this man, and this woman, should not be joined together in holy matrimony, speak now or forever hold your peace. This is your chance.'

The vicar paused to allow any such person to make themselves known. There was a deathly silence, as if the entire congregation were trying to hold a collective breath. Wilf looked at Tom, his lips twitching with amusement. Tom looked back, wide-eyed, shook his head violently and drew his finger across his throat while motioning towards Gertie and Susan. Somewhere at the back someone who had fallen asleep snorted themselves awake. The vicar looked in the person's direction, blinked his eyes at the person's partner holding a hand clamped over their mouth, and quickly looked at another part of the congregation.

'Inspector Summers!' demanded a voice from the back of the church.

The congregation turned to discover a harassed-looking traffic policeman entering the church.

'Ah,' said Geoff Keene as he realised that he was the centre of attention. 'Ah, yes. Um, sorry, it can wait. I'll just hang around outside, shall I?'

The congregation, breath still tightly held, turned back to face the front as Geoff Keene tiptoed away as fast as he could. The vicar scanned the crowd one last time to make certain that, if anyone did have objections, they had sufficient time to announce them.

'Very well,' he said finally, 'let us continue.'

There was a group outpouring of breath and the explosions of several restrained sneezes.

'Sorry, did someone say something?' asked the vicar.

Another holding of breath ensued. It took the vicar some seconds to presume that no-one had said anything, and then to find his place in the missal and continue. Frieda felt like smacking him. He was going on again. Couldn't he get to the important bit? If only they had chosen a female vicar. She wouldn't have rambled on.

Finally the vicar got to the important bit.

'Do you, Frank Summers, take this woman, Frieda Garold, to be your lawful wedded wife?'

There was absolute silence as Frank turned to look at Frieda, a smile on his lips and a twinkle in his eyes. She knew that twinkle. It was the announcement that Frank Summers was about to indulge in mischief-making.

Oh, no, he couldn't ... not now, please, not now. She could feel her hand involuntarily clench into a fist, ready to smack him the hardest shot she could give it if he even thought about being funny.

He licked his lips.

'I do,' he said with a broad smile, a little drop of sweat trickling down his brow. Frieda almost fainted with relief. Just one more question to go.

'And do you, Frieda Garold, take this man, Frank Summers, to be your lawful wedded husband?'

Did she? Did she really want to go through with it? Did she want to make the same mistake as before?

Rubbermatting right she did.

'I do.'

'I therefore pronounce you man and wife. You may kiss the bride.'

'I don't know what all the fuss was about,' the Chief Inspector whispered to Pete Phillips as Frank and a tearful Frieda kissed.

'Me neither, sir,' Pete Phillips replied, poker faced. 'I always knew everything would go off smoothly.'

'Bloody liar,' commented the Chief Inspector.


'Happy, Mrs Summers?' Frank asked Frieda as they sat watching the others dance. She sat turned towards him, a gloved hand on his shoulder, as if to declare to the world that he was hers, or possibly just needed the sense of touch to

Bill Dughaille

convince her it wasn't a dream.

'I've never been happier, Mr Summers,' she replied. 'It's been a perfect evening so far, touch wood.'

'You leave my head out of it.'

'Silly. Your father is certainly enjoying himself.'

'He always does once he feels at home. He's always been over-shy of strangers. He was terrified of meeting you. I think he expected some right-wing disciplinarian who would think him a woolly left-wing liberal. And then when he made the mistake of thinking you were my secretary he didn't know where to put his face.'

'I think he's cute,' Frieda replied. 'Don't laugh, but I thought he wouldn't look at me because he didn't like me.'

'Tsk, tsk, Free. A silly mistake like that, and you a professional police officer.'

'I suppose we all let our imaginations run away with us, given the right conditions.' She looked at Frank. 'Sorry about my mother, she can be a bit overbearing at times. She wasn't always like that, she just seems to have become worse since my father died.'

Frank smiled.

'She needs someone in her life. And I think Angler One is in danger of becoming that someone.'

'My boss going out with my mother? That could cause problems.'

'I don't know. After all, I ended up marrying my boss.'

'Your ex-boss,' smiled Frieda. She sighed. 'You know, I'm so glad it's all over. I've been terrified for weeks that something would go wrong.'

'Me too.'

'You were worried? You didn't show it.'

'I didn't want to get you worried.'

Frieda paused before replying.

'I wasn't worried about you, darling,' she said.


That night they spent in the honeymoon suite of the Wellbury Railway Tavern. Frank insisted on carrying Frieda across the threshold, despite her concern for his leg.

'I'm only ever going to do this once, might as well do it properly,' he said. Once inside they exchanged wedding presents.

'A clarinet!' Frieda exclaimed, having unwrapped hers. 'Oh, darling, you remembered. But it must have cost you a fortune!'

'We'll probably spend the next few years in penury,' he said, unwrapping his present. 'What with the cost of the wedding and everything. But the clarinet was worth every penny. Got it from a special little shop in London. Oh, wow! A Sax! Free, you are the most wonderful woman in the world! Give your hubby a kiss.'

'Just a minute, Frank. London? When did you manage to get to London?'

'Ah, well, you remember that day I said I had food poisoning? Well, it was what you might call a small little tiny white lie.'

'A white lie? I was worried sick! Frank, that isn't funny.'

'Sorry,' he said in a little-boy voice, hanging his head. He peeked up at her. 'By the way, when did you find the time to pick up a Saxophone? One that you wouldn't be able to find in Wellbury. Not of this quality.'

'I know how to manage my time, Frank,' she replied in what would have been a stern voice had it not also had a guilty quality.

'That visit to the Chief Constable,' he said. 'I should have guessed. There was no reason to take Tricia with you. And you've never spent an entire day with the Chief Constable.'

'Well, I could hardly tell you where I was going, could I?'

'And then you had Trish delay me outside of your office while you were hiding the evidence. I'll bet she knew exactly what overhead transparencies were.'

'Well, maybe ...'

'And you even had the temerity to invite me along to the so-called visit to the Chief Constable, knowing I would avoid it if I could.'

'Well, perhaps ...'

'Frieda Summers, you are a bad, bad woman. Come, give us a kiss. I like bad, bad women.'


The next morning they returned to Frieda's house to drop off surplus luggage. The surplus luggage did not include the clarinet or saxophone. They weren't likely to start learning to play them on their honeymoon, but both wanted them along.

Well, Frieda wasn't likely to start learning to play the clarinet. She suspected that she might have to convince Frank that the first noises coming from a trainee-Saxophonist would probably not endear them to other guests in the hotel.

Their parents accompanied them to the station where they waited for the London train.

'What a wonderful idea,' Frank's father said. 'A flight to Paris and then a train to Normandy. When I last visited the battlefields I went across by steamer. Very conventional. Train from Paris down – well, you might get an idea of how the Germans felt travelling towards the invasion area.'

'They're called ferries now, my dear,' said his wife. 'And I don't think Frank and Frieda are interested in how some silly German soldiers felt. Now, Frieda, remember not to let Frank have his own way all the time. This is your honeymoon too, you know.'

'I think I've got the hang of this thing now,' said Katherine Garold, holding a digital camera which had somehow failed to work the previous day. 'Come, you two, smile. Cheese!'

Frank and Frieda smiled for the camera. It still wasn't working. In Katherine Garold's hands it never would.

'Hello, here's the whole gang,' Frank said, spotting Tricia with Squishy, Jeremy, Susan, Tom, Gertie, Wilf and various other members from the station coming onto the platform as the train drew in. 'Looking a bit the worse for wear, some of them. What time did you lot finish up last night?'

'About five o'clock this morning, Frank,' said Percy Hanson. 'I feel like I could do with two month's holiday.'

'We'd better get aboard, darling,' Frieda said, spotting an irritated looking station assistant looking at them and pointing at his watch.

'Now you have got everything, darling,' fretted Katherine Garold, watching Frank load their luggage into the train. She still could not understand how a woman could go on her honeymoon without anything less than ten suitcases.

'I've got everything, mum,' Frieda said, giving her a kiss on the cheek. She repeated the process with her new mother-in-law and father-in-law. The father-in-law tried to hide the fact that he was blushing beetroot red. But a very happy beetroot red.

'Don't forget to send a postcard,' Percy called as the doors began to close.

'We won't. Just try not to destroy the station while we're away,' Frank replied.

'Look who's talking,' called Pete Phillips as the train began moving. Frank and Frieda stood at the window to wave goodbye until the station disappeared from sight.

'Ah,' sighed Frank as he slumped into a seat, Frieda making herself comfortable against his shoulder, 'a week of bliss awaits, my darling. No Pete Phillips to cock things up. No Percy Hanson to get the wrong end of the stick. No mad Wellburians inventing stories of ghosts, aliens and other bizarre ideas. No, instead we can look forward to the professionalism of those who know how to do things. Clear run to London. Piccadilly Line to Heathrow. Flight to Paris. The renowned French railway to Normandy. And then a lovely little family-run hotel.'

Frieda put a finger on his lips.

'Do me a favour, darling,' she said. 'Do not say anything silly such as "nothing can go wrong".'

'Course not, Free,' he said, taking her finger and kissing it. 'Not even I would be that stupid.'

Which was just as well. The train sat outside Kings Cross St Pancras for twenty minutes with no information of the reason for the delay, nor how long it would be until they got to their destination. On the Underground the tannoy was describing the service as a "Good service running on all Underground lines", while the driver of the tube they caught mournfully suggested that they tried other methods of transport, as "severe delays" were occurring.

They made Heathrow with minutes to spare. Frieda was only holding on to her goodwill by reminding herself that they were on their honeymoon, and nothing, but nothing was going to stop them enjoying themselves. Even Frank was wearing at the fringes. Especially when they got to check-in.

'Sorry,' said the assistant, a young woman with blonde hair on top of her head and nothing inside it. 'I've got a Frank Summers and a Frieda Summers, but no Frieda Garold.'

'We were married yesterday,' Frank said through clenched teeth, trying to keep a smile going.

'Oh, that's nice,' replied the assistant. 'I'm going to get married as soon as I find Mr Right.'

'I'm happy for you,' said Frank. 'Right at this moment my wife and I are about to start our honeymoon. And the reason her passport has the name "Garold" on it is because we only got married yesterday.'

'Sorry, I still can't find a booking in the name of Frieda Summers,' the assistant replied, tapping at the keyboard in case the computer had changed its mind. Fortunately for her, as both Frank and Frieda had the maniac looks of people about to commit murder, an older woman appeared.

'It's your tea break, Marlene, I'll take over,' she said.

'Oh, thanks, Mrs Hendersy,' said the blonde. 'This is Mr and Mrs Summers. I can find a booking for him, but not for her.'

'That's okay, Marlene, off you go.'

Marlene twittered off to her tea break while Mrs Hendersy made herself comfortable on the vacated stool.

'Sorry about that,' she said. 'Unfortunately she isn't the sharpest knife in the cutlery box. Actually, I don't think she is in the cutlery box. An egg-timer has more brains, I'm afraid. Now. You're on economy to Paris. Well, I've just spotted a couple of empty seats in First. Be silly to waste them.'

She punched a few keys and the boarding passes appeared.

'Have a lovely honeymoon, Mr and Mrs Summers,' she smiled.

'Thank you,' said Frank. 'We were beginning to wonder if the world had gone mad. And thanks for the upgrades. It's very kind.'

'Not at all. And when you've worked here for a couple of years you realise the entire world has gone mad.'

'There you go,' Frank said as they hurried to the departure point. 'Fifteen arseholes and then you come across a human being. Makes the world seem a slightly better place.'

Frieda glanced at him. When Frank Summers spoke like that you knew that he was really, really angry.

'Darling,' she said, stopping.

'Yes, Free?' he asked, turning. 'The plane's waiting.'

She let go of her luggage, stepped up to him and gave him a kiss which had all the other passengers pausing to admire. A couple on the conveyor belt fell over.

'Stuff the plane, my sweetheart. It will just have to wait for us.'

It didn't quite wait. The truth is that they made it on time. And from there on in it was champagne and good wishes.

Even the French train took them to Normandy on time. And the French taxi-driver who drove them to the little hotel was cleanly and neatly dressed, didn't smoke Gaulloises, and had absolutely no hint of garlic about him. He even knew how to smile.

'I think we should complain to the Trading Standards Authority,' Frank whispered. 'He could at least have a couple of onions rolling loose.'

Frieda giggled.

The dream had finally come true. Now nothing could go wrong.

## Living Appily Ever After?

The motherly-looking woman looking after the bar-cum-foyer of the small hotel greeted them with a smile.

'You ar, how you say, in the honeymoon?'

'Mais oui, madame,' replied Frank.

'Ah, so sweet. Your room, it is on the first floor.'

'Merci beaucoup, madame.'

'I call for mon mari to carry your luggage, one moment, please. He is in the hotel nearby.'

'Oh, don't worry Madame, I can carry the cases,' Frank assured her.

'Ah, if you are certain, monsieur.'

'I like these small family hotels,' Frank said as they walked up the stairs with their luggage. 'That little bar where the locals pop in for a chin wag. Good service without artificial smiles. I can't stand the large ones with fawning attendants rushing around, carrying your cases, tugging their forelocks, while you know they're really looking down on you. I can never relax.'

'And relax is the operative word,' Frieda replied. 'I fancy a bath, and then dinner, a slow stroll around town, a nightcap, and then bed.'

'And after bed we might try sleeping.'

'Frank!'

'Now, Mrs Summers,' Frank said, opening the door, 'you aren't going all coy over me, are you? The look that concierge gave us was x-rated. At least here, in bon France, they understand l'amour.'

'I am definitely having a bath first before l'amour,' Frieda replied as they put their suitcases down. She took him in her arms and gave him a long kiss. 'And while I'm inspecting the bathing utilities, oh husband of mine, you can pour me a glass of scotch.'

'An excellent idea. I might join you in one, if I can find a glass big enough.'

Frieda shook her head.

'Frank, I married you despite your terrible jokes, not because of them.'

She gave him another kiss.

'Back in a short while,' she said.

Frank hummed to himself as he inspected the small drinks cabinet. Relax. Yes, now he could relax. No doubt there would be good times and bad times ahead, but he was now happily married, on his honeymoon, in a small town in France. Good food, good wine, languid strolls in the Autumn days, not a worry nor a cloud in sight. He poured two little bottles of whiskey into two glasses, added ice and took a sip. He licked his lips at the taste and turned around to take Frieda her drink.

'Darling, could you come here for a moment?' Frieda called from the bathroom.

'Only a moment, darling?'

'Well, there's something you should see.'

'You are a temptress, Frieda Summers.'

'It's not that, Frank. It's a body. In the bath. And she's been dead about an hour, I think.'

End of book five

Other novels by Bill Dughaille:

**The FFSG series (aka the Wellbury Chronics)**

## *Summers*

The first in the FFSG series.

Detective Sergeant Frank Summers is a man on a mission: to keep his head down, stay out of trouble and enjoy the relaxed atmosphere of the easy-going, genteel town of Wellbury, his new posting. It's a town just made for him, where, he believes, even the criminals take bank holidays off. But, while perceptive in his professional life, he tends to miss the subtleties in his private life. In this case he fails to realise that his own tranquillity is being threatened by three women and a philanderer. The fact that the women in question are his boss, his constable and the local pathologist adds just the touch of danger to his life that he had hoped to avoid. The philanderer has been dead several decades. The women are very much alive.

## *The Eighty-five-percenters*

The second in the FFSG series.

Detective Sergeant Frank Summers is faced with an unexpected crisis as the staid citizens of the genteel town of Wellbury rapidly descend into disorganised anarchy after a sociology professor announces on radio that eighty-five percent of the population will die in a coming cull. The prediction appears to be coming true as apparently total strangers are felled one by one according to a list of the ten-most-disliked Wellburians, from nagging neighbours to estate agents ... and the police, at a poorly performing number ten. But Frank fails to realise that there is a graver danger closer to home. Three women have decided that he is their responsibility: his boss, his constable and the local pathologist have agreed to become best of enemies. Now they intend to re-arrange his fate the way it should be. And they aren't asking anyone's permission.

## *Fakes, Fraud and Deception*

The third in the FFSG series.

Detective Sergeant Frank Summers is in the doghouse, despite having recently arrested an internationally sought con-artist. And since he is in the doghouse he has no intention of pointing out that there is something very strange about the attractive French police woman who has come to interview the arrested man, not to mention the two detectives claiming to be from Scotland Yard. Oh, no, he is going to stay well out of the way this time. Definitely.

## Jokers

The fourth in the FFSG series.

The doctors have pronounced Detective Sergeant Frank Summers physically fit following recovery after his shooting, but his colleagues fear that his sense of humour was extracted along with the bullet. They are, as always, more than willing to interfere in his life in the pursuit of a good cause. If that wasn't enough, a bunch of criminals calling themselves the Joker Gang are laughing at him, the university students are creating mayhem during their rag week, and someone called The Shocker is trying to kill him. The only advantage is that it take his mind off of the ultimatum the three women in his life have given him, one that he has only until the Sunday to resolve. Or leave town.

## Loonymoon

The sixth in the FFSG series.

The Inspectors Summers have tied the knot and embarked on their honeymoon in a small family-run hotel in Normandy. She has very definite ideas of what she wants out of a honeymoon: to set a seal on their love, and to form a foundation for life-long devotion. He just wants to nick a French police officer's kepi. He had a Bobby's helmet nicked from him once by a French girl while he was on crowd duty one New Year's Eve in London, and now he intends to return the favour. Neither is about to achieve their aim unless they can solve the mystery of the woman in the bath and the missing heroin. Which means pitting their minds against the French Inspectors Simenon. That's Mr and Mrs Simenon, whose marriage has gone beyond the rocks and is now beating itself to death against humdrum reality. One or either or both or neither could be the guilty crumpet. More importantly, is their marriage a portent of what could become of the Loonymooners? Ultimately the decisive question could well be: which side do the peas go?

**Others:**

## *The Window*

Jim Allbright, ex-bobby and now easy-going window washer, innocently responds to an advert for window washing placed in the newspaper by the local council. The response is a torrent of paperwork, political correctness and a computer system doing exactly what it was told to do, but not quite what was intended. But if the system cannot be beaten, the interchange of letters can be used to have a little fun and get to know some of the people struggling behind it. There's Sandi, who signs herself as "(pp the Administrator)"; her four-year old little angel Helen; Graham, a shadowy computer programmer who definitely has too much time on his hands, and a slew of Project Managers and Senior Administrators eager to ensure standards are upheld no matter how many problems they create. Against a run of bad luck and circumstances Jim and Sandi aim to meet up one day, eventually. Hopefully. The window might even get washed. Maybe.

## *Diary of a Sane Man*

In a cross between 'Last Of The Summer Wine' and 'One Flew Over The Cuckoo's Nest', set against a backdrop of the brave new world of New Labour's end of honeymoon, Fred is the Last Cynical Optimistic Realist.

Believing that he's found the perfect niche – three square meals a day plus all the newspapers he can read just for occasionally pretending to be mad – he's not going to be the one to rock the apple cart. Oh, no.

Safe from the wiles of women and the woes of the world, he's not going to rock the boat. Oh, no.

No, he's just going to sit and observe, and comment quietly on the insanity of life outside.

Well, maybe just little one tug of the loose strand of wool on life's jersey ...

Did you know they elected a monkey as mayor in Hartlepool?

## *The Weekend At Longwood*

A whodunnit in the classic sense, set against the backdrop of World War II and the trials, tribulations and romances of nine suspects.

A group of friends get together during the last weekend of August 1939 at the rural retreat named Longwood, just a few miles from Portsmouth. They are there to celebrate the last time they will see Georgina Riley, famed American novelist and socialite, for some time, as she is scheduled to leave for her native New York in order to marry her childhood sweetheart. During the afternoon they good-humouredly assign to each other the most suitable names of the nine muses, the daughters of Zeus and Mnemosyne:

Calliope: the muse of epic poetry and rhetoric

Clio: history

Erato: love poems and mimicry

Euterpe: lyric poetry

Melpomene: tragedy

Polymnia: hymns to the gods and heroes

Terpsichore: dance

Thalia: comedy

Urania: astronomy, astrology and prophecy

The following morning Georgina is discovered in her bedroom covered in blood, her throat slit, barely alive. Her American maid is dead. A tiara Georgina had been flaunting the day before has disappeared.

Detective Inspector Rudman arrives to investigate. But with Georgina in a coma and no solid evidence there is little he can do apart from haunt their lives. With Germany's invasion of Poland a week later they disperse across the land, some to the air-force, some to the army, others to reserved civilian jobs.

But Rudman does not give up. Wherever they are he can be found. Whatever other duties he is tasked to, he will find time to keep tabs on them. Whatever the defeats and victories of the Allied cause, he has only one aim: to find the person responsible for the murder done that weekend in Longwood.

The war ends; some of the Muses have survived, some not. Some have prospered, some married, some matured, others have found despair. And then comes invitation to spend another weekend at Longwood. The message is that Rudman has found the evidence he has been looking for.

And so one of the surviving couples motor slowly down to Portsmouth, remembering the original weekend, the trials and the tribulations of the past years, and wonder: what will be revealed during the coming weekend at Longwood?

## Firelight

A modern-day tale of an ordinary family gathering at Christmas; the good, the bad, the dysfunctional and the forgotten.

George Browne and his wife Winifred have retired to a large, run-down pile in the country. Rumour has it that it was once the abode of a mad aristocratic family with a penchant for Satanism, and that both they and their victims still haunt the corridors. Other rumours are that it was a lunatic asylum for much of the nineteenth and twentieth century, and bodies of the inhabitants are buried around the large gardens in unmarked graves.

The Brownes are an unremarkable retired couple who, depending on who you might ask, have bought it as an investment, or alternatively as somewhere with enough bedrooms to accommodate their children, grand-children, and the little baby great-grandchildren. Too often in the past excuses have been made at special times, the most common of which has been of the "I don't want to put you to any trouble" variety. That excuse can no longer hold water.

Now it is approaching Christmas. Winter has set in, but the house is snug with oil heaters and real fires. As the various relations arrive, or don't arrive, it becomes clearer why invitations might have been refused in the past. The men of the family believe in having their way. The women of the family are strong-willed in their own different ways, and have various means of getting what they want.

The guests of the family - friends, boyfriends, girlfriends, wives and husbands - discover that their partners have a totally different side to them as the explosive hatreds of long-nurtured fights and feuds simmer to the surface before quickly boiling over.

One evening Winifred Browne encourages them to each tell a story as they sit in the lounge with the large fire warming them, the television off, no access to broadband, computers or mobile connections. Reluctantly at first they begin. As each evening passes: with different members taking turns, they announce in stories the feelings and hopes they cannot voice in public.

Finally it's the turn of Winifred Browne. Her story will be the one that tells them who they are, where they come from, and maybe why they have turned out the way they have.


For further details on these visit:

www.dughaille.info

www.ingramcontent.com/pod-product-compliance
Lightning Source LLC
Chambersburg PA
CBHW071633260626
47170CB00001B/84